THE ADJUSTMENT

ALSO BY SUZANNE YOUNG

The Program Series
Book 1: *The Program*
Book 2: *The Treatment*
Book 3: *The Remedy*
Book 4: *The Epidemic*
Still to come . . . Book 6: *The Complication*

Hotel for the Lost

All in Pieces

Just Like Fate
(with Cat Patrick)

A PROGRAM NOVEL

Book 5

THE ADJUSTMENT

SUZANNE YOUNG

SIMON PULSE

New York   London   Toronto   Sydney   New Delhi

SIMON PULSE

An imprint of Simon & Schuster Children's Publishing Division

1230 Avenue of the Americas, New York, New York 10020

First Simon Pulse hardcover edition April 2017

Text copyright © 2017 by Suzanne Young

Jacket photographs of models copyright © 2017 by Michael Frost

Jacket photographs of backgrounds copyright © 2017 by Thinkstock

All rights reserved, including the right of reproduction in whole or in part in any form.

SIMON PULSE and colophon are registered trademarks of Simon & Schuster, Inc.

For information about special discounts for bulk purchases, please contact Simon & Schuster Special Sales at 1-866-506-1949 or business@simonandschuster.com.

The Simon & Schuster Speakers Bureau can bring authors to your live event. For more information or to book an event contact the Simon & Schuster Speakers Bureau at 1-866-248-3049 or visit our website at www.simonspeakers.com.

Jacket designed by Russell Gordon

Interior designed by Mike Rosamilia

The text of this book was set in Adobe Garamond Pro.

Manufactured in the United States of America

2 4 6 8 10 9 7 5 3 1

This book has been cataloged with the Library of Congress.

ISBN 978-1-4814-7132-9 (hc)

ISBN 978-1-4814-7134-3 (eBook)

For Mandy and Bethany,
who always let me set the air-conditioning
to below freezing
And in loving memory of my grandmother
Josephine Parzych

ENTER THE WORLD

THE PROGRAM

The Program—a memory-wiping therapy—was created to combat the outbreak of a suicide cluster. Sloane and James will do everything they can to survive both the epidemic and its cure.

THE TREATMENT

On the run from The Program, Sloane and James must figure out a way to take down the system that ruined their lives before it can expand.

BOOK ONE

BOOK THREE

BOOK TWO

THE REMEDY

Before The Program, there was the grief department. Quinn and Deacon spent their lives as closers, offering grieving families a chance to say good-bye—until Quinn discovers her life is not at all what it seems.

OF *THE PROGRAM*

THE ADJUSTMENT

Tatum and Wes undergo the Adjustment—a new procedure to replace memories that The Program erased. But what happens when the past you thought you had was a lie?

THE COMPLICATION

After learning the truth about her past, Tatum must find a way to stop the Adjustment before it sets off a new epidemic.

BOOK FIVE

BOOK FOUR

BOOK SIX

THE EPIDEMIC

Quinn will enlist the help of other closers to save a girl she hardly knows, setting off the series of events that lead to the suicide epidemic.

PART I
TO WISH POSSIBLE THINGS

CHAPTER ONE

I CAN'T REMEMBER THE LAST TIME I CRIED.

It's an odd thought to have in the middle of English class, but for years the threat of being taken, against our will, to a facility for memory manipulation had terrified all of us. Any moment of weakness, one show of emotion, and we could have been flagged as unstable. Once flagged, we would have been handed over to The Program, where the doctors would steal our memories, our experiences, and our lives—all in the name of their false cure. I barely escaped that fate.

But it turns out that although The Program no longer exists, its effect is long lasting.

I stare ahead in class at the whiteboard, the words there blurring together. Around me, pencils scratch against notebook pages and the movement of other bodies mimics learning. I sit still and apart from all of them.

I'd gotten used to small classes, some with as few as twelve students. But now we're pushing thirty in here. Former patients of The Program have been flooding in—wide eyed and confused. I mostly feel bad for them. They've been erased, some only partially.

Months ago, when The Program was shut down, there was no follow-up therapy offered to its patients. Many were sent uncompleted, un*cured*, to Sumpter High, a private school just for those who were treated: a school filled with broken people. Returners were left to their own devices, and some didn't make it. Some didn't want to.

But as the criminal trials carried on in the media, The Program decimated and supporting politicians questioned and shamed, Sumpter was shut down. One senator filed an injunction to ban returners from our district, citing the possibility of another suicide outbreak. As a result, students were left for weeks with nowhere to go—abandoned by their government. But that asshole politician got voted out of office, so returners have come back to the lives they had before The Program. Now that their lives have been thoroughly ruined by The Program.

Even now, former patients still occasionally freak out. Break down. Crack up. To them, The Program is forever.

I glance around at the other students in my class, some dressed in black, dark and dramatic. Others even wear Program yellow ironically. Some say their emotions are heightened now that we're suddenly allowed to "feel" again—built-up angst and anger getting release. Lust and love intertwining so that no one knows the difference anymore. Everything is about now. Everything is about living.

But not me. It's like I've forgotten how to feel—always set to numb. I wonder how many others are just mimicking what they think is sadness. What they think is joy. What if The Program took away our ability to feel by making us hide it for so long? What if none of us is real?

I shouldn't sit here feeling sorry for myself, though. Not when there are those worse off. I look sideways at Alecia Partridge, watch as she flinches—a post-Program twitch she hasn't lost. She occasionally murmurs to herself during class, but the rest of us pretend not to notice. Alecia talks to the ghosts of her past—a friend who died during the epidemic. A friend who was only partially erased from her memory and is, therefore, familiar enough to still be in her present.

Alecia laughs under her breath, brushing her knotted brown hair behind her ear. "Yes," she whispers to no one. "Yes, I know." She looks back down at her notebook and continues to work. She does this at least once a week. This is her normal—and by extension, ours.

I swallow hard and turn away, reminded that returners are still considered unstable, even if the purpose of sending them to The Program in the first place was to make them stable.

"I'd ask to copy your notes," Nathan says in his scratchy

voice from the desk behind me, "but you're obviously going to fail this test."

I turn my face toward him, keeping my eyes on the floor so as not to draw attention from our teacher. "Bet my F will be higher than your F," I say.

Nathan laughs, low in his throat. "No fucking way," he says. "I'll take that bet."

"Done," I say, and look toward the front. I'm almost ready to write down a line or two from Shakespeare's Sonnet 30. I get as far as picking up my pencil before the classroom door opens.

There's a flash of white fabric, and I immediately imagine crisp white jackets and blank expressions. I imagine silence and dripping fear. Although handlers have been out of our lives for months, I still have nightmares about them. And so I hold my breath until my eyes can adjust.

A guy steps into class wearing the same stupid clothing most of the returners do: a stiff button-down shirt, khaki pants, belt—like he's on his way to become our new math teacher. Most returners have had their clothing replaced, and it takes a while for them to figure out their style again.

And maybe it's because of that, or maybe I don't recognize his newly buzzed hair, but Nathan reacts to his presence before I do.

"He's back," Nathan murmurs, putting his hand on my shoulder. But I feel a million miles outside of my body, and his touch is just a breeze past my soul. My pencil falls from between my fingers and drops on the floor, before rolling under my desk.

I stare at the guy in the front of the classroom, my mouth agape, my heart racing. Guilt smacks me, scolding me for not recognizing him immediately. Several students look in my direction, anticipating a reaction. They're curious, maybe. Horrified?

"Wonderful," the teacher says, barely hiding her annoyance. "I see they still aren't worried about class size." She pauses. "Welcome back, Weston," she adds, softening her voice. "There's one last seat." Miss Soto motions toward an empty desk near the front.

Wes watches her for a moment like he's trying to figure out if he knows her, but then he turns and starts down the aisle. He sits two rows away from me. After a moment of silence, Miss Soto goes back to teaching, and the other students go back to pretending to learn.

Nathan's hand is still on my shoulder, attempting comfort, but I lean forward and out of his reach. I stare at the back of Wes's head, willing him to see me. Begging him to turn around.

As if he can sense me, Weston puts his chin on his shoulder and covertly turns. When he finds me, when his dark eyes lock on mine, tears I didn't know had welled up spill onto my cheeks.

And I smile.

Weston Ambrose is the love of my life, and I don't mean "the like," I don't mean "the obsession." We were together for two years, until the day men in white coats showed up at his kitchen door. Although handlers would occasionally take people from school, it was more common for them to come straight to the house. Most patients were turned in by someone they knew. Turned in by their parents.

Of course, parents didn't know the truth of what was happening in The Program—the lasting effect it would have. The paranoia that became the curse rather than the cure to an epidemic.

Wes's parents turned him in. The handlers arrived and pulled Wes from his home as I fought, holding on to his shirt until it tore at the collar. Until a handler physically removed me from the house.

And when Wes was gone, stolen away, his mother came and sat next to me on the curb. It was the first time I cried in public. The only time until now. Mrs. Ambrose held me tightly and let me sob into the shoulder of her blouse, and when I was done, she kissed the top of my head and told me never to come back. Fair or not, she blamed me for her son's condition.

She called them. She called The Program on her son. I'll never forgive her for that.

I blamed myself, too. I replayed the last few months of us over and over, trying to figure out what I could have done differently. Trying to take responsibility for his actions. Most of that time was a blur, really. But eventually, with therapy, I accepted that it wasn't my fault.

My love for Wes is pure, forever. And so I waited for this moment. I waited for him to come back.

SUZANNE YOUNG

But Wes doesn't return my smile, and instead he turns around and opens his notebook. He jots down what I assume are notes from the board.

My skin is on fire, waiting for him to look back. When the bell rings, Weston gets up and walks out without even a backward glimpse.

I sit still and watch after him. There is a sympathetic glance or two in my direction from other students; even Alecia nods at me like she understands how I feel. Truth is, people have wondered about my stability for a while, and I'm sure that if The Program didn't end when it did, the handlers would have come for me next.

"Tatum?" Nathan calls, his voice always set to a quiet hush that gives every word an extra layer of depth, like he's confiding in you.

I don't turn immediately, and I hear his chair scrape against the linoleum floor before he crouches down next to my seat. I turn to him, feeling my bottom lip jut out.

Nathan's eyebrows pull together as he looks me over, like I'm the most pathetic creature on all of Earth. He leans in and puts his forehead against my arm and whispers, "I'm sorry."

CHAPTER TWO

HE SHOULDN'T BE SORRY. MY NEIGHBOR NATHAN
Harmon has been my constant companion since Wes was taken
away—unwaveringly by my side. I've known him since we were
kids, and although he and Wes were never friends, Nathan was
devastated when he was taken. If for no other reason than
because of how it affected me.

When we heard that Weston had been released from The
Program, I begged Nathan to help me find him. He reluctantly agreed, and we went to Wes's house. But Wes's mother
told us he'd moved to California to live with his uncle, a devastating fact I hadn't expected. Mrs. Ambrose wouldn't give
us a forwarding number or way to contact him. She told me
he needed space.

I didn't give up, though. When the district ban was lifted,

and students started returning, I'd hoped he'd show. Fantasized about it. But, of course, I was imagining *my* Weston walking in—wearing his worn, tan leather coat. His dark wavy hair to his shoulders. His busted-up motorcycle parked illegally in the teachers' lot.

He'd walk in, wink at the teacher, and then say to me, "Come on, Tate. Let's get the fuck out of here." And then we'd be free.

I'd confided that fantasy to Nathan once, to which he replied, "Sure, that sounds just like Wes. If he were a character from *Sons of Anarchy*."

But no matter how I pictured it, I always imagined Wes would look at me and know me instantly. Know me always. And now all I can hope is that he does, but decided not to show it.

The rest of the morning passes quickly; I don't share any more classes with Wes. Nathan is in advanced courses, so I don't see him, either.

At lunch, Nathan and our friend Foster are waiting at the usual spot on the half wall near the flowers in the courtyard. There were murmurs at the beginning of the year that students would be able to leave campus for lunch this year, but it hasn't happened yet. Some terrified parent always speaks up, worried about a car accident. Most of the time, I think the parents in this district will only be happy when we're all put in individual bubbles, completely protected (and isolated) from the outside world.

Nathan must be telling Foster what happened this morning, because they both look miserable, conspiring quietly without me. Nathan is first to lift his head as I approach, his hazel eyes squinted against the sun. Foster casually sips from his soda and turns away. Neither of them speaks as I sit on the wall next to them.

I set my chips aside and try to pull back the cardboard top on my juice carton to open it, but it keeps shredding. My fingers shake. Nathan watches me, and then he takes a bite of his sandwich before putting it on top of his lunch bag.

"Gimme," he says through a mouthful of food. I hand him the carton without argument, and he refolds the triangle top and opens it easily. When he passes it to me, I murmur a thank-you.

"So . . . ," Foster starts carefully, "I heard Weston came back. That's good news, right?" He presses his freckled lips into a hopeful smile, the kind you give someone as they're loaded into the back of an ambulance.

"Seriously, Foster?" Nathan says with a heavy sigh. "I said don't bring it up."

Foster scoffs. "Yeah, I figured you knew I would anyway. Of course I'm going to bring it up—her boyfriend just came back from the dead!"

"He wasn't dead," I say quietly.

"I know," Foster whispers, reaching to pat my leg. "I was just trying to make Nathan feel shitty."

Foster Linn is cute with bright red hair, freckles, and the

12

SUZANNE YOUNG

sort of personality that makes guys and girls swoon alike. I've known him since seventh grade, when he and Nathan were on swim team together. For most of middle school, the three of us were inseparable: video games, pizza, and cliff diving—Foster being the reckless diver. Fearless, always.

But two years ago, his older brother Sebastian was taken into The Program. None of us realized he'd been suicidal, something that I know haunted Foster afterward. The entire situation was obviously traumatic. When Sebastian finally came home, he was like the other returners: quiet, reserved . . . empty. We stopped talking about him. Ever since, Foster spends his free time with his family, with his two older brothers. They work weekends in their dad's shop together.

Foster's friendship with me and Nathan is mostly lunch oriented now—which is also just the evolution of high school, I guess. We still love each other. I know he understands what I'm going through right now—better than most. And to prove it, he grabs my hand and squeezes it.

"Wes doesn't remember," I tell him, pain welling up in my chest. Foster lowers his eyes, feeling the heaviness of the moment. We all fall silent.

I'd been waiting for Wes. I'd built the future around the idea of him coming home.

"What does that mean for you?" Nathan asks, leaning forward. He may not show it the same way, but Nathan knows my devastation too. He tries to carry it for me.

I take a sip of my juice, the sour taste stinging my tongue. I swallow it down. "I don't know," I say. "I don't know who that was this morning."

The real Wes would have asked someone to move so he could sit next to me. He would have made a show of it—completely fine with his affection. A Wes who doesn't smile at me is something different entirely. And we know what it means: He's forgotten me.

Around us, the courtyard is buzzing, other people going about their lunch period, their day seemingly unaltered by the aftermath of The Program. Tears tickle my cheeks, and I wipe them away quickly.

"Tatum," Nathan says, "I know this is hard, but you have to pull yourself together. I just . . . I don't want you to get caught up in it. You were getting better," he adds, then looks at Foster. "Wasn't she getting better?"

Foster opens his mouth to answer, but I'm quick to cut him off. "No, I wasn't," I say. "And you both know it."

They exchange a look, and Foster widens his eyes and picks up his Tupperware and fork, stabbing his pasta salad.

"Okay," Nathan concedes. "Then you were good at pretending. And as the counselors say, that's part of it. Believing it can get better. I think you started to believe it."

"Then you're an idiot," I say.

"And you're being an asshole," Nathan replies just as quickly. I'm not offended—I know I'm projecting my frustration, my hurt, onto him.

As if he can't stand to listen to us argue, Foster shoves a

large bite of food into his mouth and then snaps the lid on his Tupperware to set it aside. "You two are pretty intense for a Tuesday afternoon," he says. "How about we try some deep breathing?"

Nathan ignores him and packs up his lunch before standing to face me. His eyes weaken when he looks me over. "I'm sorry I called you an asshole," he says sincerely. "But I won't indulge your misery. You forget who had to pick up your pieces last time."

Foster comes over to put his hand on Nathan's chest, leaning in to whisper, "We should really work on those apology skills."

But Nathan isn't in the mood to joke around. He steps out of Foster's reach. "Digging into the pain isn't healthy," Nathan says to me. "It isn't safe. If you want to be alone right now, fine—clearly you want to be. When you're ready to have an actual conversation, then come find me."

"Nathan," Foster says, as if he's still being too harsh, but he doesn't stop him from walking away. I don't ask Nathan to wait—not that he paused long enough for me to try.

Foster turns back to me, caught in the middle. "He's just worried," he says.

"I know," I reply. "And don't tell him, but he's right—I was getting better. Or at least I was trying to."

"I hate when he's right," Foster mutters.

I sniff a laugh. "Yeah, me too."

Foster reaches into his lunch bag to take out a cookie. He offers it to me, but I wave it off. He takes a bite, and we both watch Nathan cross the grass to go sit with Jana Simms.

Jana's new this year, sporty-cool in a way I could never be. From what little we've said to each other, she seems nice enough. Nathan swears there's nothing between him and her, but she's the first person he runs to whenever he wants to get away from me.

Foster finishes his cookie, eyeing them carefully before talking again. "Want me to stay?" he asks me.

"No, I'm good," I reply. He waits to see if I'll change my mind, but I really do want to be alone so I can think. Foster nods, and says he'll see me later, before jogging over to where Nathan is holding court.

I watch them, the easy way Nathan smiles at Jana like nothing's wrong. Jana's dark-lined eyes following his every move. Foster chatting with Arturo, whom he's dated on and off for the past few months. They all look so happy. I'd feel left out if I wasn't already aching inside.

Another girl in the group catches my attention: Vanessa Ortiz—a returner. When Jana first arrived at our school, the two of them became best friends. Normally it would be odd, but Vanessa isn't like the other former patients. She seems well-adjusted. Normal. No twitches or breakdowns. Nathan heard it was because she started a new sort of therapy—a counteractive to The Program.

We're all wary of that sort of nonsense, though. A cure to a cure only equals more fucked-up-ness, so we didn't bother asking for more details. But maybe the new therapy *is* working. It's definitely something to consider now that Weston is back.

I take a sip of my orange juice and stash the chips in my backpack for later. I'm not hungry. Instead I notice a couple on the other side of the half wall, their backs against the building. Courtney Dane, another returner, sits with her new boyfriend. Her eyes are narrowed as she glares at him, and I guess that they're in the middle of an argument.

Of course, when Courtney returned, she didn't remember that she and Joshua used to hate each other. Nothing violent, but he was a judgmental know-it-all in class while she was popular and impatient with his bullshit. I couldn't stand the way Joshua treated her, like she *owed* him her attention.

They'd had words more than once: He called her a shallow bitch, claiming she didn't want a "nice guy" like him. Yeah. Courtney wasn't swayed by that. She told him he was a loser and always would be.

But . . . what we didn't realize at the time was that Courtney had been slowly unwinding—spiraling, just like the spirals people would draw on their notebooks. A symbol of how deep and dark they were burrowing inside themselves. We heard the handlers found a stash of notebooks in Courtney's locker filled with those spirals. She's lucky to be alive.

Courtney Dane had gone out one Friday night to an underground party where she had been friendlier than ever. She laughed with friends, and even made out with a guy she knew. And then she promptly went home and jumped in her family's pool. She was unconscious when her mom found her—nearly drowned. The firefighters were able to resuscitate her, but she didn't come back to school. Instead she went into The Program.

She returned two months later, her beautiful long dark hair cropped short and preppy at the chin. She smiled politely; she looked empty. I imagine it had a lot to do with the sedatives The Program doctors had given her.

In those hazy days, Courtney started talking with Joshua, and eventually they became a couple. I found the idea terrifically sad. Could Courtney truly choose a relationship with him if she didn't remember their past?

We're not friends, but I asked Courtney once after class if she knew how she and Joshua hated each other. She laughed it off, and said people change. Especially her. But Joshua was the only person who spoke to her when she returned; her friends abandoned her.

And now she and Joshua have been dating for months.

A cool breeze blows over me, rustling the leaves overhead. I pick up my juice to take another sip, and I hear a loud gasp. And then another. I look back over to Courtney and Joshua, and see Joshua jump to his feet. I'm momentarily confused until I see Courtney clutching her throat, trying to breathe.

I'm stunned, watching as she struggles for breath, her eyes rolling back in her head. She must be choking. Joshua screams for help, but as several lunch monitors rush in their direction, I hear Courtney whisper: "I'm drowning."

My juice carton falls from my hand and hits the ground as I climb to my feet. Around the courtyard, everyone watches with trepidation. Courtney's not really drowning, but what exactly is going on, I'm not sure. The science teacher, Mr. Winston, drops to his knees next to her, his hand on her back. After a quick assessment, he starts coaching her through her breathing, and I wonder if this is a panic attack. Another returner crashback. Behind Courtney, Joshua's eyes fill with tears.

"I'm sorry I didn't tell you sooner," he says. "I'm sorry."

A crowd gathers, and I look down to see the orange juice from my carton making a river toward the grass. Courtney is lying back, labored but breathing on her own. She begins to cry.

"Just let me die," she rasps out. "Leave me in the pool."

Her words make me sick to my stomach. Courtney seems trancelike, and it occurs to me that she's not herself—she's having a flashback. She's trying to kill herself all over again.

The vice principal appears, jogging over with a black walkie-talkie clutched in his hand. I turn and look for Nathan, finding him already watching me. His eyes are wide and concerned, but not just for Courtney. He nods toward her, as if saying that could be me.

I pick up the empty carton of juice from the ground and grab my backpack to slip it over my shoulders. I make my way over to the trash and throw out the carton. I stop there and steady myself.

That won't be me. I've never wanted to die—not like the others did. I was just sad, and what everyone ignored is that there's a big fucking difference between the two. So many people were wrongfully taken.

I check back on Courtney and find her sitting up, sipping from a bottle of water another teacher has provided. Although she's shaking, Courtney's eyes are clear. The flashback has passed for now. But when Joshua reaches for her, I see her avoid his touch.

Maybe she remembered. I imagine that would shift her entire world.

And now I'm worried about Wes. The sight of a girl crashing back like that, drowning on air, even if it was only in her head, has unsettled me. I have to find Wes and make sure that The Program hasn't left him half sorted and confused like Alecia. Or crashing back like Courtney.

I walk into the building a few minutes before the bell rings. The next-period lunch students are already making their way toward the cafeteria, but I don't head toward my history class. Instead I begin searching the halls for Weston, trying to find his new locker location. I grow hyperaware of every whisper, every glance. I want a hint as to where Wes might be, and sympathetic expressions become breadcrumbs that will lead me to him.

And it's the flash of a pitying smile in the science hallway that makes me turn that way. Sure enough, I find Wes. He's standing in front of an open locker, his brows pulled together as he stares inside, like he forgot which book he was looking for. A few people glance at him as they pass, whispering. They know he went through The Program. They know he's not the same. And because of that, they'll avoid him—as if the contagion is still around us, hidden.

The epidemic may be over, but the fear is not. The fear may never be.

My heart is in my throat as I approach him. I self-consciously slide my hair behind my ears and then brush it forward again so that I don't look nearly as distraught as I feel. I won't get my hopes up. I won't.

I pause a few lockers away and watch Wes, hoping to see a glimpse of the boy I love. A sly smile, the sort that's full of mischief and desire. The smile that can melt away any argument.

Wes sighs and slams his locker shut without a book. I jump at the metallic sound, and consider disappearing into the sea of students walking down the hallway. A few people, unaware of the war going on inside my head, say hello to me. I smile politely but keep my attention on Wes, making sure he's okay. I should walk away before he notices me staring, but I can't bring myself to. I've waited so long to see his face. I've missed him so much.

He runs his palm over his shaved head, flustered, annoyed. It used to be that returners would come back well behaved and sedated. Program doctors gave them actual sedatives—not medication—when they returned. It made them too weak to fight back. But Wes is clearly not under any influence, because his emotions play across his face.

I rest my shoulder against the cool metal locker, unable to move.

He exhales, seeming to prepare himself to reenter the classroom, and then he starts to walk away. Suddenly panic—bright and red—breaks across my chest.

"Wes, wait," I call out to him without thinking. "Do you remember me?" I ask.

Wes stops, his uncharacteristic loafers scraping on the linoleum tiles. He turns slowly, and I recognize each feature as it comes into focus. The light-brown freckles dusting his nose and cheeks, the dimples that are obvious even when he's not smiling. My entire soul moves toward him even though I stay in place.

"What?" he asks, his eyes sweeping over me in an unimpressed way.

He used to gaze at me, stare and ask if it bothered me. I'd say yes, and he would keep staring anyway, making me laugh. He'd even keep his eyes open sometimes when we kissed—said he liked that my eyelids fluttered when his tongue touched mine.

"Do you remember me?" I ask again, my voice hushed. Desperate.

Once again, his dark brows pull together, like he's looking into his locker, not recognizing anything.

"No," he says simply. I expect a follow-up question: "Should I?" But he doesn't say anything else. He tightens his jaw and turns to feed into the hallway traffic.

I fall back against the locker, losing him in the crowd. I rest my head against the metal, a headache beginning to throb behind my eyes. *At least he's not having a crashback*, I think. *At least there's that. We'll be fine.*

Denial coats its way through my veins, trying to protect me from reality. Wes could be pretending to forget me, I rationalize. Or . . . he might remember later. Right? It's possible.

I hitch in a breath, choking back my emotions. Wishing for impossible things. Wishing I could go back to how we were. I close my eyes.

"What's your favorite part?" Wes asked me once, holding my hand as we left a restaurant after dinner. He'd given me his jacket, and the smell of him surrounded me—seduced me.

The parking lot of the Montage was deserted, and when we got to his motorcycle, I shrugged. "I don't know," I said. "All of you, I guess." Wes handed me the scuffed black helmet, and then reached to buckle it under my chin.

"Not good enough," he said, putting on his own helmet. "We all have favorite parts. For example," he explained, helping me on the back of the bike, "I like your smile. It's kind of wide and goofy, but in a sexy sort of way."

I dropped my hands to my sides. "Did you just call my face *goofy*?"

He laughed. "Tell me your favorite," he said, climbing in front of me on the bike. The night air was cold, and I liked the feel of his body close to mine. But I wouldn't give him the satisfaction of snuggling close now that he'd called me goofy.

"Uh, well, it's definitely not your mouth," I said.

"You sure?" he asked. Wes turned, putting his chin on his shoulder to look back at me—the way he always did. "I'm good with my mouth," he offered.

I rolled my eyes, even if the mention stirred me a bit. "I still hate you."

He hummed out that he could understand why, and then

licked his lips like he was waiting for me to kiss him. I leaned in and did just that.

It was his dimples—my absolute favorite part was his dimples and how I could see them even when he wasn't smiling.

"I love you, Tate," he whispered against my lips, and kissed me again. My fingers threaded through his long hair, his hand gripped my thigh against his side. I loved him too. More than I could say. Around us, the world was cold and dreary. But we had each other.

That was before Wes was taken to The Program.

Overhead, the class bell sounds and I shake myself out of the memory. I can't get lost in the past, in all that's been taken—it'll drive me mad. Nathan is right about that.

I push off the locker, and then notice a girl across the hall— Kyle Mahoney—watching me. She has long blond hair and sun-kissed skin. And from her pitying expression, I guess she overheard my desperate attempt to talk to Weston.

I don't break eye contact, defiant in my shame. Not even when tears drip onto my cheeks; I brush them aside with the back of my hand. Finally Kyle lowers her eyes and turns toward her locker, leaving me to wallow in my loneliness.

CHAPTER THREE

I WALK TO THE FRONT OFFICE OF THE SCHOOL AND pause outside the frosted-glass door. I take out my phone and call my grandfather. The line rings and I look around the deserted hall, the weight in my chest heavy enough to pull me through the floor.

"Hello?" Pop says when he answers.

"Hey," I say. "Any chance you can call the school and tell them I have a doctor's appointment?" I ask. The sound of my grandfather's voice protects me from myself, from the emotions bubbling up.

"Are you sick?" he asks, sounding more curious than anything.

"Heartsick," I respond. "Weston came back to school today."

The line is silent for a moment, and then I hear the creaky

springs of the recliner chair. "Yep," he says with a groan of an old man standing up. "I'll call 'em now."

"Thanks, Pop," I say, and hang up. Once he calls in, I'll be able to sign myself out. The regulations have loosened since The Program ended. Plus, I'm eighteen. If I didn't want the excused absence from class, I could just leave.

I've lived with my grandparents since I was a baby. My mother had me when she was young, too young I guess, because she dropped me off with her parents. I see her on holidays; she remarried in her twenties and started a new family. We're not hostile or anything, but Gram and Pop are my parents—both legally and emotionally. They're the ones who raised me.

My dad is in the wind, somewhere in New York, I hear. I'm lucky, though. Some people grow up without any support, but I happen to have the best grandparents in the world. I've never felt left out of the family experience. And when The Program dominated our lives, my grandfather spoke against it. Said he thought it was adding to the epidemic. He's a smart man.

We have a house in the suburbs of Portland, and Nathan lives next door to us. It's just him and his mom; his parents divorced when he was in middle school, but his dad lives only a few blocks away. He sees him every other weekend or whenever he feels like it. So I guess we're both lucky.

Unlike Wes. He has both a mother and a father, but the windows of his house were always dark, no one waiting up for him to come home. His bedroom was in the renovated base-ment with its own entrance, completely separate from his mom

SUZANNE YOUNG

and dad. He had a sister once, but she died in a car accident a little over two years ago. She was the passenger in a suicide pact. It's not something Wes talked about. Not even to me.

Wes used to tell me that his parents forgot he existed most days, and maybe he was right at the time. But then The Program got to them, sweeping them up in the hysteria. After that, his mother hovered, listened. Fretted.

I try to remind myself that she was right to be worried. We all knew something was wrong with Wes. Because one afternoon, he disappeared. Ran away. He was gone for almost a week, and when he came back, he was different. I couldn't help him—I wasn't enough. He needed therapy. Instead he got The Program.

Now he doesn't remember a damn thing.

My grandfather is waiting when I get home, like always. He retired from the newspaper a couple of years ago, while my gram still works as the patient coordinator at the hospital. Gram told me she'll work until she's in the ground and she means it. But my grandparents are relatively young, so I don't worry about them leaving me any time soon.

I close the front door and set my backpack on the bottom stair before walking into the living room. My grandfather is in his blue recliner, and he looks up at me, his glasses perched on the edge of his nose. He folds the newspaper in half.

"Do you want to talk about it?" he asks.

"I'm not sure how," I answer, and go to sit on the couch. I

pull my legs underneath me, resting my elbows on my knees, and close my eyes. "Weston came back. I spoke to him." I look over at my grandfather just as he removes his glasses.

"And?" he asks.

"No," I say. "No, he doesn't remember me."

My grandfather purses his lips, thoughtful, waiting out my wave of emotion. I don't cry—I shouldn't have cried earlier, either. In fact, I wasn't sure I still could. But I hurt just that much. When the wave passes, I lift one shoulder in a shrug.

"What do I do, Pop?" I ask. "What do I do to get him back?"

He seems to weigh out an answer, never quick to blurt out an opinion. "Does he look well?" he asks. "Because before he left . . . your grandmother and I were worried about both of you, really."

"I didn't talk to him long enough to psychoanalyze his condition," I say, and then apologize if it sounded harsh.

"Before you make any decision about what to do with Weston," he says, "I ask that you keep an eye on him first. Jumping headfirst into a shallow pool will break your neck, Tatum. So be careful."

"That's incredibly encouraging," I say, and he laughs.

"I missed my calling as a relationship counselor. Now," he says, "there is an entire basket of your laundry sitting on top of the dryer. If you wouldn't mind? My knees are killing me today and I don't feel like walking upstairs."

"Sure thing," I say, and stand up. My grandfather settles

back in his chair with the paper. "There was something else that happened today," I add, still bothered by what happened at lunchtime.

He tilts his head. "What was it?"

"A girl—a returner. She had a crashback. She . . . she seemed to be stuck in a memory. Reliving it, I guess."

He lowers his paper, thinking it over. "What sort of memory?"

"The night she tried to kill herself. She thought she was drowning again."

"That's terrible," he says. "That's the second crashback this month, right?"

I tell him it is, and Pop shakes his head, his expression gravely serious. "I guess we'll be seeing this sort of thing for years," he says. "It's still too early to know the lasting effects of The Program."

"Yeah," I say. "It was just . . . sadder. I've seen crashbacks before, but people don't typically get lost in a memory like that."

Pop exhales, folding the paper. "Let's hope it's not something new, then. And let's hope it doesn't happen to all returners."

We let that thought settle between us, unwilling to make it possible by further discussion. And unwilling to apply it out loud to Weston. I turn and walk to the stairs, pausing before I put my hand on the railing.

"By the way," I say to my grandfather. "Thanks for calling the school for me today. I needed the break."

"Of course," he says. "I'd rather you tell me than cut and disappear. But try to keep it to once a semester."

"Noted," I reply, putting my hand on the railing. "Oh, and if Nathan comes by, let him know I'm folding Mount Laundry in my bedroom."

He says that he will, and I grab my backpack from the bottom stair and head up to my room.

My bedroom is a shrine to the past. My gram asked the therapist a few weeks back if it was healthy for me to have so many pictures and mementos surrounding me. Gram worried it was keeping me low. But the therapist told her it might actually be healthy. "It helps her feel connected to the past," I heard her say in a hushed tone. I hate that my grandparents have to worry about me. I hate that The Program made the fear real. But, luckily, my therapist has been a huge help. I like her.

Therapists nowadays aren't nearly as scared of feelings. Not anymore.

I walk over to my mirror and gaze at the pictures tucked in the frame. After a moment I open the top drawer to the pictures I keep tucked away—the ones that hurt the most. I grab my favorite, letting it tear me open as I stare down at it.

There hadn't been a junior prom at my school—things like that don't exist in the middle of a suicide epidemic. But Wes and I had wanted to do something, have something of our own. We'd seen too many old high-school movies, I guess.

So we put on formal clothes and danced in my backyard near

the fire pit. Lights hung from the low-hanging tree branches; soft music played from Wes's phone. My grandparents were out of town, and Wes slept over. The entire night was impossibly romantic.

I look down at the picture we took together that night. It's perfect: the two of us lying on my bed, still in our fancy clothes. Wes is turned, kissing the side of my mouth while I held the camera above us. I'm curved against him, and my smile is pure—wide and goofy just like he described.

This photo is less than a year old, but we look so much younger. We still had possibilities.

I run my finger over Wes's face in the picture, feeling the ache build in my chest. And the terrible part is that I want to wallow in that pain. Somehow, the way it hurts also feels a little good. But then I worry that that sort of thinking led to the epidemic, and I lower my arm. I drop the picture inside the drawer and slam it shut. Then I go to the laundry room and grab the basket of clean clothes.

It's after dinner, and my grandparents are in the kitchen talking politics while I sit on the couch, my statistics book open on my lap. I haven't answered any of the homework questions yet, staring blankly at the page instead.

There's a quick knock on the back door and then the creak of the hinges opening. My gram immediately asks Nathan if he's hungry for leftover pot roast. He says yes; his mother is an awful cook. Gram tells him that she knows.

I look up just as Nathan appears in the hall between the kitchen and the living room. He stares at me a moment to see if we're still in a fight, but I wave him in and he smiles. My grandmother walks in with a plate of meat, potatoes, and a dinner roll.

"Yum, Grams," he tells her in his most kiss-up voice. "My favorite." He dramatically leans in to smell the food and then takes the plate from her hand, beaming at her like a cartoon character. She laughs before returning to the kitchen.

"For real, though," Nathan says as he comes over to the coffee table, "I fucking love your grandmother's roast beast." He sets his plate on the table and kneels in front of it. Using the knife, he saws off a piece of meat and delicately places it between his teeth. As he chews, he turns to me. "So good," he says around his food.

"What did your mom make for dinner?" I ask.

"Fake chicken, I think," he says, cutting a new piece. "I couldn't tell. I tried to fill up on chickpeas."

"Gross."

"Yeah," Nathan says, taking another bite. We're quiet for a few moments, at least until he finishes the bulk of his meal, and then he puts the knife and fork on the side of his plate. He comes to sit next to me on the couch, and the cushion tilts under his weight, swaying me slightly. I close my book and set it aside.

"Foster says I need to apologize again," he starts.

I look sideways at him. "Does your conscience think you need to apologize again?" I ask.

Nathan grins. "You first."

I wait a beat, but I actually do feel bad. I was taking out my disappointment on him. "I'm sorry I called you an idiot," I say.

Nathan grabs the roll off his plate and then sits back and takes a bite, propping up his foot on the coffee table. "Forgiven," he says. "And I'm sorry I was being an insensitive prick at lunch. I should have forced my compassion on you."

I laugh—he's kidding about the compassion, of course. But I'm sure he feels bad for walking away from me. "It's okay," I say. "You were right. I did need some space."

He lifts one shoulder as if he's not sure he totally agrees with that statement, and he rests against the couch cushion, folding his hands behind his neck. "And since we're apologizing already," he says. "Let me add—and don't take this the wrong way—but you look like shit."

"How could I ever take that the wrong way?" I ask.

"Remember in fifth grade when Mrs. Aberdeen told you that your bad decisions reflect themselves on your face?" he asks. "It's one of those moments. I heard you talked to Wes."

"Wow, news travels fast."

"Eh, well, it's kind of a big deal, Tatum. People want to know if he remembers."

"He doesn't," I say.

Nathan's throat clicks as he swallows, like the idea is hard to get down. "Did he tell you that?" he asks.

"Pretty much. He doesn't know me." The words are a dig into my soul, and I flinch uncomfortably next to him.

"Knowing Wes," Nathan says, "if he's forgotten you, he's forgotten everything. You were his world."

"He was mine," I murmur, and reach to grab my book for distraction. I open it to where my piece of paper sticks out from the pages. "And, yes," I continue. "I know I'm feeling sorry for myself, but I get to do that now. I can feel sad. I can be pissed. I can be hopeless—"

"Not hopeless," Nathan says, and I turn to him.

"At least temporarily," I say. "I can *feel*, Nathan. I have to. And once I wallow in it just a bit"—I pinch my fingers together—"I'll figure out what to do next. Deal?"

He watches me, thinking it over. Nathan and I have always made deals and bets, ever since we were kids. And when he nods, he agrees to take this deal now. We decide that I'm allowed to be miserable for at least twenty-four hours—I deserve it. I've been strong for months. He knows any judgment he passes on me now would be unfair. After all, I'm only human. I can only take so much emotional fallout before I crack.

We're quiet for a few minutes, and then he motions toward the game system connected to the television. "Want to play?" he asks.

"Not really."

"I'll let you win this time," he offers.

I laugh, and turn to him. "*Let me?* Dude, I murder you on this game."

"Prove it." He gets up and goes over to turn on the system, unplugging the controllers to bring them over to the couch.

I abandon my homework and settle in, taking the controller from his hands when he passes it in my direction.

When he sits next to me again, and we start playing, I murmur a thank-you.

"Anytime," he says, eyes glued to the television set.

And for the moment, I calm and let myself believe that all is okay in the world.

CHAPTER FOUR

I LIE IN MY BED, STARING AT THE WHIRLING CEILING fan. The chain ticks against the lightbulb, rhythmic and comforting. Like I've done most nights over the past few months, I let my mind drift back to Wes. I used to keep a journal, mostly about us. But it got lost somewhere along the way. There are still a few moments that stick out, though, and I keep them in my head like an emotional scrapbook.

I think back to this one time when Wes and I headed downtown to see his favorite local band play. The all-ages show was on the back patio of a bar; the night was clear and full of stars.

Wes had found a way to get served, and he came back to the table with a beer and a bowl of pretzels. I looked from him to the food.

"You're not seriously going to eat those, are you?" I asked.

As if answering, he gathered up a handful and shoved them into his mouth. I shook my head and turned toward the stage, watching the band set up. Wes didn't normally drink, but the day before, another one of our friends had been taken. Cole was sitting in McDonald's, staring at his french fries, when two handlers walked in to collect him.

Things around here had been difficult. With the news focused on Sloane Barstow and James Murphy running away, Amber Alerts, and propaganda about the spreading epidemic, the handlers were out in full force. They were everywhere. They were hunting.

I didn't know Sloane or James—they were at a different school in the district. But the news had picked apart their lives, put their parents on TV. Part of me wanted them to make it. But another part of me wanted them to get caught so The Program would stop being hysterical. It was selfish—but we were scared.

So when Weston downed his beer and left to get another, I worried. The week before, he had been totally fine, at least as fine as a person living in of the shadow of The Program could be. His appointed school therapist recommended him for extended therapy, and he went a few times. And then . . . suddenly he was quiet for longer. Like he was lost in his own head.

I was scared of what they were doing to him.

Weston came back to the table and sat across from me. He darted his eyes away when he noticed me looking at him. Behind us, a guitar strummed as the band tested their equipment. The patio grew busier, but the older crowd was a nice change from the people we were normally around. These people were over eighteen—the fear wasn't the same in them.

When the band started to play, I looked again at Wes. He was staring down at the bowl of pretzels like maybe they hadn't tasted all that good after all. His expression was lost; he was all alone at sea.

"What's wrong?" I asked him, having to talk loud enough to be heard over the music.

Weston lifted his eyes to meet mine, and smiled. But it was only halfhearted. "Just don't feel good right now," he said.

"Physically?" I asked.

He didn't have to answer. I could tell he meant emotionally. He felt emotionally ill. And with the world falling apart, it should have been a giant neon warning sign.

Wes watched the band, his gaze far away. A tingling began to crawl up my arms, and I was scared. Too scared to press the issue with him. I was losing him.

And then, suddenly, Wes turned to me as if I had called out to him. Despair painted in his expression. "Oh, baby," he murmured sadly, and outstretched his hand across the table.

I flinch, here at home in my bed, pulled from the past just like every time—always at the exact spot in this memory. Pained by Weston's anguish. But I dig back into the memory, unwilling to leave him in the past.

"What?" I asked, looking down at Wes's hand on the table.

He cursed, and got up to come over to my side. He held

out his hand again. "Dance with me, Tate," he said, barely audible over the sound of the guitar.

The bluesy music wasn't really for dancing, and I told him just that.

He watched me for a long moment, and then smiled. "So?" he asked. "We can do anything we want. And I want to dance with you."

I couldn't resist—I never could. So I slipped my hand in his. We walked over to the center of the patio, where absolutely no one else was dancing. Wes pulled me close, his body against mine. I loved the smell of him—like his own brand of cologne, leather mixed with the sweet smell of his shampoo. I loved everything. Especially when he leaned down and kissed me softly right there. How his palm glided over my neck to rest under my short hair. How it didn't matter if anyone was watching us.

But of course . . . they were. The handlers were always watching. And soon, school was out for summer. One day, I called Wes, but he didn't answer. I called him the next day. And again until I finally called his house and spoke to his mother. She sounded horrified to hear from me.

When I asked about Wes, she told me he'd run away. Disappeared. The police organized a search; a high-risk case going off the grid was more than a little concerning to them. I searched night and day, and Nathan showed up to help, seeming more concerned about me than Wes. Foster was away for the summer with his family in Wyoming, but he called to check on me.

And after the first few days, I started to think that Weston was dead. That he'd killed himself and I had ignored all the signs. The guilt was enough to destroy me. But then six and a half days later, Wes appeared on my doorstep. He was dirty, mud caking the ankles of his jeans like he'd been riding non-stop. His beard had grown rough and scratchy; his hair was matted down.

He stared at me from the porch, his eyes red rimmed. He didn't say anything.

I stepped up and hugged him, crying out for my grand-parents. They darted into the room, alarmed, but relieved by his presence. My grandmother checked him over to make sure he wasn't injured.

When my grandparents left the room to call his parents, I held tightly to Wes's arm, feeling how rigid his posture was. Seeing the lost expression in his eyes.

"Where were you?" I asked, leading him to sit on the couch.

He gazed out the window toward his bike, like he might just leave again, before turning to me. "You know me?" he asked. I nearly broke down right there. Wes seemed too weary, too fucking sad. He was broken—I knew that much.

"Yes," I said, and leaned in to kiss the side of his mouth, my palm on his cheek as I fought back my tears. "Of course I know you." He hitched in a breath, and then laid his forehead on my collarbone.

"I'm so sorry, Tate," he whispered. "I'll make it right. I promise."

He didn't have to apologize. I was just happy he was back. He was safe. I offered to drive him home so that his parents wouldn't have to come get him; I was greedy for more time with him. My grandparents thought it was best because they worried Wes might take off before his parents arrived. Wes didn't speak a word to my grandparents—not even a thank-you, which was totally out of character.

On the drive, I asked Wes again where he'd been, but he didn't answer me. I'd catch him looking at me, though, like he was memorizing me. When we got to his house, a police cruiser was idling at the curb and his parents were waiting on the porch. I didn't see the white van parked just up the street.

Wes's mom led us into the kitchen, tears still wet on her face as she brushed back Weston's hair, murmuring soothing words. His dad stood, jaw clenched, and at the time I thought he was mad—upset that his son made him worry. The police officer came in, notebook out, but he didn't immediately start asking questions like I thought he would. Everything felt off.

When Wes's mom moved to the back door, Wes turned to look at me—an apology in his eyes. Something deep and sorrowful—apologetic. And all I remember thinking in that moment is that he wanted to die. I knew that look. I knew what it meant. My eyes welled up with tears, blurring the scene, and then the kitchen door opened.

"I've always loved you, Tate," he murmured.

It all happened so fast. Wes didn't fight the handlers, at least not as hard as he should have. There was something dark in him. Hopelessness. Misery. But I jumped forward to keep him anyway—terrified of what the handlers were about to do to him. Horrified that I was losing Wes to The Program because that meant he would lose himself.

"Stop!" I screamed, gripping the collar of his T-shirt in my fist. "Let him go!"

I felt the brush of Weston's fingers on my arm—that simple, tender touch. And it was like I was underwater—the world slow and the sounds muffled. I met Wes's eyes as they pulled him back, tearing his shirt because I still held it.

Wes was sick—I wasn't delusional about that. He'd changed. He disappeared and came back different.

And now, because of The Program, I'll never know why.

When I wake up for school in the morning, groggy from a night of restless sleep, I take my time getting ready. Although Pop told me to observe Wes before trying to talk to him again, I know that won't happen. How can you see a person you know so well and not want to tell him? It's torture otherwise. And, besides, it's unethical to keep it from him. He should know who I am. He should know who I was to him.

Gram is at work when I leave, and I get out the door before Pop can ask too many questions about today's plans. He would disapprove, but I also know that he'll forgive my mistakes because he loves me. I've seen too many people afraid to share things with their parents. It happened all the time with The Program. But I've never had to worry about keeping secrets. And it's probably why I'm still here today.

It's a little dark as I leave the house and get behind the wheel of my Jeep, an old model with a rebuilt engine and rusting red paint. I glance at the clock and see it's too early to go to school, so I decide to stop for a coffee. Next door, Nathan's bedroom light is on, and I guess that he's probably just getting up now. I text him and ask if he wants a coffee.

Plain black coffee, he writes.

Okay . . .

Kidding. Who am I, John Wayne? Get me a hazelnut latte. Extra hot.

I text that I will, and set my phone in the cup holder. I shift gears and drive down the street, my tires rolling through the fog. I love this time of day, the way the fog clings to the road and races over the fields. It's not dangerous, just atmospheric. The air has bite. The day has possibility.

I try not to think about the past—a constant battle. I try not to think about Wes's face when I asked him if he remembered me. Instead I lower my window slightly and let the cold air chill me. Remind me that I'm alive. Present.

The coffee shop is a few blocks west of the school—a small local place that's overpriced but worth it. The woman who owns it employs all her kids, all their spouses, and even a few grandkids. It's the epitome of a family-run business.

I park near the front, glad to see it isn't too busy. Sometimes the wait is so long, I have to go to Starbucks like a traitor. But not today. I walk inside and get in the short line at the counter, comforted by the sweet scent of vanilla and coffee beans. After a moment, I move forward a step.

There's a scuff of shoes on tile as someone comes to stand behind me in line. I look back politely and feel a jolt when I recognize Vanessa, Jana's friend who has gone through The Program. I turn back around before she notices me, but my heartbeat has sped up.

It's disconcerting to be this close to a returner. Of course, that would apply to Wes, but with him, I'm sure I'll get over it.

Another customer gets coffee and I move up a spot. I'm hyperaware of Vanessa behind me, can smell her cotton-candy perfume. I have a wild craving to stare at her, check her over and evaluate her condition.

I'm reminded of what Nathan told me about Vanessa starting a new therapy, and how Jana said it made her better. What sort of therapy could be a counteractive to The Program?

I glance back over my shoulder, and just then Vanessa notices me staring. I quickly smile.

"Hi," I say. "How's it going?"

Vanessa watches me for a moment before answering, studying me—the same way most returners do when they meet people. She's probably trying to place me, figure out if we know each other. Up close, she's much different from whom I thought she was from afar. She doesn't look as steady as I thought.

Despite having been back from The Program for months, Vanessa has a fragility about her—like someone who is still shaken after losing her balance. Still tender in spots from the fall. Her shoulder bones protrude through her T-shirt, the hollows at the base of her neck are deep, the edges around them sharp and exaggerated. She wears makeup, well placed and contoured, but she's a fun-house reflection of the sad girl underneath. I think Jana and I have different opinions on what "better" means.

"Hey," Vanessa says. "Tatum, right?"

I'm taken aback. "That's me," I say. "Sorry." I wave off my hesitated response. "I wasn't sure you'd . . ." I let the statement end, not wanting to bring it up.

"Remember you?" she finishes anyway. "Sure I do," she says. "It's only the important people they make you forget."

She motions over my shoulder to the line, and I see a gap to the counter has opened. I apologize to the barista and scoot forward to place my order. I still want to talk to Vanessa, but I'm also a little rattled that she remembered me. I shouldn't be, but it's a bit scary, like a stranger calling you by name.

I pay for my coffees and go to the end of the counter to wait for them. I keep my eyes on the floor, listening as Vanessa orders two drinks. When I sense her coming over, I press my lips into a smile and look up.

She stops at the end of the counter, picking through the selection of creamers and sugar packets. "So," she says conversationally. "I heard your boyfriend came back."

"He did," I say. "Did . . . did you know him?" They weren't in The Program at the same time, so I'm not exactly sure why

I ask this. I guess because I assume there's a bond there. They both went through something horrible.

"No," she says, shaking her head. "I had a few classes with him before, but we've never talked or anything. Does he remember you?"

The bluntness of her question catches me off guard, stinging like a slap. "No," I say, feeling exposed to the word, like it signifies that Wes and I weren't close. Of course, that's not true; everyone knows the effect of The Program. But I guess we all hope we'll be different. That we'll be the ones remembered.

The coffee shop is picking up, and the line grows. Vanessa watches the people curiously, but her question has spurred on my bravery.

"What about you?" I ask her. "Did you remember when you came back?"

She laughs, and turns to me. "No way," she says. "The Program wouldn't have let that happen. I was in for the duration: six weeks of constant therapy and harassment, I'm sure. They took everything important."

"I'm sorry," I say.

She smiles sadly at my apology. "You know, when the government shut down the facilities," she continues, "the public was told that all the patients would be set free without further interference. Didn't happen. I heard they were given the black pill anyway—without the targeted memories. Some things disappeared, others didn't—past and present grinding together, making memory soup. It made their testimonies inadmissible in court. Guess The Program didn't want their patients to be able to testify against them." She turns away. "So count yourself lucky," she adds. "Your boyfriend isn't dead."

He's not dead. She's right—I am lucky for that. Too many people were lost during the epidemic, more gone from The Program. But that doesn't mean that I have to accept things the way they are.

"Tatum?" the barista calls as she sets two drinks on the counter. I walk over and place the cardboard sleeves on the cups. When I have them in hand, I turn back to Vanessa.

"How did you get them back?" I ask her. "Your relationships with people?"

A dark shadow crosses Vanessa's features. "Thank God for the Adjustment, right?" she says evenly. I furrow my brow.

"Adjustment?" I ask.

Before she can respond, the barista calls her name, and Vanessa reaches past me to get her drinks. Her jaw is held tight and she doesn't bother with the sleeves on her hot cups.

"Look, I have to go," she says, not meeting my eyes. "Maybe I'll see you around." At the last second, she lifts her gaze to mine, and I can read that she wants to tell me something.

But she turns away instead. Vanessa walks out of the coffee shop, leaving me standing at the counter with an uneasy feeling and a lot more questions.

CHAPTER FIVE

NATHAN IS WAITING FOR ME ON THE CONCRETE steps of the school. When he sees me, he zips up his jacket and stands, brushing off the back of his black jeans. He looks bored.

"I started to worry," he says, when I come to stand next to him. We stay shoulder to shoulder, staring out over the front lawn of the school as students get dropped off at the curb. I pass Nathan his coffee and he takes a sip, quiet and thoughtful.

"Have you ever heard of an Adjustment?" I ask him. A cool breeze blows over us, whipping his hair against his forehead. He takes another sip.

"Like a chiropractor?" he asks.

"I don't think so," I say. "It might be that therapy you mentioned to me once."

He narrows his eyes like he's trying to think back, but then shakes his head. "I literally have no idea what you're talking about," he says.

"Vanessa Ortiz," I say. "You told me that Jana said she was undergoing a new therapy. Something that was going to combat The Program. It worked, right? She thought it was working?"

"Oh, that," Nathan says. "I don't think it's as big of a deal as you're making it. I was out with Jana one night, we were drinking, and she said some things I half remember. Something about Vanessa not dealing well with being a returner, but after her therapy she's been good. Or good-ish, I guess. She didn't go into specifics. I'm sure being a returner sucks. Probably worse for the people they forget, though."

"Yeah. It's not awesome."

Nathan looks over. "Sorry," he says. "And I'm sorry I don't have more details. I didn't ask and Jana hasn't told me. All I know is that they've got a serious bond. They're always whispering—like they're sharing some big secret."

"Interesting," I say. "I just bumped into Vanessa at the coffee shop. She said the Adjustment helped her. Maybe she thinks it can help Wes, too."

"Maybe," Nathan replies, and takes a sip from his drink.

We're quiet, and I turn to him. "So when were you out drinking with Jana?" I ask. A blush rises on his cheeks and he shrugs like he doesn't remember. I knew there was more to him and Jana than he admitted. "You're such a liar," I say.

"Hey." He holds up one finger. "Keeping a secret isn't the same as being a liar."

"You're right. It's worse."

He reaches out to push my shoulder, and I laugh. I don't care if he sees Jana. I just don't really like him not telling me. Then again, maybe it isn't serious. Which would explain why he didn't tell me.

"Wait," I say. "Does Foster know?"

"Nope," he replies easily. I stare at him, and he looks over. "For real, I haven't told him anything either."

"You'd better not have. I won best friend privileges, remember?"

"Yeah, yeah," Nathan says. "I remember." He smiles to himself before taking another sip of his coffee.

Back in middle school, Nathan and I got in a terrible fight and didn't speak for weeks—the longest I've ever gone in my entire life without talking to him. It was torture.

So one day my grandparents invited him over, forcing us to discuss it at the kitchen table. Truth was, I was jealous of his friendship with Foster. I'm only human. But Nathan swore I'd be his best friend until the day we die and possibly even after that.

"Our ghosts will haunt the shit out of this place together," he whispered.

He bet me a million dollars, and we shook on it.

The bell rings in the building, warning us that classes will start in five minutes. I throw a glance back at the big double doors as other students head that way. I hike my backpack up on my shoulder, reluctant to go inside.

Still, my conversation with Vanessa is bugging me—what she said. Or more, the *way* she said it. *Thank God for the Adjustment, right?* The words weren't joyous or happy. They were indifferent.

"Look," Nathan says, touching my forearm to get my attention. "I can ask Jana about Vanessa if you want. I can't guarantee she'll talk to me about it, but I can check. At least figure out what this Adjustment is."

"I'll owe you," I say, and he nods his agreement.

In truth, I doubt Jana will confide in him. Another side effect of The Program: difficulty talking about anything remotely personal with people. Then again, if they go out drinking together, I have no idea how personal they get.

I link my arm through Nathan's and together we climb the stairs toward the school. There was a time when I would do this, hold on to him, so that I wouldn't fall apart. So that I could hide how sad I was. My shaky legs would have given me away to handlers in a second. Those of us who avoided detection learned ways to hide in plain sight. But now it's habit.

When we get inside, my eyes adjust to the artificial lighting. Nathan and I start toward English class, and I'm not unaware that several people watch me. They're probably surprised that I'm not arm in arm with Wes. Even though they know that no one's memories survived The Program—at least no one we know. Somehow Wes and I were supposed to be different.

"Guess we're not," I mumble.

"What's that?" Nathan asks. I shake my head and tell him it's nothing.

We part as we cross into the room. I immediately look at Weston's desk and find him there, staring down at his composition notebook. And just like that, my legs are weak again. Nathan puts his hand on my back and guides me to my seat.

"At least try to be normal," he says once we're at my desk. I look up, ready to be offended, but he smiles, letting me know he was just trying to get a reaction.

Nathan sits behind me, scooting his desk up so it's at the back of my chair, same as he does every day. I stare intently at Wes, willing him to see me. But this time he doesn't turn around. And I try to control my disappointment as the teacher walks in to start class.

I'm tempted to follow Wes out of the room when the bell rings fifty minutes later. But, ultimately, I know I have to chill. No matter how I feel, I have to play it smarter. I should be observing, not obsessing.

I tell Nathan I'll catch up with him at lunch and head to my locker to grab my books for my next few classes. My stomach growls and I realize that I haven't eaten anything this morning. I was too distracted to order a muffin at the coffee shop. The hunger brings with it a swirl of sickness, and I scrunch my nose and slam my locker door.

When I spin around, I jump, startled, coming nearly nose to nose with Kyle Mahoney. I gasp and fall back a step to keep from running into her. "Sorry," I say quickly, shifting my books to my other arm.

But rather than apologize, she stares at me. Her bright blue eyes are blazing and her blond hair looks nearly white against her tan skin. She opens her mouth like she's about to talk, but then promptly snaps it shut.

I'm motionless, trying to figure out what the hell she wants. But then, without an actual spoken word, she turns on her heels and walks away.

"Uh, okay . . . ," I call after her. What was that about? I don't even know her. She doesn't know me. Then again, maybe she's curious about Weston, wants to know if he remembers anything. She might have lost someone to The Program. So many of us have.

Despite the fact that she weirded me out slightly, I feel bad that I wasn't friendlier. She probably could have used my support.

I stand there, watching the students walk by and realize that I'm the one unbalanced here; I'm the one spiraling out of control. This isn't me. It can't be me. I wrap my arms around my books and head to my next class.

I go through the morning, actually paying attention in class. I try not to think about Wes, but it's not easy. In science, Foster stops by my lab table to tell me I look pale and pinches my cheeks for color. I slap his hand away and threaten to douse him with chemicals. Then we both laugh until the teacher tells us to get to work.

I appreciate the reminder of normalcy, though—how easy the day can be with it. Because if I plan to be of any help to Wes, I'll need to be all right myself. And so I thank Foster for being annoying and he tells me I'm welcome.

At lunch, I walk out of math and go to the courtyard to meet Nathan and Foster. The sunshine is bright today, and I wish I had sunglasses—my eyes aren't ready for the change in weather yet. It's almost spring, but sometimes spring in Oregon doesn't really mean shit for sunlight. Today it does.

I'm only halfway across the grass when I see him. Wes is sitting all alone on the concrete walkway, his back resting against the brick wall as he reads a book. The way he does this, the book folded in half without any care for the condition of the spine, used to drive me crazy. But I also secretly liked it. As if he were on a stage, about to read from it. Something about it was so very *Dead Poets Society*, and I feel that flash of attraction again. I love that my guy is smart.

Neither Nathan nor Foster has noticed me yet, and I take that moment to step out of their line of view. I know Nathan wouldn't approve of what I'm about to do. Hell—I probably wouldn't approve, but I'm not thinking clearly when I make a beeline straight for Weston.

I try to be subtle, taking a seat against the wall a few feet down from him. He's absorbed in his book, and because the pages are folded back, I can't see the cover. I wonder if it's one he's read before but doesn't remember. There's a twist in my gut at that idea, how tragic it seems. Being stripped of even the simplest things.

I open my snack bag of chips and casually pop one into my mouth. I chew slowly, trying to build up my courage. After a sip from my Sprite, I turn to look at Wes.

"Hey," I call. He glances over, not appearing startled to see me, and nods hello before going back to his book and turning the page. I feel a little slighted but remind myself that he doesn't know me. At least he didn't get up and walk away.

I almost ask if he's reading a good book, but I realize what an annoying question that would be. And as the seconds tick by, my courage fades. I'm about to gather my lunch and walk over to my friends when Wes closes his book and sets it aside on the ground.

He exhales heavily, resting back against the wall, and then rolls his head to look at me.

"Yesterday," he says. "You were the girl at my locker?"

I'm startled that he talked to me, and I have to stop the words from falling out of my mouth incoherently. "Yeah," I say, trying to sound normal. "Sorry if I scared you."

"Scared me?" Wes's dimples deepen as he smiles, and my heart swells. My anxiety evaporates off my skin. "No, not at all," he says. "I just didn't want to talk to anyone."

"I bet," I say.

He stares directly into my eyes, the kind of gaze that makes you feel invincible. It's the way he's always looked at me.

"So what's up?" he asks. "Why'd you come over here? I'm guessing we know each other."

I don't answer immediately. Around us, the courtyard is buzzing—other students gossiping and laughing. No one is watching us. Wes and I are completely alone in a sea of people.

"We, um . . ." How do I say this without sounding desperate? "We used to date," I say, immediately thinking I've made too light of it.

He looks me over, his lips flinching with an amused smile. "Yeah?" he asks. "Don't take this the wrong way, but I think you could do better."

I laugh, a blush rushing to my cheeks, and I look down at my lap. That's exactly something Wes would have said, and it's amazing because it makes me think that no matter what happens, there's still a piece of him in there. The Program couldn't take that away.

I hear my name, and turn to find Nathan staring at us. Foster has the decency to look embarrassed, but Nathan waves me over. I hold up my finger to tell him to give me a minute, but I seriously might kill him. Why would he interrupt?

"And who's that?" Wes asks curiously, looking over my shoulder. "Your boyfriend?"

"What? God, no. That's Nathan. He's my best friend."

"Am I friends with him?"

"Not really," I say. "You're both very civilized about it, though."

"Huh," he says, like that's no big deal. "And the other guy—the redhead?"

"That's Foster."

"What did he think of me?"

"He thought you were cute."

Wes glances across the courtyard at Foster and then to me. "I must have liked him, then."

I laugh. "Yeah, the two of you got along pretty well."

Wes settles against the wall, pulling his knees up in front of him. He seems to enjoy talking to me, and I feel myself lean in closer.

"And you and me?" Wes asks, motioning between us. "We had a thing?"

I nod, unsure of how to even explain.

"So . . . how was I?" Wes asks. "As a person, I mean." He flashes me a small smile to let me know he's totally flirting.

"You were great," I say.

He grins wider. "And how about us?" he asks. "How were we together?"

I should play along, casually flirt back with him. But . . . the fact that he doesn't remember me hurts. The fact that he doesn't remember us.

"We were everything," I say seriously.

Whether it's my tone or my expression, Wes's smile fades as he watches me—like I've given him an answer he isn't quite ready for. He swallows hard and lowers his eyes.

"Oh," he responds simply. "It was serious."

"Two years," I say.

He flinches, his brows pulled together. He's quiet for a moment, and then murmurs, "Good to know." Without looking at me, he reaches for his book. "It was nice to meet you . . ." He pauses.

"Tatum," I say, devastated.

Wes nods uncomfortably, and then folds back the cover of his book to start reading again as if I'm not even here. He shuts me out completely.

Pinpricks race over my cheeks and I'm about to cry, but instead I pack up my lunch. I knew this was a bad idea—what did I think would happen? What if a stranger walked up to me and professed that we were a serious couple? I'd feel violated. I'd feel vulnerable.

I grab my things and stand. "Enjoy your lunch," I say with a hint of apology in my voice.

He winces at the tone, and turns to me. But instead of asking me to stay, he holds up his hand in a half wave and goes back to his book.

I wait only a moment, and then I leave. On my way over, I see Nathan murmur to Foster, both of them watching me sympathetically. When I get to them and sit down with my lunch, Nathan sighs.

"I was going to say," he starts kindly, "maybe don't bring up your relationship yet. It might scare him."

"It did," I say, and take a bite of food. I feel like a fool. Tears begin to gather and I sniffle and try to fight them back.

Nathan scoots over and puts his arms around me, breathing into my hair that I'm going to be okay. Foster nods, and together the three of us feel sorry for me. Because I don't know how to make this right.

And the cold realization hits us all that it might never be right again.

CHAPTER SIX

JUST BEFORE THE BELL RINGS, FOSTER TAKES OFF for his next class. Nathan asks me to hang back a moment, and we wait, watching the others go inside and the flood of new lunchgoers come out. I don't see Weston, and I wonder if he left earlier. If I was the reason.

Nathan turns and looks down at me. "I didn't get a chance to tell you—Jana's not here today, but I'll go by her house after school, okay? I just . . . I didn't want to bring it up in front of Foster."

I furrow my brow. "Why not?"

Nathan shrugs. "He doesn't like her."

This surprises me. "What? Since when? I've never heard him say anything bad about her."

"No, you're right," Nathan agrees. "He's never said it out loud. But I can tell."

"Maybe you're projecting and *you* don't like her," I say, studying his expression. He laughs.

"Nice try, detective. But as I said, there's nothing going on between me and Jana Simms. Leave it at that."

"Foster probably knows you're full of shit," I say. "He could be mad about that."

"Do you still want me to do you a favor, or . . . ?" Nathan asks, pretending to be confused.

"Yes, please," I say. "And for the record, I seriously doubt Foster has a problem with Jana, but if you think he does, you might want to ask him about it."

"No, thanks," Nathan says quickly, and starts toward the school. "I'll call you later."

I wave him ahead, giving myself a moment to think as I slowly walk to class. Although I vowed only a few hours ago to pull myself together before pursuing Wes, now I'm determined to fix us—to make it real again. He was *right there* in front of me. I still feel the same way, and I know once he remembers, he will too. The Adjustment might be the key to that.

In sixth period, the teacher announces that we're going to the computer lab to work on our research reports. I don't really have any friends in this class, so when we get there, I take a seat near the end of the row in the back. Above me, the fluorescent light flickers, annoying me.

I haven't even picked a subject yet for my report (something about a turning point in American history), but I take a quick glance around the media room to make sure no one is watching me. When it's clear, I lean closer to my computer screen.

I quickly type "The Adjustment" into the search bar and click enter. An entire page of chiropractic recommendations pops up. Well, I'm pretty sure Wes would need more than a muscular-skeletal shift to fall back in love with me. I go to the search bar and add on "The Program."

The screen seems to glitch for a moment, but then the results begin to list. There is no longer any official site for The Program—not since the government shut it down. The actual web address is "under construction," which I assume is to stop other people from buying the address and turning it into a real shit show or propaganda.

But there are a dozen sites dedicated to the horror stories from The Program. Even a few fan sites and blogs; not everyone hated it. There are conspiracy theories that claim it never happened, and sites devoted to the stories of Sloane Barstow and James Murphy, the couple who ran away and blew up the entire project.

It's a self-help forum that catches my interest. I get lost reading sob stories from people who survived The Program, stories about those who didn't. The saddest parts of all are the posts about how we knew—as a society, we knew the devastating effects of The Program. Even if we weren't clear on the methods, we accepted the results.

There is post after post of people asking for help. Begging for their memories back. They say they're not whole without them. My eyes well up as I read through their desperate pleas. I feel it in my heart: their pain. Their ache.

But then one small ad pops up in the sidebar like spam. The background color is Program yellow—like the awful hospital scrubs they used to make the patients wear. Probably meant to catch the attention of returners.

I click the ad and the page lights up as yellow fills the monitor. I self-consciously look around the room and quickly minimize the page. The color fades, replaced with an empty white space. Written in black is the phrase: "Prepare for your Adjustment."

The words send a chill over my spine, and soon a phone number appears, followed by a link. I click it and a new page opens, the fine print, I guess. It's a series of paragraphs, like a magazine ad for side effects you'd see for medication. I look it over, but I'm just not getting it. What does the Adjustment do? I think maybe they're being purposely vague. But it's the bottom of the page that raises the hairs on the back of my neck.

Side effects may include:

Confusion

Blurred vision

Flashbacks

Depression

Insomnia

Stroke

Death

Death? Really, death is an acceptable side effect? I glance around the room as if someone might pop up to agree with me. There's no way I'd want Wes to risk this. I can't believe anyone would have let Vanessa take this chance. I'm worried about her now—has she been experiencing any of this? She seemed off. Has anyone even noticed?

It's The Program all over again.

"We've got about five minutes left in class," the teacher announces from the front of the room. "Don't forget to cite your sources, and then go ahead and turn off your monitors."

I shut everything down and push back in the chair, waiting there while the others finish up their work. I'm overcome with disappointment. Even though I only heard about the Adjustment this morning, I let it fill me with hope. I wanted it to give me Wes back. But it seems no better than The Program.

My phone buzzes in my pocket. Since the bell hasn't rung yet, I covertly slide it out and check the message. It's from Nathan.

You doing okay? he writes, as if he can sense my anguish from across the school.

Mostly.

Yeah, right, he replies. Betty Rasta just texted me that you're crying in computer lab.

I quickly glance up and see Betty watching me from across the room. She diverts her eyes. I sigh.

I'm surrounded by spies, I write.

Or, he writes, people care about your well-being. Feel free to expect the worst, though.

I can't help it, I smile. Why are you harassing me? I ask. Don't you have science to fucking worry about?

You know I aced this class on the first day. I wanted to tell you, I just heard Courtney Dane dropped out of school.

My smile fades. Really? Because of her meltdown?

I guess. Sad, right?

Tragic. And it really is. Whatever happened yesterday, it wasn't her fault. I just hope she'll get the help she needs now.

Bell's gonna ring, Nathan texts. But stop freaking out. I still plan to talk to Jana later.

Don't bother, I respond. Just looked up the Adjustment online. It sounds like a bad idea.

Oh, sure. Because we know how reliable the Internet is. Are you new here?

I laugh and glance up to make sure the teacher hasn't noticed me texting under the table. If she sees me on the phone, she'll confiscate it. Once it's clear, I look down at the screen.

Also, Nathan writes, can you give me a ride home? My mom had to borrow my car. She dropped me off.

Yep. Meet me at the Jeep after the bell. I turn off the screen and stash my phone. I can't decide if I still want Nathan to talk to Jana or not. I know the Adjustment is dangerous—they pretty much said so themselves on their site. But despite all my rational thoughts, my hopes climb once again.

But this time, I prepare for them to crash back down around me.

• • •

The entire sky has clouded over, cold and gray from here until eternity. My mood shifts without sunshine, the feeling of possibility I woke up with is gone as I head out to my car. My backpack is heavy, and I switch it to my other shoulder to take turns balancing the weight.

Nathan is resting against the passenger door of my Jeep as I walk up. He nods hello, and then takes my backpack and tosses it into the backseat. We climb inside, and I pull out of the parking space, both of us quiet. When we're on the street, Nathan reclines the seat and turns to me.

"So I know you like to bottle up your feelings until you explode," he starts. "But since you were crying in class, I feel I have to ask: What happened with Wes at lunch?"

"Why does it matter?" I ask.

"Just does." I turn sideways, and Nathan shrugs like it makes his point. Although I don't feel like reliving my humiliation, I tell Nathan the entire conversation. Even the parts that embarrass me.

My brakes hiss as I slow to a stop at a red light. The radio isn't on, but my engine is loud enough to fill the silence. When the light turns green, Nathan chuckles.

"He had the presence of mind to flirt with you?" he asks, as if that's the larger point. "That's so Wes."

"I mean, at first," I say. "But when I mentioned that we'd dated for a while, he sort of . . ."

"Lost that loving feeling?" Nathan offers.

"Yeah," I say, feeling pathetic. "He was probably grossed out."

Nathan laughs. "If a girl came up to me and said we'd been 'everything' to each other, I'd immediately think of sex and be pretty proud. Confused, sure. But not grossed out. Secondly, you actually *did* have a relationship with him—it's not like you were lying."

"But he doesn't know that. He doesn't feel that. So to him, what's real? Certainly not us."

I turn on Walker Road, and Nathan points out the passenger window. "Take a right," he says. "Let me buy you a slice of pizza; turn that frown upside down."

I smile, appreciating Nathan's attempt to cheer me up. I pull into the strip mall with our favorite place tucked away in the corner. It's completely unassuming and a little dingy, but Rockstar Pizza has the best slices in the Portland area—even better than downtown.

We walk in and the girl behind the counter pops her gum, glancing up at us with a bored expression. Nathan and I grab two menus and head to the back to seat ourselves. The tables are covered in graffiti and Magic Marker. The walls have limericks and love notes written by customers. A few crude drawings. The air is thick with the smell of wood-fired crust and spicy wing sauce. I'm suddenly starving.

The girl comes to our table to take our order, and after she returns with two Cokes, I lean my elbows on the table and exhale. Nathan makes an exaggerated pout for my benefit and then matches my posture on the table.

"So . . . ," he starts, tilting his head. "Jana ended up coming to school today after all. I talked to her."

I immediately straighten. "Wait, what? Why didn't you tell me sooner?"

"Because I wanted to hear about your day first," he says. "Now, I don't know what you read on the Internet, that amazing bedrock of misinformation, but Jana had some good things to say about the Adjustment."

"She did?" I ask, surprised. I assumed it would be an awful review, considering the side effects and the general secretiveness of the therapy. And the fact Vanessa didn't seem all that enthusiastic, unless, of course, I misread her.

"From her point of view," Nathan says, "Vanessa was in a dark place after returning. But after the Adjustment, she was enjoying life again. Said she was better able to process her feelings and her past. Don't know what exactly *that* means, but she said it was good."

My lips part, and there's an inflation in my chest—happiness and hope. "Does she think it would work for Wes?" I ask.

"We didn't get that far into the conversation."

The server appears again, holding two plates and sets them in front of us. The tip of my slice is too big for the plate and touches the table. "Anything else?" she asks.

"Nope," Nathan says, reaching past me to grab the red pepper shaker on my side of the table. The server leaves, and I let my slice cool a minute. Nathan folds his in half, takes a bite, and then fans his mouth. *Hot,* he mouths around the pizza.

"Was that all Jana said?" I ask.

Nathan takes a sip of his Coke. "She said she heard about it online, told Vanessa, and the two went to check it out—it's in Portland. Vanessa signed up. Now they're best friends forever and life is good."

I think about that. "Vanessa didn't seem all that good when I saw her," I say. "She seemed . . . off."

"Well, she is a returner," Nathan says. "She's going to be."

I want to tell him that he's being unfair, but I have yet to see a returner who isn't at least a little traumatized from his or her experience in The Program. So he's mostly right. And yet I still don't apply that same logic to Wes. He'll overcome this. He's gotten over every other terrible thing that's happened to him, all without help. Without interference. He'll beat this, too.

Nathan sets down his slice and grabs a napkin from the dispenser. He wipes his fingers and then smiles mischievously. "I also got an address and the afternoon off from work. In case you want to check it out."

I'm suddenly scared of opening this can of worms. Opening myself up to the pressure of doctors, the lies they might tell if they're anything like The Program. I'm not ready. "Although I appreciate your curiosity," I say, "I'm still not convinced. With the risk of death, how could it possibly be worth it? I'd rather do more research before marching down there."

"Uh, fine by me," he says. "I'd rather not kill people today. Jesus."

"I probably should have led with that."

"Always lead with the death warning," he responds.

"Besides," I add in a lighter tone, "I promised Gram I'd make dinner tonight."

"What are we having?" Nathan asks.

"Spaghetti."

He crinkles his nose. He's never been a fan of pasta, which is absolutely baffling to me. "I'd better fill up on pizza, then," Nathan says. "And about the Adjustment, if you change your mind, or when you find the next mystery to solve, let me know."

I thank him. Nathan is my best friend—no strings attached. No hidden motives. And our loyalty to each other is fierce. "You're always the first person I call," I say.

Nathan smiles, wide and bright. "Yeah, I know," he responds. "I just like to remind you sometimes." And then he takes a monster bite of pizza.

CHAPTER SEVEN

GRAM IS HOME WHEN I GET THERE, AND I HELP WITH the sauce that she's already started. Nathan opts out of dinner altogether.

At the table, I tell Gram and Pop what I know about the Adjustment. Both what I found online and about Vanessa's behavior at the coffee shop. They listen, nodding occasionally. It's my gram who offers the first opinion, a shadow of doubt in her pale-blue eyes.

"What The Program did was reprehensible," she says. "They robbed kids of parts of their lives. They stole from all of you. There was a better way, but they didn't use it. Maybe it's good to have other treatment options."

"I agree, but I'm worried, too, Gram," I say. "Then again . . . is it wrong to hope? Or at least think it over?" I lean into the table, craving her guidance. My brain is so mixed up. I'm starting to lose perspective. Since leaving Nathan, I've turned over the possibilities a million times—what if I could get Wes back but was too scared? What if I fail him again?

"No, honey," my gram says. "It's never wrong to hope. Sometimes it's all we have."

I glance at my grandfather and he presses his lips into a smile. "Your gram's a brilliant woman," he says. "We're here for you, Tatum. If you want, I'll contact a few doctor friends and gather some information on the Adjustment. No sense relying on a Google search."

"Thanks, Pop," I say, feeling partially relieved. "I just want to know as much as I can. Even if it's not a real thing, maybe they have some ideas that can help. Therapy or whatever."

My grandparents nod, and we finish dinner. After we clean up, I volunteer to take out the trash. I'm just as confused as I was earlier, but at least now I can be patient while my grandfather does research. As a former reporter, he's good at that.

It's not quite sunset when I get outside, but the blue sky fades to orange and pink at the horizon. I'm crossing the driveway toward the trash can on the side of the garage when I notice a figure sitting on the curb. I stop abruptly, the bag bumping against my shin, jabbing me with something sharp.

Wes's shaved head is an immediate giveaway, even with his back to me. He's sitting outside my house, staring at the street. I glance at the trash can and then dump the bag and quietly close the lid. My heart races as I walk down the driveway toward Wes. I have no idea why he's here. Unless he . . . remembers.

He must sense me, because Wes turns to look back at me. I stagger under his attention but quickly try to recover. "Hi," I say, holding up my hand in a wave. I immediately close my fist and lower my arm to my side, self-conscious. I don't know how to act around him anymore. "I, uh . . . I live here," I add, and hike my thumb toward the front porch.

"Yeah," he says. "I kind of figured it was you."

I notice then that his clothes are different. A worn band T-shirt with jeans and sneakers. They're not his, or at least nothing he would have worn before. But they're definitely not the typical returner collared shirt, so I appreciate the change.

"Why would you think it was my house?" I ask, walking carefully in his direction. Wes nods at the curb next to him, inviting me to sit. When I do, it feels strange to be so close to him. I can feel his energy, his heat. "I mean, how did you end up here?" I ask.

He shrugs, and scans the road in front of us. "I was sitting in my house tonight, at the dinner table, listening to my parents argue. I told them I was going for a walk and left. I didn't have any place in mind. I just kept walking, and it was like muscle memory—the way I got here. At one point, I looked up and I saw this house. It felt . . . familiar. So I figured it was a place I knew." He looks over at me, and flashes an embarrassed smile. "That probably sounds weird, I'm sorry."

"It's weird that you walked," I say. "You don't live close." He looks down the street, and chuckles to himself.

"Yeah," he says. "I guess I've been walking for a while."

We sit quietly, and I watch the side of his face, waiting for some hint of intimacy between us that doesn't come. "Do you want to go inside for a bit?" I ask.

"No," he says. "If I've been here before . . ." He pauses. "Obviously I've been here before. I wouldn't know what to say to your parents. I wouldn't be able to answer their questions."

"Grandparents," I correct. "I live with my grandparents."

"Oh, that's interesting."

I laugh. "Yeah?"

"Sure," he says. "I live with a boring old mom and dad."

"Huh," I say, like he's making sense. "Well, the good news is my grandparents like you. They wouldn't pry into your life."

"That's awesome," he says. "It's definitely not that way at my house. I wouldn't be surprised if my mother put a tracking device in my sneakers."

I smile and we both look down at his shoes. A gust of wind blows over us, and I cross my arms over my chest. When it gets dark, it'll be cold, but I don't want to go inside to get a sweater. I'm afraid he won't be here when I get back.

"Your mother kind of hates me," I confess. "Just so you know."

This cracks him up, and I like how his face lights up. "Really?" he asks. "Now, that's even more interesting. Are you horrible?"

"No," I say. "But you were horrible and I got blamed by association."

"Shit, I'm sorry," he says, like he's not at all. "But I must have been awesome to hang out with."

"Most of the time."

He nods along, shifting so he's facing me. "Okay, well, since I'm here," he says, "I have another question for you. I found a motorcycle. Is it mine?"

"Yep," I say. "You like riding everywhere on it."

"Do *you* like riding everywhere on it?"

I smile. "I did."

"That's cool," he says. "It sounds fun. It sounds . . ." He furrows his brow and looks down at the road. "It sounds normal," he adds quietly.

"We were pretty normal most of the time."

He looks up and there's sadness in his eyes—like he's missing out on something. Only that something is his life. I hate seeing him this way.

"We could . . ." I'm scared to finish my statement, but I shore up my courage. "We could go for a ride," I suggest.

Wes studies me with a look that is distant and curious, like he doesn't know me at all.

"When I asked about the bike, my parents wouldn't give me the key," he says quietly. "They treat me as if I'm fucking helpless. I tried to tell them that The Program didn't erase my motor skills, but they're not listening." He sniffs and turns away, pushing his sneaker through the debris against the curb. "Maybe they're right," he murmurs.

I'm not sure what to say to make him feel better; his outrageous confidence has been eroded. It occurs to me that I don't know him anymore either, but I refuse to let that thought linger.

"Then we should steal it," I say. Wes laughs to himself, but I double-down on the statement. "I'm serious. We should steal your motorcycle and go for a ride. That's what you would have done before."

Wes looks at me and sees I'm not joking. "That's what I would have done?" he asks. I nod.

It's true. Wes's parents took away his bike once before. Wouldn't tell him where they'd hidden the key. So Wes went down to the dealership and talked to a guy he knew there. He got a new key made and stole his motorcycle right out of the garage. I told him he was crazy at the time, but . . . . damn if I don't miss that bravery now.

Wes smiles to himself and lowers his guard. "You're completely reckless," he says. "I like it. I'm in. But just in case, do you have a grappling hook I can borrow?"

"In the back of my Jeep," I respond without missing a beat. "Right next to the fake passports and ski masks."

"Perfect," he says. "We'll need all of those. So I'll sneak into my house and grab the key off the top of the fridge. Then we'll go for a ride, Miss—" He stops dead, his smile faltering.

He still doesn't know my name. My heart crumbles.

"Tatum," I say, not letting the hurt reflect in my voice. "Tatum Masterson."

Wes swallows hard but tries to smile again. "Let's go steal back my shit, Miss Masterson."

"Okay," I say, and stand up from the curb. Wes gets to his feet, brushing off the back of his jeans. "But this," I say, motioning between the two of us, "is why your mom hates me. She thinks I encourage your bad behavior."

Wes leans in, and his sudden closeness makes my breath catch. "You do realize this is your idea, right?" he says, grinning. "So she might be on to something there."

We stare at each other, and I bite back my smile. He's totally right. "I'll go grab my keys," I say quickly, making him laugh.

"I'll wait here," he replies, and turns back to the street.

I hurry toward the house, afraid he'll be gone when I get back. Afraid he's just an apparition, a flashback. I slip inside the kitchen door, and when I don't see my grandparents, I opt not to call out to them. They'll want an explanation. They'll want to check on Wes to make sure he's okay.

But this is mine—I can't let this moment slip away.

I grab the keys off the counter and take my grandfather's sweater from where it's folded over the back of the kitchen chair. I quietly close the door and run out into the driveway to meet Wes.

I wave him toward my Jeep, and he ducks dramatically like we're sneaking out. In a way, I guess we are. He seemed absolutely thrilled at the idea, and in his grand gestures, I catch a glimpse of the person I've missed.

Wes circles to the passenger side, and when I unlock the doors, he quickly gets in and crouches down in the seat.

"You're being a *little* dramatic," I say, and start the engine.

"I can promise you," he says, lifting his gaze to meet mine, "I'm only going to get so much worse."

"Yeah, I know. So you should start at a lower point."

He laughs and slowly sits up. We back out of the driveway, and with one more glance at my house, I start down the street. I feel guilty for not involving my grandparents, but at the same time, I know they'll understand. At least I hope they will. By this time tomorrow, Wes might be able to explain it to them with me.

Wes and I drive toward his house. The streetlights turn on, and the small houses fade into expanses of woods. Wes's house is tucked among the trees.

"What if your parents are in the kitchen with the key?" I ask.

"They're not," he says. "They'll be watching TV, pretending not to wait up for me."

"They'll hear you come in."

"That's why we're *sneaking*, Tatum."

"You know this will never work, right?" I ask.

"Yes, it will," he says just as easily. When we pull onto his street, he makes me park near the stop sign at the end of the street. Tree branches hang low, obscuring us from view.

And I think we both realize how weird this is—us together in my Jeep, about to steal his motorcycle. How strange it is that we're not talking about the obvious. Not talking about us. But maybe we're both doing it on purpose.

"Okay," Wes says. "If I'm not back in five minutes, leave without me."

"Five?" I ask. "You sure you don't want to give yourself ten?"

He looks sideways at me. "You think I'll need ten?"

"You might."

"Okay, seven and a half. But if I make in it five . . ." He stops himself and then shakes his head like he was about to bargain for something inappropriate. "I'll be back." He grabs the door handle and gets out. I watch him in the rearview mirror as he jogs toward his house and then turns down the walkway to his back door.

I glance at my reflection and see the flush in my cheeks. Feel the electricity on my skin. I smile. Wes may not have done so consciously, but he came to find me tonight. Like he's drawn to me. Like his heart remembers even if his brain doesn't.

I settle back against the seat, and a sudden panic strikes me when I realize that I left my phone back at the house.

"Shit," I mutter. My grandparents will definitely call, looking for me. I hate to worry them; I just didn't think through this plan entirely. When Wes gets back, I'll borrow his phone and text them. I'll let them know I'm with Wes, and that I'll explain more later. At least that way they won't think I was kidnapped while taking out the trash.

There's a flash of movement, and I turn around to look out the back window. I see Wes at his old wooden garage door, lifting it gingerly as if trying not to make the hinges squeak. When he gets it open, he looks in the direction of my car and gives me a thumbs-up.

Wes disappears inside, and moments later he wheels his

motorcycle out. He walks it down the road toward me, and although I want to feel light and fun, seeing it brings an unexpected wave of emotion. It's a part of him. Part of his past. Part of our shared past.

I still remember the first time I rode on that bike. God, Wes nearly killed me. Or at least it felt that way. He offered me a ride home from school, and completely and utterly smitten, I said yes, even though I wanted nothing to do with his bike.

But riding with him, close to him, I think I fell in love that day. There's something so vulnerable about being on a motorcycle—so adventurous. The world around us was suffocating, but on his bike we felt free. He opened up a different part of my soul.

I check the time and turn off my Jeep. I climb out and lock the doors, tightening my grandfather's sweater around me. I wait until Wes is within shouting distance before starting in his direction.

"Six minutes," I tell him.

"Fuck," he says. "Took too long in the garage."

"Your parents didn't see you inside?"

"Nope." He stops just in front of me and pulls a helmet from the back and holds it out to me. It's not the one I usually wear, but I don't mention it.

"How'd you avoid them?" I ask.

"Well, metaphysically speaking—"

"I'm going to stop you right there," I say, holding up my hand. Wes laughs, and slips on the second helmet. I wait while he climbs on the bike, testing out where he's comfortable sitting. With anyone else, it might have looked unnatural, but Wes looks perfectly at home there. When he's settled, he turns to look at me, confidence shimmering in his eyes under the streetlights. I swear it's really him.

"You coming or not?" he asks.

And I'm breathless when I answer, "Yes."

CHAPTER EIGHT

I CAN'T LIE. WES'S DRIVING IS A LITTLE SHAKY AT first. He takes the turns slow, sliding his sneakers along the pavement. He may look natural, but it takes him a few miles before he gets the hang of riding again. I'm not sure where we're going—we just . . . left. The engine's too loud to speak over, so I keep my arms around him, and before I even realize I'm doing it, I rest my chin on his shoulder.

Wes slows as we wind up through a neighborhood thick with trees and bushes. I've never gone up this hill before, but it's beautiful. When we get to the top, there's a clearing, and Wes pulls his bike into the small lot and parks.

"Do you mind if we stop?" he asks. He rubs his palms and I wonder if the vibration has hurt his hands. Wes used to wear gloves when riding.

I tell him I don't mind, and I climb off the bike. It smells like pine trees and earth, like camping and freedom. I can't believe I've never been here before.

"I love this place," Wes says, mostly to himself. I turn to him as he gets off the bike. He reaches up to take off his helmet, but it takes him a few tries to find the button on his chinstrap. When he gets it off, he smiles sheepishly, and then takes both our helmets and sets them on the seat.

"I've never been here," I say. "It's beautiful."

"I agree," he says. "Here, I want to show you something." He motions me forward and together we start across the lawn, the grass slightly lit up from the streetlights. The farther we get into the park, the darker the world becomes. But when we get to the edge of the clearing, my eyes widen.

The top of the hill overlooks the city, lights twinkling in the distance. It's straight out of a movie. "Wow," I say. I turn to Wes and find him staring over the edge, his hands on his hips like he's admiring the hell out of it. "How long have you known about this place?" I ask.

"Not sure. Just knew I'd come here all the time."

"Really? Since you've been back?"

"Not much. From before, I think. Us?" He turns to me.

"No, I've never been here," I say.

"Then maybe I stopped coming here," he says quietly. His expression darkens and he looks out over the cliff again.

Wes had never taken me here before, but there's a chance it was special to him. Maybe to him and his sister. I see the reflection of the light in his eyes, and I long to reach for him. But as much as I want to, something holds me back. Something unfamiliar in his posture.

"I drove my mom's car here last night," he says. "Early, before it was dark. And when the sun went down and the lights came up, goddamn if it wasn't the most beautiful thing I'd ever seen. Apart from the world, but on top of it. I felt like I had control for once."

This is Wes—so deep and introspective. So casual in his brilliance.

There's a boulder nestled in the grass near the edge and I ask if he wants to sit for a while. He glances back at the bike, but we don't have anywhere else to be. We walk over and sit next to each other, not too close. The cold surface of the stone cuts through my jeans and chills my thighs. I wrap my arms tighter around myself.

"By the way," Wes says, "I'm kind of digging the old-man sweater."

I laugh. "Don't make fun of me."

"I'm not!" he says, hand over his heart. "I actually really dig it. You look like you don't give a fuck what anyone thinks."

"Oh my God," I say. "You are the worst at giving compliments."

"That's because I'm sincere. If I lied a little bit, they'd probably go down easier."

"You were never one to lie," I say. Wes seems to be proud of that thought, and he sets his hand behind him and leans back on the boulder. He runs his gaze over me, like he's trying to figure me out.

"Were we important?" he asks suddenly. "I know you said 'everything,' but were we important?" It's not leading, not begging me to validate him.

"I like to think so," I say. "We were fearless. Bold. Brave." I smile a little sadly. "Like I said, 'everything.'"

The words are heavier than I intend, and we fall silent. After it goes on for what seems like forever, Wes laughs, breaking up the melancholy.

"So, *everything*, huh?" he repeats with lighthearted innuendo.

"For someone who doesn't remember," I say, "you sure have kept your filthy sense of humor."

He shrugs, but turns away. "A beautiful girl saying she's my long-lost girlfriend and I'm not supposed to fantasize a little?"

"Technically, you're the long-lost boyfriend."

"Good point," he says. He sits up, crisscrossing his legs in front of him. Around us, the night has darkened considerably, and his image starts to pixilate like a photo taken in dim light. "Can I be honest about something?" he asks.

"Of course." My heart rate speeds up.

"Even though I have no idea who you are, have never seen you before—"

His words prick me, but he doesn't seem to realize how sharp they are.

"—at the same time," he continues, "I'm insatiably curious. Not just about you, but about who I am with you."

"I can tell you that you're very honest. You're kind. You're funny."

He smiles softly. "Well, let me make this weirder still," he says. "I was kind of pissed after lunch. I mean, it's not your fault or anything, but . . . I didn't know if you were for real."

I try not to flinch from his words. From how he dismissed me earlier. "Okay," I say.

"I tried to ask people, but big surprise—no one wants to talk to returners. So I went to the library, found a yearbook from last year. Pages of memorials. *Pages*. It reminded me that the world I left isn't what I remember. It was a nightmare."

He's right about that. The epidemic was killing us. The Program was making it worse. There were days when hope was nowhere to be found.

"But there was one picture," he says, holding up his index finger. "Just one. It was of the two of us. We were in the library, standing in the stacks . . . just looking at each other. Compared to the rest of the yearbook, it was oddly upbeat. But also . . . compelling."

I know which picture he's talking about it, but it isn't nearly as light as it appears. In fact, we weren't happy at all. Handlers had been at the school that day, hunting again. They weren't after us—not that time, but they did take someone; I can't even remember who it was. How sad is that? Whoever it was had been one of many. A face lost in an epidemic.

Wes and I were drowning, trying to hold each other up. We shared a sympathetic smile, the kind you flash when you're trying not to cry. The picture doesn't reflect our isolation and fear.

But without context, the picture would have seemed different to Wes. And I don't tell him the truth of it.

"So, yeah," Wes says, standing up from the boulder. "I thought about you all afternoon and ended up at your house. And now I feel sufficiently exposed and even a little creepy."

I laugh, watching him. He's only a silhouette against the soft glow from the other side of the cliff. I'm relieved that my lunchtime confession didn't drive him away entirely.

"I should probably take you home," he adds, "but maybe we can go for ice cream first?"

"I don't really like ice cream," I admit, getting to my feet.

"What?" He gasps. "You're a monster. Okay, then. Do you like french fries, or are you the literal devil?"

"I love fries."

"Perfect," he says as we start back toward his motorcycle. "I'll buy you some fries and we can act all normal. It'll be fun. Yes?"

It occurs to me that this is why we're here: him, grasping at normal. It should make me uneasy, the fact that this is less organic than I want. But we are together.

"Yes," I agree.

So I play along, and try not to get lost in a feeling that may not be entirely real.

Scoops is an old-fashioned ice-cream counter with different kinds of sundaes and toppings, a grill for hamburgers and fries, and it's basically the only ice cream worth having in the area.

Sadly, I'm partially lactose intolerant, so I never eat ice cream. I'll eat the hell out of some fries, though.

The shop is busier than I expect when we pull up. There are a few customers at the wrought-iron tables outside, and some of them look in our direction as we park. I don't recognize any of the people. I'm hesitant as I climb off the bike, waiting for someone to point us out, but no one does.

"Do I like this place?" Wes asks. When I look at him, he apologizes. "Sorry to ask so many questions."

"It's fine," I say, taking off my helmet and handing it to him. "And, yes. You do."

He smiles and his dimples continue to dazzle me. It's strange for him to ask me what he likes, where he's been. I don't like the power it gives me over him. As if his reality might be altered by what I say. Wes pulls open the door to the shop, and the little bells on the door jingle.

A cold breeze rushes over me, the temperature in the place set cooler for the ice cream. There's the sound of sizzling from the grill, the cook visible through the rectangular opening. The entire shop is old-fashioned, a jukebox lit up and playing Buddy Holly in the corner, vinyl-covered booths packed with people. There are a few seats at the counter, but before we take them, a couple gets up from a small table in the corner and we opt to sit there.

I sit facing the ice-cream shop while Wes looks out the large window to the street. It takes forever for the server to come over to us, and we use the time to peruse the menu, discussing the pros and cons of all the sundae options. Since I just had dinner,

I'm not very hungry, but Wes insists I get fries anyway. I think maybe he just wants to eat them.

"What can I get you?" the server asks when she arrives, pulling a notebook out of her apron.

Wes looks at me, widening his eyes like he's pleading for french fries. I laugh and turn toward the server. "Plate of fries," I say. "And a Coke."

"And for you?" she asks Wes.

"Peanut-butter-cup sundae. Extra whipped cream. Two cherries."

My heart skips a beat, and Wes looks at me suddenly. "Those are for you, aren't they?"

I nod, stupidly emotional over this tiny sliver of a memory. We stare at each other until the server scratches the order on her pad and says she'll also bring us waters. She probably thinks we're crazy, but damn if I don't feel completely validated by the fact that Wes remembered my cherries.

"Because you don't eat ice cream," he says, like he's figuring it out.

"So you'd give me the cherries instead."

"I'm fucking chivalrous," he announces, and looks around like he's waiting for applause.

"You also don't like cherries," I say.

"Correct."

I laugh, but try to temper my wide smile, keep some semblance of self-control. This is the kind of moment I'll cling to. Every peek, every reveal, of the him I know.

We're quiet, and it's only a few minutes until the server brings our food. The fries are hot and the whipped cream on Wes's sundae spills over and runs down the side of the glass dish. He plucks off one cherry and holds it out to me by the stem. I can see he's considering making a joke, but he must fight hard to hold it back.

I take the cherry and eat it, conscious of how he watches me. When I'm done, he gives me the other one, smiling to himself.

"So what should we talk about?" he asks, reaching to take a fry from the plate. "You should ask me questions since I seem to be the question king over here."

"Okay. Well, how personal can I get?" I ask.

His expression clouds over, and he reaches across the table for the ketchup. "Whatever you want," he says in lower tone, and sets the bottle in front of me. Again, the gesture fills my heart, because he would always do that, knowing how much I love ketchup.

He seems uncomfortable with the possibilities, but this might be my only chance to ask him this question. "What was it like when you came back from The Program?" I ask. "You were gone for a long time before you returned to school."

He keeps his eyes downcast and picks up the shiny metal spoon next to his ice cream.

"First few days are a little hazy," he says. "They had me pretty doped up. Next thing I knew, I was in Palm Springs, living at my uncle's house. He was cool about it, but kind of tiptoed around me like he thought I might murder him." Wes lifts his eyes to mine. "Sorry, that went a little dark."

"I imagine there are more dark moments," I say. "You don't have to spare me."

He dips the spoon in his ice cream and takes a bite. "Maybe I'm sparing me."

The song on the jukebox switches to "Son of a Preacher Man," and I salt my fries and pour ketchup all over them. I take a bite.

"I waited for you," I say softly. "I would have waited forever."

He pauses, spoon near his lips. "I'm sorry I don't remember you, Tatum."

"And I'm sorry you're sorry. It's not your fault."

He scoffs at this. "They say that a lot, but if I was stronger—"

"It didn't work like that," I say. "No one remembered."

Wes smiles. "Are you trying to say I'm not special?"

"You are entirely average," I say, like I'm not joking.

"Funny," Wes says, taking another spoonful of ice cream, hot fudge dripping from his spoon. "*Men's Health* led me to believe that I was well above average."

I nearly choke on a fry, and we both crack up. There's the jingle of the door opening, and I turn out of curiosity to look over my shoulder. My humor falters when I see it's Kyle Mahoney, her hair trailing behind her in the wind. She stops dead when she notices me—her shiny black Mary Janes skidding on the tile.

Kyle is alone, and she darts a quick look at me and Wes. Then she continues toward the counter of the ice-cream shop, sitting in an open seat there. I turn back to Wes and find him licking the back of his spoon, seeming lost in ice-cream heaven.

"Do you know her?" I ask him.

"Who?"

"Kyle Mahoney," I say, and motion toward the counter. "The blonde."

Wes glances over and I try not to feel slightly jealous as I watch his eyes travel over her, taking her in. He turns back to me and scoops up another mouthful of ice cream. "I have no idea who that is." He continues eating, but I let my fries get cold. I feel unsettled, although I can't exactly pinpoint why. I watch her, and notice when she turns her head slightly to check on us with her peripheral vision.

"Why do you ask?" Wes says.

"She keeps showing up," I say. "Ever since you came back, I've been bumping into her. I saw her near your locker twice."

"Maybe that's where her locker is," he adds logically.

"Maybe."

Wes exhales, and when he sees I'm still examining her, he asks, "Do *you* know if I know her?"

"I don't think so," I say, looking at him instead. "You might have had a class together or something."

Wes shakes his head. "My guess is that she's just curious about a returner."

He puts his spoon aside and points at the fries. "Are you going to eat those now that you've destroyed them?"

"No, go ahead," I say, pushing the plate closer to him. He

picks up a fry and when it hangs limp, heavy with ketchup, he drops it back onto the plate.

Kyle turns away from the counter with a white Styrofoam container in her hand. She keeps it close to her and walks past us and straight out the door. She doesn't stop or even hesitate. And it occurs to me that her strangeness might have nothing to do with her at all. Maybe I'm projecting. Maybe I'm the one making it weird.

CHAPTER NINE

WES PAYS THE BILL SINCE I DIDN'T HAVE TIME TO grab any money from the house. The ice-cream shop has died down, and by the time we get outside, the tables there are empty too.

"What do you want to do next?" Wes asks, as we pause at his motorcycle. I reach and grab the helmet I wore earlier.

I groan. "I should actually get home," I say. "I . . . sort of took off."

"Hey, what a coincidence," he says, climbing on his bike. "Me too. Guess we're both terrible."

"Told you so," I say, and get on behind him. He kicks the bike to life, and I slide my arms around his waist. Wes leans back into me, subtly, but I notice. And my heart is content as we drive back toward his house, where I left my car.

Again, his riding is a bit shaky, and I suggest he get some boots (Wes would have never worn sneakers), because they slide better on the pavement.

Wes kills the engine at the end of his block next to my Jeep. He parks his motorcycle, and I'm charmed when he walks me to my driver's-side door. I unlock it, but we stand there a moment longer. I don't think either of us wants the night to end.

The streetlight casts Wes in shadows, and it's still new between us, familiar, but uncharted. I'm not sure who either of us is anymore.

Wes smiles under my gaze and moves to stand next to me, his shoulder resting against my Jeep. I can see him more clearly now, and that was probably by design. He has to know how attractive I find him. As if acknowledging it, he licks his lips.

"Tatum," he says, smiling my name.

"Yes?"

"Can I kiss you good night?"

There is a flutter of butterflies, weightlessness inside me. But at the same time, I'm entirely grounded in reality. "Why?" I ask, thinking it's too soon. He still doesn't know me. And I don't know this new him.

He laughs and puts his palm over his mouth. "Ouch," he says. "Shut down."

"That's not what I meant," I say. "It's not a rejection. It's just . . . do you want to?"

"Sure," he says. "Of course I do. But it's more than that. I want to feel it. I want to know if it'll be something I remember, like the cherries."

"So I'm a science experiment?"

"No. But it is for the good of science if that helps sway you." He grins, and it melts away my hesitation. Fact is, I'd do anything to be in his arms again. Plus . . . it might actually help.

Then again, I'm curious. Will he kiss me the same way? Will it feel the same for me? Damn. I'm overanalyzing again.

Rather than step toward him, I move back against the driver's-side door. I'm scared. Because the worst thing that could happen would be for us to kiss and for Wes not to feel any way about it at all. I nod my chin, motioning him toward me.

Wes laughs quietly to himself and pushes off the Jeep. He comes to stand in front of me, and I lift my eyes to his, my heart already racing. Wes looks me up and down, his lips parted in anticipation, and then he moves a step closer, taking up my entire world.

Another step and my breath catches, my hands automatically reaching for him when he's this close. I twist my fingers around the fabric of his shirt and gasp when he moves closer still, pressing me against the door. My eyes flutter with the excitement of the impending kiss. His body heat is fire.

And slowly, torturously slow, he leans down and presses his lips to mine, his fingers grazing my jaw to bring me nearer. I close my eyes, overwhelmed.

His lips are soft just like always, only now they move hesitantly, carefully. I pull him closer, growing impatient, and when

SUZANNE YOUNG

I feel the light touch of his tongue against mine, I lose my mind. Desire floods me and I get on my tiptoes, slipping my arms over his shoulders, my fingers on the back of his neck. He responds, moaning slightly as he kisses me harder, his hands now at my hips, pulling my body against his.

"I've missed you," I murmur against his lips. "I've missed you so much."

But my words must startle him, because he suddenly pulls away, making me stagger forward a step before he steadies me. His eyes are wild and glassy, his face flushed. We're both heaving in breaths, but he stares at me, like when he was looking into his locker, trying to figure out what everything was.

I brush my hair back from my face. I'm aching inside, my emotions a roller coaster that went from high to low in just seconds, upending my reality. It was just a kiss, but when me and Weston used to hook up, a kiss always led to something more. It was always so passionate—as if we couldn't stop.

But Wes isn't saying anything now, and I'm starting to wonder if I did something wrong. Maybe I shouldn't have grabbed his shirt. Maybe I shouldn't have been so eager. He must notice my concern, because he quickly holds up his hands apologetically. But he still moves back another step.

"Sorry," he says. "That was . . ." He runs his thumb over his lower lip like it's tingling. "I'm not trying to lead you on or anything."

There's a pinch in my heart. "What do you mean?" I ask, my voice weak.

"I'm sorry if I made you think . . ." He winces like he knows this is going to hurt my feelings. "I was just trying something—I shouldn't have. If I gave you the wrong idea, I'm sorry—"

"*Wrong idea?*" I say, wrapping my arms around myself. "This isn't the first time you've kissed me," I say.

"This is the first time I remember," he says. "And it should have been . . . fun. But that was intense. Like, painfully intense."

These are not the words I wanted to hear from him. But at the same time, I don't disagree. We are intense. Not just now; we were always reckless. Passionate. Maybe dangerous. Because we never cared about consequences. We let each other take up the world.

"I'm sorry," I start to say, fighting the tears that start to well up.

"Oh, God," he says. "Please don't apologize. Seriously." He comes to stand in front of me again, ducking down so his gaze is on my level. "Please," he repeats.

"How am I supposed to feel?" I ask.

"I don't know," he says sincerely. "It wasn't just the kiss. It was . . ." He trails off and turns to look down the street, like he doesn't want to voice the thought.

"What?" I ask.

"It was a feeling," he says. "When you said you missed me, it was like emotional déjà vu. I anticipated you saying it and it made me feel . . . guilty. I felt guilty."

I furrow my brow, confused. "You shouldn't," I say. "You couldn't stop The Program. They had us on their radar. They would have come for you no matter—"

His jaw tightens at the mention of The Program, and he starts to shut down, just like he did at lunch. "You don't get it," he says, cutting me off. "This wasn't about The Program. This was something about us."

He studies the hurt on my face, and softens his tone. "Look," he adds. "It was a good night. Honest. It was nice to talk to someone. I'm glad it was you. But now I think you should go."

The rejection stings, and although I don't want to be angry, it bubbles up anyway. "You asked to kiss me," I snap. "You realize that?"

Wes steps back from me. "Yeah," he says. "Yeah, I know."

I wait, but that's it. He doesn't offer an explanation. I shake my head and turn away from him, yanking open my driver's door. I get in and slam it, starting the engine as soon as I can get the key in the ignition. Wes wheels his bike back toward his house, his head hanging low.

I watch him in the rearview mirror for a moment, my anger fading into heartbreak. I thought . . .

I stop myself. What did I think? That he would just suddenly remember and love me again? Did I really think I could beat The Program so easily?

My nose starts to run, and I grab a tissue from the center console. I shift the Jeep into drive and start toward my house. I won't cry now. I can't be weak. I even resist the temptation to pick apart the entire night, applying meaning to every word. Every pause.

So I focus on the cherries. On the ketchup bottle. On all the little pieces that added up to him. And I cling to my denial so that reality won't drown me.

The lights in my house are blazing from inside the windows. I didn't tell my grandparents I was leaving. They've probably called a dozen times, but I didn't even bring my phone. I forgot to ask Wes for his.

I bump the curb when I pull into the driveway, racked with guilt. I hate to make my grandparents worry.

The side door opens at the same time I get out of the driver's seat. My grandfather stands there, his glasses on even though he's usually in bed at this time. My grandmother appears over his shoulder and pushes past him, tightening her fuzzy sweater against the night air.

"I'm so sorry," I start, but she holds up her hand to stop me.

"I don't want to hear your apology," she says, uncharacteristically short. "Just tell me where you were? Why would you just leave?"

"It . . ." I pause, and look at my grandfather, expecting him to tell her to ease off. But instead he lowers his eyes like he's disappointed in me too, and it hurts more than any scolding could. "It was Weston," I say, turning back to Gram. "He was here."

My grandmother's posture stiffens, and she glances around like maybe he still is. "What do you mean?" she asks. "Why didn't he come inside?"

"He didn't know it was my house. He had just started

walking and ended up here. Muscle memory." I smile at this, but my grandmother is having none of it. She waits for me to explain. "I offered to drive him home, but we stopped for something to eat. It . . . it was stupid. I should have come in and told you. I was just so surprised to see him. I didn't want to ruin the moment by asking your permission."

"Telling your family you're going out and haven't been abducted isn't ruining the moment. It's responsible. Respectful." She hardens her jaw, but I see the anger fade from her eyes, replaced with relief that I'm home. She turns away and starts back toward the house.

"And you'd better call Nathan," she adds. "He's out looking for you right now."

"Shit," I mumble. I follow my gram inside, passing my grandfather, whose lack of conversation makes me feel worse than ever. I'm not sure if he's angry or if he understands in some way. But once I'm inside, he goes to his room, so I guess I'll have to wait until morning for clarification.

My grandmother goes into the kitchen to make herself some tea, and I head up to my room to get my phone. I call Nathan's number and when he answers, sounding immediately reassured, I tell him I'm home.

"Dude," he says, and I can hear his car blinker through the hands-free connection. "I'm in my sweatpants and a flannel shirt," he says. "What if I saw someone I knew? Where did you go? And why the hell wouldn't you tell your grandparents?"

"It's a long story," I say. "But I'm sorry you had to look for me." I sit down on my bed and run my hand over my comforter to smooth it out. "I went for ice cream with Wes," I say.

Nathan is quiet for a moment, and then I hear him exhale. "You're lactose intolerant," he points out.

"And fries," I say.

"Okay, well, that isn't what I assumed. Although I'll go ahead and admit that I assumed the worst. I'm about to turn onto our block. Do you want me to stop by?"

"No," I say. "I'm a little talked out."

"Cool. Well, just a piece of advice: It wasn't too long ago when people were being picked up off the street by handlers. So next time you plan to disappear, give me a heads-up. Now I'm going to enjoy my life. See you tomorrow." He hangs up, and I figure he's annoyed that he was part of my search party, rightfully so. I owe him. I'll bring him a latte tomorrow.

I set my phone on my side table and plug it in. I gaze at it for a moment, part of me expecting it to buzz with a message from Wes. But of course it doesn't. I lie back, the lamp still on, and stare at the ceiling.

My night didn't go as planned either. And although I'm disappointed in how it ended, I hold on to the fact that he found me. Wes may not have meant to, but he found me tonight. It makes me think his subconscious is fighting to get out. To set things right.

It makes me think that he still loves me—always and forever. Just like before. Even if he doesn't know it yet.

CHAPTER TEN

I'M NERVOUS WHEN I WAKE UP. NOT ABOUT HANDLERS following me or a test I didn't study for. I'm unsure of how to approach Wes now, wondering if he'll avoid me.

When I come downstairs for breakfast, I'm reminded of the consequences of my evening escape. My grandparents are both at the table, actively ignoring me. It's not that they don't care—they're obviously mad, and it's standing policy to never talk while angry. They swear it leads to regrets. So I eat my Fruity Pebbles in dead silence and then kiss them both on the head and leave for school.

I bring Nathan a double mocha chip, and all is forgiven between us. I tell him about the night before with Wes, and ask what he thinks it means. All on the way to English class.

"I don't know," Nathan says. "It sounds like he's definitely still in there—like maybe The Program wasn't able to take it all." Nathan turns to me and smiles supportively. "He remembered your cherries."

"But what about the kiss?" I ask.

"Well," he says seriously. "That was definitely an example of you oversharing with me. But if I have to comment, I'd say you reminded him of what he lost and it scared him. I'm just guessing, though. Maybe you want to share more of your intimate details with me?"

"Be quiet," I say, pushing his shoulder. "I wanted your opinion. You don't have to—"

He quickly leans in like he's going to confide in me. "I'm sorry," he says seriously. "But I mean it—there was a lot of good that happened last night. Just . . . these things take time. Don't lose perspective. And try not to be so extreme," he adds.

"I'll dial it back," I say, admitting that he's right. "None of this is easy, though."

"I know it's not. But you've got this. Okay?"

I smile, appreciating his support. "Yeah, okay."

We walk into English class and I see that Weston is already in his seat, and he looks up when I enter. I pause, and Wes holds my gaze for a moment before looking at Nathan, as if trying to guess our conversation. Nathan ignores him completely, touching my arm in a good-bye, and heads to his seat.

It's not hostile; he and Wes weren't enemies or anything. But when your girlfriend's best friend is a guy, there tends to be a little jealousy. Not the macho, possessive kind—more like jealous of the time split between them. Or the fact that they know everything about each other because of me. Their personalities don't mesh, but they each mesh with mine individually. So they tolerated each other and mostly joked about being rivals.

Wes leans forward in his desk. "I'm sorry," he says loudly enough to get my attention. And the attention of several others. "About last night," he continues, "I—"

"Shh . . ." I move quickly toward his desk. "Don't talk so loudly," I say in a hushed voice.

"I fucked up," he whispers. "I'm sorry."

"You . . . didn't," I say, looking around uncomfortably. I see one girl bite down on her lip as she pretends not to listen. "I mean, it's fine," I add. But when I turn back to Wes, I see that it's not fine. The skin under his eyes is dark with shadows from lack of sleep. He tilts his head like he wants me to admit that what happened was not okay at all.

The bell rings and the rest of the class comes rushing in, along with our teacher. She glances at me, and then at Wes.

"Miss Masterson," she says, "that was the bell."

I nod an apology to her, and head back to my desk and take my seat.

As class goes on, Wes looks back at me a few times, impatient, and it's completely throwing me off. Even Nathan leans up to whisper, "You sure he didn't like that kiss?"

I honestly don't know what to make of Wes's behavior. I get

that he's confused, but I never thought he could be confused about us. I guess I'm just as lost as he is in this.

When the bell rings, Wes holds at his desk like he's waiting for me. I turn to Nathan, and he fills up his cheeks with air and blows out a breath. "Might as well hear him out," he says. "I'll catch up with you at lunch?"

"Yeah," I say, distracted. "See you then."

Nathan leaves, and I walk to the front of the room. Wes stands at his desk, and shoves his hands in the pockets of his jeans. He looks at the teacher, and then motions toward the hallway so she can't overhear us. I adjust my backpack, fidgeting, and follow him out of class.

"Can I say something?" Wes asks when we get into the hallway. Several people look at us as they pass, mouths open with surprise. Before the end of The Program, this wouldn't have been allowed—a returner and a former relationship partner talking out in the open. But no one is monitoring us now.

"You can say whatever you want," I tell Wes. He winces, and I realize my tone was colder than I intended.

"You were right," he blurts out, surprising me. "Last night when you said the kiss was my idea—you were right. And I was an asshole to just send you away like that. I didn't know how to explain how I felt. I honestly still don't. But I'm sorry if I hurt your feelings. I felt guilty all night."

His words should make this better, but they don't. Guilt isn't the intended emotion. And the fact that it's all he's feeling right now isn't reassuring. I swallow down the bitter taste, and accept his apology.

"I'm still saying the wrong thing, aren't I?" he asks.

"Sort of."

"This will probably make it worse," he says. "But . . ." He furrows his brow and runs his palm over his shaved head. "Can we be friends?" he asks. "Can we start there?"

The stab to my heart is sharp and rusty. To go from loving someone so completely to just being friends . . . it seems almost cruel. False, at least on my part. But Wes doesn't love me like he used to. I have to admit that to myself.

"Sure," I say, diverting my eyes. I'm afraid to blink because tears might fall onto my cheeks. "Friends."

He waits a moment, doubting my response, I assume. But when I don't offer anything more, when I don't look at him for fear I might cry, he sighs out his frustration and turns to walk the opposite way.

When he's gone, I watch after him. I see a few people nod politely in his direction, but no one speaks to him. No one gets too close. It's like he has an invisible shield, repelling them. And seeing that makes me realize Wes is going through a lot—for him to feel outside his own life must be tortuous. He could use a friend.

And so that's what I'll be.

I'm standing in front of the soda machine on my way to lunch, and I count through the change in the front pocket of my backpack. I haven't seen Wes since first hour, and when I texted

Nathan to tell him what happened, he didn't answer. Not even to say I'm oversharing. Foster's not at school today, so I couldn't even get his opinion during lab.

"Hey," a girl calls. I turn and find Jana Simms standing there, smiling pleasantly. Her dark hair is in a tight knot at the top of her head, her liquid liner a perfect cat-eye swish. She's always pulled together; from her baby-blue Nike sneakers to the delicate gold necklace resting in the hollow of her neck, she's effortless. "You okay?" she asks with a flash of concern.

"Oh," I say, and swipe my hair behind my ear. "Yeah. I'm good."

Jana gets in line behind me. "I saw that Weston came back," she says conversationally, and her eyes sweep over me like she might be able to tell how it's going. "Nathan mentioned he was your boyfriend. Or used to be."

"Yep." I don't say more about it, but I wonder how much Nathan has shared with her about my situation. I shift uncomfortably and go to the machine to put in my coins. I'm ten cents short.

"Here, I've got it," Jana says, just as I start to rummage through my bag again.

"Thank you." I step aside as she puts in a dime. When she moves back, I hit the button for a Coke and listen as it falls to the bottom of the machine with a rattle. "Appreciate it," I say, ready to flee for the courtyard.

"I know why Nathan was asking about the Adjustment," Jana says. I turn back to look at her, glad that the other people in line are distracted. "I know how it feels to watch someone you care about struggle. If I can offer any advice," she adds, "it's that sooner or later, they all want their memory back. It's cruel to keep it from them. It's just another form of manipulation."

Her words are a slap in the face. Even though I'm not the one who took away Weston's memories, it makes me think I should be doing more to get them back.

"Is that what happened with Vanessa?" I ask, stepping closer to her. "She felt manipulated?"

"Something like that," Jana says. "As I'm sure you've noticed, not everyone can deal with the aftermath of The Program. Not everyone is strong enough." She subtly nods to the right, and I look over to where Derek Thompson rests against a locker, his phone close to his face as he reads from it, his shoulders flinching up every so often. He's alone—always alone, like most returners.

Derek has been back for months, but he never really acclimated. And when I think about it, none of them truly have. The returners are the social pariahs of our school, even if it's through no fault of their own. Derek lifts his gaze from his phone, maybe feeling us staring, and I quickly look away. Jana presses her lips together sympathetically and turns back to me.

"Can the Adjustment help?" I ask her seriously.

"It saved Nessa's life," she says. "It's going to save a lot of lives."

Several girls from the basketball team—a sport newly reinstated after The Program's ban on athletics ended—pass us, and it's like Jana flips an entirely different switch when they call out to her. She goes over to them, and they slap hands. She doesn't even give me a backward glance, as if I've disappeared from her vision.

I turn away, surprised to find Derek, still at the locker, staring dead at me. His eyes are dark and shadowy; he lifts the corner of his mouth in a crooked smile, and damn—it sends a chill right down my spine. But I smile back politely and rush toward the courtyard for lunch.

When I walk outside, I notice Weston sitting at the wall, reading. He glances up from his book, and there's a flutter in my chest when his eyes meet mine. He nods a hello, watching me the entire time I pass him.

I find Nathan at the half wall, all alone and looking sullen in our usual spot. I drop my bag on the ground at his feet and sit next to him, setting my soda on the wall between us.

"You're late," he murmurs. "I didn't think you were coming today."

"Is that why you have such a sad face?" I say with an exaggerated pout, trying to make him laugh. But instead, when he turns to me, I see actual hurt there. I quickly ask him what's wrong.

"Not about you," he says. "It's about Foster."

"What about him?" I ask, my stomach dropping. "He's not in school today. Is he okay?"

Nathan stares down in his lap. "It's his brother."

My blood runs cold and it's like he doesn't even need to

tell me. I can read it all over his face, feel the shift in the world. "Sebastian," I murmur.

Nathan picks up my can of soda and stares at the tab, flicking it with his thumb. "Yeah, so he's dead," he says darkly. I cover my mouth, horrified. Nathan stares down at the can, and I watch as his eyes well up and a tear drips onto the thigh of his jeans.

Sebastian Linn was only seventeen when The Program took him two years ago. We heard it during class, heard the shouts echo down the hallway. Foster was with us in class, and he couldn't even react for fear they'd take him, too. He had to listen to his brother scream.

I can still see Foster at his desk, fingers curled around the edges. Nathan was sitting behind him with his hands on his shoulders, holding him there. Giving him strength. Foster's eyes squeezed shut, the girl next to him weeping at the horror of it all.

We listened to Sebastian yell for help, and then he was silent. Then he was gone.

Nathan brought Foster back to my house, and along with my grandparents, we stayed with him, comforting him. My grandfather promised to use his connections at the paper to check on Sebastian's condition. It turned out . . . it wasn't good. Sebastian had bought a bottle of QuikDeath, one they recovered from his house. He nearly died.

So although we never wanted anyone to go The Program, we hoped it could help him.

But now he's dead anyway. What was the point if he's dead anyway?

"Oh my God," I say. "Foster. Have you talked to him?"

Nathan quickly wipes under his eyes and sets the soda can aside. "Yeah," he says. "That's how I found out. He called me before physics; could barely understand him. He thinks . . . Sebastian was having a tough time with his lost memories. Angry, I guess." Nathan looks at me and I know that Foster is wrecked—the pain, the deeper way it hits when you know it was self-inflicted. The guilt.

And all I can think is: *We've lost another one*. I grab Nathan's arm and pull him into a hug. He doesn't hug me back; he just leans against me for support. Sebastian wouldn't be the first person to commit suicide after The Program. Although the epidemic is over, there are still too many deaths.

Nathan sniffles again, and straightens, grabbing his lunch bag like he's ready to carry on. But it's obvious that he's not okay. "Foster won't be in school the rest of the week," he says. "Maybe longer."

He takes out his sandwich and bites off a piece, chewing it like it's a piece of cardboard. "I just . . ." He pauses. "I just saw Sebastian last week. He helped me change the oil in my mother's car. He . . ." Nathan stops, closing his eyes, his face scrunched up. After a moment, he takes a breath and exhales heavily. "So much for a cure," he murmurs.

I feel sick. I can't even pretend to eat, thinking about Sebastian. About Foster. And worst of all, thinking about the damage The Program has done. The lives it continues to take.

I look over to where Weston is sitting, holding a book in

one hand, a cookie in the other. He seems content and peaceful for the moment. But Sebastian might have been like that too. They don't all have an obvious twitch.

Maybe Jana is right: Eventually all the returners will want to know. I think about Courtney, about her meltdown in the courtyard. Was it because she didn't have her memories back fully? And Sebastian . . . I wince, pricked by the grief. I can't help but wonder if he could have been saved by the Adjustment. What if there was a chance?

I look back at Nathan, finding him shattered. I lean my head on his shoulder, and he reaches to put his hand over mine. We've lost today. But I won't lose tomorrow.

I think it's time to find out a little more about the Adjustment.

CHAPTER ELEVEN

I'M ONLY GOING THROUGH THE MOTIONS OF SCHOOL, set apart by worry for Foster. I text him how sorry I am, and he thanks me—short and to the point. Even now, we try to hide our grief. Even now, The Program has robbed us of that.

My teacher tells the class to head to the library to continue researching for our reports. I'd hoped to use the computer lab to gather info on the Adjustment, but at least I have my phone. Although service in the library is sometimes spotty.

The teacher disappears into the stacks to help students pick additional books, but I grab the first one on the cart and find a table near the back of the room. I take a seat at that large wooden table and open the textbook to a page about the *Challenger* disaster. I take out my notebook and jot down a few notes, just in case the teacher comes by to check. I keep my phone under the table.

This time I know where to look, and I find the site for the Adjustment fairly quickly. When I search for testimonials, however, the Internet is silent on the matter. How that's possible, I have no idea.

I go back to the site and click the contact page, seeing the office is in Portland. I take a deep breath and fill out the appointment form with my first name. They have an opening later today. With my stomach in knots, I accept the time and click out of the page. I have no idea what I'll say when I get there.

The chair across from me is pulled out, and Alecia Partridge sits down at my table. My breath catches, and her dark eyes lock on mine.

"The teacher told me to sit here," she says, as if I'm about to kick her out.

"I wasn't . . ." I stop and glance around. Several people watch us. "It's fine," I say. "How are you?" I tack on the end so that I don't sound like a jerk, but I have to admit I'm rattled to be so close to her. Not just because she's a returner. Not just because my friend's brother died. But because she scares me with her instability.

She smiles, slow and creepy. "I'm good," she says. "Thanks for asking."

I realize then that she's not trying to be creepy; she's honestly surprised that I asked her. I wonder if anyone ever asks how she is anymore.

I give a polite return smile and slip my phone into my pocket, going back to the research.

"It's funny, right?" she says, startling me. I lift my head.

"What is?"

"How most of you study disasters—as if all of history is death and destruction." She licks her dry lips, chapped and cracked in the corners.

"What are you doing your report on?" I ask, truly curious.

"The Nineteenth Amendment," she says. "It won some of us the right to vote."

I look down at my book, looking at the names of those who died trying to get to space. How easily I selected the topic. How distant it felt. But now, after Sebastian, their deaths feel closer. I shut the book.

"Can I ask you something?" Alecia says, leaning into the table. Her right eye twitches, and she shakes her head like she can clear the tic.

"Sure," I respond, matching her posture.

"What's it like to remember?" she whispers.

The question is horrifically sad, and it's a blow to my chest. I straighten up, overcome by her situation. Alecia flinches again, and at my nonresponse, she smiles and looks down at the page of her book, running her index finger along the lines until it's off the table and onto her lap.

"Time has a way of going backward," she says quietly. "You'll see."

"I don't know what you mean."

"Did you ever think that they're the ones who are crazy?" She nods out to the room. "And the returners are the only ones who are real?"

Alecia brushes some of her tangled hair behind her ear. She looks down, mumbling something under her breath, but I don't think she's talking to me anymore. I wish I could remember what she was like before The Program, but the truth is, most of us were too scared to notice much of anything. Now she's here, and still . . . no one notices her.

"I'm going to get a different book," I say, grabbing the heavy volume off the table. Alecia keeps her head down as if she doesn't care if I come back.

I walk toward the stacks and put the book on an overcrowded cart at the end of the aisle, scanning the spines for something else. I grab an encyclopedia at random, ready to search for a topic, when I feel a prickle of needles across the back of my neck, as if someone is watching me.

I quickly turn, dart my eyes around the room, and find Kyle Mahoney. My heart jumps. Kyle is sitting alone at a table, a textbook open in front of her. She must have study hall this hour, but despite her book, her eyes are unmistakably trained on me.

It's obvious that she needs to ask me something, and now is as good a time as ever. I hold the book to my chest, and start in her direction. My teacher appears at the end of a row and looks at me. I motion as if asking permission to move spots and she nods that I can.

I cross the room toward Kyle, and she quickly lowers her head and turns the page in her book, like she was studying all along. I sit down at her table, and she waits a beat before closing her book. She looks directly at me, as if her shy act was just that.

"What's up?" I ask in a hushed library voice. "I see you everywhere. Do you need to talk to me about something?"

She takes a deep breath, and then leans back in her chair. Pink rises high on her cheeks. "Weston," she says quietly. "When he came back from The Program, did he remember?"

"Why do you want to know?" I ask. My boyfriend's state of mind isn't really any of her business.

"Because people have had memory crashbacks—meltdowns or whatever. Some can remember," she says. "Some can't. For instance, your friend Alecia over there is a little bit of both, isn't she?"

"She's not my . . ." But I don't finish the sentence. Again, my life is none of her concern. "So?" I ask.

"I was . . ." She seems thrown. "I was just curious where Wes fell on that spectrum."

"Curious?" I ask. "Are you doing a study on him?"

She laughs as if my question is ironic. "Let's say I am," she states. She turns around her textbook so I can read the title: *Memory Manipulation in the Modern Age*. "I'd say The Program qualifies as an important moment in history. I'm in Mrs. Klein's third-hour class."

Well, I feel kind of stupid now. I ease back in my chair. "No," I say. "Weston doesn't remember anything."

Kyle blinks quickly, as if my answer surprises her. "But I saw you two together," she says. "I thought he remembered."

I watch her, trying to figure out exactly what she wants from this. Report or not, she's not allowed to pry into our business. Part of me wonders if she's trying to find out information for another returner. "Nope," I say, pushing back my chair. "He doesn't remember a thing. Sorry."

I stand and Kyle leans forward, her blue eyes suddenly desperate. "If he does remember, though," she says quickly, not bothering to whisper, "you'll let me know?"

I furrow my brow, not sure why she thinks we have any kind of a deal here. "No offense, but it's not really any of your business, Kyle. This is kind of personal."

She looks hurt, but I watch as she tightens her jaw and sits back in her seat. "You're right," she says. "Never mind."

I look around the room, the other students working and chatting away quietly. I want someone to agree with me that this is a completely bizarre conversation, but I'll have to settle for texting Nathan about it instead.

"Look, I'm sorry," I add before walking away. "I hope you find what you're looking for."

Kyle stares down at the closed book but doesn't answer me. I tell her to have a nice day, and then I walk back to my table.

Alecia looks at me, seeming surprised that I returned to sit with her. We don't say anything, though, and after a moment, I open up the encyclopedia and flip through the pages. I don't want to write about death and tragedy. In a life where we're completely immersed in it . . . I just can't.

The image of Foster, crying on my sofa—wondering if his brother will ever come back from The Program—plays across my mind. We promised he would. We promised it'd be okay.

But we were liars.

I sniffle, and Alecia shifts in her seat, as if drawn to my sadness. But I don't want to break down, so I look at the book again and find the history of the moon landing. I opt to focus on something positive for a while. Just long enough to dull the sharp end of my pain.

I don't see Wes the entire rest of the day, and when the final bell rings, I jog to Nathan's locker just before he slams it shut and turns around.

"Have you talked to him again?" I ask, wondering about Foster.

"No," Nathan says. "He texted me to say he was with his family, and that he's not ready to talk about it."

I rest against the locker next to him, and look sideways. "Well, do *you* want to talk about it?" I ask.

"Not really," he says. "Not right now, at least."

"Okay," I say. "But if you change your mind—"

"Yeah, I know, Tatum," he interrupts. He pauses and tries to force a smile. "Can we change the subject?" I nod that I will, and we start toward the exit.

"Are you working tonight?" I ask. Nathan works a few

nights a week at an office as part of the janitorial staff. It's not terrible and the money and hours are amazing. My grandparents don't want me to get a job until after graduation because they're concerned it'll affect my grades. Nathan is brilliant, so he doesn't have to worry about that. I, on the other hand, actually have to study.

"Not until tomorrow," he says. "Why?" he asks, looking at me suspiciously.

"I thought we might do that investigating after all," I say. The halls are packed with everyone trying to get out for the day, but I notice Jana and Vanessa hanging by the exit doors.

"I'll have to get the Mystery Machine first," Nathan says. And when I don't laugh, he elbows me in the side. "Hey, I thought we were trying to feel better?"

"Sorry," I say, distracted. I watch Jana and Vanessa talk . . . more like arguing, I guess. Jana's expression is sour as Vanessa stares right back at her, stoically. Like she doesn't give a shit what she thinks.

I'm about to point them out to Nathan, but together they must agree on something before Vanessa finally smiles and they walk out together. That was weird.

"Well, don't keep me in suspense," Nathan says. "What's the plan?"

"Oh," I say, looking over. "Remember how we were going to find out more about the Adjustment?"

"Clearly."

"You still down for that?"

He pauses, and I watch grief cross his expression before he buries it. Sebastian Linn could have been a candidate for the Adjustment. What if it could have saved him?

"Okay," he says simply, holding my gaze. I smile sadly, wishing we didn't have to do any of this, and loop my arm through his.

"Well, good," I say. "Because I already made us an appointment."

The Adjustment office is in a small strip mall without any advertising. The building itself is unremarkable, with nothing architecturally interesting about it: flat roofed with gray-paneled siding. The only reason I know this is the right address is because the sign with the suite number painted on it is lemon yellow.

I've seen pictures of The Program facilities online and on TV before they shut them down. They were large and hospital-like, some with expansive green lawns and iron fencing. This unassuming office is less intimidating. But as I park my Jeep in front of the frosted-glass door, I note that the parking lot is deserted. The other storefronts are all closed down, some even boarded up. I turn off the ignition and look at Nathan.

"Uh . . . ," he starts, "this is a little spooky."

"That's why we're checking it out, right? Also, keep in mind that The Program had nice facilities and it sucked, so don't judge an experimental, mind-altering business by its storefront."

"Funny," he says, like it's not funny at all.

"Come on," I say, and we both climb out. I glance up at the gray clouds wearily, and walk to the door. Nathan grabs my arm before I pull it open.

"Just to be clear," he says. "This is only a fact-finding mission, right? You're not committing me to something that will steal my identity."

"Your memory is safe," I say. "I just need to know the details. Seems no one wants to talk about it, so we have to go to the source. Plus, I'm pretty sure they only adjust returners."

"Never assume anything, Tatum. So when I say leave, we leave. Got it?"

"Deal."

I pull on the door handle and find it locked. I furrow my brow and look around until I see a small buzzer next to the door. I guess it's for security, and I ring it and look up to the small black camera set above the doorway. There's a buzzing noise, and the click of locks opening. Nathan sighs like this annoys him more than anything else, and then he pulls open the door and we walk inside.

The waiting room is brighter than I imagined, white and clean. The chairs are all yellow. There is a pretty girl with long dark hair behind a receptionist's desk, and she smiles as we enter. A candle burns on her desk, filling the room with a soft scent of sage. I glance around and there is nothing on the walls but one framed picture of a man I've never seen. He's older, and I assume by the serious style of the frame that he's either dead or the creator of the Adjustment.

"Can I help you?" the girl asks without losing her perfectly straightened smile.

"I have an appointment," I say, my voice hitching higher. It's cold in the room, and I wrap my arms around myself. "I . . . um . . . I scheduled it online."

"Your name?" she asks. She opens a file on her desk, glances down, and then back to me.

"Tatum," I say. She stares at me, and I'm not sure if she's waiting for my last name, but I didn't use it for the appointment, and I don't give it now. After a second of awkward silence, she closes the file.

"Thank you," she says. "You can have a seat. The doctor will be with you in just a moment."

I glance at Nathan and I see that although he's trying to play it cool, his complexion has paled considerably. We go over to the yellow chairs and sit down. I hear his throat click when he swallows. I know he wants to tell me this is a bad idea, but neither of us speaks. I think we're both scared to. My heart pounds harder and it feels like an eternity—although it's only a few minutes—until the door opens.

I sit up straighter and Nathan reaches over to put his hand on my arm, both of us staring at the door. A man appears in a white doctor's coat, an older version of the same man from the picture.

The doctor looks at Nathan and me, a flicker of compassion in his blue eyes behind his glasses. My dread eases slightly.

"Hello, Miss Masterson," he says. I'm rattled that he knows my last name even though I hadn't given it. Nathan's grip on my arm tightens.

"My name is Dr. McKee," he continues, before smiling warmly. "Welcome to the Adjustment."

PART II
THE ADJUSTMENT

CHAPTER ONE

DR. MCKEE LEADS US THROUGH THE DOOR AND into a long hallway. At the end is a set of wide double doors, and I have a moment of panic when I think that's where he's heading. But he stops at the first door on the right, opens it, and steps aside to let Nathan and me enter first.

His office is unlike the rest of the building. It's warmer, still white walled, but there are several silver picture frames on his desk, books on shelves, although I can't read the spines to see the titles.

The doctor motions for us to sit down while he rounds the desk to sit in an oversize leather chair. He gathers a few papers, one that looks like a folded brochure. Nathan gives me an annoyed look and then crosses his sneaker over his knee.

"Noticed your picture in the lobby," Nathan says to the

doctor. "Do you also have a huge oil canvas of yourself above your mantel at home?"

Dr. McKee laughs, and leans back in his chair. "I do not. And I've kept the other one because my daughter took it, a few years ago now. I'm sure you've noticed I've aged."

"Yeah, I did," Nathan says. I shoot him a look to let him know he should stop being a dick, but I guess whether or not he should remains to be seen.

I almost ask about Dr. McKee's daughter, but, ultimately, that's not why I'm here. "How did you know my name?" I ask. "I didn't give my last name when I made the appointment."

The doctor leans forward, folding his hands in front of him on the desk. "I apologize if I startled you," he says. "We've kept all the records we could find on returners, and by extension, their significant others."

Nathan scoffs, but the doctor holds up his hand to stop him. "It's not quite as sinister as it sounds. Many of the records were lost and we've spent a significant amount of time and resources trying to get back what information we could. It helps with the process. With that said"—he looks at Nathan—"I didn't catch your name, son."

The corner of Nathan's mouth turns up. "No, you didn't."

"Look," I say to the doctor, drawing his attention once again. "I just want to know how you're any different from The Program."

"First," Dr. McKee says, "we aren't erasing anything. We're putting back what was stolen, or at least a memory close to it.

The process is complicated, but the biggest difference between us and what became known as The Program is that we're not trying to control your lives. If anything, we want to put the control back in the hands of the patients."

There's that word again: "control." Seems a simple concept, but in reality, it's harder to define. One person's freedom may equal another person's control.

"I appreciate the theory," I say. "But The Program said it wanted to help too. A lot of people, a lot of parents, bought into it. How do I know you're not just another helpful company that's going to end up killing us with your side effects?"

"You don't," he allows. "Sure, I can sit here and promise, but what weight does that hold? For you, what this comes down to is Weston Ambrose. How badly does he want his life back? I assume you're here about him?"

Again, he catches me off guard. I nod that I am here about Wes.

"Well," Dr. McKee continues. "From what I've seen, former patients will do just about anything to have their memories back. But not all are good candidates. Not to mention, you disregard the other side of this: Weston will suffer side effects regardless.

"I know you've seen it," he continues. "The crashbacks. The returners need our help. We still don't know the permanent effects of The Program, but what we're seeing . . . it's alarming. Crashbacks have become more common, especially in those who didn't receive any follow-up therapy. Even some who did. I believe we're facing down the start of a new kind of epidemic among returners. I want to stop it. I want to set things right."

Nathan shifts uncomfortably, and I realize that there have been more crashbacks. More returners who are unstable due to the tampering of The Program. Courtney to Sebastian to countless others. I have to admit that he's right about that. But a new epidemic . . . that's terrifying.

"So what *is* the Adjustment?" I ask.

"Memory implantation," Dr. McKee says. "We—"

"Like *Total Recall*?" Nathan interrupts. Dr. McKee smiles at him, as if he actually enjoys Nathan's humor.

"Not exactly, but if you need an image, then sure."

"Then how is it?" Nathan asks more seriously. "How do they get their memories back?"

"It's less sci-fi than you'd think," the doctor says. "And, technically, we aren't giving them *their* memories; we have no power to bring them back. But we help by implanting smaller memories around the desired ones, hoping to trigger a controlled crashback."

"And how do you get those smaller memories?" I ask.

"We use donors," the doctor says. "A person close to the patient donates a few memories. They re-create that memory in their subconscious, relive it, calling up even the minutest details. We map out the parts of the brain that are being stimulated, creating a pattern. Then, using light, we stimulate that same pattern in the returner's brain. There will be gaps, but our brains are amazing organs. It will try to fill those gaps, make sense of them. Your brain, for all intents and purposes, jumps to conclusions."

"I still don't get it," Nathan says for me. "You're not technically using their memories, but someone else's memory of them. How's that working out?"

"Pretty well so far," Dr. McKee says, and looks at me and smiles. He turns back to Nathan. "And we've only just started. The results thus far have been promising—some even recover their own memories. We've applied for a fast-track patent. We're currently the only treatment available that can combat the effects of The Program. We want to rush to market. We want to change lives."

"And the drawbacks?" I ask. "That was a pretty hefty list of side effects on your site."

"That's because we have nothing to hide, Tatum. Unlike The Program, we're not operating under a veil of secrecy."

Nathan smiles. "Like in an unmarked building?"

"We're taking precautions with our advertising," the doctor says. "This isn't for the general population; it's not some wish fulfillment for people who are bored with their lives. In the wrong hands . . . well, technology like this could be very dangerous. We won't let it get twisted into something like The Program."

"So only returners?" I ask.

"Yes. And like I said, not everyone's a candidate, and that alone offends people. But safety is imperative. We're at an important stage in development, and we'd rather not have negative attention until it goes through. And . . . there are others, from politicians to activists, who will try to shut us down, and if they can't, burn us down. So I assure you, the subtle signage is intentional, but when it comes to the procedure, I will be up front with Weston about the risks."

"What sort of risks?" I ask.

"The crashbacks could come unexpectedly," Dr. McKee says. "Or, he could reject the memory. But we have safeguards in place to try to prevent that. A colleague of mine invented a truth serum; she likes to put it in tea, but for this it's injectable. The Program used a similar drug, but it was not with consent. We use this method because one of the most important pieces to this is honesty. We're not trying to create a perfect world—life is messy. Life is painful. Returners need to know what things were really like for them, not an idealized version."

Dr. McKee leans back in his chair, folding his hands again. "So the truth serum would be for you, the donor," he says. "We want to make sure that your memory is as accurate as possible, fresh in your mind. If not . . . the contradiction between fact and fiction could cause a complete meltdown for Wes."

"This just keeps getting better and better," Nathan says. "And how much does this probably-not-even-legal procedure cost?"

"Nothing," Dr. McKee says. "This is an experimental

treatment. Weston would be part of a study group."

"Okay," Nathan says, and stands up, taking my arm to help me up too. "Thank you for the explosion of information, but now we have to go."

Dr. McKee stands politely, not looking too shocked by Nathan's sudden desire for exit. I wonder if this happens often—the first meeting ending in people running out.

"We really do want to help you," Dr. McKee calls to me. "I've taken the time to review his file, and based on his medical history, and your . . . stability—I really think Weston would be an excellent candidate for the Adjustment. If either of you has any further questions, my door is always open."

I narrow my eyes slightly, trying to figure him out. Trying to understand this man who wants to right the wrongs of The Program. But will he just make them worse?

"Thanks, doc," Nathan calls dismissively, and pulls open the office door.

Dr. McKee tilts his head, a small smile on his lips. "You know," he says to Nathan, "you remind me of my son-in-law. He's a pain in the ass too. But he's a good guy."

"Thanks for that completely unsolicited information," Nathan responds, and puts his hand on my back to lead me out the door and into the hallway. I half expect the doctor to follow us, but the long narrow hallway stays empty.

"This is easily the dumbest shit you've ever gotten me involved in," Nathan mutters to me as we walk back into the lobby. The receptionist stands when we enter, seeming surprised that she didn't have warning that we were leaving. Nathan offers her a mock salute.

"Wait!" she calls after us. "Do you want to schedule your next appointment?"

Nathan looks at me and laughs, and then he pulls open the glass door and leads us out without responding to her.

We sit in my Jeep, still parked in front of the Adjustment office. My phone is dead, so I stash it in the cup holder. Nathan and I are quiet at first as I try to take in all that Dr. McKee said. The fact that the memories are donated, my memories. And then, from those, Wes might get back a few of his own.

Nathan glares over at me. "Don't tell me you're actually considering this."

Although I usually appreciate Nathan's opinion on matters, count on it, in fact, he's starting to annoy me. "And why not?" I ask. "If they're my memories, I know they'll be true. He was right, you know," I say. "There have been more crashbacks. Wes could be next."

"That doesn't mean we knee jerk into a worst-possible-scenario reaction," he says. "There are other options, Tatum. Therapy. And . . . you. You being there for him. Neither you nor Wes has to do this Adjustment bullshit."

But it's my own self-consciousness that stings me. "But what if I'm not enough?" I say, my voice lowering. "What if I don't do enough, and Wes . . . ?" I stop when Nathan flinches, the effect of Sebastian's death still raw, too new to scab.

I close my eyes, taking a breath before looking at him again. "Don't you think it's worth a shot, Nathan? Wouldn't you do it for someone you love—a chance to make them whole again?"

Nathan lowers his head, sadness reflected in his expression. "No," he says. "Because good intentions aren't enough. And if I was so distraught to think I would let my friends get their minds tampered with, I'd hope you were there to stop me."

His words come with the devotion of friendship—the life-long kind. He's begging me not to continue down this path because he cares about me. I have to look away.

"You know I love you, Tatum," Nathan says in a low voice. "And maybe I haven't always been there for you. . . ." He stops and runs his hand roughly through his hair. "I'm here for you *now*," he says, looking at me. "So if you really are hell-bent on ruining everything, I suggest we find out more about the Adjustment."

"Didn't we just do that?" I ask.

"Not the bullshit sales pitch," he says. "We need to talk to his clients."

My heart rate speeds up. "Vanessa?"

"I was thinking we could start with Jana," he says, looking out the window. "We'll go over to her house together, get in her personal business." He smiles, and I'm reminded of why I'm here with him in the first place. Nathan always has my back.

"Am I bad cop?" I ask, making him laugh.

"Nah," he says. "You're always good cop. But how about we try sympathetic cop/dickhead cop?"

"I know which one you'll be."

Nathan laughs and gives me directions to Jana's apartment. And just like that, we fall down another rabbit hole.

CHAPTER TWO

JANA LIVES IN A DUPLEX ON THE WEST SIDE OF town. I park, and Nathan and I get out and stand in the driveway. The duplex has red-shingle siding, bright blue shutters. It's actually adorable, and I think, *Of all the places she could live, this really suits her.* Behind the first-floor window, I see a curtain swish aside like someone has been watching us.

"You should go first," I tell Nathan, pushing him in front of me.

"I will," he says. "But don't act weird or she'll think we're hooking up."

"Ew, stop."

He chuckles. "Okay, listen," he says. "I'm going to have to use my powers of persuasion, so be cool."

"*Persuasion?*" I repeat. "Gross, Nathan."

He snorts another laugh, and then together we walk up the wide front-porch steps, and he rings the doorbell for her apartment. We have to wait only a second before the door swings open. Jana stands there in yoga pants and a tank top, her hair pinned back.

"Hi," Nathan says brightly, as if he and I come here all the time. Jana looks at Nathan, then at me, and then back to Nathan before she smiles.

"Hey," she responds to him sweetly. "What's up?"

"I know I could have called," he says, boyishly adorable, "but I thought we'd just stop by unannounced. Can we come in?"

I'm a little taken aback, although I'm not sure why. It wasn't like we were going to pick her brain out here on the front porch. Jana doesn't seem all that overjoyed, but she glances behind her and then pushes the door open wider and steps aside for us to come in.

Jana's house smells slightly of smoke, and when we get into the living room, her mother sits on an old-fashioned green-patterned sofa, smoking a cigarette. Jana introduces me, and her mother nods politely. She says hi to Nathan, and I'm reminded that he's been here before.

"Let's go to my room," Jana says, and leads us toward the back bedrooms. As we pass the small dining room, a black cat stretches out its front legs on the table, eyeing us lazily. The kitchen is quaint, with a pile of freshly washed dishes drying on the rack next to the sink.

Her room is just past the kitchen, and when we walk inside, it's an explosion of color. Clothes are everywhere—all styles, like a mishmash of taste. Flowy skirts and leather jackets. Sandals and black boots. It's weird because Jana is consistently well put together and sporty.

Jana kicks some papers into the closet, closes the door, and turns to us. "This is about the Adjustment, isn't it?" she asks. She goes over to make her bed and then sits down. Nathan sits next to her, while I stand awkwardly near the door.

"I'm sorry to keep asking about it," he says. "I'm not trying to invade Vanessa's privacy. But . . . we just came from the Adjustment office. I mean, is the place legit? Is Vanessa having any of the negative side effects they mentioned?"

Jana stares at Nathan for a long moment, reluctant to answer. "I'm not sure what you want me to say here," she replies. "Everything has side effects, Nathan. The Program had side effects. So I guess the real question is: Which is the greater evil?"

"I'd rather avoid evil altogether," he says. "But I'm here for your opinion."

"Nessa got back some of her memories," Jana says. "It helped her cope with her loss. And I truly believe she's alive because of it."

"How did it work?" I ask, drawing her attention. "The procedure, I mean."

"I wasn't in the room," Jana says. "Her brother was her donor, and the way Nessa tells it, they put sensors on her big bro and together they all took a trip down memory lane. Said they avoided the painful stuff."

"Like what?" I ask.

"Her suicide attempt," she responds. "Her brother told me the toughest part was trying to find the right small moments, ones that would hold bigger meaning."

"And she had memories on her own after that?" Nathan asks.

"A few," Jana says. "Her crashbacks have been increasing, but Dr. McKee's observing her closely. They say they have it under control."

"I bet," Nathan murmurs, and then looks at me like now we have all the proof we need to avoid the Adjustment. But if anything, this only spurs me on more. If Wes could remember too . . . God, if I could just get him back, I'd do anything.

"She has one more session left," Jana adds. "Four in total. But I'm sure the doctor mentioned to you the most important part is to tell the truth and try to describe everything you can. From the color of your shirt to the background noise to the smell in the room. There is no detail too small. That description will implant in their mind; their brain will create the image. Give them enough info."

"What, did you read the manual or something?" Nathan asks her.

Jana smiles, something private and flirtatious. But it feels more like a distraction than anything. "Of course," she replies. "I usually research medical procedures before I let my friends get picked apart by doctors. Kind of like you're doing right now."

"Point taken," Nathan says.

"How did Vanessa feel after the procedure?" I ask.

"Great," Jana says. "Said she felt like she remembered it for real. That there was almost no way to tell the difference between a real memory and an implanted one."

"I still think I prefer the real thing," Nathan says.

"Yeah, well," Jana says. "Isn't it nice for you to have that option?"

Nathan widens his eyes, and Jana exhales and says she's sorry. "It's been tough, okay?" she says to him. "Never mind how The Program scared us, made us fear for our lives. It actually erased *us*. We're the ghosts here, not them." She nods in my direction. "So if there's a way to set it all back the way it was, I'm in. I'm all in to make things right, even if there are complications."

Her words are dangerously close to what parents said when calling The Program on their children. Fear blinding logic. Nathan keeps his eyes downcast, and Jana stands up from the bed and begins to pace.

"So, yes, if you're wondering," she says, "I'd tell Nessa to do it again. I think all returners should have that chance. Especially now."

"What do you mean?" I ask. "Why the urgency?"

She scoffs like it's obvious, and when Nathan and I exchange a confused look, she's taken aback. "You heard about Alecia Partridge, right?" she says.

I still, fear curling in my stomach. I just saw Alecia in the library. She was fine. Or . . . as fine as she could be. "What about her?" I ask.

Jana's lips part as she seems to realize that we really don't know what she's talking about. "Just an hour ago," she says, lowering her voice. "She died."

I gasp, and Nathan sways—already rattled by Sebastian's death. Before I can ask what happened, Jana goes on.

"I don't know the details," Jana adds. "But she had some sort of breakdown after school. It's on the news." She motions out toward the living room. "She . . ." But Jana trails off, not finishing the story.

Nathan and I sit quietly, and my mind races to put the pieces together. I asked Alecia how she was, and she seemed so happy that I just *asked*. That someone cared enough to ask. Why didn't I say more? Why didn't I do more?

I hitch in a breath, and Nathan puts his hand on my back supportively, staring at the floor like he's trying to make sense of things too.

All those times I didn't pay attention to Alecia. It feels so incredibly selfish that I didn't notice her, help her, and a rush of emotion builds in my chest and burns my throat. Nathan stands abruptly.

"Let's go," he says to me. I shoot a look at Jana, and she takes a step back from us as if offended. "Tatum," Nathan adds, his voice raspy. "Please."

I don't know what he's thinking, but the honest pain in his

voice is enough to make me jump up. Jana swallows hard, and then walks to the door to open it for us.

Nathan and I follow her through the house again. I say good-bye to her mother, and Nathan holds up his palm in a wave. Silent. When we get out onto the front porch, Jana calls his name.

He doesn't look back at her, but Nathan waits as she comes over and puts her palm on his cheek, gazing up at him. The move is so intimate that I feel suddenly out of place, and I turn and go back to my Jeep. When I get in, I stare down at the steering wheel. I can't wrap my head around the fact that Alecia's dead. She . . . I just saw her. She was alive. And I think about what Nathan said about Sebastian—how he just saw him, too. How much harder that makes all of this.

And for a second . . . I wonder if they can really be dead if they're still alive in our memories.

I look over at Nathan and Jana, and I'm surprised to see how they're talking. How close they are. Nathan leans in to put his forehead against hers. They exchange a few more words, and then Nathan pulls back to look down at her. I can't see his face, but I can see Jana's. Her eyes are teary, but beyond that is admiration.

I think she's in love with him.

I shift uncomfortably, not because I'm jealous, not in that way. I'm just used to having Nathan by my side. He's never had a serious girlfriend, and it occurs to me how this might affect his judgment. How it can change him.

But I don't mention any of this when he gets in the Jeep and closes the door, burying his face in his hands and submerging us in heavy silence.

Nathan doesn't talk the entire way home, and I think the grief over Sebastian is finally too much. He murmurs good night when I park, but I sit in the driveway for an extra minute. Two deaths in one day. Another crashback. Dr. McKee is right—there is something bigger going on here. Are all returners in danger? Is Weston?

I had thought that maybe Nathan was right about the Adjustment being too dangerous, but now I'm not so sure. Maybe doing nothing is the dangerous part.

I get out of the Jeep and cross the driveway, but when I pass the gate, I'm surprised to find my grandfather in the garden; it's nearly sunset. I pause in the driveway, debating whether or not to go in because I'm not sure if he's speaking to me yet. When he glances back at me, I wave. He nods, and I opt to tell him what I've learned about the Adjustment.

I sit on the little stone bench that my grandmother bought at a swap meet while my grandfather digs up some vegetables. He's wearing an Oregon Ducks baseball cap and his multicolored sweater. A trickle of sweat runs down under the side of his glasses even though it's not hot.

"Found out some stuff today," I offer when he doesn't speak. He glances up, not giving away his thoughts just yet. "About the Adjustment," I clarify.

This seems to pique his interest, and he pulls his handkerchief out of his pocket to wipe his hands before sitting back on his heels.

"And how did that go?" he asks, his voice measured.

"It was okay. Nathan came with me. We talked to the doctor who does the procedure."

My grandfather tucks his handkerchief back in his pocket. "You spoke to the doctor?" he asks. "You didn't sign up for anything, did you?"

"No." I shake my head. "We just asked him how it worked. Got the info for Wes, although I'm not sure he'd be interested. There are some pretty hefty side effects."

"Is that it?" my grandfather asks. "Did the doctor say anything else?"

I think back, and tell him everything we talked about. About the procedure, about the application for a fast-track patent. Even the details that Jana provided. My grandfather takes it all in, and I pause before I tell him the rest.

"What's wrong?" he asks, standing and brushing dirt off the knees of his pants.

"Sebastian Linn," I say, lifting my eyes to his. "Foster's brother died."

My grandfather's expression falls and I watch him work through this knowledge, the tears building up in his blue eyes. "I remember when Sebastian was taken," he says quietly. "Foster . . . he had a hard time with that. He'll need support now."

I nod that he will. Even though Foster's mourning with

his family right now, I'll text him that I'm thinking of him and sending him my love. And I'll ask how he's doing. Because we all deserve to know that people care about us, worry for us. I hope Alecia knew.

"And there was another girl," I add, drawing his weary eyes. "Alecia Partridge. I didn't know her that well, but I just talked to her today. She's had some severe side effects after The Program, but she was coming to school. She was in my classes. She had some kind of meltdown, Pop."

He exhales, closing his eyes. I sit forward on the bench, guilt and sorrow mixing in my heart.

"Two deaths," I say. "Two. You don't think something's happening to *all* returners, do you?"

My question seems to rattle him. "I hope not, Tatum," he says seriously. "For all our sakes, I truly hope not. But let's be careful here. Fear leads to recklessness."

"Of course," I say. My grandfather's a reporter. All our facts have to be backed up by research.

"I'll get some statistics and talk to doctors I trust," he says. "We'll figure this out." He holds out his hand, and I let him pull me up from the bench. Death surrounds us. To create some semblance of normal, I help him gather the gardening tools and return them to the shed.

"I'm sorry I was so angry last night," he says quietly as we start back toward the house. "When you disappeared . . . we were so worried." He stops, tightening his jaw. I feel the slap of guilt and apologize again.

"Your grandmother and I . . . You're everything to us, Tatum. We can't lose you." He turns to me and at his sadness, I instinctively reach out and hug him.

"Pop, you'll never lose me," I tell him. "And I'm sorry I worried you guys. I'm a jerk." I pull back and smile at him, but his sadness doesn't quite fade.

"We just want to do right by you," he says. "It's all we've ever wanted. And this Adjustment, the risks involved . . . If you weigh out all the possibilities, I'm still on the side of caution. For now, until we know more, I don't want you around any more doctors. We want you just as you are."

I understand his worry, especially after the terror The Program put us through for years. But I see my grandfather preparing to say something else, and his long pause makes me dread his next words. "And so after discussing it with your grandmother, we think that maybe you should give Wes a little space too. We don't know what he's going through. It might be best—"

I take a step back from my grandfather, stunned by his suggestion. "What?" I ask. "Pop, Wes is home. How could you . . ." I shake my head, trying not to get angry. My grandparents have been there for me. They watched me grieve when Wes was taken away. Watched me wait. This is a betrayal, like I'm the kid in the bubble now, being protected from the world.

"No," I say, finally. "I won't stay away from him. I can't believe you'd even ask me to."

My grandfather lowers his eyes as if he's ashamed, like it's something he never expected to say. I walk past him and pull open the door, pausing to look back. "I won't run off again," I say. "But I won't abandon Wes either. I hope you can understand that."

Pop looks over at me, tilting his head. "All we've ever wanted was to keep you safe," he says in a quiet voice. "And during the days of The Program . . . you have no idea how difficult that was. Stay away from this Adjustment, Tatum," he adds. "Let us keep protecting you."

"The Program's dead, Pop. It's time you let me protect myself." I hold his gaze a moment longer and then pull open the door. I'm surprised to find my gram waiting just inside the hallway, listening to our conversation. She didn't stand up for me. She didn't take my side.

I murmur hello to her and go up to my room. For the first time, I feel apart from my family. I feel misunderstood. Controlled. More than anything, my pop's suggestion has had the opposite effect.

It makes me realize how much I'd give to be with Weston again, how hard I'd fight.

CHAPTER THREE

IN MY ROOM, I PLUG IN MY PHONE. THE SECOND IT turns on, it blows up with text messages. I drop onto my bed and scroll through them. Nathan sent me the details for Sebastian's funeral, although apparently his parents have closed it to the public. I suggest we send flowers, but it feels woefully inadequate. I ask Nathan if he wants to come by, but he declines. I sit up on my bed and glance out toward his window and see his light shut off. I rest back against my pillows.

I start to text Foster, but stop. I call him instead. The line rings a few times, and I expect to leave a message, but at the last minute he picks up.

"Hey," he says, knowing it's me.

"Hi," I whisper. We're both suddenly quiet as a thick shroud falls over us, weighting us down. Because this moment makes it true. Sebastian is dead. He's never coming back.

I hear a sniffle, and then Foster begins to cry without another word. A rattle, a sandpaper scratch over my heart. I squeeze my eyes shut, listening to him. His raw pain.

"I'm so sorry," I murmur, wiping my tears. "I'm here."

I'm reminded of when Foster was on my couch, crying about Sebastian the first time. The devastation and fear of those days crawl up my throat. It's strange that the past doesn't haunt us more, honestly. It was so horrible. How do we even go on when that fear alone could have killed us? Is it because we've grown numb to it? Become desensitized?

I feel it now—the ache. The sadness. Just like I did then. And I realize it's like Alecia said—for a moment, time is going backward. Memory is life in reverse.

The phone line grows quiet except for the occasional sniffle. When Foster talks again, his voice is hoarse. "I'll be back on Monday," he says quietly. "You going to be okay?"

"I'm supposed to ask that question," I say. He hums out a small laugh.

"Yeah, well—you know me. Fucking friend of the year."

"Don't tell Nathan," I say. "And, honestly, Foster . . . anything you need. You know I'm here, right?"

"Of course I know," he says. "Thanks for calling, Tatum. It means a lot to me."

I smile, wishing I could be there in person. But I won't

invade his family's grief. I'm here for him when he's ready. I always will be.

We say good night and I hang up, setting the phone next to me on the bed. I clear away all my tears and stare at the ceiling, trying to process all that's happened today. I'm emotionally exhausted, and I feel myself sink into the bed. My eyes flutter closed, and then I'm asleep, the grief washed away for now.

There's a buzzing sound, rousing me awake. I blink and look around the room, seeing it's darker outside. Next to me on the bed, my phone continues to vibrate with several incoming messages. I glance down and my breath catches when I see it's Wes. I quickly open the message.

I know what I said last night, he writes. My heart sinks because I don't know where he's going with this. And I know what I said today, he adds. But any chance I can convince you to sneak out with me again?

My lips part in surprise, but not all-out excitement. Sure, he may be the one who went through The Program, but that doesn't mean he can mess with my feelings. Besides, I'm a little tender after today.

Don't you think that might give me the wrong idea, friend? I text back. I have to admit, it's a pretty cold response. And I nearly regret it when the phone rings.

"You didn't block my number, so that's good," Wes says as a way of answering.

"Not yet," I tell him. "But I guess it depends on what you say next."

He laughs, his voice hushed and sleepy. I smile and let myself thaw out a little bit.

"I'm lonely," he says.

"That was absolutely not the right—"

"And I realized," he says, louder, like I interrupted him, "it was because I missed you."

I fall silent. I don't even know how to respond, don't know what this means.

"After lunch," he says, "I looked for you. I wanted to apologize again. I thought up ways to make it up to you. I thought about you all damn day. And as I was lying here in my bed, I was *still* thinking about you, Tatum." He pauses. "You're quiet and now I'm worried that I've scared you away."

I sit up, cradling the phone to my ear. "I'm listening," I say, a little disappointed. For a second, I thought he remembered us. But if he did, he would have called me Tate.

"See, the thing is," he starts again, "I don't know what to do with you. And I don't know what to do without you, either. And, yes, I know that sounds shitty and unfair, but I want to be up front here. When I'm with you . . . it's like there's two of me: one who's running toward you and one who's running away. How does that make sense?"

I close my eyes, more hurt by his words than encouraged. He's telling the truth—I'm sure that's exactly how it feels to him. He's scared of how I feel—the pressure that puts on him.

But he longs for a connection. It's not something I can fix. So what should I do? This is the person I love.

"Wes, what do you want from me?" I ask, my eyes still closed. "Why did you call?"

"Because I want to see you," he answers miserably. "Don't you want to see me?"

My heart sways, and I open my eyes to stare across the room at the pictures on my mirror. In this moment, I know exactly who Wes is. I've heard him murmur that same phrase late at night, when he needed me. When the epidemic was suffocating him. I won't turn my back on him now. Not with everything happening around us.

"Yes, I want to see you," I say quietly.

"That makes me so happy," he says with a heavy sigh. "Do you want to come here?" There's a rustling on the line like he's tangled in the sheets of his bed. And I can picture his room, just as he left it. I wonder if his parents changed it when he went to The Program. Did they put away his Little League trophies, which were standing on his dresser covered with dust? Did they take down the picture of us from his mirror? I'm sure they did. They had to erase me.

"What about your parents?" I ask.

"They won't know. I have my own entrance to . . ." He stops. "You already know because you've been here. So basically we won't tell my parents. You in? I have pizza."

I smile. "Let me clear it with my grandparents first. They're still a little pissed about last night." I decide not to tell him about my conversation with Pop and how he asked me to stay away from Wes. "I'll text you."

"I'll be here," he says.

After we hang up, I take a deep breath. I forgot what it was like to have a boyfriend waiting for me. Always choosing to hang out with me, above everyone else. I set the phone aside and grab my things.

I go downstairs to ask my grandparents a huge favor, worried they'll actually say no. I find them both sitting on the couch, midconversation. They stop when they notice me.

"I promised I wouldn't run off without telling you," I say, looking at them. "So I'm asking: Wes just invited me over to hang out and have pizza. Can I go?" Although I'm not trying to, there is a bit of hostility in my voice.

My grandfather turns away, not angry, but conceding. My grandmother watches me a long moment, and then purses her lips.

"You're old enough to make your own decisions," she says, speaking for both of them. "However, after disappearing last night, after scaring us like that, I feel it's only fair that you have some consequences."

My heart sinks, and I open my mouth to argue, but my gram holds up her hand to stop me.

"You have an hour," she says. "Consider this your grounding."

An hour isn't much time, but I know she's right. I do deserve the consequences. More than anything, I'm glad she's letting me go at all.

"Thank you," I tell her. I quickly jog over to the couch,

conscious of time, and kiss both her and my grandfather good-bye before grabbing the keys to the Jeep. But just before I walk out the door, Gram calls my name. I look back at her.

"I'm sorry about Sebastian," she says. I flinch at his name, and nod—heaviness settling over the room. "We'll send Foster's parents our condolences," she adds.

"Thank you," I say in a quiet voice. "I think that's a good idea."

"You be careful out there, honey," she says, studying me. "Keep us updated."

I nod that I will, and then, somberly, I open the door and leave.

The truth is, I'm glad Wes called, not just because I want to hang out with him, but because I want a distraction. An escape from the grief and worry. A chance to live.

I park down the street from Wes's house, same place as last night, for good measure. I wait a moment and check my reflection. I practice smiling once, checking to make sure the muscles remember how. There I am. I grab my keys and get out of the Jeep.

I smooth back my hair and get to the basement entrance on the side of the house. But before I knock, I pause, nervous about seeing him. What if he's changed his mind again? Just like the kiss.

The door opens, startling me. Wes smiles broadly, like he can't even control how happy he is that I'm on his doorstep.

"I thought I heard someone creeping around out here," he says.

I laugh, my guard lowering the minute I see those dimples. "Wasn't creeping," I say, and then glance at the second-story windows, worried I was too loud. I'd hate for his parents to catch me sneaking in; I haven't even seen them since he returned. This isn't the impression I'd want to make.

When I look back at Wes, expecting him to tell me to be quiet, I instead find him watching me with an amused expression.

"No old-man sweater tonight?" he asks. "I'm disappointed."

"You're wearing white basketball shorts," I say, as if that's the bigger fashion travesty.

"Ouch. All right, now get in here before you wake up my parents."

I smile and follow him inside.

Wes lives the good life down here. The basement consists of three different rooms and a large bathroom. He uses the smallest room for his bedroom; another one has a pool table, and the other a couch with a monster TV and video game system. We opt for the couch.

I sit next to him and see he's watching some Discovery show about building motorcycles, but he passes me the remote in case I want to change it. I leave the channel where it's at and set the controller next to the closed pizza box on the coffee table.

I lean my head back on the couch, and Wes mimics my movement, the two of us gazing at each other. "I probably shouldn't lead with this," he says, smiling adorably, "but about that kiss last night . . ."

He lets the words hang there to gauge my reaction, and heat rushes to my cheeks. "The kiss you pulled away from?" I ask.

"I did do that, didn't I?" he asks. "Past Me is an idiot. If it helps at all, I promise not to stop any future kisses."

"If only you could find someone to kiss you," I reply.

"If only . . . ," he repeats. We're both smiling, drawn to each other in so many ways. I think he's funny. I think he's smart. And, yes, I want him to kiss me again. I just don't know what he wants. Not really.

"Were you avoiding me today?" he asks, quieter, more self-conscious. "I mean, I don't blame you if you were. Just curious where you disappeared to."

My smile fades; the chance for distraction crumbles. "It's actually been a super terrible day," I say, sitting up and breaking our gaze. "My friend Foster—the redhead? His, um . . . his brother died."

"Oh, God," he says. "I'm so sorry."

"Thanks," I say. "Sebastian was older. I haven't even really seen him since he got back from The Program." Wes flinches at the word "Program." I don't blame him; I'm still scared of handlers and they didn't even take me. He slowly sits up, lifting his eyes to meet mine.

"What happened to him?" he asks.

"He, uh . . . he killed himself. And there was another girl, Alecia, in our first hour? Turns out she died today too."

Wes swallows hard. "Was she a returner?"

I nod, and he looks away from me and rests back against the couch. I can't imagine how this feels for him, as a returner. A spike of worry he doesn't want to put into words. Although I planned to tell him about the Adjustment eventually, I didn't want to do it tonight. Not like this.

"This girl I know has a friend who's trying a new therapy to deal with the fallout from The Program. It seems to be working. Jana told Nathan—"

"He's the tall one?" Wes asks, his brows pulled together.

"Yeah. Nathan's my neighbor, my best friend. Anyway, he asked Jana about the therapy for me. And then Nathan and I went and investigated. It's called the Adjustment. Have you heard of it?"

"Of what?"

"The Adjustment," I say. "It's for returners."

"No," he says. "What is it—a drug?"

"Not really. It's some sort of trigger for memories."

Wes winces suddenly, and rubs his temple. It's then that I notice the haunted look that his smile hid earlier.

"You okay?" I ask.

"Yeah," he says, waving me off. "Just . . . I get headaches sometimes." He pauses for a moment, and then, as if the pain has passed, he straightens to look at me, his eyes narrowed. "So what, that was your day?" he asks, his tone colder. "You and your friends searching for a way to cure me?"

"Hey," I say. "That's not fair. And no . . . I'm not looking for a cure. I was looking for help. Do you want to hear about the Adjustment or not?"

He waits a beat and then shakes his head no. "Sorry. But it sounds like Program two point oh to me," he says. "I'm fine being just this fucked up."

"You're not fucked up," I say, reaching for him before I can think about it. He tenses out of my reach, and it's like a rejection. I pull my hand back into my lap.

"Sorry," he whispers. "You catch me off guard. How easy it is for you to touch me. It's still new for me."

But this isn't new. I've never had to think twice about being close to him. Wes watches me for a long moment.

"Can we . . . ?" He opens up his arms, inviting me into them. He seems hesitant, even scared.

There's a flutter in my chest, and I realize I'm scared too. But slowly I move closer until I'm resting against him, his arms wrapped around me. I close my eyes, seduced by the familiar way he feels. His fingers slide under my hair, cupping the back of my neck, and his cheek rests on the top of my head.

"This is kinda nice," he says.

I laugh softly, and move to put my hand over his heart. "'Kinda'?"

"It's nice," he whispers. He moves his mouth over my hair, like he might have kissed it. "You smell pretty," he adds.

His heart is beating fast. I pull my legs under me, and wrap my arm around his waist to snuggle closer. He hums out a relaxing sound and settles in with me.

"I'm not sure how I'm supposed to act," he says. "I feel like I know you, but I don't. I don't know your favorite color, your favorite band. I don't even know if you like pizza."

"I like pizza," I murmur.

"Oh, good," he says. "We might have had a serious problem otherwise. But I also don't know how you feel about me—this me," he continues. "Because I don't remember us. I don't remember how to kiss you. Don't remember how you like to be touched. I'm not the same person anymore. And I'm not sure I can be."

I squeeze my eyes shut, the pain in his voice cutting straight through me. I can't imagine what I'd do in his place: if I'd embrace or run from my past.

"I like you even more than pizza," I say, making him sniff a laugh. I can't tell him that I don't know the answer. If he really is different . . . I don't know if I love him anymore. I guess I just don't believe he's actually different.

We sit quietly for a while and Wes trails his fingers down my back and up again. There's a shiver that goes along with his touch, and I shift to look up at him. His hand pauses on my hip as he gazes down at me, his eyes heavy lidded.

"I know I said some bullshit about us *just* being friends . . . ," he says.

Maybe it's just physical. Maybe it's muscle memory, like him walking to my house. But I put my palm on his chest and lean toward him. And this time, when we kiss, he keeps his eyes open.

Wes is slow at first, careful. But each time our tongues

meet, our breathing becomes faster, more frantic. So when the intensity grows, when he eases me back on the couch and kisses me harder, I want it to be real. I want it all.

And as he kisses my neck, his hands touching me over my clothes, I'm sure this is him—it's Wes, the real one. It could be denial, but I believe it. I love him. I love him and I've missed him too much. My mind is spinning as I slip my hand inside his shorts. He moans, his kisses hungry, his body burning hot.

"You don't have to," he murmurs, his teeth grazing the skin of my neck. But there's little conviction behind his words.

"I know," I say. I think we both just want to feel and forget everything else. Forget it all.

And so we do this until Wes is slumped against me, his forehead resting on my jaw. I wait for a sign, that moment where he says that he loves me. That he's back for good.

But that moment doesn't come.

Wes kisses me quickly on the lips, and says he'll be right back. He runs to use the bathroom at the top of the stairs. I watch him leave, and then walk to the other bathroom with a dull ache in my chest—a familiar pain that I can't quite place.

I stand at the sink, washing my hands, and look up at my reflection. I see the redness around my mouth from kissing, the tangles in my hair. The despair in my expression. I stare at myself, my eyes welling up with tears, the water of the faucet ice-cold over my fingers.

Although he didn't mean to, Wes hurt my feelings. I feel

stupid and embarrassed. I turn off the faucet and dry my hands on the hanging towel. I smooth down my hair.

What the hell am I doing?

I lean my back against the sink, knowing that I made a mistake coming here, hooking up with the guy I want to be my boyfriend rather than the guy who actually is. I can't make him real. I don't have that kind of power.

I take a moment to pull myself together, and then I walk out of the bathroom, ready to leave for home. But I find Wes standing at the bottom of the stairs, staring at me wide eyed. My stomach drops and I'm scared something's wrong, but suddenly he laughs.

"What?" I ask, breathless.

Wes licks his lips and smiles widely. "I think I just had a memory."

CHAPTER FOUR

I NEARLY TRIP OVER MY FEET TRYING TO GET across the room to Wes. "What do you mean?" I ask. "What did you remember?"

He looks proud, and places his hands on my upper arms. "I remember you and me," he says. "It was just a snippet— no context—but we were here, and you told me if you had to watch one more motorcycle reality show, you'd kick in my TV. That's it." He laughs. "That happened, right?"

I smile, a reaction to his, but I can't call up that specific memory. It would be so small in our vast history, but I don't doubt it. "I'm sure it did," I tell him. "It definitely sounds like us."

"It's you," he says. "It's because of you that I remembered." He gazes down before wrapping his arms around me and leaning in to kiss me softly on the lips. "Thank you," he whispers.

"You're welcome."

He kisses me again. "And *thank you*," he repeats with innuendo. I smile, but I'm embarrassed that our hookup went further than I intended. Because looking at him now, he's not changed by it. It didn't mean the same thing to him.

"I should go," I say, untangling myself from him. "My hour's almost up."

Wes slips his feet into a black pair of sandals, and grabs a baseball hat off the coffee table and puts it on backward. He sighs, his hands on his hips, clearly disappointed that I'm leaving. "Let me walk you to your car," he says.

I agree and together we walk out. We're side by side, not touching. He may not think that's strange, but to me, it's like a river has opened between us, ready to wash us away if we get too close.

"My favorite color is red," I offer, drawing his attention. "And my favorite band is Radiohead."

He smiles. "My favorite color is—"

"Green," I say for him. But Wes furrows his brow.

"No," he says. "It's black. I think it's dark and sophisticated."

"Oh." We walk quietly for a bit, the mood between us off.

"So about earlier," he says, looking sideways at me. "You okay with us?" And I see a touch of insecurity in his eyes. "With everything?"

"Are you?" I ask.

"Yeah. I mean . . . I still think we should take it slow. . . ."

SUZANNE YOUNG

He waits to see if that offends me. What can I say? He's not trying to be cruel, not trying to use me. I knew he was confused before coming here, so he isn't lying to me. We've gotten too far ahead of ourselves.

So I swallow down the hurt, and I tell him I agree. I'm the one who's lying.

When we get to my Jeep, I climb onto the driver's seat and leave the door open while Wes hangs there to talk to me. He seems more confident than he was when I arrived.

I rest my head against the seat, wishing he could remember me. Wishing the old Wes would just swoop in and tell me he's sorry for making me wait and that he loves me. That he always did.

Wes perches his arm on the bar above my door, stirring me out of the fantasy, and looks down the darkened street. "So how about you explain this Adjustment to me," he says.

The request surprises me. "I don't really know a ton about it yet," I say honestly. "I went by their offices and met with the doctor. He seems to have good intentions. Of course, we know that doesn't always mean anything."

"Exactly," Wes says.

"But he said the Adjustment doesn't take memories; it implants them."

Wes listens as I tell him all about Dr. McKee and his new procedure. I explain to him about visiting Jana, and how she thinks keeping memories from people is just another form of manipulation.

"I don't agree with her," he says. "I think of it more like gambling. You keep trying to better yourself but end up further in debt. Losing more of yourself each time."

"There's something else," I say, worried about how he'll react to this part. "The doctor's worried about returners. He, uh . . . he said he thought there may be another epidemic among them."

Wes's expression tightens. "Meaning?"

"He said the long-term effects of The Program are still unknown, but that there's a strong possibility that some—many—won't be able to handle them. He thinks there will be a spike of deaths in returners. He said the Adjustment can help."

"Do you believe that?" he asks. "That returners are . . . what, defective somehow?"

"No." I shake my head. "Not like that. And my grandfather—he used to be a reporter—he's looking into it. He won't have any ulterior motives to cloud his judgment. But on the plus side," I add with a shrug, "Jana said her friend Vanessa got some of her own memories back. She said she's doing really well."

Wes stares at me, and I can see how this tortures him. The possibility hanging there. "Tate," he says, tilting his head. "I'm sorry. I can't."

He called me Tate. Despite this, my heart still sinks. "I understand," I say.

"I don't know how much you know about The Program," Wes explains, and his voice cracks. "Hell, I don't know how much *I* know, but there's a wound in my heart. A deep cut from something I can't remember. And it hurts. I'm scared they'll only make it worse. And I'm scared that pain will kill me."

"Then we don't do it," I say. "It's not about me, Wes. I'll always be here to tell you anything you need. We won't do it, okay?"

He closes his eyes as if this doesn't make him happy either. But after a moment, he looks at me again. "Will you eat lunch with me tomorrow?" he asks suddenly, changing the mood entirely.

"I usually eat lunch with Nathan and Foster." I pause. "It'll just be Nathan tomorrow, though," I add quietly.

"Ah," Wes responds. "Nathan. And we hated each other, right?"

I laugh. "Not really. You would sometimes pretend, though."

"I'll pretend again," he jokes, and takes a step back from the Jeep. "And if you decide to eat with me, you know where I'll be."

We say good night, and he holds up his hand in a wave, waiting for me to leave before walking back toward his house.

And as I drive alone, I start to cry. Not because of regret or fear. But because without the Adjustment, the Weston I know might never come home.

Even if he finally remembered my name.

It's Friday, and I bring Nathan his morning latte. We stand outside the school for a while in the cool air. Yesterday's tragedy hangs between us, both of us somber, and I turn to him.

"How are you?" I ask. Nathan presses his lips into a sad smile.

"I've been better," he admits. "But I talked to Foster for a while last night. Seems Sebastian had been acting a little strange. Headaches, nightmares. He, uh . . ." Nathan chokes up a little, and in turn, I feel the grief in my chest. "He didn't say good-bye. Foster said that was the worst part. That he died without saying good-bye."

I pull Nathan into a hug, wishing I could take away the pain. But for now, all we can do is be here for each other.

"It's okay," Nathan says after a moment, and straightens. He sniffles back his tears. "Foster said we could come to the funeral if we wanted, but that it would really be best if we didn't—for his parents' sake. They're not taking it well and they want privacy."

"We'll do whatever Foster wants," I say.

Nathan nods that it's a good plan, and then he turns to me and sputters out a laugh like he's embarrassed he just fell apart. "So how was your night?" he asks.

"Fine," I say. The bell rings behind us, and I take Nathan's arm to steer him toward the front door of the school. "I saw Wes. We're friends or . . . whatever."

Nathan lifts his right eyebrow. "Whatever?" he asks. "Sounds inappropriate."

"It's whatever," I say, not wanting to tell him the details. The rejection I feel. "He asked me to eat lunch with him today," I add.

"Hell no," Nathan replies, and takes a sip from his latte as we turn down the hallway toward English class. "You don't just get to trade out friends. Besides, Foster's not here. Am I supposed to eat alone?"

"You're right," I say immediately. "But just for the record, you sometimes ditch me for Jana. What's up with her anyway? You two had a moment yesterday. Does that happen often?"

"I have no idea what you're talking about." He smiles at me, basically telling me to stay out of his relationship business. I guess he and Jana are more serious than I thought. It could be why Nathan thinks Foster doesn't like her. He's probably trying to figure it out too.

"Speaking of Jana, though," he adds, "she called me last night asking about you—what you were going to do about the Adjustment. She was acting kind of weird yesterday, right?"

"I don't know her normal setting of weird."

"She's not usually. But something's off about her. Has been since . . ." He stops, but I'm curious.

"Since when?" I ask.

He pulls his eyebrows together. "Since Weston came back."

We pause just outside our English class. "She might be wondering about him," I say. "He's a returner like Vanessa. Or she could be doing a research report like Kyle Mahoney."

Nathan looks down at his coffee. "Could be it," he says. "Either way, I just didn't want her to convince you to go for an Adjustment. Her concern didn't feel . . . genuine. Does that make sense?"

"I agree she was acting a little sketchy," I say. "But she also likes you, so she clearly has problems."

"Ouch." He laughs and pushes my shoulder.

"And you don't have to worry," I add. "Wes and I agreed on the Adjustment. It's not going to happen." I don't let my disappointment show.

Nathan blows out a relieved breath and reaches out his coffee to cheers me. "Finally some good news," he says. "Your grandparents had me worried."

"What?" I ask. "They . . . talked to you about it?"

"Last night," he says, seeming surprised I didn't know. "Pop called and told me to talk you out of it. I informed him that I don't have the power to talk you out of anything, but I said I'd offer my opinion. Which is a big fat no," he adds, leaning in to accentuate his point.

"I get it," I say, turning away. My grandparents didn't mention talking to Nathan about this. I don't like that Pop went behind my back.

The final bell rings and a few students jog by us to get to class.

"Listen," Nathan says, offering a truce. "Have lunch with your man," he says. "Your absence is excused for today." He bows cordially, releasing me from today's lunch date. I feel bad; I really wouldn't ditch him. But that's why we're friends. We don't hold the other hostage.

"Thank you," I respond.

He walks into class before me, and when I head in, Weston

looks up from his seat. He's dressed in a vintage-looking T-shirt, and he's wearing boots—more like himself than ever.

Wes doesn't say anything, but he smiles. Before I can smile back, I notice the empty desk, like it's an open wound. Alecia's desk. I'm scooped out by fear that I'd put off; another returner gone. I walk past Weston without stopping to talk to him.

Nathan pushes his desk to my seat, ready for our usual banter, but he catches me staring at the desk. He looks sideways at it and falls quiet. He sits back in his chair.

Several other people glance at Alecia's spot, a mixture of guilt and fear in their expressions. Maybe each is wondering if they could have done something different. Or maybe they're afraid. Afraid it's happening again.

CHAPTER FIVE

WES GOT CALLED OUT OF CLASS EARLY, AND I USED the opportunity to walk alone to my next period. I'm not sure how to feel anymore. I almost preferred the time when I was numb. Because this sucks.

By lunch, my nerves have mostly settled. It's a subdued day; everyone's quieter than usual. Most have heard about Alecia already, and a few ask me to send love to Foster for his brother.

Nathan texted me earlier to say he's using his free lunch period to catch up on science, and that he's not even mad about it.

I'm late getting to lunch, and as I step into the courtyard, I find Wes in the same spot, his lunch and a book in front of him. For a moment, I imagine him the way he was last year, lost in a book while I ate with Nathan and Foster. I take out my phone.

I'm here, I write. I watch when Wes gets the text and immediately looks up and finds me. He doesn't wave me over or anything dramatic. He leans back against the wall and puts down his book, like he's content to wait.

I cross the courtyard and take a spot next to him, setting my lunch between us. He looks at me, his dimples deepening when he smiles.

"Thought maybe you decided you hate me," he says.

"Nope," I reply, unfolding my paper bag.

"Not even a little bit?" He waits a second. "You sure?"

I pinch my fingers together. "A tiny bit," I say. "But not more than usual."

Wes nods seriously, and then picks up his sandwich. "I can handle that," he says, and I laugh. "So how are you today?" he asks. "You didn't talk to me this morning and it made me sad."

"Well, I'm here now, talking to you." I grab my Tupperware of leftovers and set aside a Baggie with chocolate chip cookies. I don't like sweets, but Wes does. He eyes them as we eat our food, talking about simple things: movies and books. When we're done eating, we rest back against the wall.

He adjusts his position so that his shoulder is against mine. I notice a girl glance over at us, and I'm sure she must think I've gotten my life back. If only it was that simple to explain.

"Tate, were we happy?" Wes asks in a low voice, as if he

expects me to say no. I think about the question, and although there are no easy answers, it's mostly a yes.

"Kind of, yeah," I say, turning toward him. He nods to himself and falls quiet. The crowd in the courtyard goes about their business, living their lives. But Wes's expression grows sullen. He doesn't look at me.

"Then how did I end up in The Program?" he asks quietly.

His words hit me in the gut, a punch to the stomach. They're not accusatory, although, honestly, maybe they should be. He doesn't know if this is my fault. He was quick to trust me.

"I'm not sure how exactly you ended up there," I say. "But you changed."

This draws his attention, and when he turns to me, his brown eyes look darker. "Tell me," he says.

I begin to wring my hands in my lap; the thought of dredging up the terrible moments, having to relive them, is daunting. But I remind myself again that this is Wes's recovery. I promised I'd always be there for him, and that means through the bad stuff.

"There was a bridge," I say. "Crescent Bridge, out on the coast. We only went there twice, but we went there with heightened emotions. We went there to escape our lives, to escape what was happening around us. We went there to escape The Program."

"We failed," he says.

"I guess." My eyes tear up, and I gaze at the school, trying not to let the sadness overwhelm me. We did fail and I lost him because of it. "The second time we went there, you were different."

"How?" Wes asks.

"Devon Winston had just been taken. You two were friends. Do you remember?"

"No, of course I don't."

"Sorry." It's a bad habit to assume he remembers anything, especially anything that The Program might have taken. "Devon had gotten picked up by handlers that day," I tell Wes. "And you were feeling down about it. You . . . you busted up your knuckles punching a mirror in the bathroom."

Wes starts at the comment, seeming surprised that he would do something like that, regardless of cause. He's not wrong. Wes is a pretty passive guy. He looks down at his knuckles and there's a small sliver of a scar still there.

"We left school early and I bandaged you up," I continue. "We went to the bridge because you said you felt helpless. Hopeless. I understood, and I wanted us to be free so I took us to the bridge. There's a little area beneath it and we laid out a blanket and stayed together, quiet and content. Except you started to flinch at your thoughts. You said your mind was going too fast. You told me you weren't sure how to make it stop."

I pause, a deep ache in my heart as I remember the moment. Wes looked so terrified that night. He was sorry, as if every bad thing that had ever happened was his fault. His guilt was painful to watch.

"You said that you loved me too much," I continue. "Then you promised that we'd run away together."

"I'm guessing we didn't run away?" Wes asks.

"You ran," I say. "But not with me."

His lips part in surprise, and he sits up. "I did? Where'd I go?"

"I don't know," I say. "It was in the summer, and when you didn't call me, I knew something was wrong. You were gone for an entire week. The Program was waiting for you when you got back. You never got the chance to tell me where you'd been."

I cringe at my own words, that feeling of someone walking over my grave. I shiver and wrap my arms around myself.

"I'm sorry I left you," Wes whispers, and I turn to look at him. "I'm sorry that I didn't take you with me. I'm sure I had a good reason, or at least thought I did."

"I'm sure you did too," I say. But the truth is that no reason would have been good enough. He abandoned me and left me to think the worst. That grief alone could have killed me. It could have brought the handlers down on me. But, of course, when Wes came back, the slate was wiped clean. He came home; he was alive. That was all that mattered in the end.

I don't tell him the rest, how under the bridge he grew eerily quiet, lying with me and stroking my hair. He muttered, flinched. He wasn't himself. He kept saying he was sorry. And maybe that was the last bit of him; he drained away right then.

He *let* himself get taken into The Program. He didn't fight it. He didn't fight for me. And I'm not going to tell him that.

"I've been thinking a lot," Wes says, quiet and introspective. "About what you said."

"What did I say?"

"The Adjustment. After you left last night, I kept thinking about that moment I remembered. That one small memory felt more real than anything I've done since being back—like that's my real life. So I looked up the Adjustment and I read all night. Rather do that than sleep anyway. . . ." He lowers his eyes, and his expression holds all his heaviness. His doubt. His loneliness.

My heart quickens its pace. "But you said it was Program two point oh."

"Every day," he says, "I walk around like a visitor in my own life. I avoid people's eyes because I'm scared I'll see recognition there, that they'll know me when I don't know them. I'm completely lost here. Haven't you noticed that you're the only person who talks to me?"

He's right—I haven't seen Wes talk to anyone else. Not since he's been back. He used to have friends, but none of them talk to either of us now. People don't associate with returners.

"They will in time," I say, trying to sound encouraging. "People are just afraid—"

"That's the thing," he says, leaning toward me, his eyes blazing. "I don't want people to be afraid of me. And if I knew the truth about myself, about all of *you*—" He runs his palm over his face, and I feel slighted at how he included me with the masses. Like I'm not nearly as special as I thought.

"It was just something I was thinking about," he says, his tone clipped. His face flinches, and he quickly shakes it off. "Forget it," he says.

"Wes, if you want to talk about it, we can—"

"What are you doing tonight?" he asks, glancing over at me. "Will you come out with me? I promise to be super fun and awesome."

It's then that I notice how pale and drawn he's become. His freckles are darker on his white skin, the purple and blue shadows under his eyes more pronounced. It worries me.

I reach to touch his forearm, and he pulls back from my touch. Wes curses and closes his eyes, obviously upset with his reaction—like he can't control it. I don't let my hurt show, and bring my hand into my lap.

"I'm sorry," Wes whispers.

"Don't be," I say, trying to sound light. "But, hey, you'd better deliver on fun and awesome tonight or I'm definitely never stealing a bike with you again."

The corners of his lips turn up, and I love the sight of it. "So, yeah?" he asks.

"Yeah," I say. "I just have to go home and see my grandparents first. Then we can meet up."

Before he can think about it, Wes leans in and kisses the side of my head. It's a casual movement—muscle memory.

SUZANNE YOUNG

Then he leans back against the wall, ignoring the cookies that I saved just for him. He pulls his knees in front of him and looks sideways at me.

"Do you have any aspirin with you?" he asks. "I have a headache."

CHAPTER SIX

AFTER LUNCH, I WALK ALONE DOWN THE HALL toward my class. I mean to stop by my locker before next period, and I'm surprised to see Vanessa waiting there for me. She lifts her head just as I arrive. She smiles, but the effect distorts her features. It's too false.

"Hey, Tatum," she says.

I fold my arms over my chest. "Uh . . . hi," I say. "What's up?" Vanessa steps aside, opening a path to my locker. I spin my combination and grab my history book from inside. When I close it, I turn to her.

"I heard you and Wes are together again," she says. Her tone isn't judgmental, mostly just curious.

"We're figuring things out," I say, noncommittal. "Why?"

She brushes her hair away from her face, stalling, it seems.

Then she exhales like she doesn't want to go on but will. "Just be careful, okay?" she says. "I don't know either of you, but you're cool. I wouldn't want to see you get hurt."

"What does that mean?" I ask.

"There's a reason we ended up in The Program," she says. The side of her lip hitches up on her molar, almost like a snarl, as she talks. "Just make sure you know that reason before you jump in again."

"You mean the Adjustment?" I ask.

"They promise to bring it all back," she says, tapping her temple. "But how can you tell the difference between a lie and a memory if they feel the same?"

Vanessa steps closer to me and I hadn't realized how much taller she was. "And here's the secret," she says. "We're surrounded by lies every day. Surrounded by people who lie. Have been for a long time. So be careful whom you trust. Not everyone's who they seem."

"Jesus, Vanessa," I say, pushing her back when she gets too close. "You're freaking me out."

She stares at me a moment, like she's just seeing me for the first time. She blinks quickly, her lips twitch. She runs her fingers through her bangs, and laughs. "Just kidding," she says breathlessly. "Sorry. Tremor."

I stare at her, shocked. A thin line of bright red blood begins to trickle from her nose.

"You're bleeding," I say, pointing.

"Oh, shit," she says, touching under her nose and checking

the blood herself. "Not again." Without a good-bye or an explanation, she spins on her heels and heads for the bathroom.

I watch after her, alarmed, but mostly worried. I take out my phone to text Nathan. Jana might have an idea what Vanessa is talking about. I plan to type out the text, but then I see Vanessa come out of the bathroom a moment later, all cleaned up. She doesn't even glance in my direction again, walking away like nothing's wrong at all.

The doctor at the Adjustment said the controlled crashbacks would need follow-up therapy. Vanessa seems confused right now, but Jana said that Dr. McKee was watching her closely, so I assume she's getting it. They might want to step that up a notch.

Still . . . it feels cruel to rat her out when she's already dealing with a lot. So after a long pause, I slip my phone back into my pocket and don't tell anyone about what she said.

"I'm home," I announce as I walk in the door after school. I'm surprised when there's no answer. I can't remember the last time my grandfather wasn't waiting for me. I take a few moments to wander the house, looking for my grandparents. When I'm sure they're gone, I sit on the couch, staring at the blank television screen.

I'd planned to confront Pop about talking to Nathan behind my back, but now that I'm here without him or my gram, I feel suddenly vulnerable. Clearly Pop was just worried about me, and it's that worry that's kept me safe. It would be unfair for me to judge him for it now.

I take out my phone, resting back on the couch, and text my grandfather.

Where are you? I write.

A speech bubble surfaces immediately. Research, Pop says. Thought I'd be back by the time you got home. Everything okay?

I hate that I've been fighting with him and Gram. It's just not like us. I'm all good, I write. Turn up anything in your research?

Not yet.

I don't ask what he's researching, assuming it's the Adjustment. But I don't want to talk about that right now. I just want to pretend that everything's okay between us.

Your grandmother will be home around six, he adds. I might be later.

I furrow my brow but don't press the issue. Is it okay if I go out in a little while? I ask, using his distraction to my benefit.

Home by curfew, he writes, without asking where I'm going. It's strange that he doesn't ask for details. It makes me think he's trying to avoid the conversation, same as me. So I tell him that I love him and that I'll talk to him soon. He says he'll let my gram know I'm going out.

And with that, I go upstairs to do my homework.

It's starting to rain, so I offer to drive. Wes reluctantly agrees—itching to ride his motorcycle—and I go by his street to pick him up at the usual spot around five. It's earlier than I planned, but I agreed when Wes said he couldn't stand to be in his house a moment longer. I could hear it in his voice—the scratchiness, the beginning of desperation. It reminded me of the time before The Program. I grabbed my keys and rushed out.

Wes gets in the passenger side of my Jeep, glancing around at the interior. His hair is a little wet from the rain, and he puts his hands in front of the heater for a moment to warm them. Above us, the tree branches hang low enough to touch the top of the Jeep. It's private here.

I watch him, and when he turns to me, he smiles. "Hi," Wes says. "You look nice."

I feel myself blush, even at such a simple compliment. I hadn't realized how much I missed hearing them. "Thank you," I say. "You look exactly the same as you did at school."

He laughs. "Sorry, my white basketball shorts were in the wash; otherwise, I would have worn them for you."

"Thank God for laundry day."

"I did bring you something, though," he says, biting back his smile in the most adorable way. It sends flutters over my skin.

"You did?" I ask. "What?"

Wes takes out his phone and turns it toward me. All I see is a bar code, so I move the screen up. My breath catches. "Tickets?"

"To see Radiohead," he says, like he hopes I'll like it. He takes the phone back. "This summer in Seattle. I got two tickets, but if you want to go with—"

"You didn't have to do this," I say, smiling widely. "I still would have gone out with you tonight."

He chuckles. "Yeah, but I promised awesome."

"This *is* awesome. Thank you."

He holds my gaze. "You're welcome, Tate," he says in a quiet voice, his eyes searching mine. And I can feel it, him looking for a connection. I don't know if he finds it before he turns to look out the passenger window.

"So," he says. "Where should we go tonight?"

"I thought you'd already have a plan," I say. "You invited me."

"I did, right? Hmm . . . well, it's already late, so I'm guessing the coast is out?"

"Plus, it's raining," I add, leaning forward to glance up between the branches at the cloudy sky. "The mist will block the view of the water." I think for a moment. "What about a movie?" I suggest.

This seems to appeal to him. "I'm not sure how you feel about blowing shit up," Wes says, "but there's a movie at the dollar theater. One with the Rock?"

I laugh. "First, I love a good explosion. But that came out last year. We've already seen it." But when Wes doesn't return my smile, I realize what I've done.

"Oh," he says, looking down at his lap. "I don't remember what happened."

I hate knowing his life when he doesn't. Knowing the simplest things like what movies he's seen. I know his secrets better than he does. I've known him for so long that he has all my secrets too, even if he can't remember them. That thought sticks with me—the damn tragedy of it.

"I'm sorry," I whisper, but he's a million miles away. I reach to touch his hand, and Wes flinches, just like before. His reaction pulls me down, drowning me in rejection. That's what it feels like even if it's not his fault. I stare out the windshield as rain taps the glass.

"Kiss me," Wes says, startling me from my dark thoughts. I turn to him, miserable, and find his eyes have welled up with tears. "Kiss me and make me remember."

And he's the one who looks sad and lonely. He looks so sorry. I lean in and he keeps his eyes open, studying me. I rest my hand on his chest, waiting to see if he'll move away. And when he doesn't, I kiss softly at his bottom lip, then the top. Wes doesn't react at all, like he's testing the feeling. I kiss him again and he breathes heavily, his hand sliding onto my thigh.

"You make me feel so goddamn much," he murmurs. And just like that, he comes to life; he wakes up.

Wes kisses me hard, using me as a shield against his pain. Despite the problems with that, my body reacts, and I know we're both using each other. Both blocking out reality with something that feels good. Something that can dull the pain. Before I know it, Wes is pulling me into the backseat and I'm working off his jeans.

Earlier, Vanessa had warned me to know everything before I jump into a relationship with Wes—know how he ended up in The Program in the first place. But he can't remember, so it's not like I can ask him.

"Should we go inside?" I gasp out as Wes kisses my neck.

I'm half out of my mind, my thoughts blurring together, clouded with desire.

"No," Wes says, yanking off my shirt. We crash together again, parked along the wooded street, half a block from his house. The windows of my Jeep are fogging up. It's so irresponsible. We would have never done this before—but maybe that's why it's happening. A new memory rather than reliving an old one.

And yet, the idea of sneaking into his house, into his bed, into his arms, is what I miss. It occurs to me that those are the moments I'm chasing. I'm in love with my memories.

The backseat of the Jeep is cramped, but Wes slides over and takes off the rest of my clothes, kissing down my body. My heart is racing so fast.

I've never been with anyone other than Wes. We were each other's first and only. It made things easy. It made us feel connected. But Wes isn't a virgin. Neither am I. But in another sense, he is. He doesn't remember doing this before. And it strikes me that I would give anything to have my old Wes back, how easy and casual it would be—like we could or couldn't and neither mattered. So long as we were together.

Wes comes back over to kiss me, and I close my eyes, squeezing them shut to block out the memories that I want to be here instead. There's a rustle as Wes reaches for his wallet in his crumpled jeans on the floor. He kisses my hip before straightening, looking down at me.

He murmurs how beautiful I am. I open my eyes and look

up at him. He smiles, deep dimples, shiny eyes. I don't recognize him. I'm cheating on my boyfriend with my boyfriend.

And I miss him. I love him so much that it's absolute agony. It's tearing me to pieces. I want my Wes. I want him to come home.

"Tate," Wes whispers, concern crossing his features. "Holy shit," he says, tossing his wallet aside. "You're crying." He reaches to wipe my cheeks, and moves to crouch on the floor. "I'm so sorry," he says. "Did I—"

But I wave off his worry. This isn't his fault. I sniffle hard and reach for my shirt, pulling it on. Wes looks wrecked, guilty.

"We should have gone inside," he says. "Or, wait. I shouldn't have asked you to kiss me. Tate," he says, his voice sounding desperate. "What did I do? I'm sorry."

But my stray tears begin to turn into a full-on sob. Here, with Wes, I have never felt more alone in my life. Wes curses again, and moves to sit next to me on the seat, close but scared to touch me.

"Please talk to me," he says, his voice shaking like he might cry. "What can I do? How can I fix this?"

And between gasps, between tears, I look over at him miserably, and I whisper, "I don't know."

CHAPTER SEVEN

WES AND I BOTH GET DRESSED, AND WHEN WE realize the rain has let up, we climb out of the Jeep and sit on the curb. The night has grown colder, and I wrap my arms around myself. The tears have dried on my cheeks, making my skin feel tight.

Next to me, Wes sniffles every so often, and we both stare down at the pavement near the tire. I tried to explain why I was crying, tried to do it in a way that wouldn't make him feel bad, feel inadequate. He doesn't say anything until now.

"You're in love with him," he murmurs. Surprised, I turn to him, but he doesn't meet my gaze. "You're in love with me. Just not this version."

"That's not it exactly," I say, although it's closer to right than I want to admit.

"Can you imagine how that feels?" he asks. "To not remember. To feel like he was a better version of me. I see it in the way people at school look at me. The way *you* look at me."

"No," I say, my heart breaking for him. "I didn't mean—"

"You wish I was somebody else," he says, like it's simple. But when he turns to me, tears drip onto his cheeks. His skin is ghostly pale even in the low light. "I see it. And I feel it every time you touch me—how much you wish I were him. I'm not stupid."

"I'm sorry," I say. "I just . . . I miss our life together."

Wes swallows hard, lowering his head. He wipes roughly at his cheeks, clearing the tears. "I've been thinking about that," he says. "And . . ." He looks over at me, his expression softening. "I'm going to get an Adjustment, Tate," he says, and my breath catches. "But I'm not just doing it because of you," he adds. "Or because of the others."

"Why, then?" I ask.

He rubs his temples. "You remember how you told me about the other returners and how the doctor thought it could be the start of another epidemic?" he asks. When I nod, he continues.

"Well, I understood," he says. "I didn't want to admit it then, but there's something in my head. Sometimes it's an itch; other times it's a throbbing pain. It's like . . . it's like a memory fighting to get out. And the nightmares, God, the nightmares. Every night I'm trapped in a white room. Trapped in restraints. I stopped sleeping. The Program is still coming for me, even if it's only in my head."

"Wes," I breathe out, horrified. I had no idea this was happening to him. That he wasn't sleeping, growing more drawn each day. This sounds like what was happening to Sebastian, too. "Why didn't you tell me?" I ask.

He shrugs, skidding his foot along the concrete. "Because it's gotten worse. Since I came back to town, since I've been seeing you . . . it's gotten worse."

His words devastate me, and I rock back. But Wes is quick to look over at me. "I don't mean it like that. You're not causing the pain, Tate. Being with you, it's making me fight. I'm fighting the effects of The Program every day. But I'm not winning. It's pulling me under; it's making me sick," he whispers. "Will you help me?"

I have a million reasons why he shouldn't get an Adjustment. It's dangerous. It's untested. It's completely scary. But I also had no idea how much he was hurting. He could end up like Sebastian or Alecia. Or any one of the countless others. This is what it's like to be a returner—never-ending fear. The torture of it is almost incomprehensible.

Wes holds out his hand to me, palm up, his eyes pleading. And even though I don't know if this is the answer we're looking for, I won't turn my back on him. I slide my hand against his and let him pull me closer. Hopeless in my devotion.

"Of course I'll help you," I say as I lean against him. "I'd do anything for you, Wes."

"We won't let them control us anymore," he says. "I'm going to control myself."

"You were never good at self-control," I murmur, trying to get past my fear by joking.

Wes laughs, and his lips brush my forehead. "I can imagine. And I'm sorry I asked you to kiss me earlier. It wasn't the right time."

"It's okay," I say. "I really like kissing you."

I feel him smile. "Yeah, I mean, before you started crying, I thought things were going pretty well."

I laugh, and straighten to look over at him. The tears still fill his eyes, even as he smiles. "I always knew your mouth was my favorite part," I say.

"I bet." We wait a moment, and then Wes takes a deep breath and focuses on me. "I'm ready," he says. "No more taking it slow. I'm ready to dive into this with you. So what do you say we stop feeling sorry for ourselves? Have one normal night in our completely abnormal lives? Just this once."

And I decide that I'm ready too. No more longing for a memory—I'm ready for the real moments. The real us. I'm ready to bring Wes home.

"How about that movie?" he asks. "Can you stand to see it twice?"

"No spoilers," I say, crossing my heart.

Wes stands, helping me up. And then a subtler version of us climbs back into the Jeep. We talk about nothing, laugh and smile. Neither of us mentions the Adjustment again until I drop him off later that night, and Wes asks me to make an appointment. And so I do just that.

• • •

Wes and I climb out of my Jeep in the strip mall parking lot Saturday morning. Our appointment is at ten a.m., but my grandparents think that Wes and I are going to brunch. They seemed slightly uncomfortable with the idea, but I told them we're just friends for now. It was easier to lie.

Wes looks at me over the hood. "When life is finally falling back into place," he says, "the only thing to do is try to fuck it up, right? At least, that's what we might be doing."

"Uh . . . your confidence is encouraging."

Wes comes to stand next to me in front of the office door. We've tried to joke since I picked him up this morning, mostly to relieve the anxiety. But nothing helps right now. We're a bundle of nerves.

Wes twists his baseball hat around backward, and stares at the building, unimpressed. He glances over. "Tell me this isn't a mistake," he says.

"I can't," I admit.

"Perfect," he says, like we're completely screwed. "So, should we go see what they have to say?" We both look at the door, but neither of us moves.

We have an appointment—I can't say we've thought about the implications beyond that. The decision was made, and from there, we've drifted along. We also decided to keep it a secret for now. I made the appointment online, but Wes didn't tell his parents.

We're conspiring. If that's not a huge red flag, then I don't know what is. And yet—here we are.

Wes and I stand outside the frosted-glass door, and I look at him. He's still pale, and I notice how sharp the angle of his jaw has become. How thin he looks. Maybe this is how we fix everything.

"You sure you're sure?" I ask.

He smiles and lifts one shoulder in a shrug. "Sure," he says.

I go over and ring the bell next to the door. There's a loud clink as the door unlocks, and Wes and I walk into the waiting room. The same girl sits behind the desk, and she smiles pleasantly as we enter, not seeming at all surprised to see me again.

"Dr. McKee will be with you shortly," she says to us. She doesn't ask us to fill out paperwork, and I'm reminded how unlike a doctor's office this really is. I don't know if that should reassure us or not.

Wes taps the toe of his boot on the floor. There's music playing softly in the background—a song from the Cure, ironically. Although we decided to come here, we have the stipulation that if either of us changes our mind at any point, we'll walk right back out the door. I'm already close to doing this when the office door opens.

"Tatum," Dr. McKee says like we're old friends. He outstretches his hand and I shake it more out of uncomfortableness than actually wanting to interact.

"And you must be Weston," he says, turning to him. Wes doesn't shake his hand, and the doctor slips his hands into his coat pockets like he doesn't notice the slight. "Please," Dr. McKee says, holding open the door to let us pass through.

"Megan," he tells the girl behind the desk, "clear my schedule for the day."

She smiles. "Absolutely."

Wes and I exchange a look, and walk into the back hall. Dr. McKee motions us into his office. I notice that the picture from the lobby, the framed one of himself, has been moved into his private office. I wonder if Nathan embarrassed him by bringing it up. I stare at the image for a moment, and then take a seat next to Wes while the doctor rounds the desk to his leather chair.

"I can start," the doctor says, "but perhaps you can just tell me why you're here, Weston. And then I can tell you if we can help."

I like that he's to the point. The last thing we're here for is a sales pitch.

Wes leans forward, his elbows on the knees of his jeans. He takes a moment before speaking. "Were you a part of The Program?" he asks, surprising me. Dr. McKee doesn't even flinch.

"No, son," he says. "My partner, Marie, and I fought against The Program from the start. Fought against its creator. In the end, even Arthur Pritchard realized the danger it posed. When The Program ended, Marie and I finally saw our chance to right the wrongs. Yes—I was part of the initial phasing. Have you heard of the grief department?"

"No," Weston says. "Sounds awful."

"Yes, I suppose it was," Dr. McKee says, taking off his glasses and setting them aside on the desk. He rubs his eyes. "I lost a daughter."

I swallow hard, my eyes finding the picture again. Dr. McKee notices my gaze, and shakes his head like it's not her he's talking about. He turns back to Wes.

"I lost my wife and my little girl more than fifteen years ago, but there isn't a day that I don't mourn them, don't miss them," the doctor says. "The grief drove me close to insanity. And Dr. Pritchard used that to make me agree to things I wouldn't have normally done. But that's the thing with pain—you'll do anything to make it stop. I'm not proud of myself. I'm not proud of the things I've done. But if there's anything I am proud of, it's this." He motions around us. "The Adjustment will set things right—like how they should've been from the start. Whether you know it or not, Weston, your heart is grieving for all that you've lost. All that they took. That sort of pain will find its way out somehow."

"It's already started to," Wes admits, like he's embarrassed. "Nightmares. headaches. I'm afraid . . ." He looks over at me, and then leans closer to the doctor. "I'm afraid of crashing back hard. I feel it coming."

Dr. McKee nods, and I see him thinking this over. I wonder if it will disqualify Wes as a candidate. "Then it's good you're here," the doctor says. This seems to set Wes at ease, and he rests back in the chair.

"Tell me how this Adjustment works," Wes says. "How can it stop me from getting worse?"

Dr. McKee pushes back in his chair and stands. "Better yet," he says. "I'll show you."

• • •

We take a tour of the facility, starting with the recovery room. Unlike the starkness of the lobby, the room is cheerful, colorful. As if the world has come into focus. I wonder if they decorated this way for just that effect. So a waking patient will feel more alive, suddenly enlightened.

The recovery room has deep-blue walls, with gorgeous gold-leaf art, orange accent pillows on a couch. There is a hospital bed, but the blanket is woven and beautiful. Dr. McKee turns to me.

"My assistant decorated this one," he says, sounding amused.

"She did a good job," I respond. There is an eclectic sense of home about it. A sense of good intentions.

The doctor then leads us through a swinging double door to another room, this one in total contrast. The walls are white, like the lobby, and there is an alarming amount of medical equipment. The kind of stuff straight out of a science-fiction movie.

On one side of the room is a metallic reclined chair with a series of controls on the arm, a screen on a rolling cart, and a heart-rate monitor standing next to it. Across from the chair is an exam table with white paper draped over the top. At the end of it is a machine with a circle cut into it—similar to an MRI machine. But it's the metal crown set on the edge of the table that catches my attention. The outside is smooth metal with snaps, while there are lights all along the inside. There is a pile of sensors with sticky pads on a metal tray between the chair and exam table.

"This looks intense," Wes says, wrapping his arms around himself. He's definitely having second thoughts.

"Not at all," the doctor says, going over to pick up the metal crown. He flips it over to show us the inside. "These sensors distribute light, stimulating parts of the brain following a pattern. That pattern will help create images. When it's all said and done, you'll remember—or your brain thinks you do—the events of the pattern. In time, your own memories may fill in the gaps. It's how the brain works logically."

Wes listens as Dr. McKee goes on to explain the rest, much of what he'd already told me and Nathan. Some of it is technical, a lot of it philosophical: *People shouldn't have the right to erase memories. It's the same as killing a younger version of you. No one wants a life half lived.*

These are sayings we've all heard before, but now, with the possibility of reversing the damage, they suddenly have more weight. It reminds me again of Alecia—*Time has a way of going backward.* Isn't that what this is? Us, living backward?

Dr. McKee finishes his speech and sits on a stool near the computer, like he's waiting patiently for us to decide. Wes turns to me, and I expect hesitation, but instead I see hope.

He lifts the corner of his mouth. "Sounds too good to be true," he says with a smile.

"Exactly," I reply.

"Only this time," Wes says, "no matter what: It's my decision, not the government's. Not my parents'. *Mine*. And I choose to deal with my shit. Even the bad shit." He looks at the doctor. "And this will stop me from breaking down, right? Stop the crashbacks?"

"Not stop it," Dr. McKee says. "Manage it. We still have to be careful, Weston. Every implanted memory will open a door. We can't let everything flood in at once. We'll take it step by step. And, luckily, I'm confident in your donor." He smiles at me. "A clear memory is invaluable. A memory that hasn't been corrupted by alcohol or emotions. Tatum is a perfect specimen."

"Geez, doc," I say. "You're making me blush." Wes snorts a laugh.

"I'm just being honest," Dr. McKee says easily. "And, Weston, after the first implant, we'll start therapy to temper the headaches and nightmares. You won't be actively fighting the erasure anymore, so it should give you some relief."

Wes closes his eyes as if this is the best news of all. It occurs to me that I've been selfish, worrying about getting him back and not about what he is going through here and now. I should have seen it. I should have known he was getting sicker.

"You're in good hands, son," the doctor adds. "I wouldn't even consider doing it if I thought otherwise."

Wes glances at me, and then turns to the doctor. "Sign me up," he says.

"Wonderful," Dr. McKee returns, and hands him a clipboard and a pen. "I have an opening right now if you're ready. And, really, I'm so happy for you both. You deserve this. Truly, you do."

Wes smiles, filling out the paperwork. Dr. McKee picks up the phone on the wall and murmurs something into the receiver. It's all moving so quickly, a runaway train.

The lab door opens and a black woman with long braids and a lab coat walks in. Dr. McKee steps over to introduce her.

"This is my partner, Dr. Devoroux," he says fondly.

"Nice to see you," she says to me, holding out her hand. "And please call me Marie." Her red nails are filed sharp, a shiny gold watch on her thin wrist. I shake her hand and it's warm. Her temperament is peaceful, confident, and competent. She turns to Weston.

"And it's good to meet you," she says kindly. Wes says the same, and actually shakes her hand when she offers it. "Now," she continues, "I'll be assisting on your Adjustment. Tatum, if you wouldn't mind taking a spot in the chair."

I shoot a panicked glance at Wes, but he's watching Marie with an expression of absolute trust. So I swallow hard and walk over to take a seat.

"Just relax," Marie says. She wheels over the metal tray from the other side of the room. I sit back in the chair, reclined at an uncomfortable angle. I try to shift my shoulders, and rest my arms at my sides. I look over at Wes as Marie helps him onto the table. Once settled, he stares up at the ceiling. I can see his chest rise and fall quickly.

What are we doing?

Marie returns to my side and picks up a thin plastic sheet with round circles stuck to it. She slowly peels them off and then places them on my temples and along my forehead; the sticky side is cold and I shiver. I'm not sure if it's from the temperature or fear. She asks me to pull up my top, and then places a few others on my chest, near my heart, and I gulp as she begins to connect wires into the tabs.

"Is this how you get my memories?" I ask. My voice is hoarse, and I clear my throat. She presses her lips into a smile.

"Well, these measure your heart rate." She tugs on the wires from my chest. "That way we can tell if you're lying. As I'm sure Dr. McKee mentioned, lying can skew the results. So recall the memory exactly as you know it. And these"—she lovingly brushes my hair away from the tabs on my head—"detect the patterns."

"Will actual images show up, or just . . . lines?" I ask. Even though the doctor explained it to me a few times now, I still don't quite understand what they'll see.

"No," she says. "On our end, we'll see different parts of your brain light up, the parts you're using for recall. We record the pulses to the finest point, and then we re-create it, stimulating that exact pattern in Wes's brain." She leans in and wipes the inside of my elbow with an alcohol swab. "I'm going to give you an injection now."

"Injection?" my voice squeaks the word. Marie looks at her partner, then back at me.

"The truth serum," she says. "Dr. McKee already explained it to you."

"Oh . . . ," I say, and turn toward Wes.

"Hey, do I get one of those?" he asks.

"No," Marie responds.

"Thank God," Wes says, and then he shrugs an apology at me. I laugh and lay my head back against the chair. I'm glad he's still trying to make me laugh.

"It's imperative we get the true memory from the donor," Marie says quietly to me as she aligns the syringe with my vein. "But this won't affect you in any other way. It compels you by relaxing you, lowering inhibitions. Don't worry," she says with a smile. "We won't be asking intrusive questions—just details on the memory. Triggers for his." She nods in Wes's direction. I like this woman; she seems to get it. I trust her. And with that, I try to let go of my fear.

The needle tip pricks my skin and I wince. There's a burning sensation up my arm, but it fades quickly. Marie removes the needle and puts a bandage over the tiny hole.

She pulls a blanket up over my legs and walks to the other side of the room with Dr. McKee. "We're ready to begin," she says.

CHAPTER EIGHT

DR. MCKEE ROLLS THE STOOL OVER TO MY SIDE and sits facing me. He brings the computer cart in front of him, and begins typing. Marie attaches the wires to the cart, and, I assume, it feeds information into the computer.

She then goes over and talks to Wes, only her voice is low and I can't hear what they're saying. I look at Dr. McKee.

"You're sure this is safe?" I ask.

He pauses in his clicking and glances down at me. "I swear it," he says. "Safe enough I'd perform it on my own daughter if I could." Only he says it with a bit of loss in his tone, and rather than comfort me, it makes me more apprehensive.

Wes laughs at something Marie says as she puts her hand on his shoulder encouragingly. And with that, all is decided. We're moving forward. I can see the corner of the screen the doctor is working on, and pulled up is a series of numbers and words I can't quite read from here.

"Weston is ready," Marie says, and comes to stand between us. I glance sideways and see Wes is wearing the metal crown, only now there are lights on, coloring the skin on his forehead different shades. It doesn't look silly like I thought it would. It looks dangerous.

"Let's get started," Dr. McKee says, and the heart monitor begins to beep quietly. Marie sits in a chair between me and Wes, keeping a close eye on both of us. I'm embarrassed at how quickly my heart is beating, the sounds blending together. Wes watches the monitor too, like he's concerned. I wish the sound were off, because I feel exposed. Just another way I can't lie, I guess.

"Memory," Dr. McKee says, watching his computer screen, "is really just a series of electrical pulses generated by neurons. If we put an electrode there and monitor it, we're able to map out the memory. Tracking the electrical signals in your brain creates a pattern, and each pattern represents a specific experience. Look around this room, Tatum," he says.

I do just that, taking in the white walls, the door that seems farther away than it was when I first walked in. "Your brain," he says, "has just created a series of pulses. Next time, when you want to recall this memory, your body will repeat those pulses to call up the image. Along with the image, the brain attributes feelings. Fear, I'm assuming?"

I nod, and the wires breeze over my neck.

The doctor looks thoughtful. "Sadly," he says, "there isn't much I can do to re-create the feelings—those will be interpreted by the brain. Your memories are implantable. Your emotions are not. That way, you can't entirely force your will on someone else. It's your body's safeguard."

"Okay. . . ." I worry that he's accusing me of something, but I must be projecting my guilt, because he glances at his computer screen without judgment.

"Now," he says, "once we have the pattern of an event, we'll compress it and then send those exact pulses into Weston's brain. The mind wants to understand things—it's a miracle. We make logic jumps every day—images we see are interpreted. We make natural assumptions to form an understanding. Weston's brain will interpret the pulses, only it will see his part of the memory and apply it to him. He won't think he's you; we're not creating a false identity. We're re-creating a situation and activating his brain's desire to make sense of it.

"When it's done," he continues, "Weston will feel as if he was there. He saw what you saw, took part in it. There will be no distinguishing reality from the memory. For him, for all of us, really, they are one in the same. We will do this with four triggering memories. Afterward, Weston's mind will put together the filler between events—jumping in logic and plugging up the holes."

"But today we're just starting with the first memory," Marie adds. "We want to make sure it takes before moving forward. So after we extract your memory, we'll streamline the pattern and then implant it—although that will take several hours. Wes will stay under our constant supervision during this time." She looks over at Wes. "Does everything we've talked about so far make sense to you, Weston?" she asks.

"About as much as it can without a degree in neuroscience," he says.

"All you need to know is that we are not The Program," Marie says. "We will take care of you."

Marie's words send a chill over my skin, raising the hairs on the back of my neck. I look at Wes and see him tighten his jaw.

"So," Marie asks us both, "are we ready to begin?"

Weston turns to face the ceiling. "Ready," he says evenly.

"Good," Marie says. "I'm going to give you something to help you relax. It may make you sleepy, but that's all right. It'll open your mind."

As Marie picks up another syringe, Dr. McKee taps a button on his keyboard and I feel a slight buzz go through the electrodes stuck to my temples. It's not uncomfortable, just a soft motion to let me know they're there. I notice that the beating of my heart has slowed.

"What is your name?" the doctor asks me.

"Tatum Masterson," I say.

"And can you describe yourself, Tatum?" he says. "It will help the memory isolate you and, therefore, separate you from the identity of Weston."

"Oh, uh . . . I'm five foot six, short brown hair. Brown eyes." I pause. "A wide, goofy smile." Across the room, Weston laughs, and I wonder if it's because it's his compliment, even if he doesn't remember saying it.

"Good," Dr. McKee says, using a red pencil to mark on a paper. "Now," he says, "we're going to start with something simple, but important. Can you please tell the story of how you and Weston met? Tell it exactly how you remember it, with as much detail as you remember. Be the observer. Don't talk to me. Just . . . recall."

I swallow hard, suddenly nervous. The beeping on the heart monitor speeds up again.

"It's okay, Tatum," Dr. McKee says. "Lean into the memory. Live it."

And so I close my eyes, and I do just that.

"It was at a funeral," I start. I'm pulled out of the memory, worried about how the story will sound to Wes. But the drugs in my system are clouding my judgment—they're making me want to talk. Want to live in the past.

My eyes flutter closed again.

It started as a sunny day two years ago, although the weather eventually grew overcast. I was at the river, saying good-bye to someone. It wasn't technically a funeral, more of a makeshift memorial.

I was with Nathan and Foster, honoring their friend Malcolm. He and a passenger in his car had died a few months earlier, drove off the bridge and straight into the river. We were paying our respects along with thirty or so others—funerals weren't allowed back then because it was feared they would elicit a reaction.

I was standing at the edge of the water, a cool breeze blowing through my hair, when I looked over and noticed Weston sitting on a boulder upriver. He was wearing a black hoodie and jeans and smoking a cigarette. I couldn't believe he was wearing black. No one else ever did, because we were too afraid of catching the attention of the handlers and getting flagged for The Program.

I watched as Wes inhaled and then slowly let the smoke drift out of his mouth as he stared at the water. I didn't know who he was, so I elbowed Nathan—who was midconversation with Foster—and nodded my head in Wes's direction.

"Who's that guy?" I asked.

Nathan looked over with a bored expression and then lifted one eyebrow when he turned back to me. "You mean James Dean over there?"

"Sure," I responded flatly, to let him know he could keep the jokes—they weren't funny.

"That's Weston Ambrose," Foster said, taking a sip from his coffee. "He's cute, right?" he added. "I think he's dangerously cute."

"Do you know him?" I asked, taking Nathan's coffee from his hand and drinking from it. He scoffed and grabbed it back from me.

"Sadly, no," Foster said. He nodded at the river. "But that was his sister."

"He's Cheyenne's brother?" Nathan asked, his expression growing serious.

"Cheyenne?" I repeated with a sinking feeling in my stomach. "The girl who died?"

"Yep," Foster said. "She was Mackey's girlfriend. It was some fucked-up shit too." He shook his head, glancing over to where Weston was sitting. "Mackey and Cheyenne drove right off the bridge. Heard they planned it."

"Damn," Nathan said, sounding more sympathetic now. "Didn't realize that was him." We were quiet for a moment, feeling sorry for Weston. Then Nathan added, "I heard he's starting at our school. Maybe he already did."

"How do you know?" I asked.

"What can I say, Tatum? I know what all the good-looking guys are doing." He nodded at Foster, and Foster beamed back like he was proud to be his source of information.

"Well, I haven't seen him," I said. And I would have noticed someone like him—someone so unlike the others who had fallen into line. I liked that he was different.

"Definitely intriguing," Foster said, still gazing in Wes's direction. He exhaled. "But probably a bad idea," he added. "I mean, he just looks like trouble." He offered me a small smile as if telling me I should find out more about him anyway.

"Don't listen to anything Foster says," Nathan announced as he looked sideways at the woods, where a few people had disappeared to have a drink or two. "He's a terrible influence."

"It's literally why I exist," Foster said, holding up his coffee in cheers. I grabbed Nathan's coffee to tap his cup, and we both laughed before Nathan snatched it back from my hand.

Nathan took one last look at the river, and then motioned toward the woods. "I'm going to get something else to drink," he said. "You coming?" he asked me.

"Nah," I said. "I'll stay here a little longer."

He watched me for a moment before nodding. "Fine. I'll let you know when we're ready to leave," he said. And then he and Foster headed to meet up with the others, leaving me alone by the river.

It was the wind—a quiet howl of wind that made me look over at Wes again. The sound was like a long cry—like mourning. Misery. I didn't have any siblings; I couldn't imagine what that loss would feel like. I'd lost friends in the epidemic. Classmates. But not a sister.

Weston stared down at the burning end of his cigarette, as if questioning why he was smoking it. He put it out on the bottom of his boot, and slipped it back into the pack. He looked like the saddest person I'd ever seen. It wasn't even his face; his eyes were shaded by his hood and his hair was poking out near his neck. It was more his clothes, his slumped posture. He looked devastated.

Maybe I was curious, or maybe I wanted to help. But I found myself walking along the edge of the river in his direction. I got all the way to the boulder and he never lifted his head. Not even when I sat next to him, both of us facing the water.

　　　　　　　　　　　　　　　SUZANNE YOUNG

I expected to smell smoke, but this close to the river, all I could smell was wet earth. Wes didn't look at me, although he must have thought it strange that I was there.

"I'm sorry about your sister," I said, a bit of pity in my voice. He didn't seem to like it, and he sucked at his teeth.

"You from the counseling office?" he asked. "Did they send you over?"

"No," I said. "I was here for the memorial. I sort of knew Malcolm."

Wes turned suddenly, and I expected his face to be hard and unapproachable. But instead I found his dark-brown eyes bloodshot and red rimmed, like he'd cried so much, there would never be any more tears. I had a deep ache in my heart for him, and it felt as if I would do anything to take away his pain. Even if he was a stranger.

"I'm so sorry," I whispered, trapped in his gaze. He watched me for a long moment, never diverting his eyes. He licked his lips before he spoke again.

"What's your name?" he asked.

"Tatum," I said. He smiled, small and private. Like he'd never forget.

"Thank you for coming over, Tatum," he said. "You're a really nice person."

I laughed softly. "Not always this nice."

"Ah, I bet you are," he said, and turned back to the river. "And you didn't know Cheyenne?"

"No."

"Too bad," he said, more solemnly. "She would've liked your hair."

Absently I reached to run my fingers through my short hair, shaved on one side. Wes picked up the pack of cigarettes and shoved them into the pocket of his hoodie, standing up from the boulder.

"Do you smoke?" I asked.

He laughed. "No," he said. "They belonged to my sister. Sort of thought . . ." He shook his head. "Never mind. It was dumb."

There was a wave of sadness when I realized he thought it would make him feel closer to her. I understood. And I liked the vulnerability in it.

"Tatum!" Nathan called. I looked over to see him and Foster waiting by the river like they wanted to leave. I turned back to Wes.

"I'd better get going too," he said, as if giving me an out from our conversation. But then he tilted his head to the side, smiling adorably. "I'll see you around, Tate," he said. And damn if that nickname didn't make me fall for him right then.

"Yeah, maybe," I said, trying to play it cool, although I was sure my blush had already given me away. I held up my hand in a wave and started toward Nathan and Foster.

As I walked away, I thought I wanted to know more about Weston Ambrose. I wanted to know how to fix his broken heart. I wanted to be the reason it could be fixed.

He showed up at school the next week, and maybe it was because I was the only person he knew there, but we became close. For nearly two years we were inseparable. He wasn't flagged in all that time. And then, for some reason, he changed. And then that Wes, the one I loved, was gone forever.

CHAPTER NINE

WHEN I STOP TALKING AND OPEN MY EYES IN THE treatment room, I realize how dry my lips have grown. I don't even know what I was saying—the words tumbling out as I lost myself in the memory. There's a soft touch on my arm, and I glance over and find Marie watching me with a mixture of sympathy and pity. I know the difference between the two. Sympathy is what people gave after my friends died. Pity is what they offered when Wes was taken away and I was trying to keep my head above water. I look beyond Marie to Wes, and find his eyes closed, his chest rising slow and steady like he's asleep.

"That will do for today," Dr. McKee says on the other side of me. I turn just as he types a few lines on the computer. He does it so fast that I don't know how the words could possibly make sense.

I sit up, the wires still attached to my body. I don't want to stop the session. I want to stay lost in the memories.

"You've done a great job, Tatum," Dr. McKee says, closing the laptop. "Very detailed. Your recall is . . ." He glances at Marie, and then back to me. "It's all we could have hoped for, really. Now, we've mapped out the sequence, and the next step is implantation. After that, we'll monitor Weston. If everything goes well, we'll bring you back for the next session."

"Do you think something will go wrong?" I ask. "You said—"

The doctor holds up his palm to stop me. The alarms on the heart monitor go off—the beating too fast—and Dr. McKee motions for Marie to assist. She puts her hand soothingly on my arm before beginning to remove the sticky tabs and wires. I wince each time one is plucked from my skin.

Weston makes a breathy sound, and I turn to him, concerned. I want to wake him up and make sure he's okay. But Dr. McKee must sense that.

"The memories haven't been implanted yet," he says. "We need to modify the pattern to fill in some of the larger blanks. Then we'll let his brain do the rest. He'll be here another few hours, and we'll call you with an update when we have one. Weston has you down as his emergency contact."

After the wires are cleared, Marie helps me to stand, holding my arm like I might fall over at any moment. There is a quick second of disorientation, but it passes. She tells me that the medication should wear off at any moment.

I glance at Wes longingly, wishing he was awake already. It's strange to leave him here. I look at the doctor.

"I could just wait," I offer.

Dr. McKee shakes his head. "I'd rather you didn't," he says, not unkindly. "It's better to go about your day, take care of yourself. Being here will only rattle you, skew your memory for next time."

"But you'll call me as soon as he's awake?"

"Yes," he responds. "I promise."

I rub roughly at my face, trying to clear the last bit of fogginess. I walk out of the room, a bit drained, a bit dreamy.

And it's like I can still feel the cool wind from the river in my hair. Like I really was there. It reminds me of how powerful memories can be. And how sad it is that Wes lost his. I quickly call up the moments again to make sure they're still there, a concern I hadn't thought of before. They are, all the same details. Paranoia goes hand in hand with memory manipulation, I guess.

I'm acutely aware of how real it all seemed, like that moment still existed, replaying again and again in time. I understand what Vanessa might have meant when she said it's hard to tell the difference between lies and memories. Because part of me wants to deny the difference between memories and reality.

When I get out into the lobby, the receptionist smiles warmly and offers me a Jolly Rancher candy. A wave of reality crashes over me as the medication fades, and I murmur, "No, thank you."

SUZANNE YOUNG

I rush outside, and once there, I swallow down the metallic taste in my mouth. *I should have grabbed the candy*, I think as I lean against the exterior of the building. There is a small bench near the door, and I sit down, the edges of my mind still a little fuzzy. I take out my phone and click on Nathan's last message—nothing new from him.

He doesn't know where I am; he doesn't know what I've done. What Wes and I have started. I know I should tell him.

My fingers hover over the buttons, ready to type out the words, but in the end, I click out of his messages. I write to Foster instead.

Thinking of you, I text. Part of me hopes he'll invite me to the funeral so I can see him. But at the same time . . . there have been enough funerals and memorials over the past few years. I'm not sure I could even sit through another one.

My phone buzzes. We need to talk, Foster responds.

I quickly look up and dart my eyes around, paranoid that he knows about the Adjustment. I swallow hard. About what? I ask.

Just between us, he writes. But can't talk right now. Will call you later.

I wait to see if he'll say more, but minutes pass without another response. Could Foster possibly know about the Adjustment? Or did something else happen?

I almost text Nathan to ask what it's about, but Foster said it was just between us. I'm not sure what that could mean, but

I can't betray his trust if it's something he doesn't want Nathan to know. At the same time, I can't imagine him keeping a secret from Nathan.

Yet, here I am, keeping a secret from Nathan. I'm keeping the Adjustment a secret.

And with that thought, I click off the phone and slip it back into my pocket.

I'm a nervous wreck by the time I get home twenty minutes later. I wait nervously for an update on Wes, even though I know it'll be hours before I hear anything from the doctor. My grandparents are at the farmers' market, so for distraction, I clean my room, organize my closet, and then look through old photos. It's nearly one in the afternoon when my phone buzzes. I practically jump out of my skin to grab it.

Saw you get home while ago, Nathan writes. You haven't left since. Haven't texted. Are we fighting?

I sit on the edge of my bed, letting my heart calm. Nope. Just cleaning my room.

That's weird. Are you grounded?

I have to tell him about the Adjustment. He's my best friend—I know I shouldn't keep this from him. I swallow hard, trying to build up my bravery. Want to come over? I ask.

Sure. Be there in a few.

Before going downstairs, I check once again to make sure I didn't miss any calls, even though I've had the phone with me the entire time. But there's no word from the doctor; nothing

SUZANNE YOUNG

new from Foster. I hear the kitchen door open, and I put my phone in my pocket and head downstairs.

Nathan is already on the couch, the game turned on and the second controller waiting on the coffee table. He glances over his shoulder at me when I get to the bottom of the stairs and I freeze. I should tell him everything. He'd tell me.

"You all right?" he asks. "Where is everybody?"

"Uh . . ." I head over to the couch. "Farmers' market." I take a spot next to him and join the game without a second thought.

"I hope Gram gets that salmon dip again. That shit was gooood," he says, and at the same time blasts my character across the screen. I slap his shoulder and immediately recover my stance in the game.

"So where were you this morning?" he asks. "I was surprised your Jeep was gone when I came out to get the paper for my mom."

I hold off a second, trying to guess the intention of his question. But it seems completely innocent and without suspicion. And although this could be the perfect moment, I chicken out.

"I went to the coffee shop," I lie. "Craving a scone."

"Understandable. Well, last night got a little wild for me," he says, clicking buttons and not looking at me while he talks.

"How so?" I ask.

"Met up with Jana."

"Gross, Nathan." I push him over. "The last thing I want to

think about is you and Jana getting 'wild,'" I say, setting down my controller.

"Hey, hey," he says, looking sideways. "Relax over there. Not the kind of wild I'm talking about." He pauses the game and sets aside his controller. "I ended up drinking a beer in my garage because I was so stressed."

"Why didn't you call me?" I ask, my concern spiking.

Nathan looks down in his lap, his brows knitting together. "I wanted to think about it first. Jana told me something."

"What did she say?" I ask.

"She wanted to talk about Vanessa. But not in a normal way, you know, like a normal person. We were sitting at her house, and she just looked over at me and said, 'Do you think Vanessa's going to kill herself?'"

Sickness crawls up my throat. "What else did she say?"

"She started rambling, and was all, 'She was my responsibility. I should have watched her more closely.' And I'm thinking, what are you talking about? I'm telling you, Tatum—she's been really off lately."

"Maybe not as much as you think," I say. "Vanessa was at my locker yesterday. She said she had a tremor." I go on to tell him about the incident with her, the cryptic words, the nosebleed. When I'm done, Nathan leans forward, his elbows on his knees.

"Shit," he says. "Jana was right."

"It's definitely not good," I agree. "What was her plan for Vanessa? Was she going to tell her parents or anything?"

SUZANNE YOUNG

"I don't know. She mentioned that doctor, but it got me thinking . . . maybe it was the Adjustment."

My stomach drops. "What do you mean?"

"Vanessa got the Adjustment, right? She has all of those negative memories back. But maybe they're skewed too dark, or too many at once. Hell, they're not even *real*. We have no idea what they put inside her head. What if the Adjustment isn't a cure at all?"

"I understand your distrust," I say, careful not to get too defensive and give away that Wes and I had started down that path. "But I think there's something to the doctor's theory on the returners. Even Pop said we don't know the long-term effects of The Program; what if this is it?"

Nathan's expression clouds over with concern, and he stares at me. "Why do you say that? Have you . . . Has something happened?"

I look away from the intensity of his gaze. "All I'm saying is that there have been a lot of returners getting sick lately. I don't think we can blame this on the Adjustment. Sebastian didn't have an Adjustment."

Nathan grows quiet, and I regret bringing up Foster's brother. It's a few moments later before Nathan talks again, more subdued. "So do you think I should tell her?" he asks.

"Who?"

"Jana," he says. "Should I tell her about Vanessa acting strange yesterday?"

"Probably," I say. "If she's really in danger, someone has to help her. Foster . . ." I stop myself from telling him about the text messages. "Foster would agree," I say instead.

"Yeah, he would," Nathan says, resting back against the cushions. "He'd Jiminy Cricket that shit. Always let your conscience be your guide and all."

I laugh. "Tell Jana," I say. "It might be good for her and Vanessa to get on the same page."

"I should go over there right now, huh?" he asks, and I can see that he's still worried. Something about what I said hit him harder than I expected.

"It's up to you," I say. "But, yeah. You should."

Nathan stands, clicking off the game system. "She did mention you again, by the way," he adds before heading to the door. "Jana said you and Wes would be great publicity for the Adjustment. I told her you weren't looking to be famous."

"Cool," I say sarcastically. Honestly, I don't understand why she wants to be in my business so much. Sounds like she has plenty of problems of her own.

My phone buzzes in my pocket with an incoming call. I don't want to react immediately, so I let it buzz several times until Nathan walks out the door. The second he's gone, I quickly grab the phone. It's the Adjustment office.

"Hello?" I say, my voice high-pitched from nerves.

"Tatum, it's Dr. McKee," he says. "Everything went well. The memories were implanted and Weston is awake. He's asking for you."

I put my hand on my heart. "He's okay?" I ask.

"He is perfectly well," the doctor says, sounding proud.

"Did it work? Does he remember?"

He's quiet for a moment too long. "That part is uncertain," he says. "It takes time to smooth out, but yes—he has the memory. It's just not quite his yet. He'll have a few gaps that his mind will have to fill in. But he's doing fine. I'm encouraged so far."

I'm slightly confused, but I just want to see Wes. "Let him know I'm on my way," I tell the doctor. And after we hang up, I grab my keys and head out the door.

CHAPTER TEN

THE RECEPTIONIST BUZZES ME IN BEFORE I EVEN ring the bell at the Adjustment office. The entire drive over, my nerves continued to ratchet up. The doctor said Wes was fine, but had it *work*? Will he remember?

"They're waiting for you in the recovery room," the receptionist says, and I pull open the door and head down the hallway. I pause for only a second—a second of total fear—before pushing inside the room.

I find Wes sitting in one of the chairs, his eyes downcast. I quickly dart a look over to Marie, who's standing at the computer cart, typing something. She looks up at me first.

"Tatum," she announces, pushing aside the keyboard. "You got here quickly."

Wes immediately looks at me, and at first his expression is

unreadable. He sweeps his gaze over me like he's seeing me for the first time. I have another spike of fear, but then Wes lifts one side of his mouth in a smile. It's slightly devious, so very Wes. I think my heart actually skips a beat.

He stands, and I run over to hug him. His arms wind around me, his hand resting on the back of my neck. "Are you okay?" I ask, close to his ear.

Wes slides his fingers into my hair, and when he pulls back, he smiles. "Your hair's different," he says. "But I think Cheyenne would have liked this too."

I gasp, covering my mouth, and Wes's eyes tear up. "You remember?" I ask. Across the room, Marie watches us, her head tilted, both examining and empathizing with us.

"Somewhat," he says, holding up his hand to tip it from side to side. "Right now it's kind of like a movie I only half remember."

Wes places his palm on my cheek, an intimate move that sends sparks over my skin. I don't want to cry in this office, but I'm not sure I can help it. There's hope.

Wes turns to Marie. "So when's the next session?" he asks, taking a step back from me to address her.

"We usually like to wait twenty-four hours before—"

"No," Wes says, shaking his head. "I'm ready now."

Marie bristles slightly under his determination. "Weston, please."

"It's working," he says. "The Adjustment's working, I can feel it. And it's so close." His voice hitches on his heightened emotions. His eyes blaze with energy, like the memory has given him new life. "I can almost touch it," he says. "I think I can unlock everything. We have to keep going. Right now."

I put my hand on his arm, about to caution him about pushing too hard. But it's Marie who speaks first. "I understand," she says. "But I can't."

"Where's Dr. McKee?" Wes asks. "I'll beg him, then."

Marie exhales heavily, standing from the stool. "He's not here at the moment," she says. "After he contacted Tatum, he had to go check on another patient. He'll be back tomorrow morning."

"Then it has to be you," Wes says, shaking his head. "Please. This is almost worse—like I'm suddenly able to feel again, hurt again—only I can't figure out what I'm hurting for. What I'm aching for. Just one more memory, Marie. Please," he repeats. "I want to be whole."

I quickly think back to what Nathan said about the memories not being real. That they may even be causing problems. But looking at Wes now, his hunger for more of his past, the slight change in his demeanor and confidence . . . I know that Nathan was wrong. The Adjustment isn't the problem. The Program was.

Marie sighs, and turns to me. I expect her to refuse outright, but there must be something about Weston that evokes her sympathy. She looks at me. "Would you . . . would you be willing to donate another memory, Tatum?" she asks.

I'm taken aback. I'd almost forgotten that I'm the donor, that I'd be involved in this. "Oh, uh . . ."

SUZANNE YOUNG

"Tate," Wes begs, turning to me. It's like a fix, a high he needs to re-create. I should say no—it doesn't feel right. But I can see that he really believes it will work. I can't deny him that chance.

So I make my way over to the chair.

Wes and I go through the motions once again, the uncomfortable angle of the chair, the sticky tabs on my chest and temple. Even the truth serum, although this time it comes with a wave of sickness. Maybe from taking the doses so close together. Marie watches me as the drugs take effect.

"I'm sorry," she says quietly.

"For what?" I ask.

"I should have known he'd want more right away. They always do." She turns and walks over to Wes to get him situated, and I wonder why she said yes in the first place.

"Is this safe?" I call out. Marie straightens, and then glances over her shoulder.

"I wouldn't do it if it weren't safe," she says, like I'm accusing her of something.

"Why break the rules for us?" I ask. "Assuming there are rules about this sort of thing."

Marie gives Wes the sedative, taking her time before answering my question. "Like Dr. McKee, there are moments from my past I'd like to take back. If we had acted sooner, maybe we could have stopped The Program. If we had just fought a little harder. But we'll never know that now." Marie fits the metal crown on Wes's head, and then walks over to the computer and taps a key to make my sensors buzz. "So if you want to know why I'm doing this, it's because Weston's memories should have never been stolen in the first place. You have yours . . ." She pauses. "It's only right that he has his. And if there's even the small possibility that Weston could remember everything, then I'll take that chance. I'll take a chance on all of you."

Wes smiles, and meets my gaze from across the room. We watch each other, even as I feel the warm splash over my chest that tells me the medication's kicked in, even when Wes's eyelids flutter under sedation.

"Wes," I call, trying to draw him awake. He looks at me lazily. "Are you sure?" I ask, my heart beating fast, beeping on the monitor.

"Tell me everything," he whispers.

Although reluctant, I promise that I will. I turn away and stare up at the ceiling. Marie sits down next to me, and I focus on the sound of the heart monitor, willing the beats to slow while Marie asks a few baseline questions.

Once that's done, we're ready to begin.

"What would you like to focus on this time, Tatum?" she asks. "Something about the two of you that can help Weston make connections. Something emotional for him."

I turn my head on the pillow and see that Wes is listening, but his eyelids look heavy, and each time he blinks, they stay shut a little bit longer. I don't want him to drift away. I want him to listen.

"The first time he said I love you," I say in a low voice. It's incredibly intimate, and I'm happy it's just Marie in here. As if she'd understand better than Dr. McKee.

Marie types something into the computer, and tells me to go on. And so I close my eyes and spill my guts.

It was raining, and had been for the past few months. The time of year in Oregon when it seemed like it had never *not* been raining. Weeks would go by without even a hint of sunshine. And for a town buried in the misery and fear of the epidemic, it was constant gloom.

The weather affected Weston more than me because he couldn't ride his motorcycle. He would either have to borrow his mother's car (which he hated to do) or depend on me for rides. I didn't care even one bit, but I think he missed the power of his motorcycle. Now he rode shotgun and controlled the stereo.

The day was cold, and Wes had the heat on full blast. Even though he was wearing a beanie and a heavy jacket, I could see him shivering.

"You okay?" I asked.

"Yeah," he said, but I didn't believe him. A quick check of his person and I could see his cheeks were flushed. I reached over and put my palm on his forehead.

"Wes," I said. "You're burning up."

He turned his head out of my reach. "Burning up for you, baby," he joked, only he sounded exhausted when he said it.

I saw a Walgreens coming up on our right and I pulled into

the lot. "Aw, what," Wes mumbled. "Seriously, Tate," he said. "I'm fine."

I parked near the door and glanced over. "Uh, clearly you're not. Stop being stubborn. I'll be right back." I ran inside and grabbed some aspirin and a Gatorade. I'd never once seen Wes sick before, but I wasn't surprised he was going to try to reduce his fever by sheer will.

When I got back into the Jeep, I made him take a few pills, and then I drove to his house instead of going to the movie theater like we'd planned.

His parents weren't home. This was back when they mostly ignored him, and he said he thought they might be gone for the night. We went inside his basement room.

I took Wes's temperature and confirmed that he did have a fever. He didn't look too sick, but he was a little pathetic in an adorable way. I helped him into bed as he shivered uncontrollably, and I lay at his side, brushing his hair away from his forehead.

He groaned and rested against me. He said he hated feeling helpless. "Will you stay with me tonight?" he asked, gazing up at me with glassy eyes. Normally, I would have said no, but this time I didn't want him to be alone and sick. I shrugged one shoulder as if reluctantly saying yes. I'd call my grandparents later and let them know where I was, and that I'd be taking care of Wes that night. I never lied to them.

Wes lifted the corner of the sheet, wanting me closer, and soon I was resting against him, fully clothed and tucked up right under his chin. His skin was fire against mine, but it was also comforting. He sighed, like having me there made all the difference.

I ran my fingers over his arm, soothing him as he breathed steady and deep. And just when I thought he had fallen asleep, he whispered, "I love you, Tatum Masterson. I love you so fucking much."

I was his girl. His love. He said it all the time after that, recklessly and with abandon. In front of my grandparents, and eventually in front of his parents. He even said it once during an English report in front of the class.

Our love burned bright, hot and feverish just like his skin that day.

And now I'm in a treatment room with wires hooked to me, openly sobbing for that boy. I wish for every second of that day back.

"Good," Marie says, startling me. I reach to wipe the tears off my cheeks, but I'm not sure how the story sounded out loud. When I look at Wes, he's asleep.

"I'm proud of you, Tatum," Marie says, standing up from the stool to begin removing the tabs and wires. "That was not an easy memory for me to catch—you felt it very deeply, I assume. It was real. It was really yours."

"Yeah," I say, sitting up. "And it hurts."

"I can tell," she says. She doesn't dismiss me right away when she's finished. Instead she walks over to check Wes's vitals. "It conveys, you know," she says. "Although the emotions can't exactly be transferred, pain that deep—it shows in the memory. Just so you know."

"Is that going to mess things up?" I ask with fresh concern.

She shakes her head but doesn't look at me. "It just means Wes will have to be closely monitored. It could cause a crash-back." She turns to me. "It could also trigger his old memories," she adds. "All of them."

"What?" I ask, getting to my feet. "Are you saying it's possible that Wes could remember . . . everything? Like, from his perspective? Right now?"

"Everything."

Hope fills my chest and I wish Wes were awake to hear this. "That's great," I say. "How come Dr. McKee didn't bring up this possibility?"

"Because he's taking a more methodical approach. He doesn't want to rush it. My personally held belief, though, is that we have to overload the system to reboot it, so to speak." She looks down at Wes, a touch of sadness in her expression. "He reminds me of someone, you know," she says quietly. "An employee named Reed—a friend. I didn't get a chance to save him before the epidemic. I should have done more. So this time, I will do everything I can." She looks at me, and I can read her loss. Her regret.

The moment is heavy, and by the time I leave, Marie has already started condensing the patterns to implant. Like Dr. McKee, she asks that I leave. She promises to transport Wes home once she's sure he's stable.

I only agree when I see her working on the computer, tapping away with stony concentration. It's familiar somehow, seeing her so focused. I realize that I trust Marie. I trust her with our lives.

I get home, eat at the kitchen table with my grandparents, and continue on like nothing happened today. My stomach is slightly upset from the injections, and I worry that its effect is long lasting enough that if my grandparents ask me about the Adjustment, I'll confess everything. But they don't ask. And the medication fades.

I sit and watch TV with them, my grandmother knitting in the recliner while my grandfather seems distracted, even though he's facing the television. I take out my phone to check for messages, worried that I haven't heard from Marie. But also worried that I haven't heard from Foster.

I click on Foster's name and text him. Hey, I write. Haven't heard from you. You okay?

I wait through the remainder of the show, but he doesn't respond. Tomorrow is his brother's funeral—it's understandable he might be busy or tired or just too damn sad to talk to me.

I look over at my grandmother in the recliner. "Are you sending flowers to the Linns?" I ask. She glances up, her expression immediately stricken with grief.

"Yes, of course," she says. "I'm going to bring a salad by the house too. I heard the funeral is private."

I nod, and she purses her lips like she doesn't agree with the decision. "When will they ever learn?" she says quietly, looking at my grandfather. "Hiding grief isn't the answer."

My grandparents watch each other for a long moment in silence, and then my grandmother goes back to her knitting. Their exchange leaves me slightly uncomfortable, but no one brings up the Linns again.

A little while later, I tell both of them good night and head upstairs.

Marie calls eventually to say that Wes is fine, recovering at his house, and I'm relieved that he's okay. She says he'll have to sleep off the sedatives, but that he was responsive and upbeat when she woke him. He even asked for me.

I thank her for her help, wondering what she'll tell Dr. McKee about this. Wondering if he'll be mad. Then again, she might opt to not tell him at all.

CHAPTER ELEVEN

AT AROUND MIDNIGHT, MY PHONE LIGHTS UP MY room from the nightstand. I pick my head up off my pillow and glance over, sleepy eyed. When I see it's Wes, my heart leaps. I quickly grab the phone.

Hi, he writes. You awake?

I am now, I respond. I'd call him, but my grandparents would hear me on the phone, and I wouldn't want to wake them. How are you?

A speech bubble pops up, but then disappears. It does the same thing again. Are you okay? I write, starting to panic. Marie said she brought him home, but maybe I should have checked on Wes sooner. I was scared to wake him.

It's working, Tate, Wes writes. The Adjustment is working.

Tears spring to my eyes, and I bite down on my lip to try to stop them when they blur my view of the screen.

What do you mean? I ask. What do you remember?

I remember you. The day by the river. The night in my room. And I feel more, just below the surface. It's coming back. You're coming back to me.

Tears sputter between my lips as a cry finds its way out despite my attempt to hold it back. We text a little longer, but then Wes tells me he's still tired and that he'll call me in the morning.

I'm tempted to write that I love him, that I love him so much. But I don't want to put that pressure on him.

We say good night and I set the phone aside. I lie back down on my pillow, and the room is dark with the absence of light from my phone. I squeeze my eyes shut, thinking about the other times Wes will remember about us. About our love.

But just as I think that, there's a small glitch—a sharp pain in the side of my head that makes me wince. It's gone just as quickly, leaving behind a dull ache in its place. I rub my temple over the spot, waiting to see if the pain will return.

Eventually it fades, and my body grows sleepy. And I drift off.

Wes and I decide to keep his treatment secret a bit longer, at least until the process is finished. We don't want anyone to interfere or try to stop us, especially when Wes tells me he slept through the night for the first time in weeks.

So for now, we'll try not to draw attention. We'll keep this secret.

SUZANNE YOUNG

Wes and I spend Sunday texting, but we don't see each other. It's strange how quickly we fall in together—whether it's the memories or the secret keeping, something is bonding us. I don't want anything to ruin that.

I spend the day with my grandparents, although my grandmother leaves for a little while to drop off food to the Linns. Nathan and I decide to honor their wishes and stay away from the funeral. I send my love to Foster, but he still doesn't answer. Nathan said he talked to him briefly and that Foster would be at school tomorrow, so I know he's all right at least.

Nathan goes to his father's for the afternoon, saying he needs to get away. He doesn't mention Jana, and I wonder if he told her about Vanessa's behavior at school. I hope so.

While it's sunny, I help my grandfather in the garden. He doesn't talk about his research and I don't bring it up. At this point, any talk of the Adjustment would be unwelcome—for either of us.

And so we all play our parts, keeping our thoughts to ourselves.

On Monday morning I meet Nathan on the front steps of the school with coffees per usual. He takes a sip and looks sideways at me. The day is windy, and his jacket flaps against his chest.

"Anything new?" Nathan asks. I have a quick fear that he knows about the Adjustment, but when I turn to him, I see he's just making small talk.

"Not much," I say. "You?"

"Eerily quiet," he responds. "I told Jana about Vanessa's bloody nose, and all she said was, 'Thank you for the information. I'll let her doctor know.' And then I didn't hear back from her again."

My heart speeds up. I wonder if Jana was talking about Dr. McKee. It occurs to me that Vanessa might be the patient that the doctor had gone to see when Wes had his second Adjustment. "Hopefully he can help her," I say, trying to keep my voice steady.

Nathan hums out his discontent. "We'll see. Life has been better, which can only mean it's about to get much worse. No ups without downs, right?"

Although he might be making a sober observation, it sounds oddly prophetic.

"Have you seen Foster?" I ask.

"No, but my mom went by the house yesterday." Nathan lowers his eyes. "Said the place was draped in black, whatever that means. Only adults except for the Linn kids." He takes a sip of his drink and looks at me. "That's weird, right? That it was all adults?"

"I don't know what's weird anymore," I say. I'm reminded of Alecia and how she said that maybe the returners were the sane ones. She's partly right, I think now. The rest of the population still clings to their denial and fear, while returners want to get back to their lives. Which of us is living in the altered reality?

I take a fast gulp from my coffee, wincing when I burn my throat. I cough, and Nathan dramatically pats me on the back.

"You all right there?" he asks. "We usually try not to pound extra-hot lattes at eight in the morning."

I laugh, pushing his arm away. The bell rings behind us in the school, and we both groan and reluctantly grab our stuff and head inside.

My phone buzzes on the way to class, but I don't check it in case it's Wes. I wouldn't want Nathan to accidentally see a text about the Adjustment. I have to play it cool. And yet . . . when I get to English class, it's hard for me to see Wes and not react.

Wes is at his desk, his phone out. When I walk in, he lowers it, nodding politely when I pass but saying nothing. The weight of our secret is heavy, but there's also the pull, the need to be together.

Last night Wes and I talked when I could find some time alone. He didn't suddenly remember everything like I'd hoped, but the memories I donated have stuck. He's able to make sense of them, even expand on them a little. They are almost exactly the same with the exception of a few tiny details: hair color here, time of day there. But Wes is convinced that the memories are building out—that he is slowly remembering on his own. I'm not sure, but I know he wants to believe it, so I'll believe it too.

I get to my seat and my phone buzzes again. I wait until Nathan is settled, notebook open on his desk, and peek at the message under my desk. There are a few missed messages asking if I'm coming to school, and a new one from after I got to class.

This is torture, Wes writes.

What is? I ask.

Pretending that I don't want to drop everything and be with you. We could skip. Go to the coast.

I look up at the back of his head in the front of the room, and put my fingers over my lips to try to hide my smile.

"You're grinning like an idiot," Nathan says in a low voice from just behind my shoulder. "Are you sexting?"

"Ew," I say, and laugh. I turn around and push him backward by the face. "And no, I'm not."

Nathan glances from me to Wes, and then smiles despite himself. "Things are going well with Weston, then?" he asks.

I smile. "Yeah. Pretty well."

"I'm glad you're happy," Nathan says. "I was getting tired of watching you be miserable."

"Oh, thank you." I turn and Wes must have heard my voice because he looks back curiously. When he sees me talking to Nathan, he lifts his eyebrows questioningly and turns around.

"He must be getting back to his old self again," Nathan says. "Maybe he remembers how much I don't like him."

"Oh, stop."

"Okay, so maybe I don't hate him," Nathan allows, "but he's certainly not my favorite person."

"Do you even know why?" I ask.

"Easy," he says. "You. No boyfriend wants his girl to have a smokin' hot friend like me. Too bad you're your own person with feelings and brain cells. I bet that really burns him up."

"Oh my God, don't," I say, and laugh. "You know he's not like that."

"Maybe sometimes," he reasons.

"And sometimes you're an asshole. So I guess we're all equal."

"Point goes to you, Tatum."

Just then the teacher walks in with a bundle of copy paper pressed to her chest. She puts the stack on her desk, and then before speaking to us, Miss Soto begins to pass out the papers from the front of the room. Nathan and I exchange a confused look, and then the person in front of me spins and holds out a paper to me. I read it as I pass it back.

Are you feeling lonely or overwhelmed?

"It's an assessment," I say. Dread curls in my stomach. We haven't had this type of questionnaire since The Program ended.

"What the hell is this about?" Douglas Miami asks from the front of the room. He pushes the paper to the side of his desk, his posture rigid, fear tightening his voice. "This is some Program shit right here."

Several people in the class shift uneasily. The girl next to me drops her pen on the floor but makes no motion to pick it up; another kid crumples up his page like he's already decided he wants no part of it.

"Watch your language, Mr. Miami," the teacher says to Douglas in a warning voice. "This isn't about The Program. The school board is . . ." Her careful words falter slightly. "They are concerned. Seems several members are worried about another outbreak. A parent brought it to their attention."

Douglas laughs bitterly. "That's every week," he says. "What's changed?"

Miss Soto crosses her thin arms over her chest. "This is fact-finding. They're only conducting a survey to gather information about—"

"A survey, huh?" Douglas asks. "Yeah, we've all heard that before."

"It's about the returners," the teacher adds, and the class falls silent.

Wes sits rigidly at his desk, but rather than turn to me, he takes out his phone. My phone buzzes; I covertly read the message under my desk.

Not good, he writes.

I chew on my lower lip, worried this has to do with the Adjustment. But it's more likely they've noticed the outbursts too. The way the returners have been breaking down. Dying. But there are larger implications to this, ones that become glaringly obvious.

"Returners?" Douglas repeats. "Then why not tag them instead? Why all of us?"

I see a few others nod their heads, and I worry about the fears getting stoked. Returners are already outcasts. Our teacher shouldn't have said anything. I think she realizes it too.

"Because this *is* about all of you," Miss Soto says. "All of your well-being. In case you forget, the epidemic affected everyone. We still don't know why."

"If you ask me," Douglas continues, sweeping the paper off his desk and leaning way back in his chair, "it looks like The Program is still trying to control us." Several other students agree. Douglas isn't a returner, but like most of us, he feels cheated by what The Program took. Our ability to feel, to talk about feeling. They made us dead in our skin, all under the guise of saving us.

Miss Soto tightens her jaw, but I realize it's not because she thinks Douglas is wrong; she thinks he may be right. If The Program taught us anything, it's not to be complacent. We can't wait to be saved. We have to save ourselves.

"The assessment is voluntary," Miss Soto says. "You don't have to take it if it makes you uncomfortable. However, I will have to note the refusal."

"Sounds like monitoring to me," Douglas says.

Miss Soto walks over to pick up Douglas's paper from the floor and sets the page on her desk. "Please take five minutes," she announces to the rest of us, her voice softer, "and I'll be around to collect them."

My phone buzzes again, and I don't like how ominous Wes's words are out of context. Or even in context. I turn my paper over, leaving it blank, and set my pen aside.

Don't answer any of their questions.

Weston leaves class without me, seeming rattled by this development. I can understand it. I see the blank stares, shock, on the faces of others as Nathan and I walk down the hallway. They must have sent the questionnaire out across the school.

"Did you fill it out?" Nathan asks. "The assessment."

"No," I say. "You?"

"Hell no," Nathan says. He turns his shoulder as we cut

through the crowd jammed up at the end of the English hallway. "It just felt too creepy, you know?" he adds. "Same fucking wording and everything."

"I noticed," I say. "It made me feel—"

There's a loud metallic bang and I reach to grab Nathan's arm as he falls back a step. The crowd of students swells, reacting to something, and then they contract inward. There's another clang, and Nathan gets up on his toes to see over the crowd.

He pulls out of my grip, pushing into the crowd. He peels them back, and I watch him as he fights toward the middle of the circle.

There's a loud screech of a girl's voice. "Don't fucking touch me!"

The other students move back, terrified by an outburst— like we'll all get flagged for witnessing it. Some fade to the back, and my heart skips when I see who has been yelling. Vanessa stands in the middle of everyone, her hair tangled and clumped near the scalp. Her lips twitch, distorting her features, and her eyes are wild. She's almost unrecognizable.

"Nessa," Jana says, stepping toward her with palms raised. By her frazzled appearance (neck of her T-shirt stretched out, scratch on her cheek), I assume she's the one Vanessa has been throwing against a locker. Nathan stands next to Jana, as if ready to protect her. Together, they have Vanessa cornered.

"You did this!" she shouts, pointing a shaky finger at Jana. "You did this to me!" Vanessa's having a meltdown. Another one.

"I didn't do anything," Jana says, understanding and calm.

She puts out her hand toward Vanessa, but her friend slaps it away. The sound cracks through the air, and Jana winces from the pain and pulls her hand to her chest.

Nathan pushes Jana behind him, like he's the last line of defense between the two girls. I quickly scan the hall, wondering where the hell all the teachers are. Maybe everyone was too stunned (scared) to go get one.

"Vanessa," Nathan says. "What's going on?" He's trying to sound supportive, positive, but knowing him as well as I do, I can hear the hint of anger in his words. He's not going to stand aside and let her kick Jana's ass.

"Are you seriously that clueless?" Vanessa asks him venomously. "That dumb?"

Nathan tilts his head, allowing her insults, although I'm sure his patience is running thin. "We don't know what you're talking about," he says, motioning around him like he's speaking on behalf of the entire crowd.

An eerie calm falls over the storm of emotion on Vanessa's face. Her gaze flicks from face to face, pausing when she reaches mine. And when she smiles—strangely, bitterly, it's like the bottom falls out from underneath me.

"They're watching you," she says. "It's all a lie." She turns to look at Jana accusingly. "They're all fucking liars," she whispers.

Jana tightens her lips, as if telling Vanessa to stop. But then Vanessa growls out in anguish. She balls up her fists and runs full speed down the hallway to ram headfirst into the metal lockers, crumpling to the ground in a heap.

PART III
A NIGHT LIKE THAT

CHAPTER ONE

I'M SICK TO MY STOMACH. CLASSES GO BY WITH-out a word about the incident, not from teachers, not from other students. Everyone sits there shell-shocked. I think about Vanessa coming to me, and I wish I'd done more. I feel partly to blame.

When I arrive at science class, I take a seat at my usual lab table. I glance around, waiting for Foster—hoping he's in school today. I notice that there are several people absent, including my lab partner. Whether the others have left or were never here, I'm not sure.

I look down at the black tabletop, my hands leaving prints on the dull surface. Proof of my existence. I close my eyes, try-ing to block out the sight of Vanessa falling to the floor in such an unnatural way. It's haunting me.

"Is this seat taken?"

The sound of Foster's voice is an absolute godsend, and I lift my head and find him at the end of my table. I immediately jump out of my stool and hug him, and he returns it with the same ferocity. We hug out his loss, our fear, and our joy at seeing one another again. I hear him sniffle, and slowly release him. Tears shine in his eyes.

"I needed that," he says, pressing his lips into a sad smile.

"Yeah, me too," I say. Because the truth is, I'm unsettled in a peculiar way, down to my core. And it's not just Vanessa. It's not just the Adjustment. It's something about that assessment. It's wormed its way into my consciousness.

Foster takes the stool next to mine, and when I look up at the teacher, he doesn't seem to mind the switch. I'm sure he's heard about Foster's brother, so he might be cutting him a little slack today.

The bell rings, and the teacher tells us all to work on yesterday's lab project. I've finished mine, so instead Foster and I scoot closer to catch up.

He doesn't say much at first, staring down at my finished notes. I watch him—the skin under his eyes is puffy, his T-shirt wrinkled. He's mourning, and I put my hand over his to draw his gaze.

"I'm sorry I wasn't there yesterday," I whisper.

"Don't be," he says. "Hell, *I* didn't want to be there. Me, Jake, and Daphne were the only people under thirty," he says about himself and his siblings. "And of course Sebastian," he adds quietly.

Foster squeezes my hand and then lets go. I'm quiet, overwhelmed by his grief. I falter with the right words in my head.

"I saw your gram, though," Foster says, forcing a smile. "She makes an awesome salad. Extra croutons like a boss."

I laugh. "I told her more cheese, too," I add.

"Loved it."

We watch each other a long moment, and then Foster rests his elbow on the table. He glances around to make sure no one is watching us. "During the funeral," he says to me, "all those people, do you know what they talked about?"

"What?" I ask.

"Not about The Program," he says, as if it's what they *should* have been talking about. "They said nothing. Not one relevant conversation. I sat on the sofa, Daphne crying next to me, and some asshole asks her about her grades." Foster shakes his head. "Who gives a fuck, right? The Program did this to us. Our brother *died*. He . . ." But Foster clenches his teeth and turns away. "My brother died," he adds softly, "and no one talked about why."

I want to hug him again, but Foster clears his throat and looks back at me. "So, anyway, it was all dreadful and I'm glad you were spared." His words are abrupt and I know he doesn't want to talk about it anymore.

"Now," he says, lowering his voice conspiratorially, "I heard about Vanessa today. Were you there?"

I tell him what happened at the locker, the horror of it all, and I see the concern grow in his expression. He runs his hand roughly through his red hair.

"She's partly why I wanted to call you on Saturday," he says. "Damn."

"What do you mean?" I ask.

Foster checks the room again, and it's almost paranoid the way he does it. As if someone really might be watching us. Our teacher sits at his oversize desk, red pen in hand. Other students are filling up beakers with water or measuring solvents.

But one . . . one small girl in the corner with short black bangs is watching us from her lab table. When we notice her, she quickly diverts her gaze.

Foster swallows hard and leans in to me. "Handlers," he whispers. "I think there are handlers."

I lift my eyes slowly to his, the blood draining from my face. It's like an automatic response, the way the fear completely takes over. My fingers begin to tremble; my throat tightens. "Wh—what?" I ask.

"Those assessments," he says. "I don't think they're the only form of monitoring."

I want to check the room again, make sure there aren't any men in white coats ready to drag me away. Steal me from my family, friends, and society. But I know it can't be true.

"And I think Vanessa figured it out," he continues. "The day Wes came back, I sat with her at lunch, you remember?" I nod that I do. "Well, she was acting kind of strange. I assumed that was just her way, but she would have these moments where she'd ask me a question and then study my face, as if she was trying to tell if I was lying. As if she *could* tell. She was paranoid for sure, but . . . there was something else, too. I couldn't put my finger on it.

"And then, after Seb died," he says, "I got a message—a text. Arturo told me Vanessa thought she was being watched. He sort of laughed it off in a sad way, but it occurred to me . . . what if she was right? What if there really are still handlers?"

I stare at him, my heart thudding loudly. I'm speechless, too terrified to believe it. "The Program's over," I whisper to Foster. "And the handlers are gone. At least . . . they're gone from school. I think they'll live on in our nightmares for a while."

"It's just a theory," he allows. "I mean . . . clearly Vanessa has much bigger problems. And I didn't bring it up to Nathan because I didn't want it getting back to Jana. I don't think she can keep a secret."

"Nathan doesn't think you like Jana," I say.

"I don't," he says simply, shocking me.

"Okay, everyone," the teacher announces suddenly from the front of the room, gathering our attention. "Hand in your reports, and then open to lesson four point one. Top of the page."

"Let's keep this between us for now," Foster says, stooping down to match my eye level. I tell him that I will, and he leaves to hand in my paper.

While he's gone, my pulse starts to return to normal, or at least a steadier version. It was just a wild theory, and yet, I find myself drawn to the girl in the corner.

But I'm surprised when I look over and find her gone.

● ● ●

Foster and I make our way to lunch, neither of us mentioning our earlier conversation, almost like it didn't happen. Nathan is waiting in our usual spot. He's pale, and he eats without speaking. The entire school has gone quiet, fallen into a hush.

Nathan gets to his feet and grabs Foster by the arm to pull him into a hug. "I'm so sorry, man," he says quietly. "I'm so fucking sorry."

It's the first time he's seen Foster since his brother's death, and the two of them exchange a few grief-soaked words. I give them some space. Eventually Foster thanks him, and the two of them sit down, talking quietly.

The conversation is somber, and I sit on the other side of Nathan, my feet dangling off the half wall. I listen to Foster tell him about the funeral and, again, how glad he is that we didn't have to witness any of it.

Once they're caught up, Nathan takes a deep breath and leans back. The wind tries to blow away his chip bag, but I slap it down and hand it back to him. He stares down at the crumpled paper.

"So I got an update on Vanessa," Nathan says. "She managed to crack her skull—at least that's what one of the paramedics said when he was wheeling her out. They're not sure she's going to wake up," he adds, looking over at me. "Jana texted. She's pretty wrecked right now."

"It's awful," I say, feeling guilty. "I should have told you something was wrong with Vanessa the minute I talked to her at my locker."

"It wouldn't have mattered," Nathan replies. "Vanessa's been . . . she's been a mess for a while." On the other side of him, Foster nods along as if confirming it.

"I mean," Nathan continues, "we can pretend otherwise. But in a way, she was right. We are all liars. We've seen the people getting sick, saw it during the epidemic. We chose to turn a blind eye. We're still fucking doing it. And where were the teachers? Her parents? Her goddamn doctor? We saw her at school every day. No one helped her. We let this happen."

"It's like the people at the funeral," Foster adds quietly. "Pretending like there wasn't a dead nineteen-year-old in the casket. All we do is pretend . . ." He stops and shakes his head.

"So what should we do?" I ask them both. "How do we help the other returners?"

Nathan looks over, studying me. "Not the Adjustment, if that's what you're going to suggest. Because no matter what Jana says, it's partly to blame. You don't get to just mess with people's heads and not expect consequences."

I know that Nathan would be upset if he found out that Wes and I went to the Adjustment. But I don't agree, not after talking to Wes. He's getting better. The Adjustment is saving him. It's not the cause of this.

"What else did Jana say?" Foster asks, looking over. His expression doesn't give away his earlier confession to me.

Nathan blinks quickly, like he's trying to recall her exact words. "She claimed it was 'faulty wiring,'" he says. "Those were her actual words. She said The Program put Vanessa back together wrong in the first place and that the assessment this morning triggered her meltdown. She says she doesn't think it has anything to do with the Adjustment."

"The Program has been known to cut corners," Foster agrees. "It's too bad no one was watching out for her."

"Any idea what Vanessa and Jana were even fighting about in the hallway?" I ask.

Nathan shakes his head. "All I saw was Vanessa punch Jana in the face and throw her against the locker. They struggled for a bit until I pulled them apart." He pauses. "But Vanessa . . . she was like an animal, completely feral."

"I'm glad you were there," I say. I'm proud of how he stands up for others.

"Yeah," Nathan says. "It's just, with everything going on . . . I'm worried it's happening again. I'm worried The Program's coming back." His eyes weaken. "I'm scared for the returners."

I have to fight to keep my expression clear. "That will never happen," I say.

But I want to run off and find Weston right now, get on his motorcycle and escape before things get worse. That's not exactly rational; it's another outburst. And I can't imagine how the school board would react to that.

I pull my legs up to wrap my arms around my knees, hugging them to my chest. I look over my shoulder to where Wes usually sits during lunch. He's not there. His absence is a gaping hole in the courtyard.

"Have you seen Wes?" I ask.

"Unfortunately, no," Foster replies, taking an apple out of his lunch bag and biting into it. "It's disappointing."

"I haven't seen him either," Nathan adds. "Not since English."

I stand, and look around again, as if I just missed him. But each second that passes makes me worry more. Why isn't he here?

I take a few steps forward, and then check my phone to make sure I haven't missed a text from him. When I see that I haven't, I type out a message.

Where are you? I write.

I wait, but as the seconds tick by without a response, my panic grows.

"What's wrong?" Nathan asks.

"It's Wes," I say. "He's not at lunch."

Nathan comes to stand next to me and glances around. "He might be staying after class," he offers. But when I don't agree with that excuse, he lightly bumps me with his elbow. "You should go look for him," he says. "Foster's here to be my friend." He smiles, as if that'll help calm my worry.

Foster takes another loud bite of his apple. "Yes, I'll keep Nathan out of trouble. But bring your boyfriend back here when you find him. I haven't even said hi to him since he returned."

Foster and Wes really do get along well—and not even just to annoy Nathan.

"I will."

I tell them both I'll catch up with them later, and I gather my stuff and escape into the courtyard. A teacher watches me as I walk back into the building, and I can't help feel a bit vulnerable under her gaze. Feel watched. I swallow hard, and take out my phone again.

Seriously, I text Wes. I need to talk to you.

Still no answer. Nervously, I start toward his locker. As I pass others in the hallway, all of them keep their eyes downturned—trying to hide in plain sight. The subtle ways of not being noticed.

When I turn down the hallway, I see Wes isn't at his locker. I go there anyway, resting my shoulder against it. I'm not sure where to look for him right now. He might be in class. He could have left for the day. But there's a greater fear under my skin.

The Program isn't coming back, I tell myself. We wouldn't let that happen. We have to figure out how to stop the returners from falling apart and maybe all the rest of this will go away. The Adjustment might be our only shot at that.

I glance up to check for Wes again, but instead I see Kyle Mahoney walking in my direction. She doesn't see me at first, but then she looks toward Wes's locker. Her jaw tightens when she notices me.

I straighten, expecting her to come over, but she continues down the hall, her shoes clacking on the linoleum floor. I watch her pass, and I'm not sure what comes over me. I feel a sense that I'm not part of a bigger conversation that's happening around me.

"Hey," I call. Kyle stops, but it takes her a second to turn around. When she does, her eyes are narrowed slightly. Now that she's facing me, I don't even know what I planned to say to her. My resolve fades.

"Never mind," I start to say, but she cuts me off.

"He's in the office," she says. "Weston. I just saw him there, if that's what you were going to ask."

It wasn't. I don't know what I wanted to ask her. I just wanted her to acknowledge me, acknowledge that I'm not making up the weirdness between us. But I'm glad she told me where Wes is.

I mumble a thank-you and hike my backpack up on my shoulders. I rush down the hall. I don't know why Wes is in the office—it can't be good. But I'm not going to leave him there alone.

Kyle doesn't say anything else, but I feel her eyes on my back as I turn down the other corridor.

The office is crowded when I pull open the glass door and walk inside. Several parents wait in chairs, along with a handful of students. Two uniformed police officers stand near the principal's door. Whatever is going on looks a lot like panic.

"Tate."

I turn and find Wes in the corner, sitting alone. His backpack is at his feet, and I notice immediately how sickly he looks under the fluorescent lights. Strung out, even though he said he's been sleeping better. I glance around at some of the other students, and see they're suffering with much of the same.

I cross the office toward Wes and crouch down next to his chair, against the wall.

"I texted you," I say quietly.

"Yeah, sorry," he says. "I didn't want to scare you."

"It scared me more that you didn't answer."

"Now I'm extra sorry." He tries to offer an apologetic smile, but I don't return it. His smile fades. "How'd you know I was here?" he asks.

"Kyle Mahoney."

"Really?" he asks. "I didn't see her."

"I don't want to talk about her right now," I say. "Are you here . . . voluntarily?" I ask in a hushed voice. Nathan's comments have made me paranoid.

"Sort of. I mean, I guess I could have refused when they came to get me out of class."

"They came and got you? Why?"

"I think they're talking to all returners," he says. "I thought it might be best to not flip out when they asked, proving them right for being worried." He exhales heavily. "I heard about Vanessa."

"I was there," I say, and sit cross-legged on the carpet, resting my shoulder against his knee. "And it was bad, Wes," I whisper, not wanting the others to hear me talking. "She looked right at me."

"You? Why?"

"She said people were watching us," I whisper. "She said they're all liars. What does that even mean?" I ask. "Who's lying?"

I see his Adam's apple bob, but he doesn't offer an opinion right away. Instead he reaches absently to run his hand over the back of my hair.

"So now Foster," I say, "is starting to think there are handlers again—something that Vanessa got into his head. And Nathan, well, he's somewhere between blaming the Adjustment and thinking The Program's coming back." I lift my eyes to meet his. "I'm not a fan of any of those opinions. But Nathan doesn't know about . . ." I glance around to make sure no one's listening. "He doesn't know about the Adjustment. I hate keeping it from him."

"Then tell him," Wes says.

I furrow my brow. "I can't," I say. "He'll be mad. At least when you remember everything, it'll all make sense why we did it."

"Well, if it helps," Wes says, "I don't think Vanessa's outburst had anything to do with the Adjustment. But . . ." He pauses to think it over. "Foster might be on to something."

My stomach sinks. "What does that mean?" I ask.

"I was listening to a girl in my history class last hour," Wes says. "And she was talking about how she knew Vanessa before The Program. The girl said it was weird, that when Vanessa came back, Jana came with her—like a built-in new best friend.

Said Vanessa never talked to her again because Jana wouldn't allow it."

"So . . . what? Jana is possessive and they had a fight? Or . . . are you saying, what—Jana's a handler?"

"No," Wes says, shaking his head. "That's not what I mean. That girl in my class has been saying this stuff for a while, gossip, really. But for someone who has been in The Program, paranoia is a given, right? A few off moments and all of a sudden . . . you can't trust anyone. What if Vanessa cracked up and thought Jana was a handler?"

"There are no handlers," I say.

"I know," Wes agrees, and lowers his voice. "But it kind of makes sense she'd think that. Look how easily Vanessa's words made Foster worry about handlers. All of us are living in a perpetual state of panic. What could one murmur do? What if it could cause a meltdown? What if we *all* could melt down?"

"That's dark, Wes."

"It's just one possibility I'm working on." He leans in to kiss the top of my head as if he's talking mathematical equations and not the end of civilization.

"You know," I say, resting my elbow on his knee. "Nathan's been sort of dating Jana for the past few months. Do you think he's heard about any of these possibilities?"

"Would he tell you if he had?" Wes asks.

My immediate answer should be yes, but it's *I don't know*. He didn't tell me about him and Jana in the first place. Just like I'm not telling him about Wes's Adjustment. It's a sudden realization that Nathan and I . . . we're keeping secrets with other people.

"Then again," Wes says, sighing and leaning his head back against the wall, "it could have been the Adjustment. I mean . . . what if it worked and she suddenly remembered everything? That would include the bad stuff too."

"That's true," I say, considering his words. How would this affect Wes if it happened to him—all his anger, loneliness, depression—what if it all hit at once, on one day, at one hour, one moment? Would it break him? I should have thought of that before.

Wes looks down at me, and he shrugs. "That would mean the Adjustment works, right?" he asks, barely a whisper. He starts to smile when a small woman appears from the guidance counselor's office. I've never seen her before.

"Weston Ambrose?" she calls, even though she's looking right at us. I instantly don't trust her. Her gray wool suit and pinned-back hair. She's severe.

"Should I wait here?" I ask Weston as he stands.

"No," he says, helping me up from the floor. "Go to class. I'll text you when I'm done." He runs his hand over my arm before turning away, and it occurs to me how easily he's been touching me, no longer flinching away. It must have something to do with the Adjustment.

I try not to look shocked and watch him walk toward the woman. She lets her gaze linger on me a moment longer, but when Wes gets to her, she motions to the office, and together they walk in and close the door behind them.

CHAPTER TWO

I WANT TO WAIT. I ALMOST DO. BUT THE INQUISITIVE stares of the office staff and the concern of other parents makes me uncomfortable. I end up a few minutes late for my next class, and everyone is looking around; the room is only half filled. Returners are either gone or being pulled throughout the day. None of them comes back to class.

I continually check my phone, not worried if a teacher scolds me. They don't. From the expressions on their faces, I'm starting to believe they're worried too. They don't want another Program.

Nathan is waiting by my Jeep when I get out of school. I thought about texting him to tell him people are blaming Jana for Vanessa's breakdown; some might even be insinuating that she's a handler. But I figured I'd tell him in person.

They're only rumors, but still . . . he should know what people are saying.

"Yes, I heard it's all Jana's fault," Nathan announces just as I arrive at the Jeep. "And, no, I don't believe it for a second."

I stop in front of him, looking him over. His shoulders are slumped, his face worn. It reminds me of how he looked the day he heard that Sebastian died. I hate to see him so torn up.

We lean against the Jeep for a moment, watching the rest of the students leave school. Nobody looks okay. What are they doing to us?

"Jana and Vanessa did have an intense friendship," Nathan says. "And, yeah, I noticed how closely Jana would keep an eye on her. I even mentioned it once." Nathan turns to me. "She said she was making sure she stayed safe. That's why she didn't want her with her old friends. That's why she asked her to get the Adjustment. She was looking out for her."

We're quiet for a few moments, and then I bump my shoulder into his. "Got time for a slice?" I ask.

"Yeah," he replies with a heavy sigh. "Sounds great."

On the way to the pizza place, I tell Nathan that I saw Wes in the office, and we talk about how the returners are all being interviewed. I don't mention Foster's concern about handlers, and I definitely don't mention his feelings about Jana. Nathan and I get to Rockstar Pizza, grab our regular table, and order.

"Is it legal?" I ask him. "Pulling returners out of class to talk to them without their guardians?"

"I guess it depends on what they were talking to them about and who was asking the questions. You said there was a lady you'd never seen before?"

"She wasn't with our school," I say. "Detective, maybe? That seems a bit over the top."

"School board member?" Nathan offers.

"Not sure they have that kind of power."

"You'd be surprised," Nathan says just as the server appears at the end of our table. He's got tattoo sleeves on both arms, and a long beard. He sets our slices on the table and asks if we want anything else.

"We're good," Nathan tells him. The server walks away and Nathan reaches for the crushed red pepper. "Now," he says. "The real question is *what*. What information are they trying to extract?"

"I think they want to assess the returners, see what sort of side effects they're experiencing. But . . . it might also be about the Adjustment," I say, guilty to even utter the word in front of him again. "Dr. McKee did say they were applying for a patent. They might be investigating it."

"They should," Nathan says, picking up his slice to bite the end of the triangle. "And they should shut it down."

I stare at him, expecting him to qualify the statement, but he doesn't. It's then that I notice the dull headache that has creeped up, throbbing behind my eyes. I press against them with my fingers before looking at Nathan again. "You can't mean that," I say.

"Why not?" he asks.

"Because those memories are locked away. Why shouldn't returners have them back?"

"Uh . . . because they run headfirst into metal lockers when they can't handle the fucked-up reality. Look," he says, pushing away his food to put his elbows on the table, "you and Jana are both telling me it's not the Adjustment, right? And I'm sorry to point this out, but both of you have ulterior motives. Vanessa and Wes. Do I think those two deserve their memories back? Hell yes, I do. But the fact is, those real memories are gone."

"We don't know if this had to do with the Adjustment," I say. "When Vanessa came to me, she was worried about me knowing the truth. She didn't warn me about the Adjustment. If she was really concerned—"

"Seriously?" Nathan says. "Do you really think she was in a place to give advice? No," he says. "Either way, if they're investigating, I imagine the Adjustment will be shut down before the end of the week." He picks up his slice and takes a big bite. He talks around his food and adds, "And then we'll wait to see what the next failed attempt for a cure is."

When I arrive home, I'm surprised to see my grandfather's car gone once again. I don't text this time, because since the pizza place, my headache has gotten worse. It could be stress. Or I could be getting sick. Either way, I drop my bag at the bottom of the stairs and go up to my room.

I lie across my bed, checking my phone one last time to see if there's anything from Wes.

I'm okay. Will call you later, he'd sent while I was at the pizza place. I plan to still ask what happened, but then there is a crack across my skull as the headache intensifies. I squeeze my eyes shut, burying my head in the pillow as I groan out in pain. The minutes tick by as I wait for it to pass.

And suddenly I fall back into a memory—the same one I told Wes about at lunch the other day; the memory about how he ended up in The Program.

Wes and I, under the bridge. It was growing dark and we lay side by side. He turned away when I tried to kiss him. His expression was sad as he stared up at the underside of the bridge.

But then the memory changes, becomes different from how I recited it for Wes. Different from how it actually happened. The memory goes on, slightly fuzzy at the edges.

"I hate hurting you like this," Wes said in a low voice. "You know I do, Tate."

And this time . . . I was the one flinching. I was the one sad and lost.

"Just talk to me," Wes begged. "I couldn't live if you hated me."

I looked at him then, my stomach an empty pit, my chest hollow. And there was a drip as a tear fell onto my cheek, making him crumble. And I was glad. I wanted him to know how it hurt. How he made me hurt.

"This is why," he said miserably. "This is why."

. . .

"Tatum?" The sound of my grandmother calling my name from downstairs startles me awake. I sit up with a gasp, wincing the moment I do because my head pounds. I quickly reach up to put my palm on my forehead and try to blink away the pain.

But emptiness lingers in my chest, the fading memory—*dream*?—sticking with me. Had I fallen asleep?

"Tatum?" my gram repeats, sounding concerned as she knocks and opens my door. I look over at her, and her eyes widen. She quickly rushes to the bed. "Honey," she says, reaching to pluck a few tissues from the box on the nightstand. "You're bleeding."

"What?" I'm disoriented. Confused as emotions flood back into my chest all at once.

My grandmother holds the tissues under my nose, and then pulls them back to show me the blood. She folds the tissues in half, and dabs under my nostrils.

"It's okay," she says, crouching down at my knees. "It was just a little bit." But even as she tries to soothe me, I can tell by the way she's pressing her lips together that she's worried. She takes away the tissues, wrapping them in another.

"There," she says, and reaches to brush back my hair. "All better."

Gram tosses the tissues in the trash, and then comes to sit next to me on the bed. I'm off center, and she must read it because she feels my forehead.

"You're a little warm," she says, even though I hadn't noticed a fever earlier. "Come downstairs and I'll make you some soup and give you an aspirin."

I let her help me up, glad when the headache releases to a dull throb. But as she leads me to the door, I pause and turn to her. I'm disoriented.

"Gram," I start. "Wes and I . . . we were okay before he was taken into The Program, right? I mean, on a personal level."

She furrows her brow, seeming surprised by the question. "Of course, honey," she says. "Why do you ask?"

I blink quickly, trying to call up the details of the memory, but they only get further away. "Never mind," I say. "I must have . . . I must have fallen asleep. I had a weird dream."

"Sounds awful," she says, tightening her grip on my arm. "All right, let's get downstairs so I can call your grandfather. And I'll get you a cold washcloth for your head."

We start out of the room, and I'm slowly getting my bearings again. I run my hand down the bannister as we descend the stairs. "Where is Pop?" I ask.

"He didn't tell you?" she asks, surprised. "He's gone back to work—just accepted a position this morning. He'll be at the paper two afternoons a week."

This is a strange development. My grandfather had retired, citing his distaste for *entertainment news*—how so much of journalism had gone that way. And until the story broke about The Program, everything my grandfather had written criticizing The Program's methods had been buried.

So, yeah—I'm stunned he'd go back now. I'm also curious why he didn't tell me himself.

I follow my gram into the kitchen, and she has me sit while she gets a washcloth from the linen closet. She runs it under cold water, and then grabs a cup of juice. She opens a cabinet and I hear her shake out a few pills.

Damn. I left my phone upstairs. I hope I don't miss a call from Wes.

Gram returns and hands me the cup and the two pills. They're not the usual aspirin I take, and I look up at her. "What are these?" I ask.

She tilts her head like she doesn't know what I'm talking about, and presses the cool washcloth to my forehead.

"The pills," I clarify when she doesn't answer.

"Oh," she says. "Those are mine. They're for migraines."

I stare down at them, oversize and chalky looking. "How'd you know I had a headache?" I ask.

"You've got that dreamy kind of look," she says, smiling warmly. "Should help with your fever too."

Again, I don't feel feverish, but I pop the two pills into my mouth anyway, and wash them down with a sip of juice. Gram pats my shoulder and then tells me to hold the cloth on my forehead. She leaves the room to call my grandfather, and the moment she's gone, I get up and go to the cabinet.

I find the prescription bottle, and after checking to make sure she's still gone, I grab the bottle and read the label. It's made out to my grandmother, but I can't pronounce the name of the medication. The label doesn't list Dr. Goldsmith, her usual doc. All it has is the name "Attending Physician" in the right-hand corner along with a phone number.

I hear my gram hang up the phone in the other room, and I quickly put the bottle back in the cabinet and dart over to the chair, pressing the washcloth to my forehead just as she walks back in.

"Pop says he'll be home by six. He's bringing pizza." She smiles broadly as if it's just for me. She pauses at the counter and looks me over. "How are you feeling, honey?" she asks.

"Better," I say.

"Good. Now would you like some soup?"

I'm not the least bit hungry. "Not really," I say. I lower the washcloth, and she comes to take it from my hands. As I watch her walk back toward the sink, the room tilts and I feel myself sway.

"Why don't you go lie down on the couch?" she calls. "Those pills are pretty strong. They always knock me out." She says it like it's a good thing.

I hold the back of the chair as I stand. "I'll just head up to my room."

"No," she says quickly. "I want to keep an eye on you for now. Just go into the living room. I'll join you in a second. I have some knitting I can do."

I don't protest, feeling a wave of sleepiness crash over me. I try to remember the name of the pills she gave me so I can look them up later, but I can't keep a clear thought in my head. I lie across the gray-patterned sofa and rest my head on the pillow.

I feel like I'm sinking through the couch and into the floor. I'm heavy. And every time I try to think, the images are cloudy. Until there's nothing but darkness.

Fingers brush across my forehead, and I wake up to my gram staring down at me lovingly. "There she is," she announces. I blink rapidly, glancing around the room. My body still feels heavy, relaxed.

"It's time for dinner," Gram says. I look out the window and see it's after dusk. Sleepily, I follow my gram into the kitchen and find my grandfather at the table already. He smiles at me.

"How're you feeling, kid?" he asks. "Your grandmother told me you had a fever."

"Better," I say, taking my spot at the table. My headache is gone completely. I look at my gram. "Although you may have been a little heavy on the drugs there, lady."

My grandmother winces guiltily.

"What'd you give her?" Pop asks.

"Just my migraine medicine," she says quietly, and pours iced tea in my glass. I take a sip, the cubes rattling.

There's a bowl of salad in the middle of the table and I put a small scoop on my plate. "Heard about your job," I say to my grandfather. "Didn't know you wanted to go back to work."

"I didn't," he says, poking his food with his fork. "But while I was doing some research for you, I found the best way to snoop out some information was with press credentials."

I glance up at him. "You did it for me?"

"I did it for the information." He smiles. "For you."

My grandfather's awesome. A good reporter. A good person. "Find out anything so far?" I ask.

"Not much. Not enough to share at least. But I am meeting with a woman later this week. We'll see what she turns up."

I almost ask him if it's Marie Devoroux, but I can't remember when I first met her. Was it when I was with Nathan? Or when I went back with Wes? I furrow my brow, my thoughts getting mixed up.

"Is that all you're going to eat?" my grandmother asks, motioning to my plate.

"Sorry," I say. "Guess I'm still full. I had pizza with Nathan after school." I remember then that my phone is upstairs. I must have missed a call from Wes by now. I'm not hungry, but I quickly shove a forkful of salad in my mouth. I go on like that, none of us talking, until my plate is mostly clear.

"I'll do the dishes," I say, standing up and taking my plate with me. I waver the minute I'm on my feet and grab the back of the chair. My gram stands after shooting my grandfather a concerned look.

"Why don't you head upstairs," she suggests. "I'll get the dishes."

I thank her, and round the table to put my plate in the sink. I place my hand on my grandfather's shoulder as I pass him and escape the kitchen.

My body's just catching up after the medication coma. Maybe one pill would have been enough.

I get upstairs and shut my door before heading over to my bed where I left my phone. I drop down and check my messages. I see three missed calls from Wes's number. Quickly, I hit return call.

Wes picks up on the first ring. "That took too long," he says jokingly.

"Yeah, right," I say, relaxing back into my pillows, immediately comforted at hearing his voice. "Says the guy who waits until seven to call back. You're lucky my gram drugged me or I would've been freaking out. How did it go in the school office? What did they want?"

"Uh . . ." He laughs. "Did you just say your grandmother drugged you?"

"Nothing illicit. And not the point I was trying to make," I tell him. "What did they say at the office?"

He's quiet for a moment, and then he lowers his voice. "What are you doing right now?" he asks. "I planned on sneaking out. Want to meet?"

I glance at the time out of habit, but I doubt my grandparents will let me go anywhere after I've spent the better part of an afternoon sleeping off a fever on the couch. "I would, but—"

"Come on, Tate," Wes says, sounding adorably mischievous. "There's a playground near you on the corner of—"

"Yeah," I say, and smile. "I know where it is." The Hearst playground is just a few blocks away. Back when Wes and I first starting dating, still a little shy, we'd meet up at the playground and talk. I'd twist around on a swing and he would tell me stories about riding to California on his motorcycle with his uncle when he first turned sixteen. I thought he was the coolest.

"So . . . ten minutes?" he says. "Swear I'll tell you everything."

I take stock of my condition, and I feel relatively fine. I'm not quite sure my grandparents will see it that way, though. I'll figure something out.

"Yeah," I say to Wes. "See you then."

CHAPTER THREE

I ACTUALLY DO CONSIDER SNEAKING OUT, BUT ULTI-
mately I can't imagine how badly it would scare my grandparents if they came upstairs to check on me, only to find me
missing. So I put blush on my cheeks to give me color and I
smooth down my hair. Then I head downstairs.

My grandparents are still at the dinner table when I appear
in the doorway, startling them midconversation.

"Tatum," Gram says. "Thought you were going to lie
down?"

"I'm actually not tired," I say. I pause, but my grandfather is
narrowing his eyes like he can tell I already have a plan. "And . . .
Wes just called," I say.

My grandfather sits back in his chair, like I've proven him
right in his suspicion.

"Would it be okay if I ran out for a few minutes to talk to him?" I ask. "He's just over at the park. I don't even have to drive anywhere."

"And how is Wes?" Gram asks, concern painting her features.

"He's good, Gram," I say with a smile. "I really think he's good." Which is true—compared to how he used to be.

Gram tells me she's happy to hear it, but warns me not to be out too late. "And if you don't feel good, come right home. Understand?"

"Definitely," I say. I wait another beat to see if they'll change their minds, and when they don't, I grab a sweater off the hook near the kitchen door and flee outside.

The light is on in Nathan's bedroom, but I've never felt more apart from him than I do now. It's like we're in different orbits. There's a twinge of sadness at that thought, but I keep walking down the driveway and turn left toward the park.

When I get to the playground, it's deserted, with the exception of a motorcycle that pulls in just as I get there. The park is open until ten, but I promised my grandparents I'd be back before then.

Wes climbs from his bike and takes off his helmet, flashing his dimples when he smiles. They still make me absolutely crazy for him.

I walk over, my heart full. It feels like I haven't seen him in days. I've missed him. I'm entirely aware of how quickly things are changing between us, and I'm not sure if it's because of the memories or if I just need to believe in us that badly.

"I'm glad you're all right," I say. "But next time you wait several hours before letting me know, I'm going to punch you in the throat."

"Yikes," Wes says. "I'll keep that in mind." He motions toward the swings. "Want me to push you?" he asks jokingly.

"No. Last time I let you, you tried to make me jump the bar. I nearly died."

He laughs, but when I don't, he drops his mouth open. "Seriously?"

"Yep. You're the worst playdate ever."

Wes laughs and we walk together toward the picnic table, the one with a weeping willow tree beside it. I'll probably have a million bug bites before this night is over, but it's the prettiest spot in the park, so it's almost worth it.

We sit on the tabletop, our feet on the seats, and I rest back on my hands. And I think we both realize it's time to be serious. "So who was that woman in the office?" I ask.

"Her name's Dr. Wyatt," he says. "She's a monitor."

"*Monitor?* What the hell is that?"

Wes shifts his boots on the picnic table seat. "She said she was hired by the district to check on us. A parent filed a complaint claiming that returners are a threat to the general population—like we willingly chose to get our minds altered and come back like this? Idiots."

"What does this monitor want from you?" I ask.

"My cooperation. At first she was just meeting with the returners that the school had concerns about. But then she heard about Vanessa's meltdown, so by the time I got to her, it was more like an interrogation."

My heart beats faster, scared of the implications. "Does she know about the Adjustment?"

"No," he says. "At least I don't think so. But it's only a matter of time. Dr. McKee said they filed for a fast track, so it could be part of public record. And if she's interviewing everyone, I'm sure we're not the only ones who've had it done. If she hears about it, she'll want to shut it down. She's already not fond of returners. Figures she's the one they'd send to check on us, right?" He sighs, as if the entire world has gone crazy. He looks over at me, smiling slyly.

Wes takes my hand and slides his fingers between mine. His touch is startling.

"I thought about you today," he says, and his voice takes on a dreamy quality. "When I was in that office, talking to Dr. Wyatt, I had a memory."

My breath catches, and Wes laughs. "I figured you'd be happy. I wanted to tell you in person."

"What was it?" I ask. "What did you remember?"

"Nothing big," he says. "But it was definitely my memory. And we were here, under this tree." He motions above, and I notice that the streetlights have come on and the stars are just starting to shine through the dark-blue sky.

"We were here?" I ask, my voice soft. I squeeze his fingers, and he brings my hand to his mouth, kissing it softly and then holding it to his cheek.

"On this picnic table," he says. "You told me you were thinking of going to USC. I asked if I could come with you and be your househusband."

I laugh, remembering the moment only when he says it. He was joking, of course. Wes had his own college plans—he wanted to be a criminal defense lawyer. Planned on UCLA. But that night, Wes said he'd tag along with me instead, keep my apartment clean. He said he'd get me a puppy and raise it right.

"A respectable gentleman dog," Wes says as if he's reliving the memory with me. "And then you said—"

"That I had no problem being the breadwinner so long as I never had to do another dish in my life."

Wes nods, and says that's the end of his memory. It's nothing on a grand scale, but it feels so intimate. So private. It's ours.

"What happened after that?" he asks, turning to me.

I'm not sure I should, but I smile and lean in. He doesn't flinch when I kiss him softly on the lips. I gather up his shirt to pull him closer. Wes murmurs that he'll still be a househusband if I want.

Although this moment could intensify, and in fact did in the past, I gently pull back and smile at him. He pouts a little before lying back on the tabletop.

"That was a nice detour," he says. "But I actually did want to talk to you about something else."

"Uh-oh," I say, tilting my head. "What's wrong?"

"Nothing wrong, exactly. But that memory earlier—it felt

good. It felt good to remember. Like it released something in my heart. It covered a pain I had. And so now I'm thinking . . . if this monitor finds a way to connect Vanessa's outburst to the Adjustment, we don't have much time before she tries to shut it down. We have to get back there."

I widen my eyes. "But . . . there's a chance Vanessa's breakdown was *because* of the Adjustment. All the memories at once. Shouldn't we wait and see—?"

Wes sits up, shaking his head. "I'm not Vanessa—if her meltdown even had to do with the Adjustment. Look, I feel better than I have in weeks. Months even. I want all my memories back. They're mine, and I'm not stopping until I have every fucking minute."

"What about the monitor?" I ask.

"Who cares? I've already lost my memory, what more could she do to me?"

I want to immediately throw out another terrible option, but I know that to Wes, the unthinkable has already happened to him.

"I'm going down to the Adjustment office in the morning," Wes continues. "And if Dr. McKee won't help me, I'll go straight to Marie again. But . . ." He laughs like he forgot the most important part. "Are you coming with me? I mean . . . you are the donor."

"What about school?" I ask.

"Skip."

"They'll call home. My grandparents will flip if I cut class."

"Then call in for yourself. You're eighteen. Tell them you have an appointment."

The school will still send home an automated message that I'm not there, but now that my grandfather is working, I can erase it before either he or my gram can hear it. God . . . that's a lot of deceit, though.

Then again, if I get caught, a cured Wes would go a long way toward explaining.

"Okay," I say. "But if anything feels off tomorrow, either with the Adjustment or with the monitor, we bolt. You got that?"

"Absolutely," Wes says with his eyes open wide, like he'd never do otherwise. When I laugh, he rests back on the table again, staring up at the tree.

"I don't want to go home yet," he says. "Tell me a memory. Something hard—something sad."

I scoff. "Why would you want a sad memory?" I ask.

"Because they're usually the truest, the ones unaffected by our optimism."

I watch him a moment and then smile. "You say the smartest things sometimes."

"I read a lot."

I laugh and try to think of a memory worth telling; I almost tell him about the dream I had under the bridge, but I can't quite recall the details. Just then, a memory occurs to me. We were in my car, parked in front of his house late at night.

"It was the only time you ever talked to me about your

sister," I say to him. Wes looks over as if I've struck him, and slowly sits up. "Cheyenne would haunt you sometimes," I continue. "The memories of her. You kept it bottled up—you never talked about her. But one night, when I was dropping you off, you asked if we could stay outside for a while. You were so quiet. I asked what was wrong."

"Where would she be now?" Weston asked that night, staring blankly out the windshield from the passenger seat.

"Who?" I asked.

"My sister."

The question shocked me; I didn't know Weston's sister. The only time I'd ever heard about her was when Nathan told me the story of her death. Wes didn't talk about Cheyenne. At least not to me.

"I'm not sure," I answered softly, watching the side of his face as shadows from the moon played across his skin.

"Do you know my favorite memory with Cheyenne?" he asked, his voice softer when he spoke her name.

"What is it?" I asked.

"When we were kids, I don't know, I was maybe eight or nine, she took me camping in the backyard. She set it up all herself while our parents were at work. Put up the tent, threw in the sleeping bags, and even dragged my father's grill through the grass so we could roast marshmallows later."

"That's sweet," I said.

"Yeah. And then my parents got home and wanted to wring

her neck. My dad put the grill back on the side of the patio, and my mom immediately began packing up the sleeping bags. Cheyenne was so pissed." He laughed to himself.

"She waited until our parents went to bed and then she got me from my room and roasted those marshmallows on the kitchen stove. Made a huge mess." He started laughing harder, his eyes watering. "I can still remember the sound of my mother's scream when she went into the kitchen in the morning to see burnt marshmallow all in the rings of her stove. I'm pretty sure she had a ministroke."

"Knowing your mother, I can only imagine."

"*You burned my pan!*" he said, mocking her voice. "Cheyenne wasn't sure how to melt the chocolate, so she did it in a pan, and marshmallow got everywhere. God, she was the fucking best."

We fell quiet then, gazing at each other. Much like we do now, only this time Wes has tears streaming from his eyes, a smile on his face.

"I told you all that?" he asks. When I nod, he sniffs hard, fighting back his emotions. "I don't remember any of it," he says. "But it was . . . good. Why would they take that? Why take that specific memory—something happy?"

"I don't know," I say. "The obvious answer is because they're assholes, but we know The Program goes deeper than that."

Wes closes his eyes, and in the shine of the streetlights, the tears glisten on his cheeks.

"Cheyenne was my favorite person in the world," he says. "I

don't remember why, but I know it's true. I feel it. Her death . . . it must have wrecked me. It must have changed me."

"I didn't know you before," I say, "so I can't say for sure, but I imagine so. I'm sorry, Wes. I'm sorry I didn't ask you more about her so I could give it to you now."

"None of this is your fault," he says. "Not one bit of it. You know that, right?"

"I'm not sure what I know anymore."

To this, he smiles. "Join the club." He sighs deeply, and then leans in to give me a soft kiss on the lips. "You should get home," he whispers.

I know he's right, but I wish I didn't have to leave. Tonight . . . it feels right. It feels like . . . I'm with the real him.

I stand, but Wes makes no motion to get up. "What about you?" I ask.

"Think I'll stay just a little longer."

It doesn't sound like an invitation for me, and I feel a little left out. But I imagine mentioning his sister has opened up a new wound. An old wound, I guess.

Wes calls me over one last time and reaches to comb his fingers through my hair like he's fixing me up. "All right, gorgeous," he says, running his palm from my hair playfully over my face. I swat it away. "I'll call you in the morning," he says. "And don't let your gram give you any more drugs tonight. Just say no."

I laugh and tell him we'll talk tomorrow, and with that, we say good night.

CHAPTER FOUR

THE ADJUSTMENT OFFICE OPENS AT EIGHT, SO I GO about my morning as usual for my grandparents' benefit. I pretend to leave for school, but head to the coffee shop and pick up two drinks before heading over to Wes's house. I park down the block, and Wes meets me, leaving his motorcycle at home. I hand him a coffee, the way I know he likes it, and he smiles when he takes a sip.

"Lots of sugar," he says with a grin. "Because I'm—"

"Sweet like that," I finish for him. We both pause, sharing the memory. It used to be annoying, something he'd say every time. Now it feels a little sad.

"Let's go get the rest," he says, nodding toward the street. And with that, we drive across town to the Adjustment office.

When we arrive, neither of us gets out of the parked Jeep,

staring at the darkened frosted-glass door of the building. We didn't call to make an appointment, and I wonder if I should have contacted Dr. McKee myself, asked him about the dangers in light of Vanessa's condition, before bringing Wes down here. But I couldn't go behind his back like that.

My phone buzzes in the cup holder, and Wes picks it up to hand to me. He doesn't glance at the message, staring intently at the building instead, like he's having second thoughts.

"It's Nathan," I say, opening the text. Wes mutters that that's awesome.

Hey. Where are you? Nathan writes.

I'm not sure how to reply, but I also know if I don't, he'll call home with worry. Taking the day off, I text. Don't tell Pop.

You okay? he responds immediately.

Absolutely. Just need a minute. I'll be back after lunch, I write, although I'm not sure that's true. It sounds more responsible, though.

Call if you need me, he responds. Also, you owe me coffee.

I smile and click the phone off. When I turn to Wes, he doesn't mention that I was texting another guy.

Over the next few minutes, no one pulls into the Adjustment parking lot, and I wonder if the doctors are already inside. The lights don't seem to be on, though, and I have a flash of worry that the monitor found out and shut them down before we could get here.

But at 8:05, the lights inside flick on and glow through the frosted glass.

SUZANNE YOUNG

"Thank God," Wes murmurs, and I know he was worrying about the same thing.

We climb out of the Jeep and go to the door to ring the bell. The locks don't open right away, and I glance up to the camera. I ring the bell again. Wes checks the parking lot behind us, his posture rigid like he's worried we're being watched. There's a loud click, and the locks open; we rush inside.

The receptionist isn't behind the desk this time. Instead, it's Marie. She's wearing a lab coat, and she crosses her arms over her chest when we enter.

"This is a surprise," she announces, looking at us. Only she says it like she's not surprised at all. "Seems all our patients will be coming by today."

I exchange a questioning glance with Wes, but before we can ask what she means, Marie stands from the chair.

"Did you also meet with this monitor?" she asks us.

"Not me," I say. "They were only speaking to returners."

Marie's expression falters. "Of course," she says, and turns to Wes. "You did, then?"

"I didn't really have a choice," he says. "But she didn't ask about the Adjustment. She basically just went through a list of questions, asking how I'm doing now that I'm back. It was really annoying."

"That's because she was evaluating you in other ways. Watching you for hints to your thoughts. It's come to their attention that returners are failing. She needs to investigate. But I have no doubt that Wyatt knows you're hiding something. She's good."

"You know her?" I ask.

Marie nods. "We've worked together in the past. She used to oversee a branch of the grief department after being an advisor there for years. You'll be relieved to know she was not involved in The Program, and in fact she fought against it."

"We didn't hear much about anyone fighting against it," Wes says. "At least no one in power."

Marie smiles bitterly. "Yes, I'm sure you didn't. Ask Wyatt how that went for her next time you speak to her. On principle, she's opposed to any mind-altering procedure. And that includes this one. Now, let's head back. I assume you're here for your next Adjustment?"

She walks to the office door and holds it open for us. "Tom will be with us in a moment."

Marie leads us to the same office we started in, and we take our seats while she sits at the desk. She is pushing through some scattered papers, biting on one long red nail, when the phone on the desk buzzes. Marie clicks on the intercom.

"You're here," she says, sounding annoyed.

"Sorry, Marie," the receptionist says. "I thought I was being followed, so I—"

"What do you want, Megan?" Marie asks, cutting her off.

"Sorry," Megan says. "But there's a guy up here to see you. He, uh . . . he says his name is Michael Realm."

Marie is perfectly still, poised. "Thank you," she answers professionally. "Please let him know I'll be with him shortly."

"Yeah, I told him that," Megan says. "But he—"

There's a quick knock, and then the office door opens. "But he didn't want to wait," a guy announces for her. There's a tick in Marie's expression, and she moves her finger off the intercom and stands.

"Michael," Marie says, forcing a smile. "How nice of you to stop by. Unannounced."

He laughs. "Sorry to pop in like this, but you said you had . . ." He pauses when he notices me and Wes for the first time. "I didn't realize you were with clients," he tells Marie, sounding a little irritated that she didn't warn him. Even though he's totally the one who busted in here.

She motions to us. "Tatum, Wes—this is Michael Realm. He is both a former Program patient and a returner." She looks pointedly at him. "Among other things."

"Hey, there," he says to us awkwardly, avoiding my eyes. I don't think he likes the reference to The Program.

Michael is tall with dark-brown hair and eyes; he's cute. But the most noticeable thing about him is the jagged pink line across his neck. Judging by the violence of the scar, I think I know why he was in the Program in the first place.

"So, Marie," he says, his voice hushed. "You said you had some files for me?"

"I do," she responds, crossing to the filing cabinet. She pulls out a stack of folders and walks over to hold them out to him. Michael takes them, flipping through them quickly to read the tabs. When he's finished, he presses them to his chest.

"Looks good. I'll take these and head over to James's place to pick him up."

The door opens wider and Dr. McKee appears, stopping abruptly when he sees Michael.

"Michael Realm," he says, darting a glance at us before turning back. "How are you, son?" He shakes his hand.

"All right, I guess," he says. "Have you, uh . . ." He pauses to look at us like he doesn't quite trust us. "Have you heard about the monitor?" he asks in a quiet voice.

Dr. McKee presses his lips together and nods curtly.

"We're keeping an eye on the situation," Marie says for him. Michael turns to her, and I can see he's worried. I also see that he has serious baggage weighting him down. He seems miserable.

"Make sure you do," he says to Marie.

Next to me, Wes exhales loudly, as if reminding them all that we're still here. Michael is the first to look over at us, and then he steps toward the doorway.

"I've taken up too much of your time," he says to Marie and the doctor, oddly formal. "Thank you for this." He holds up the files.

"Of course. It helps us too," Dr. McKee says. "Good luck."

Michael looks back at us. "It was, uh . . . good to meet you," he says. And then he gives a quick wave and walks out. Once he's gone, Dr. McKee shuts the office door. He turns and stares at us, disapproval clear on his face.

While Marie waits at the file cabinet, Dr. McKee walks over

to his desk and takes a seat. He removes his glasses to clean them with a handkerchief he pulls from his pocket. "And how are you feeling?" he asks Wes, his voice tight.

"Good," Weston responds. Marie excuses herself and leaves the room. Dr. McKee puts his glasses back on and leans his elbows on his desk.

"What you did was dangerous," he says. "Marie shouldn't have implanted that second memory so quickly. It was unethical."

Wes smiles. "No, unethical was taking my memories in the first place. Giving them back is heroic."

Dr. McKee laughs, and sits back in his chair. "No need to flatter me, son," he says. "I'm glad it worked. Have you had any setbacks? Any discomfort?"

"No," Wes says. He goes on to tell Dr. McKee about the memory he had on his own about us in the park. I see the doctor's eyes light up. He thinks he's saving lives—his intentions really are pure, it seems.

"And you want more?" Dr. McKee says when Wes finishes talking.

"Yes," Wes says. "I think I can get it all back."

Dr. McKee nods. "I think you can too. And how about you?" the doctor asks, looking in my direction. "Have you had any complications?"

I'm surprised by the question. "Uh . . . actually, I did have a headache. But my grandmother gave me some migraine meds and knocked it right out," I say with the wave of my hand. Dr. McKee swallows hard, and looks down at the papers on his desk.

"I'm glad the headache passed so quickly. We'll be sure not to double-dose you on the truth medication. It can have that effect."

I nod and tell him that that is probably a good idea. "Also," I say, just before he seems ready to dive back into a conversation with Wes. "I was wondering about Vanessa Ortiz. She—"

"I'm sorry," Dr. McKee says quickly. "I can't talk about any of my other patients with you. For confidentiality reasons. I'm sure you understand—especially with a monitor poking around."

"Sure, "I say. "But if there was a problem with the Adjustment, you'd tell us, right?"

"It wasn't the Adjustment," he replies. "That I can assure you. But, yes, I would tell you." Dr. McKee puts the papers in a neat stack and turns to Wes. "Now," he says, "are you ready for your next session? I imagine you're growing restless."

Wes stands, and although I'd still like more clarification, I do too. If I push too far, Dr. McKee might turn us away. And I don't think Wes would appreciate that.

The three of us head out and walk back into the Adjustment room. It feels colder than usual when I sit down in the chair. Marie is at the computer, typing in some notes. She doesn't look at me. I wonder if Dr. McKee scolded her for helping us with the extra memory. I wonder if it's strained their relationship, because they don't speak a word to each other until we begin.

The injection kicks in, and it's like my insides are coated

with warm wax. I lazily look over at Wes, and this time he's still awake, the sedative affecting him differently.

"This is the third of four sessions, Mr. Ambrose," Dr. McKee states. I wonder suddenly if he's recording this somehow, and glance around until I find a small camera in the corner of the room. But it might have always been there.

"We are in the final stages of your Adjustment. After this, you should notice a few more memories coming into focus. It may be disconcerting at first, so we'll want you to communicate with us. Keep us aware of any problems you might have. Any questions. Any crashbacks."

"I'm ready," Wes says. He doesn't look at me, just straight ahead, like he's looking into his future—or his past, I guess.

"Wes," I whisper, but he still doesn't turn to me.

"We deserve this, Tate," he says. "We deserve to have it all back."

I stare at him, knowing by the adamant tilt of his chin that I couldn't change his mind even if I wanted to. So I dive into the past with him again.

"Fuck The Program," I say.

He smiles. "Fuck The Program," he repeats. And then Wes closes his eyes and waits for me to begin.

CHAPTER FIVE

"LET'S FAST-FORWARD THE TIMELINE," DR. MCKEE says. "Let's find a moment from when Wes was struggling. It's not pleasant to talk about, but it might be key in helping him recover a larger part of his memory. These would be specifically targeted memories that The Program would have taken, so if we can replace them, it might help build bridges between all his memories."

It seems like a huge responsibility to remember the perfect moment to do that. I try to think back, and at first, I don't know where to start. The time around Wes disappearing has always been fuzzy. There was so much going on—the world had gone mad. With the constant fear of The Program, none of us was really being ourselves.

My first thought is from that evening when we went to

listen to the band. Wes was lost in his head but we ended up dancing half the night. He'd been so sad, not himself.

I stop the thought, opting to pass over that memory and use another. We were wrong that night, the two of us in different orbits. It's selfish, but I don't want him to remember us like that. And it's strange—as the medication makes the memory clearer than the present, I realize there are several moments just like that. I grow weary of searching, and finally dive into one.

"There was a party," I say out loud. Heat floods my chest from the medication, and my heart rate speeds up.

She was a friend of mine, Casey Jones. She was always having parties in her basement, hidden away from the public. She lived with her stepdad, who was a nice enough guy, but never around. He would tell her that he'd rather she have friends over than go out. He didn't want her to end up in The Program.

"So Casey would have everyone park blocks away," I continue. "That way the neighbors wouldn't complain. One of those nights, Wes and I headed over to Casey's. Nathan was there too."

"Describe Nathan," the doctor says, making a note.

"No need," Wes says, sounding a million miles away. "I know what he looks like."

Dr. McKee laughs quietly and asks me to describe him anyway.

"He's a little over six feet, brown hair, and hazel eyes. Good-looking," I add. Damn truth serum.

"Awesome," Wes says. "Can we move on?"

"Of course," Dr. McKee says. "Tatum, if you'll continue."

"Anyway," I say. "Nathan was meeting a girl, so I didn't really see him until it was time to go."

Casey's house becomes real around me, and I fall back into the memory.

"Ah, it's my favorite couple," Casey announced when we walked in. The upstairs was dark, only a small lamp on in the window. We had to go through her house to get to the basement door. It felt hidden, a speakeasy in the back of a market.

Her house was plain, sparsely decorated. From downstairs, I could hear the low thump of bass from a song. A small figurine vibrated where it sat on the table next to the phone.

Wes smiled at Casey but didn't respond. I told her that I liked her hair. She'd recently put streaks of blue and pink in it—cotton candy swirl she called it. She had her eyebrow pierced three times and she wore makeup to cover her freckles, something she confided in me one time when she was drunk.

"Thanks," she said, touching her hair. "Although my dad is going to kill me when he sees the bathroom sink." She grinned, and behind us there was a quick knock at the door. "Coming," she called. "Everyone's downstairs," she told me. "Help yourself to whatever drinks are left."

"Nice," Wes said, and started that way, not looking back. Casey darted a quick glance at me, and then forced a smile and walked to the door to greet her other guests.

Wes opened the door to the basement and headed down,

stopping halfway like he forgot I was behind him. I caught up, and then together we stepped into the party.

The basement ceiling was low, dropped tiles. There were two poles on either side of the room holding it up—we jokingly called them stripper poles. There was a small bar with a large mirror behind it in the corner. The space was huge, several couches and a round table for cards set up. The music was loud, but it soon switched to something a little darker, heavier.

Wes and I made our way through the room, saying hi to people as we passed them. Across the room, I spotted Nathan on one of the couches, and he offered me a wave. He was with a sophomore I didn't recognize.

I smiled when I noticed Foster approaching. I didn't think he'd be here tonight; he spent most weekends with his family.

"Hey, guys," Foster called out. He and Wes did a hand slap and shoulder hug before Foster came to stand next to me. He looked me over, his eyes narrowing slightly. "You okay?" he asked. I darted a look at Wes and then smiled.

"I'm good. How are you?"

He shrugged, taking a sip of his drink. "Same." He turned to Weston. "And where have you been?" he asked him. "I texted you yesterday about a pickup game in the park. Thanks for answering, dickhead."

Wes laughed. "Sorry. I was . . . I was busy." He leaned to look past Foster at me. "I'm going to head to the bar," he said. And then to Foster. "See you around?"

"Yeah," Foster said, watching him. "Sounds good, man."

Once Wes was gone, Foster moved in closer, his arm against mine. "Do we want to talk about this?" he asked quietly. Wes had been withdrawing, and his friends were starting to notice.

"No, thanks," I said.

"You sure? Because he—"

"I'm sure."

Foster waited a second, and then took another sip of his drink, allowing me to change the subject. We both looked toward the couch where Nathan was talking with the sophomore, flirting.

"What's her name?" I asked.

"Kesia Boone," Foster said, motioning in her direction. "But Nathan doesn't like her," he said as if I'd asked. On the couch, Nathan must have felt us staring because he looked over and held up his bottle in cheers. Foster air-clinked it from next to me.

"How do you know he doesn't like her?" I asked Foster.

"I just do."

I laughed, turning to him. "Well, you're rarely wrong about him. Too bad, though. She's cute."

"Eh," Foster said as if she was just all right.

"I better go catch up with Wes," I said.

Foster gave me one last weary glance. "Okay," he replied, and reached to put his cool palm on my cheek affectionately. "Have fun." I smiled, and he went over to the couch to hang with Nathan.

I turned toward the bar—

• • •

I'm suddenly pulled out of the memory, blinking quickly, here in the chair at the Adjustment office. I saw Wes at the bar of the party. But he was sitting with . . . he was sitting with Kyle Mahoney. I didn't remember that until now.

I turn sideways and see Wes's profile as he stares up at the ceiling, listening to my story. "You were at the bar talking to Kyle," I say.

Wes turns, the lights on the metal crown casting shadows over his brow. His eyes meet mine, questioningly.

"Okay," he says, as if asking what the bigger accusation is.

My heart rate spikes and I can hear the sound of it on the monitor. Marie shifts uneasily next to me, and she reaches to press her thumb over my pulse point.

"Do you remember her?" I ask Wes. He shakes his head no.

Marie says my name, drawing my attention. "Stay focused," she says calmly, examining my face. She lifts her eyes to Dr. McKee, and although they don't say anything to each other, I feel they've communicated.

"Maybe we should try a different memory, Tatum," Dr. McKee says, studying whatever signal my brain is putting out on his monitor. "We can begin again. We don't want you to—"

"It's fine," I say. "I can go on."

The doctor is quiet, and he doesn't stop me. So I close my eyes, and the memory comes back, clearer than before.

Wes was sitting at the bar, looking down at his drink, and turned fully toward him with one elbow on the bar was Kyle, her blond hair cascading over her shoulder. She smiled and moved closer as she talked. Wes smiled back—the first time I'd seen a real smile in weeks.

"Weston?" I said as I walked up. He paused, but didn't turn to me immediately, even though he obviously heard me. Kyle sat back in her seat, and drank from her cup. Why didn't Wes look at me? I didn't like it—it stung.

I stopped at the bar next to him, glaring at the side of his face, and before he said anything, he turned and took my elbow. He stood and began to pull me away from the bar. I looked back at Kyle, but all I saw was the swing of her blond hair as she got down from the stool and left.

"What was that about?" I asked Wes.

He dropped my arm, turned away, and took a long sip from his drink. "What was what about?" he asked in a low voice.

I stared at him, but then Casey appeared at the bottom of the stairs. She smiled broadly and looked around at all of us, like she was proud to have brought us together. To have fooled The Program.

"Who wants to play a round of bullshit?" she asked.

"I do," Wes announced, holding up his drink. He left my side to walk toward her, avoiding my question. I ended up playing cards too. But he—

I flinch, sitting up in the Adjustment chair. I reach to touch my head, my fingers tangling in the wires. "Ouch," I say as a headache prickles the skin, spreading warmth across my brain. Marie gently puts her hand on my shoulder, but I tell her I'm all right.

"Sorry," I say, shifting in the chair as I relax back. The pain fades. "That was weird," I murmur.

I close my eyes again and the memory changes; it's later that night. The sound of my heartbeat evens out, and I feel the rush of medication in my chest.

"I took Wes home after the party," I say out loud in the Adjustment room as the picture becomes clearer in my mind. "We were parked outside in the rain. I told him I loved him."

The memory covers me like a blanket and I see it all.

Me, climbing into the passenger seat to sit on Wes's lap. We kissed, his hand up the back of my shirt. Passionate. We kissed until we were both breathless. But it had gotten late and I was going to miss curfew. He said he had to go.

But as he left, Wes looked back at me and said, "I don't deserve you, Tatum. You know that, right?"

I smiled. "Sometimes you do."

He laughed, and then as if he couldn't hold himself back, he dived back into the Jeep, sweeping me into a hug and burying his face in my hair. "I love you so much," he whispered.

Wes kissed my cheek, lingering a moment longer, and then disappeared into the night.

The treatment room is quiet when I finish the story, and it takes me too long to acclimate to the room. I can still smell the smoke from the party; I taste Wes on my lips. I still feel the suspicion in my heart.

I hear clicking as Dr. McKee types on his computer, and then the sound of Wes's breathing, steady. I feel like I should say something more, but words are failing me so I just wait.

"Thank you very much, Tatum," Dr. McKee says curtly. "That will be all for today."

I slowly sit up in the chair and turn to look at him. He's so formal—there's no closure to the session. "That's it?" I ask.

"That's all we need for now," he says. "This is a very complicated memory. It will take some time to pattern it. It'd be best if you left." He looks up at me, his face expressionless. "We'll call you when the procedure's done."

"I don't understand," I say as Marie comes over to unhook my monitor and remove the electrodes. "Is something wrong?" I ask, looking from her to the doctor.

"No," Marie says immediately. "You just have a lot of emotions tied to that memory. We want to make sure we get it right."

"Wes," I say, but when I turn to him, his eyes are closed from sedation. But halfway across his temple, I see a tear running down from the corner of his eye.

I start to pull off the rest of the tabs and wires. But before I jump down from the chair, Dr. McKee reaches out to put his hand on my shoulder.

"He's fine," the doctor says. "Can I please talk to you in the hall?"

"But . . ." I want to argue, but his vibe leaves no room for compromise. I reluctantly agree.

SUZANNE YOUNG

Dr. McKee leads me toward the door. "Marie," he calls behind us, "tend to Weston, please." She nods and takes a syringe out of her pocket, flipping off the orange cap. I don't know if that means she's going to sedate him further. How deep can he be under?

Dr. McKee ushers me out of the room, and once in the hall, he lowers his head to stare right into my eyes. "You're highly emotional," he says. "And your pattern was all over the place. We can't project that—the brain will pick up a pattern that strong. All you had to do was recite what you remembered."

"What . . . what did I do wrong?" I ask, my voice cracking. I'm scared that I might have endangered Wes.

Dr. McKee straightens, and a sympathetic expression crosses his features. He takes off his glasses and begins to clean them. "I apologize," he says quietly, focusing on wiping the lenses. "I didn't mean to imply you did anything wrong, Tatum. We . . ." He pauses and slides his glasses back on. "We didn't anticipate how complicated that memory would be."

"I still don't understand," I say. "Wes was reacting to hearing the memory—why?"

"Yes. He was emotional too," Dr. McKee agrees. "But the simple truth is, Weston left you—he did. He ran away before The Program ever got to him. And I imagine he has some guilt over that. Something is troubling him, at least."

I take a step back from the doctor. Did I tell him about Wes disappearing? Or maybe it was in the file . . . or in the memory?

"I should talk to Wes," I say, starting toward the door of the treatment room.

Dr. McKee holds out his arm, blocking me from going back in. "At this time, I'm going to ask you to wait at home. We're doctors. Let us do our job."

"Then why are you sedating him more?" I ask.

"We're not," he says, turning away to move toward the door. "We're trying to wake him up."

I feel my expression fall, and before I can ask a follow-up question, Dr. McKee goes back inside the room, leaving me here to worry.

The serum is still in my veins. It messes with my emotions, the way I feel them. The way I process them. The waiting room is empty with the exception of the receptionist. Her dark hair is scraped into a top bun, and she's staring at her computer monitor, clicking her mouse every few seconds. I imagine she's playing solitaire. The phone rings and she answers, talking casually with someone, maybe a friend. She doesn't seem worried about Wes, no alarm bells go off, and I let that encourage me.

I decide to stay. I rest my head back against the wall behind the chair, lost in my thoughts. Time gets away from me as I turn to the memory of the party again and again, trying to find more details. Worried I'd messed up somehow in the recollection of it. There's a tug inside my chest, in my soul, telling me things aren't quite right. Like I'm missing a piece of the puzzle. Or maybe I just don't know what the picture is supposed to be.

I take out my phone to check my messages; I'd better call Nathan to let him know I won't make it after lunch. I begin to text him, when suddenly the door to the back office flies open. Marie rushes out and taps her knuckles on the desk to get Megan's attention.

"I've been calling up here," she says to the receptionist. "I need an ambulance now. Now!" she says when the girl doesn't move fast enough.

My heart leaps into my throat, and I clamor to my feet. "What's wrong?" I demand. "Oh, God—is it Wes?"

Marie spins to me, seeming stunned that I'm still here. The receptionist talks hurriedly on the phone and then holds it out to Marie.

Before she grabs the receiver, Marie purses her lips. "I'm sorry, Tatum," she says. "But there was a problem with the memory."

CHAPTER SIX

I'M SHAKING. I LISTEN AS MARIE TELLS THE EMER-
gency line that Weston is having trouble breathing, that he
won't wake up. I grow frantic, on the verge of hysterical—the
medication in my system makes me unable to mask my panic.
Marie tells me to wait there, and she runs to the back.

I begin to pace, my hand over my mouth as I try to calm
down. I ask the receptionist repeatedly to check on Wes, but all
she says is that the ambulance is on its way. When they arrive, I
try to go back with the EMTs, but they stop me.

"Please wait here, miss," one of the EMTs says, pointing
to the chair. But I can't sit. I stand on the side of the room,
and when they wheel Wes out on a gurney, I start to cry. He's
unconscious with an oxygen mask over his mouth, an EMT
squeezing air into his lungs.

I have never been more scared, more regretful. I know in that instant that this wasn't worth it—no memory is worth losing him completely.

What have we done?

The medication is mostly worn off when I drive to the hospital behind the ambulance. I assume they've called his parents by now, so I opt not to. Sure, it's not brave, but the doctors can explain the situation better than me. In fact, I don't even know what's going on. Dr. McKee told me in passing that he'll consult with me later. And he suggested I get checked out as well, although for what, I'm not sure.

Then my headache returns, first behind my eyes. It's the same pain I've had before, like a medication hangover. But this time bothers me more. When I stop in back of the ambulance at a red light, I glance in the rearview mirror. My eyes are bloodshot, a thin line of pink along my lower lids. I'm pale.

I watch as my lower lip begins to quiver; water floods my eyes. This is my fault. I brought Wes to get the Adjustment. I might have just killed him. I might have ruined everything.

A car beeps behind me, startling me, and I see the ambulance is far ahead now. I press on the accelerator to catch up, swiping my palm over my cheeks to clear the tears that spill over.

I can't let this pain overwhelm me. I have to be strong like I was after I left Weston's house the night he was taken into The Program. It would have been so easy to give up then, almost like my body wanted to give up.

As if giving up was the familiar.

An ache started in my chest and hollowed it out. Slid into my muscles, whispering that it was too hard to keep fighting. *You're not strong enough*.

I remember lying on my bedroom floor, wishing to be sucked into the wood boards. Wishing it would all end. But then that moment would pass. Happen again, and then pass. I held on until it became less frequent, and when it was over, I was so grateful that I didn't die. Sure, it still hurt. It was misery. But I found hope. I found hope and I imagined that Wes would find it too. He'd come home.

And so I struggle to find that hope now, watching the back of the ambulance with familiar pain. Wes will be okay. He'll come home.

I won't believe anything else.

My fingers and hands are numb as I park in the hospital lot, and I make my way through the emergency room entrance. Wes is already being admitted, so I let the desk nurse know I'm here and that I'm looking for Dr. McKee. She has me take a seat in the waiting area: another person pushing me aside, making me wait.

The smell of burnt coffee hangs in the air, and there's an old man sitting by himself, a handkerchief balled up in his hands. He doesn't look at me.

I'm scared that Wes's parents will come through the doors at any moment. What will I say to them? How can I explain that we did this? I consider calling my grandparents, but I

SUZANNE YOUNG

want to wait until I know more about Wes's condition. I nervously rub my neck and shoulders. I just need to know what's going on.

I hear the tapping of footsteps and look up to see Dr. McKee coming down the hallway. His face is set in a stern expression, and I jump up to meet him halfway across the hall.

"Tatum," he says, and his voice holds a hint of anger.

"Is Wes okay?" I ask immediately.

Dr. McKee crosses his arms over his white jacket. "Weston has been stabilized," he says. "He will recover. Physically, at least."

My stomach sinks. "What does that mean?" I ask.

"It means the memory was corrupted," Dr. McKee says. "His system rejected it."

"I don't understand," I say. "What did you do?"

He seems to resent the remark and he lowers his arms to his sides, his chest puffed up. "Before this all started, I told you how important honesty would be. It was everything. The Adjustment can't work without it. You've compromised us all."

"What?" Is he seriously blaming me for this? "I told you exactly what I saw!"

He shakes his head like I'm not understanding. "The memories were wrong from the start, Tatum," he says with agitation. "What you don't get is that although patients have lost their memories, they haven't lost the feelings associated with them. I purposely asked for ones that should have been clear."

He waits, but I have no idea what he means by this. When I don't speak, his defenses lower slightly.

"The memory doesn't match up with the emotions in his system," he says. "It doesn't match with *your* emotions. So you've been lying to yourself, as well. And by extension, lying to us. Call it denial. Call it whatever you want, but Weston is having a reaction. In plain terms, his heart and head don't agree. I'll say it again, the memory is corrupted. I just don't understand how."

"But . . . it's all true," I say, feeling confused myself. I run my fingers through my hair, and walk past him, pacing. I think back again to see if I missed something.

Dr. McKee studies me a moment, and then he nods down the hall. "Look, Tatum," he says more softly, "memory is a funny thing. It's all a matter of perspective. Normally, we can pinpoint the right moments, find a way to fill in the blanks. You both seemed like perfect candidates; I wouldn't have taken your case otherwise. But . . . until this is sorted out, I can't perform any more Adjustments on Weston. There's too much at stake."

"But . . . you can't abandon us," I say. "If he's messed up, you have to fix it!"

"Weston will recover from this," he says. "But with a corrupted memory, there's no way for me to move forward with him. It would only endanger both of you, and I can't allow that."

"What are we supposed to do, then? What about the other returners getting sick?"

He nods and crosses his arms over his chest. "Yes," he admits.

SUZANNE YOUNG

"Without the Adjustment, he does run that risk. But at this point, the only way out is through. Weston will have to manage the symptoms on his own."

"What if . . . what if we find the anomaly in the memory?" I ask. "Would it help?"

Dr. McKee wilts at my suggestion. "Theoretically, yes, I guess it could trigger his final Adjustment—a flow of memories. But it wouldn't be controlled. It would be dangerous. And, Tatum, you're under so much stress. You both need to see someone. I have the name of a great therapist who could—"

"I'm fine," I say, my mind racing. "This isn't about me."

The double doors at the end of the hall slide open, and I recognize Wes's parents immediately. His mother jogs toward us, her fuzzy blue sweater saggy and misshapen, and her hair pulled into a messy ponytail.

But the moment she sees me, fire burns in her eyes. Guilt attacks my conscience, and I take a step backward, afraid of her reaction.

"Where is he?" she asks loudly, as if I'm keeping him hostage somewhere. I open my mouth to answer, but the doctor makes a move toward her, holding out his palm.

"Mrs. Ambrose, I assume," he says. "I'm Dr. McKee. I've been treating your son for the last—"

"With whose permission?" she demands. "Hers?" She spits the last word, pointing her finger in my direction. She intimidates me, and as her husband approaches, I want to shrink back inside myself.

"With all due respect," the doctor says, "Weston is over eighteen. He doesn't need your consent."

Mrs. Ambrose narrows her small eyes as if the doctor just said exactly the wrong thing. Her husband stands at her side, and the doctor asks them both for their discretion before he can explain what's going on. They reluctantly agree, and Dr. McKee gives them the shortened version of the Adjustment—and how Wes is rejecting a memory.

Wes's mother spins to face me. "This is your fault. You couldn't just leave him alone, could you?" she asks venomously. "You never could. You won't be happy until you kill him."

My lips part, and I swear I want to hurt her. Because Mrs. Ambrose's words do what she intended and my soul crumbles with guilt. Because what if she's right? What if my pursuit of happiness will kill him?

"Well, at least I didn't call The Program on him," I say bitterly, and she recoils as if I've slapped her. I wrap my arms around myself and walk through the hospital doors.

When I get to my car, my head still aching, I decide I can't go home, not like this. I'm broken down, emotionally drained. I sit in the driver's seat and take out my phone—it's past three and school's out.

I have to talk to Nathan; he'll understand why I did this. Why I agreed to the Adjustment in the first place. He'll know what to say to make it better. But this isn't something I can tell him over the phone. Although I'm scared of his reaction, I'm willing to risk his anger. Because I need his support. I need his help.

I need Nathan.

I drive toward my house but don't park in the driveway. I'm not ready to face my grandparents. Not alone, at least. I go to Nathan's front door and knock, trying to stay hidden under his porch awning.

I glance nervously at my house, seeing my grandmother's car in the driveway. I blink rapidly, my eyes burning from the tears I refuse to let fall. I know if I see my grandparents like this, I'll melt right into a puddle of despair. And I still don't have any answers to what went wrong. Or . . . if things will be okay.

No one answers Nathan's door; I knock again, louder. A shadow passes by the window, and I see Nathan heading down the steps of his split-level home. I know he's going to be so pissed when I tell him about the Adjustment.

The door swings open and Nathan is half squinting, his hair a mess like he's been sleeping. "Hey," he says.

"Were you asleep?" I ask, because I'm afraid to get right to it. "It's not even four."

"Long day," he says, rubbing his palm over his face. "Where did you go? I looked for you all day. Foster pointed out that Wes wasn't in school either, and then hummed 'Afternoon Delight' all lunch period."

"I, uh . . ." The words get caught in my throat and I stare at him, unable to answer. It only takes a second for him to realize something's wrong, and he steps aside and motions me into the house.

"Get in here," he mumbles, and I walk past him into the foyer.

Nathan's house smells like various plug-in air fresheners, none of which are the same. There's vanilla and Hawaiian breeze and peach blossom. It's not a bad scent necessarily, just . . . convoluted. But I know it as well as I know the scent of my own home.

"What happened?" he asks, closing the door and turning to me. His jaw is set hard like he's ready to take a punch. And although I thought I could bravely tell this story and defend myself, the emotions burn in my chest.

"He's in the hospital," I choke out.

Nathan's eyes widen and he takes a step toward me, putting his hand on my arm. "Who is?" he asks. He waits to read it on my face, and it occurs to me that his first thought is my grandfather.

"It's Wes," I say. "Wes is in the hospital."

"Holy shit," he says. "Is he going to be okay? What happened?"

"Can we . . . ?" I point up the stairs toward his living room and I watch him debate the answer. His mother isn't home from work yet; she works until six or seven most nights.

"Yeah," he says, like he knows it's going to be bad news. He leads us upstairs, and I sit on the couch while he drops in the chair, facing me. I wring my hands in my lap as he waits impatiently, tapping his socked foot on the carpet.

"It's the Adjustment, isn't it?" he asks. I look up and find him watching me. I don't have to answer. He already knows. "I'm not fucking stupid, Tatum."

Shame washes over me. Nathan is my best friend, but because I knew he'd try to talk me out of it, I lied to him. I hate that I lied to him.

"Wes shut down today," I say. "His body shut down. The doctor said he's rejecting the memory. And I—"

Nathan's anger fades from his expression and he leans forward in the chair, his hands hanging between his knees. "Which memory?" he asks.

"The most recent one," I say, but furrow my brow. "Although, what if it's not just this one? What if it's all of them?"

"What exactly did the doctor tell you? I can't believe you let them inside your head again."

I stare at him. "Again?"

He pauses and takes a cleansing breath. "Again," he says. "Like, multiple times, multiple memories. Okay," he says in a calmer voice. "Start from the beginning."

I nod that I will, glad that Nathan's in this with me. Then again, I knew he would be—that's why I'm here. I knew he'd have my back. He offers me a small smile, and I'm ready to tell him everything. I dive into all the details. I tell him about the memories, about the flirting and texts. How Wes decided to get the Adjustment. I spill my guts all over his living-room floor.

Nathan sits quietly and after I finish talking, I glance out the window and see that the day has turned to dusk. His mother will be home soon. My grandparents will be worried.

"The basement party," Nathan says, startling me. "That was the last memory?"

"Yeah."

"I can barely remember that night," he says, running his hand through his hair. "You were . . ." He stops. "Well, I definitely don't remember seeing Kyle Mahoney," he adds. "You sure she was there?"

"I . . . yeah," I say. "I think so."

"Maybe she's the difference in the memory," he says. "The anomaly. Because if it weren't for the last week of her acting weird around you, you might not have noticed her in the memory."

Nathan could be right about that—I wouldn't have remembered Kyle so clearly otherwise. The present is influencing my perspective on the past.

"It wasn't even just that she was there," I say. "It was the feeling that . . ." Sickness bubbles in the pit of my stomach. "That maybe she and Wes . . ." I don't want to put words to the thought, but Nathan tightens his jaw.

"Let's not jump to conclusions," he says. "For now, she's just a girl he was talking to at a party."

I nod, but I must not look convinced. Nathan sits back in the chair and crosses his legs.

"I'm worried about you," he says. "Why did you have to dredge all this up? You were doing better."

I'm surprised by his reaction. "Because I wanted Wes back," I say.

"He was back, Tatum." Nathan watches me, his eyes growing sad. "The Program nearly destroyed you. I don't want to lose you. This isn't worth it. Why couldn't you just leave it alone?"

I'm not sure what he means, and I lean forward to ask for an explanation. Nathan lowers his head, smiling sadly.

"Do you remember the last time you came over like this?" he asks quietly. When he lifts his eyes to mine, there is vulnerability there. There's a sting on my heart, but I have no idea what he's talking about.

"When?" I ask.

Nathan closes his eyes and shakes his head. "Never mind. It was a long time ago." He jumps, and takes out his phone. Once it's out, I hear it vibrating with a call.

"It's your pop," he says, clicking it off. "We'd better get over there." Nathan stands, holding out his hand to help me up. When I'm facing him, he stares down at me intensely, like he's trying to read me.

"What?" I repeat.

Nathan reaches to slide my hair behind my ear, a move more intimate than I'm used to. "Do me a favor," he says. "Let's not mention the Adjustment to your grandparents yet. We'll deal with Wes first. I'll take you back over to the hospital."

"You will?"

He nods, and then we walk out. I'm mentally and emotionally exhausted. Ready to lean on him for support. And together we go over to my house.

CHAPTER SEVEN

MY GRANDPARENTS WERE WORRIED, AND WHEN I show up with Nathan a few minutes later, they scold me about not calling. Nathan does his best to take the blame, distracting them from my reddened eyes and disheveled appearance.

Nathan tells them we have dinner plans that I owe him from a previous bet, and when they look to me for confirmation, I nod quickly. I hate continuing to lie to them, but if I need more time, I have to lie to get it.

I grab a few Motrin from the medicine cabinet for my headache, bypassing the pills my grandmother had given me before, and then Nathan and I head out. I let him drive as I wait for the headache to fade.

I use Nathan's phone to call the hospital to check on Wes,

but since I'm not family—and due to his parents' request—they won't tell me anything.

"You look terrible, Tatum," Nathan says, glancing sideways at me. "That stuff they did to you for the Adjustment . . . Are you sure it isn't messing you up too?"

I rub my forehead, closing my eyes for a little relief. "I don't know," I say. "It's not supposed to." I look over at him, and we both laugh shortly. It's an unsanctioned procedure. I knew the risks; I didn't care. Who knows what will happen to me now.

"Wes's mom is at the hospital," I say, scrunching up my nose. "Maybe that's stressing me out. She scares the shit out of me."

"I won't let her near you again," Nathan says. "And definitely not if she's going to threaten or intimidate you."

"She's not entirely wrong," I say.

"Maybe not," he says, stopping at a red light. The color plays across his face. "But it doesn't mean she's not a total and complete dickhead."

I snort a laugh. With Nathan there, I actually don't think Wes's mother would harass me as much. As if I'm in the inner family circle she can cuss out at Thanksgiving but not on a regular basis in public.

"Okay," I say. "So long as you have my back."

"Shit, Tatum," he says. "You know I'm going down with this ship."

I lean my head on the back of the seat, watching him. Grateful. "Thank you," I whisper.

His mouth twitches with a smile, but he doesn't say anything else. He doesn't have to.

A few minutes later, we arrive at the hospital. The lot is almost full, but Nathan finds a spot relatively close. My breathing has quickened, and I'm so nervous that I'm shaking. After we park, Nathan turns off the engine.

"Wes is going to be okay, Tatum," he says, and looks sideways at me. "And he loves you. He always has—with or without his memories."

I press my lips into a smile, thanking him for his kindness right now. But I have no illusions—this is partly my fault. I should have accepted Wes as he was. I should have loved him anyway. But I know it wouldn't have mattered. Wes had been getting sicker. He needed help. We were doomed from the start.

"We'll figure it out?" I ask, hopefulness in my voice. Nathan nods and then reaches to pat my knee before opening the driver's-side door.

We get to the sliding double doors, and I stop as they open, staring down the hallway in case Wes's parents are waiting for me. Rationally, I know they're not. They have bigger concerns. But until I'm sure they're gone, I wait there.

Nathan walks in ahead, and then waves me forward. With him at my side, I'm braver. Or, at least, I tell myself I'm braver. I glance at the information desk, and the nurse there is on a call and ignoring us.

I lead Nathan to where I last spoke to Dr. McKee, and

just then, as if I conjured her up, Kyle Mahoney and another girl stand with the doctor. Seeing her drops me dead. It feels like a betrayal even though I have no reason to lay claim on Dr. McKee.

"So am I not supposed to say anything?" Kyle asks, annoyed. She doesn't realize I'm here yet. She looks sideways at the other girl, and I realize it's Jana Simms.

"I can't stop you," Dr. McKee tells Kyle. "But if you care . . . then yes. I'd expect you to stay out of it for now. The memories are—"

Jana notices me first, and taps the doctor on his arm. Dr. McKee looks over to find me standing in the middle of the hallway, dumbstruck, as I stare at them. He slips his hands into the pockets of his coat. Am I imagining that he looks guilty?

Kyle furrows her blond brows, and then turns in my direction. She sways at the sight of me. I take in her appearance, how thin she seems—her clavicle is sharp through her worn white T-shirt. Kyle crosses her arms over her chest, seeming unsettled by my presence here.

A lock of blond hair falls over her left eye, but she doesn't swipe it aside. The only hint of color rushes to the high points of her cheeks. Dr. McKee looks from her to me, and then nods without explanation.

"I'll let you know if there's a change," the doctor says to Kyle in a low voice. He exchanges a pointed look with Jana, and then he walks away. Were they discussing Wes? I feel like I'm losing my mind. I'm the one who brought Wes to him; I'm the one who's been keeping the secret. He should be confiding in me.

"Jana?" Nathan calls, coming to stand next to me. "What are you doing here?"

"Vanessa," she says. "They think she had a stroke earlier, but she's stable now. Thank God."

Kyle uses that moment to start walking out, determined in her steps. But I don't think she was here about Vanessa at all. My fingers begin to tremble, dread curling through my veins.

"I need to talk to you," I call to Kyle before she can leave. Her blue eyes widen at my directness, and I'm not imagining that Jana winces. Kyle looks back at her before turning to me.

"Sure," she says evenly. She uncrosses her arms and slowly walks in my direction. Overhead there is dull music playing from the speaker—no words, just a jazz version of a popular song. It's haunting in a way, especially when Kyle stops in front of me, pale and thin as an apparition.

"Tatum," Nathan says softly from behind me, but I ignore him. A million thoughts run through my mind, but I'm not sure where to start.

Kyle must notice my hesitancy, but she doesn't start the conversation either. I think back to the first time I saw Kyle in the hallway, watching me that first day Wes came back—she wasn't confident like she is now.

"What are you doing here?" I ask, careful not to sound nervous.

SUZANNE YOUNG

"Dr. McKee tracked me down," she says. "Nice guy." Although she says it like she can't stand him.

"Why?" I ask. "Why would he call you?"

"Maybe he was worried that Wes was going the way of Vanessa," she says bitterly. "It was stupid, you know. Bringing Wes to him. He didn't need an Adjustment."

I hate how she's judging me right now. How she knows all the details. "Why do you even know about the Adjustment?" I ask. "You're not a returner."

"Remember that research I was doing?" she says like I'm an idiot. "I have my reasons, Tatum. And I certainly have bigger concerns than you."

"Like what?" I ask.

Her posture stiffens, as if I've somehow crossed her sharing line. She casts a glance over my shoulder toward Nathan and Jana, and then looks back at me.

"I'm sorry," she says. "It's late. I have to go."

She starts to walk away, but it feels like my heart wants to tear from my body. I can't stand not knowing anymore. Can't stand my own insecurity. And I can't keep the misery out of my voice when I call after her, "Were you seeing Wes behind my back?"

The words are a wrecking ball, and across from me, Nathan groans with the honest pain in them. Kyle stops and slowly turns to look back at me. There is a moment of vulnerability in her expression, her own brand of pain, I guess.

She shrugs like she can't answer the question, and without another word, she walks out of the hospital.

She didn't deny it. I stand still, frozen. I try to wrap my brain around this situation.

And I try to understand if my entire history with Wes is a lie.

After Kyle leaves, I demand to talk with Dr. McKee, but the nurse at the station tells me he won't be available until tomorrow. I ask for Marie, and when that doesn't work, I beg to see Weston. But all my requests are declined.

Nathan and Jana stay with me, and it's only a little weird when she comes to dinner with us in the hospital cafeteria. I'm used to a thin layer of hostility between us, but that seems to have dissolved. She has a bruise on her cheek, a scratch. I can't forget that her friend is in the hospital right now. I ask how Vanessa is.

"They're not hopeful," Jana says, picking at a plate of chicken tenders and fries. Her voice is thick with grief; little fly-aways stick out from her top bun. I want to apologize a hundred times, but I know it won't make a difference. I can see she truly cares about Vanessa, and I realize how hateful the gossip about Jana has been. She would do anything for her friend.

Nathan puts his arms over her shoulders in the booth, and she leans into him, closing her eyes. He turns to kiss her forehead, and I stare at my salad.

They're not hopeful. I feel the emotions welling up. People are dying. Something is killing us again.

The three of us sit quietly until Jana's phone buzzes on the table. She sniffles and grabs it, holding it close to her chest as she reads the message. She slips it into her pocket and looks up at us.

"It's my mom," she explains. "I have to go. I, uh . . . thanks for dinner," she says absently to Nathan, climbing out of the booth. She seems distracted.

Nathan tells her he'll call her later, and Jana says good-bye to both of us, watching me a second longer than necessary. "Wes *will* be okay," she tells me. "Just hang in there."

I thank her, saying that I will, and she walks out of the cafeteria.

"Remember when I said things were going to get worse?" Nathan says in a low voice, staring down at the table. "Well, I'm an asshole. I take it back."

"What are we going to do?" I ask.

He looks up suddenly, and I see he's completely torn up inside. "It's you I'm worried about, Tatum," he says as if I'm missing a larger point. "Jana told me again that it's not the Adjustment, it's all returners. There was another kid at school today."

I curse, fear climbing over my skin. "You don't have to worry about me," I say. "I'm fine. Wes and Vanessa are the ones in the hospital. And I don't know how to help them."

Nathan leans his elbows on the table, his face in his hands. "I don't know either," he says.

I'm not used to seeing Nathan so tortured. I reach out and pull his hand from his face, holding it on the table. "We survived The Program," I whisper. "We'll survive this."

His expression crumbles, but he quickly pulls it back together. Like I've brought up something too painful for him to bear. I squeeze his hand, and he nods like he's better.

"We're good," he says. "We're all good." He takes his hand back, and uses it to pull Jana's plate in front of him. He doesn't eat, though. "So what was up with Kyle Mahoney?" Nathan asks. "It was super sketchy of her to be here."

"Yeah," I say self-consciously. "Is it jumping to conclusions to say that Wes was cheating on me?"

"Still jumping," he says, but there's less conviction in his words. "She didn't come out and say that, you know," he adds. "But if there's a problem with Wes's past, I'd say it definitely starts with her."

I grab my Coke and bite down on the straw, chewing it between sips. "Did Jana talk to her?"

Nathan shakes his head. "Not that she mentioned. Then again, she's pretty torn up about Vanessa right now."

I feel for Jana, having to watch Vanessa fight for her life. It's not fair—it's not fair that returners have already suffered so much, only to end up no better off.

Nathan picks up a french fry and takes a small bite. "It sounds like Wes is going to be okay. though. Jana heard Dr. McKee talking about him."

"Dr. McKee," I repeat bitterly. "He won't do any more Adjustments; we have no way to stop Wes from crashing back like the others. Like Vanessa. But . . . he did say that if we find out what's wrong with the memory, if we find the truth, it might trigger a landslide. He advised against it, of course."

"Of course," Nathan repeats.

"We have to take that chance," I say. "Figure out what's real."

Nathan shifts uncomfortably. "And you think Wes cheated," he says.

"I don't know what to think. The only time I saw them together was for a second at a party. I would have known, right? There would have been more signs."

"Yeah," he says, barely audible. "You would have known." He reaches across the table to grab a napkin from the dispenser, wiping his hands loudly with the stiff paper.

"I was thinking," I say. "Over the summer—"

Nathan's eyes snap to mine.

"Wes was going through something; it's all a blur now. But when he didn't call me, I found out it was because he'd run away. I'll never know what happened because of The Program, but . . . do you think he could have run away with Kyle?" My voice cracks and I have to force myself not to believe it. But it actually would make sense. So what does that mean for me and Wes?

"I don't know the answer," Nathan says. "But ask yourself if you really need to know. Let Wes fight his own demons. People got sick, Tatum. They did things . . . things they regretted. They weren't themselves." He pauses. "Wes is in the hospital right now. Let the therapists deal with it. It doesn't have to be you."

I stare at him for a long moment, seeing the logic in his

eyes. "You're right," I say, and look across the cafeteria. My emotions eat away at me, devouring me from the inside. Love, loss, betrayal, grief—I run the gamut.

And I think that The Program had at least one thing right: The past has the power to destroy us if we let it.

CHAPTER EIGHT

I DIDN'T SAY MUCH AFTER LEAVING THE HOSPITAL with Nathan, focused on Wes's recovery. When I get home, I research the best therapists in town, ones who specialize in returners. I'm happy to find that my therapist does just that. And I trust her completely. I plan to set an appointment for Wes as soon as he agrees.

I wake up the next morning in my bed, and when I sit up, my head *still* aches. I can't decide if it's the same headache or a medication hangover. There are no messages from Nathan, and when I call Wes's phone, it goes directly to voice mail.

It's time I came clean with my grandparents. I owe them at least that much. I quickly get dressed and head downstairs to talk to them. I'm scared, but when the other person will still love you unconditionally, it makes the talk go much easier.

I start from the beginning, and I tell them everything.

I'm sitting on the couch, my grandfather standing at the fireplace with his elbow on the mantel. My gram has cried at least three times, once for not realizing sooner what I was going through, and once at the memories—how painful they must have been. And then, of course, when I tell her that Wes is in the hospital.

"I'm not going to criticize you right now," my grandfather says. "It's not the time, but we will have that conversation later, Tatum. We've always stood by you—more than you know. We always will. Perhaps if you would have trusted us with your plans for the Adjustment, it could have saved everyone some pain. In fact, the moment you leave, I'll be having a conversation with Dr. McKee myself."

"I just don't understand why he would do it," my grandmother says, wringing her hands. She and my grandfather exchange a look, and she lowers her eyes.

Pop turns back to me. "I told you to stay away from the Adjustment," he says, sounding disappointed.

"I know," I say, ashamed. "I thought . . ." I pause, realizing that my excuse doesn't change the facts. "I'm sorry," I say instead.

"I know you are," he allows. "Now, what's the latest on Weston's condition?"

"I'm not sure," I say. "I couldn't get in to talk to him. His parents—"

"I'll call Michelle," my grandmother says immediately,

referencing Wes's mother. "She's not going to leave you here to worry like this. She at least owes us that much." She stands from the chair and goes to the kitchen. My grandfather moves to follow her, but then pauses to look back at me.

"Why don't you take the day off from school?" he says. "You don't look well."

"I have a headache," I admit.

He nods like it proves his point that I shouldn't go. "Let me get you something for it," he says, leaving the room. When he returns with a glass of water and two large white pills, I pause. These were the same ones that my gram gave me the other day, the ones that knocked me out.

My grandfather waits for me to take them, and I put them in my mouth and take a sip of water. I smile, and hand him the glass. When he walks back into the kitchen, I quickly spit out the pills into my hand, the chalky coating bitter on my tongue. Before my grandfather comes back, I grab a tissue from the coffee table and wrap up the pills and stuff them in my pocket.

Although I have a headache, I don't want to sleep. I get up, holding the edge of the sofa as I do. I plan to take some regular medicine when I get the chance.

My grandfather comes back into the room, and asks if I want any help getting upstairs. I tell him I'm fine. "You'll let me know as soon as you have an update on Wes?" I ask.

"Of course," Pop responds.

As I start to walk back to my room, my grandfather calls my name. "I'm glad you're back," he says.

He means I'm back in their trust. Back in their care. And so I smile and walk upstairs.

My grandmother stops by my room a short while later. She couldn't get hold of Wes's parents, but says that she and Pop are heading there to speak with them.

"And if they're not home, we'll go over to the hospital," she says. "In the meantime, I want you to take it easy. Understand?"

I tell her that I will and she kisses my forehead and tells me to be well. I see her glance at my phone, and for a second I think she's going to ask for it. But she doesn't. My grandparents have never taken my phone away before, so the intent surprises me.

She leaves and I wait in bed, listening. When I hear their car pull out of the driveway, I go downstairs and into the kitchen. I open the cabinet, grab the bottle of pills, and pick up my phone.

I type the name of the drug into a search and set the bottle down. I click through the list of uses, leaning my hip against the granite counter. Although migraine treatment is among the possible uses for the drug, it's something else that catches my eye, and my heart kicks up its beats.

There are several articles, consumer warnings, and charts. They all list this medication as a drug used for deletion of memory, a way to suppress and erase traumatic events and affect the brain's ability to recall them long-term. It was one of the medications they used in The Program.

They call it the forgetting pill.

SUZANNE YOUNG

"Oh my God," I whisper, and with a shaky hand, I grab the two pills from my pocket that I spit out earlier. I toss them into the disposal and run the water.

My mind is spinning as I try to come up with a rational explanation as to why my grandparents would give me a drug like that. Could it be a coincidence that my gram was taking that medication?

I pick up the bottle again, checking for the phone number of the unlisted physician. I dial it, and as the line rings, my heart beats in my throat.

It has to be a mistake.

"Thank you for calling the Adjustment office. This is Megan."

I freeze. Megan repeats her greeting, and I slowly lower the phone and stare at it. The line goes dead.

Why does my grandmother have pills from the Adjustment office? And why the hell would she give them to me? To make me forget? What am I supposed to forget?

I wince, another flash of pain in my head. I press the heel of my palm hard against my temple, and then reach for the regular aspirin. I take three and wash them down with water directly from the tap. Water drips from my chin, and I wipe it away with the back of my hand.

I'm not sure what to do. Who to call. I pick up my phone, ready to try Nathan again, when the line suddenly rings, startling me.

I'm relieved when I see it's Wes. He's okay. I quickly bring the phone to my ear. "I've been so worried," I say. "How are you?"

I'm met with a moment of silence, and I listen closer. I hear breathing so I know the line isn't disconnected.

"Wes?" I say, my worry spiking.

"Where is he?" his mother asks, her voice thick like she might be crying. "Where's my son?"

I spin to look around the kitchen, as if he's in here but I didn't notice. I grow frantic as his mother's voice continues to ring in my ear.

"He left the hospital, Tatum, against his doctor's advice," she says. "I want to speak to him now."

"He's not with me," I say. Would he have run away again? Like last time. Kyle was there yesterday. Could he have . . . ?

"I have to go," I say, and hang up before his mother can argue. She must have his phone, which means he left it behind. I run my hand through my hair, taking stock of the situation. I have to find Wes. But I don't know where to look.

Everything is falling apart. Although I have to figure out my own situation, this takes precedence. I have to make sure Wes is okay.

Without giving away what I know about the medication, I call my grandfather; I need his help. Pop answers on the first ring, and I'm barely holding it together as I try to tell him that Wes is missing. He and my grandmother are on their way to the hospital since no one was home at Wes's house.

"I'm scared, Pop," I say. "What if he's gone? What if he's hurt—maybe even because of the Adjustment?"

"Tatum," he says softly. "Stay calm, honey. It's going to be fine."

"It's just . . ." I try to sound steadier. "I can't let him down this time," I say. "Wes ran away before, and look what happened to him. I didn't do enough. I won't make that same mistake. He could be in a ditch somewhere—" My voice cracks and I quickly pull the phone away from my mouth so my grandfather won't hear.

"We're going to make some calls, okay?" Pop says. "Talk with his mother. You wait at the house, just in case he shows up."

"Good idea," I say. Because when I think about where Wes might go, I remember how he showed up at my house. Showed up after he ran away the first time. And showed up again when he returned from The Program. *Muscle memory*, he called it.

"Check in every hour so I don't have to start calling around about you, too," Pop adds.

"I will," I say, pacing the kitchen. "Thank you."

"I love you, honey," he says. There's sadness in his voice. Concern. It tells me that my earlier worry will have a rational explanation. Because my grandparents love me unconditionally. And that means they would never try to manipulate me.

I spend the next hour online, looking for any update on social media that might give me some direction as to where Wes is. But there's nothing. I check in with my grandparents and they don't have an update either.

The phone rings around eleven, and I practically jump out of my skin to answer it. It's Nathan.

"Hey," I answer. "I called you."

"Yeah, sorry about that," he says. "They had us shut off our phones."

I close my laptop and get up from my bed. "They?"

Nathan exhales loudly. "Mandatory assembly. A half hour lecture from a monitor—Dr. Wyatt. She told us all about the dangers of memory alteration. *Any* form of memory alteration. She basically called out the Adjustment without naming it specifically."

"Shit," I say, pausing midpace. "Well, what does she want?"

"Names," he says. "She wants names of students suspected of messing with their heads. She's trying to get us to turn on each other. Several people walked out of the assembly, including me and Foster. Before I left, she said the school board voted on taking action. I don't know what that means. But I'll tell you one thing, we were complacent last time. We won't make the same mistake. We'll refuse to meet with her. She's bringing in all the returners, though. Have . . . have you met this woman?"

"No," I say. "Although I saw her in the office when she was about to talk to Wes."

"She's terrifying," Nathan says. "Steer clear."

"I'll try," I say.

"They called off school for the rest of the day," Nathan says, his voice dropping lower. "There's something else. Late last night . . . Vanessa died. She, uh . . . she had an aneurysm, a side effect of her brain injury. She didn't make it."

My breath catches, and I take a step back, horrified. I blink and tears spill over onto my cheeks. "Jana—"

"I'm going over there right now," he says.

"Please tell her I'm so sorry, Nathan. And if there's anything I can do . . ."

"I will," he says. "But, um . . . I wanted to tell you to be careful. Whatever parts of Vanessa's brain were stimulated by those doctors became overactive; it made her paranoid, delusional. The memories came back too fast and she wasn't able to handle it. Tatum, I'm not sure anyone can. I know you were only a donor, but I'm worried it might have affected you. You should—"

"I'm fine," I say, not wanting him to worry. I'm devastated for Vanessa's family. Her brother. Her parents. She was a survivor, but now she's gone.

"And keep an eye on Wes," Nathan adds. "That kid who also had a breakdown yesterday, he wasn't in school. I . . . don't know how many more there will be. Returners are seriously in danger."

There's a tingling that starts in my cheeks, pins and needles when you realize something terrible. It races down my chest, curls in my stomach. "About Wes," I say. "His mother called me. He's missing from the hospital."

"Jesus," Nathan breathes out, frustrated. "This fucking day."

"I'm waiting here in case he shows up, but I think I'm

going out to look for him. Should I meet up with you and Jana?"

"No," Nathan says. "Find Wes. I'll pick up Jana and bring her back to my house. She doesn't want to be alone and her mom is working. I'll keep a lookout for Wes."

"Thank you," I tell him. We hang up, and I stay for a moment, unable to move. A shadow creeps over me, and I feel it soak into my skin. It won't be long until that monitor rounds up all the returners, and not just for an interview. This is the start. Panic isn't far behind.

I look around my empty house, feeling vulnerable. Afraid. I have to find Wes and make sure he's okay.

I dash over and grab my keys, and go outside, heading for the Jeep. Only when I get out to the driveway, my heart leaps. Weston is walking down the middle of the street in my direction. I drop my keys and run to him.

I nearly stumble off the curb but catch myself as Wes hurries toward me. He's wearing the same clothes he went to the hospital in, a plastic ID bracelet still on his wrist. Bruises line the inside of his left arm, where he's had multiple injections and blood draws.

His eyes are wild, and when he looks at me, it's like I can read his soul. How desperate he was to see me. How he needed me. And without a word, we crash into each other, clinging together. I wrap both my arms around the back of his neck, standing on my tiptoes; his hands grasp tightly at my shirt.

"When I woke up, you were gone," Wes whispers at my

neck, sounding panicked. "I nearly broke out of the hospital in the middle of the night to find you. They wouldn't give me a phone." He cups the back of my neck and looks down at me as if I owe him an explanation.

He's okay. He's here. I feel like I've just gotten home from a long trip. Homesick for him. And I want to say that he seems better, but it's not true. His dark eyes are bloodshot, and there's scruff on his chin. He looks exhausted and worn down. The Adjustment hasn't fixed him at all. It might have made him worse.

"Come inside," I say, taking his hand. "And . . . you'd better call your mother."

CHAPTER NINE

WE GO INTO THE KITCHEN, WHERE I GRAB WES SOME water and tell him to sit down. He seems confused, looking around the house, and I realize it's the first time he's been inside since he returned from The Program. I'm not sure if he remembers it, but I'm not going to ask him. I don't want to overwhelm him with unimportant stuff.

I hand Wes my phone and try not to listen when he calls his mother. But I can hear her voice from the kitchen island, demanding he come back to the hospital. Wes tells her to calm down, he's an adult, and says he'll see her later. Then he hangs up. I'm sure she loved that.

When he's done, I sit at the table with him. Wes scoots his chair closer, his hand on my leg, like he's afraid I'll disappear. I wait as he gulps down a few sips of the water.

"What the hell happened yesterday?" he asks. He sets the glass down on the table with a *clank*. "Last thing I remember," he says, "we were in the Adjustment office, and you were talking about a party. . . ." He shakes his head like it gets foggy from there. "The party . . . I told you after that you were the best part of me." He pauses to verify if he got that right, and I smile at him, encouraging him to keep talking.

"Next thing I know," he says, "it's two in the morning and I'm in a hospital bed with Dr. McKee shining a light in my eyes. He said I rejected the memory. What does that mean?"

"I'm not entirely sure," I say. "But he accused me of not giving him the whole story. That's not true, Wes. I told him everything."

"Of course you did," he replies easily. He squeezes my leg and I put my hand over his. "I don't get what went wrong," he says. "Last time it worked so well. But this one . . . it left me with this . . ." He shakes his head. "It left me feeling sick, Tate. Like, sick to my stomach, pain in my chest. I don't know what they did to me."

"I'm sorry I left," I say, feeling guilty. He must have been terrified when he woke up. "Your parents . . . Your mom was there. She wouldn't let me see you. She told me I was selfish and that I'd eventually kill you."

Wes closes his eyes, breathing out an annoyed sigh. "My mother doesn't know what the hell she's talking about."

"I told her that at least I wasn't the one who called The Program on you," I say. "Sorry about that."

"She deserved it," he says. "She has no right to talk to you that way. You're the one who's trying to help me."

"Yeah, but . . . I'm scared she's right," I confess. "I'm scared I've been selfish."

"Tate," Wes says, leaning in to put his forehead against mine. "She's not right. I'm here with you because I want to be."

I put my palm on Wes's cheek, sighing deeply. "It's good to see you," I say, unable to hold back my smile when I'm this close to him. He takes my hand and kisses the inside of my palm, then my wrist, before letting my hand go.

"You had to know I'd come back for you," he says, flashing his dimples. "I always do."

In the other room, I hear my phone buzz on the table. I stand up to grab it, but pause in the doorway. "Things are a mess right now," I tell Wes. "I'm not even sure where to start." The phone stops in the other room, and I opt to leave it.

"How so?" Wes asks. "I mean, in comparison to the mess they normally are."

"Vanessa Ortiz died last night," I say quietly.

Wes rocks back in his chair and stares down at the table. "She's . . . she's dead?" he asks.

I nod sadly. I lean against the door frame, and we let the thought settle between us. Another death. Another person torn away.

"It was related to her injury," I say. "But the way she was acting . . . I wonder if she had a corrupted memory too. Or if this is just what's happening to all returners. I thought maybe therapy would be enough, but now I'm not sure. I'm scared."

"Look," Wes says, as if I'm too far ahead of myself. "I'm sorry to hear about Vanessa. I mean, it's horrible. But I promise you that we'll figure this out. Okay?"

I nod, slightly braver because of his words.

"There's more?" he asks hesitantly.

"Yeah," I say. "The monitor was back at the school today, asking for names of people who've gotten their memories altered. She might be able to track you down."

"We can't worry about that now," Wes says. "By law—unless the law is changed again—she can't do anything to me." But he swallows hard because we both know how quickly those rules can change.

"And then there's this," I say, walking to the kitchen cabinet. I take out the pill bottle and set it on the table in front of Wes. He looks it over, and lifts his eyes to mine questioningly.

"And these are . . . ?"

"I'm not sure. They might be migraine meds, or they might be memory erasers. Which do you think it is?"

"What?" Wes says, picking up the bottle. "Is this your gram?" he asks, pointing to her name.

"Yep. But when I called the number for the doctor, it was the Adjustment office."

Wes's mouth falls open and we stare at each other, both of us trying to find an explanation.

"I will say," I start, "that my grandfather's a reporter. It's possible that he went there to talk to Dr. McKee, but why would he let him treat my grandmother? And why would she give these pills to me—unless she didn't know what it was . . ."

"I'm not really going to side with the conspiracy on this one," Wes says. "Your little old gram working for . . . what, The Program? Doubt it."

I smile, because when he says it like that, it's obviously ridiculous. Still, I'll have to get to the bottom of it.

Wes pats the kitchen chair, telling me to sit down. When I do, I watch him for a moment, and the last worry starts to work its way over me. Tightening my muscles. Wes sees my apprehension.

"Is there seriously more?" he asks.

"It's about us," I say, my voice a little shaky. "I know I've told you how much we loved each other, how we were everything—and I believed that. I still do. But when Kyle Mahoney showed up in that memory . . ." Wes tilts his head at the mention, and I wait for a flicker of guilt or recognition. Instead he screws up his face.

"What the hell does Kyle have to do with anything?" he asks.

"She was there," I say. "I told you."

"She was *where*?"

"In the memory."

Now Wes reacts, pushing back from his chair to stand up. "What do you *mean, in the memory*?" There's a sudden flash of distrust in his eyes, as if I've been keeping something from him.

It strikes me how vulnerable he's been. At any point, I could have changed my interpretation of his past. I *could* have lied. I didn't, but I could have. That thought must occur to him now.

"The party," I say. "I told you in the Adjustment office."

He looks around like he's trying to think, but shakes his head. "I don't remember that," he says. "She's not in the memory I have of that night. Tell me about it," he demands.

I don't know why it's not in his memory. Could Dr. McKee have taken it out when he patterned it? But . . . why?

"It wasn't anything huge," I say, although my mind is racing to make sense of the discrepancy. "But Kyle was at the party and the two of you were talking."

"About what?" he asks. "I've never seen her before in my life."

"I'm not sure what you were talking about; you didn't tell me. But she was there. And it felt wrong—like she didn't belong in the story of us."

"A lot of things feel wrong," he mutters.

I narrow my eyes, working through that statement. "What does that mean?" I ask, a hitch in my voice. "What else feels wrong?"

He winces. "I'm sorry," he says. "I didn't mean it like that. It's just that the other memories—although I can picture them . . . I don't entirely feel them. Not like the one I had on my own. I asked Dr. McKee about it before, asked if it was normal."

"And he said it was," I respond, but Wes's pause makes my stomach turn.

"No," he says. "He said it's *not*. He said the memory itself should trigger matching emotions in my brain. Only mine don't match."

His words stun me. "Your emotions?" I repeat. "You don't . . . feel . . ."

"Not us," he says immediately, reaching for my hand. "That I can feel. I told you that." He puts his other palm over his heart. "I feel you right here. It's just the details—the emotional details that seem to be wrong."

I look down at my hand in Wes's, thinking how perfectly they used to fit together, but that somehow they don't quite match up anymore. I slide my fingers between his.

"Kyle Mahoney was at the hospital, too," I say.

"Why? What does she have to do with any of this?"

"I, um . . . I asked her if you were cheating on me with her."

"What?" Wes asks, sounding offended. He pulls his hand from mine. "Well, what the fuck did she say?"

"She shrugged. She didn't answer, which makes it sound . . . like maybe you were. I don't even know anymore. Nathan said to not let my past—"

"*Nathan*," Wes repeats with an edge. "Yes, what did your good-looking best friend have to say on the matter of our relationship?"

"Hey," I snap. "You don't get to do that. Nathan has been there for me—he's got my back. But we're just friends."

Weston looks ashamed, and apologizes. We're quiet for a moment, and then he lowers his eyes. "Do you believe that?"

he asks in a low voice, one filled with hurt. "Do you believe I was seeing someone else?"

My lips part, but I don't answer immediately. It hurts to not trust him. But I'm also not stupid. I won't be willfully ignorant. "I don't know," I say. "It could be. You were gone for an entire week, and—"

He turns away, and I see the muscles in his jaw flex. He shakes his head, adamant, and turns back to me. "No," he says. "I wouldn't do that, Tate. You've been telling me that we had this amazing relationship. I believe you. *I feel it.* And now . . . what? That was a lie?"

"No," I say. He blinks quickly and presses the heel of his palm against his forehead like it hurts. "Wes," I say, softer, worried about how I'm affecting him. "We were amazing. I didn't lie about that. But Kyle's been showing up ever since you came back. And like I said . . . you disappeared."

"And you think I was with her?" he asks.

"I don't know. I hope not. But you were sick; you weren't yourself. And when you came home, you wouldn't tell me where you were. You hardly said anything at all. And then The Program took you."

Wes starts to pace, and I can see how the idea of this bothers him. Wes is an outstanding guy—he doesn't lie. He doesn't cheat. But he wasn't himself at the end.

"We have to find out," he says. "Call and make an appointment with the Adjustment office. One more and—"

"I can't," I say. Wes stares at me.

"Why not?"

"Dr. McKee said he won't treat you anymore. He said no more Adjustments because the memory was corrupted. It would be dangerous . . . for both of us, I guess."

Wes's expression sags, like he's just been abandoned. "What am I supposed to do, then?" he asks. "How—"

"He suggested therapy," I say. Wes scoffs, but I hold up my hand to tell him to listen. "I asked about the corrupted memory—what would happen if you figured out the truth."

Wes's eyes widen. "What did he say?"

"He said it might trigger all your memories. He warned me against it, though—"

"That's what we have to do, then," Wes says, shaking his head. "We need the truth. There's no other option."

"There is," I say, but Wes won't hear me.

"No," he says. "We have to find out. I don't want to depend on someone else's version of my life anymore. And if I was with Kyle Mahoney . . . well, other than being an asshole, I'll have more questions than answers. But at least I'll know the truth."

Wes sways suddenly, and he reaches out to hold the top of a kitchen chair. I go over to steady him. His eyes are closed, but when he looks down at me, there's concern there.

"I'm mixed up, Tate," he says softly. "I'm starting to . . . You said my mother called The Program on me?" he asks.

I'm startled by the question. "Uh, yeah," I say. "They picked you up the same day you came back."

Wes looks at me, and for a second I'm afraid he's going to

pass out. "I'm starting to get confused," he whispers. "I'm . . . having trouble figuring out what's real."

"I'm real," I say. He pulls me into a hug, and guilt attacks my conscience. "I'm sorry I ever told you about the Adjustment," I say. "I should have known better. We should have both known better."

Wes slides his fingers under my hair. "Probably," he says, resting his chin on the top of my head. "But this is where we're at. I have to find out the truth, because I'm telling you, my memories are wrong somehow. They hurt because they're wrong. And if I can sort them out, maybe the pain will go away."

The terrible part is I know he's right. But what does it mean if *my* memories are wrong? I'm scared of the answer. Of the truth. And of the fear that I'm going to lose him once again.

After telling Wes everything relevant I can think of, I grab a sweater and we walk out to my Jeep. I left a message for my grandparents when they didn't answer their phone. I let them know that I was with Wes, that he was okay, and that we're going to try to figure out some of his missing pieces. I don't have to lie to them anymore about me and Wes, and the relief of that is a huge weight off my chest.

We know there's only one place to start, so Wes and I look up Kyle's address. Rain has started to fall, and I click on my windshield wipers as we drive toward her house.

"So Kyle Mahoney knows me," Wes says, looking out the passenger window. "Do you think she kept a diary?"

I turn to him and laugh. "You're going to ask to read her diary?"

"Oh," he says, looking over. "Is that too personal? She showed up at the hospital and talked with my doctor. She wouldn't clarify about an affair I may or may not have had with her. I think she'll understand if I ask to read any diary entries she has about me."

"I think you're joking," I say. "But just in case you're not, we are not going to ask to read her diary. I still actually value privacy."

"Fine," Wes says. "We'll do it your way." The corner of his mouth curves up, and I know he was joking. I want to lean in and kiss him, but I don't. And I can't explain, but for the first time since he came back, I feel completely connected to him. Inexplicably drawn to him, the way I used to be.

I reach for his hand, and he doesn't flinch. He holds it in his lap, casually, like he's done it a million times before.

And I can't help but think that this is why. This moment right here, despite the absolute shit show of tragedy surrounding us, this is why we did it. This is why we risked everything. Whether it was worth it remains to be seen.

I look at Wes as he stares out the window, see his sharp angles. How worn down and broken he's become. And I worry what I've done to him. What we've both done to him.

SUZANNE YOUNG

CHAPTER TEN

WES IS QUIET THE REST OF THE RIDE OVER TO Kyle's. He seems lost in his thoughts, and every so often, he'll flinch for no reason. Each time he does, my panic heightens. I don't know much longer before he shuts down again. It seems inevitable. All the returners are failing. This might be the only way to save him.

I park in front of Kyle's house, a modest one-story with a big grass front yard and a steep roof. I have a moment of regret, concern this was a bad idea. That I'm opening a door I can't close. I look at Wes, and find him staring at the house.

"Is it . . . is it familiar?" I ask.

I hear his throat click when he swallows. "Yeah," he says quietly, and climbs out of the Jeep. I sit there alone for a moment, allowing myself one last chance to be ignorant. This might change everything.

But I have to be brave. I am brave.

I open my door and get out, meeting Wes on the sidewalk. Together, we go to Kyle's front door and knock. I'm shaking, part fear, part humiliation. I feel completely vulnerable.

The door swings open, and Kyle's eyes widen when she sees us. Her confidence falters, and she crosses her arms over her chest like armor.

"What's this about?" she asks, looking from me to Wes. "I thought you were in the hospital."

"Yeah, about that," Wes says. "Can we come in?"

Kyle pauses long enough to make me wonder if she'll say yes, but then she steps aside and motions for us to walk in.

Wes and I sit on the couch in Kyle's living room, and I glance around. There are pictures on the wall and some along the fireplace mantel. The place is homey and comfortable. I can't help but compare it to my home.

Kyle walks in and takes a seat on one of the matching leather chairs across from us. "My parents are at work," she says, in case we were wondering. She watches Wes carefully, but he avoids her gaze. It is easily the most awkward situation I've been in all week.

The three of us sit quietly, no one willing to ask the first question. Kyle exhales.

"Did it work?" she asks, like she's been waiting to ask for a while. "The Adjustment—did it work? Is that why you're here?"

Wes finally lifts his eyes to meet hers, and I'm not imagining the flinch of a smile that crosses Kyle's features under his attention.

"Not really," Wes says. "I mean, I got memories—but not my own. With the exception of a little piece here and there."

Kyle swallows hard, biting on the inside of her lip. "Too bad," she says, trying to sound cool about it, even though it seems to hurt her feelings. "So then why are you here? Why *both* of you?"

I'm so confused about her behavior, her questions. I want to just scream, *What is your deal? Tell us everything!* But that would be giving her a lot of power. Power to tell the truth, but also, the power to lie. I don't know what to ask.

"Kyle," Wes starts, surprising me. "Can I read your diary?"

She laughs, and I turn to him in disbelief. We talked about not asking that.

"Uh, no, Weston," Kyle says. "You may not. Why would you want to, anyway? I'm sure Tatum can fill you in on your past. The rest doesn't matter."

But when Kyle says the last part, her expression weakens. She was saying she doesn't matter. And with that, I know. The pain in my chest grows because I know.

"Tell me about you and Wes," I say in a small voice. I feel Weston look at me, but I can't bear to turn to him.

Kyle watches me, a touch of sympathy in her expression. She leans back in the chair, crossing her legs, and she turns to look at the group of pictures on the mantel. She points to one of them, and I see her hand is shaking.

"Did you know that I had a brother?" she says to neither of us. She presses her lips together, staring at a picture of a little boy and a younger version of her on a backyard swing set.

The air in the room grows heavy, and when Kyle turns, she looks at Wes pleadingly. "You really don't remember?" she asks.

"No," he answers evenly.

Her eyes well up with tears, a great sense of loss. "Well, damn," she says, like a fresh wound has opened. She looks at me. "We bonded over our dead siblings," she explains. "I told Wes about my brother and he told me all about Cheyenne." Wes shifts uncomfortably.

"When did this . . . When did you bond?" I ask her. *She knows his sister's name.*

Kyle casts another glance at her brother's picture before resting her head against the back of her chair. "Wes was barely functioning when I met him after school one afternoon—both of us just going through the motions of life, lost souls searching for an escape. I told him I hated his boots and he told me he hated people. We connected over our mutual misery. In fact, it made us smile. Like someone understood us."

Her words sting because I was there. And I understood Wes. I always understood him. My mind starts to loop through the past, thinking back to that time, but it keeps coming up with the same memories I told at the Adjustment office. Things were . . . fine.

"So you started seeing each other?" I ask. My throat tightens, and it's a fight to keep going. Like I'm purposely putting my hand on a hot burner.

"Yeah," she says. "Wes and I started to meet up."

"Fuck," Wes says under his breath. I stare straight ahead at Kyle, unwilling to flinch.

"Understand it was a different time," Kyle says. "We were just a means of escape for two really sad people. We began to spiral together." Kyle looks over at Wes, but he can't meet her eyes. She turns to me. "He'd talk about you sometimes," she offers.

"I think I'm going to be sick," I say, getting to my feet. My head is spinning, complicated by the headache that's working its way into my neck muscles. Wes starts to stand to help me, but I turn on him so fiercely, he drops back down.

I keep one hand on my throat and begin to pace, telling Kyle to continue. She looks doubtfully at Wes, and after a moment he nods.

"He loved you once," she says kindly. "He really did. He told me that everything was his fault because after Cheyenne's death, he'd been slowly dying too, falling away piece by piece until even you weren't enough. You weren't enough to fix him, Tatum. And he couldn't fix you."

I watch as Kyle cringes at her own words, even though they're hurting me. I resent the fact that she's calling me broken, as if she knows anything about me. But I wasn't there. I don't know what Wes said. What he told her about us.

"One night," she continues, "Wes had me meet him at a park overlooking the city. The plan was to run away, figure it out from there. We were both a mess."

He planned to run away with her. The thought is devastating. And the park . . . that was the park Wes took me to after he returned. Only he'd never been there with me. It was with *her*.

The room spins faster, the revelations too much to comprehend. The ache intensifies behind my eyes and I wince. Wes calls my name, but I hold up my hand and tell him I'm fine.

"He never showed, Tatum," she says, as if it will help. "I thought maybe you found out about us, but I didn't see you again until school started this year. And by that time, Wes had already been in and out of The Program. They'd already stripped me away."

"I didn't know," I say miserably. "I'm not sure why he didn't show up because I didn't know about the two of you." Despite how hard I worked to hold it together until now, tears flood my eyes. "I didn't know he was cheating on me."

I turn to Wes and he hitches in a breath, a tear dripping onto his cheek. His face a mask of betrayal—betrayal of himself.

"What are you talking about?" Kyle asks. Her reaction surprises me, and I wipe my face and look at her. "Jesus, Tatum," she says. "He wasn't lying about your denial, was he?"

"My denial?" I repeat, confused.

"We weren't cheating," she says like it's distasteful. "The two of you were already broken up."

I turn to Wes and watch him stiffen, his eyes wide. I look at Kyle.

"Wes and I never broke up," I say.

"Uh . . . yeah, you did. Weeks, maybe even a month, before I met him. I mean, he told me you both wanted to keep it low profile because it might tip off The Program and get you flagged. But I'll be honest . . . it felt more like the two of you were looking for a reason to stay together. Either way, you still acted like a couple in front of other people. At least you did until this one party, Casey Jones's? I told Wes he needed to deal with you. I didn't want to be in the middle."

The party—the memory. Kyle was there. She was . . . she was there with Wes? My thoughts begin to swirl, threatening to spin away like a top, and I have to take a seat in the other leather chair.

"You're saying that Tatum and I weren't together anymore?" Wes asks in a tight voice. I don't know what he could be thinking right now. He might think I lied to him about everything—but I didn't. Maybe he lied to Kyle.

"You were no longer a couple," Kyle says to him. "But . . ." She looks over at me, pities me. "You did tell me she was having a tough time with the breakup. You didn't want to hurt her. It was maddening to watch from my perspective." She turns back to Wes and shrugs. "It made me jealous. You said you didn't love her anymore . . . but I sure wish someone didn't love me that much."

"That's not true," I murmur, mostly to myself. "We never . . ." I continue to think back, kicked out of my head as it plays the same memories on a loop. "Wes," I say, looking over at him. "Tell her we never broke up."

But Wes is staring at me like he's seeing me for the first time. "Tate," he starts, a bit of misery in his voice. "I think she's right." And he hates it, I can see that he hates the idea. But it's not possible. It's not true.

I look back at Kyle, accusingly. "You were his girlfriend?" I ask.

"We weren't exactly like that. It wasn't serious. Tatum," she says, like I'm being petty. "My little brother killed himself when he was thirteen. It wrecked me. And, Wes"—she turns to him, the remains of adoration in her eyes—"he understood. Cheyenne and her boyfriend committed suicide. He told me everything about her—we'd talk late into the night. We dug into our pain together."

Kyle winces at her next thought. "Before she died . . . Cheyenne came to you, Wes. She came and told you she was going to kill herself. And you called her stupid, said it wasn't funny or cute. You got mad at her because you thought she was just fighting with Mackey. You didn't believe her. But she killed herself that night and you hated yourself for it."

I have to cover my mouth, shocked, horrified for Wes, especially when he chokes on his cry. I didn't know any of this. In all our time, Wes never told me that. I'm starting to feel completely left out of this conversation. Like maybe I was never truly part of his life. Like I'm the lie here.

"You said it was your fault that she was dead," Kyle continues. "And that Cheyenne haunted you. You said you were toxic. You said you were death, you said Tatum—"

"Stop," he murmurs, holding up his hand as he squeezes his eyes shut. Kyle watches him sympathetically for a moment. Wes looks like he's barely holding himself together, at odds with who he thought he was.

"I told you about my brother," Kyle continues with a new breath. "You told me about your sister. Like I said, we bonded."

Wes shakes his head as if this is all too much to take. "I don't even know you," he says, and looks over at her. "I don't remember you."

"But I remember you," she says. "How it felt to be with you—like I was chasing you and you were always just out of reach. I figured it was because of Tatum."

My eyelids flutter as another wave of sickness crosses me.

"But at the beginning of the summer," Kyle continues, "you promised it was finally over with her. And we planned to run away before The Program could close in. We'd planned it all out, Wes, one late night on the coast, drawing spirals in the sand. You told me your only choice was to run away. You wanted to escape Cheyenne. You said you wanted to forget Tatum completely—bury her deepest of all. Because you couldn't live with how you hurt her. You couldn't live with how you broke her heart. You said you were emotional poison. You said you wished you were dead."

Kyle sighs, and I see that she cares about him—or rather, the other version of him. The one that I loved too. "Instead," she continues, "I waited in the park until morning, but you didn't come. After that, I never wanted to speak to you again.

And when I heard you went into The Program, part of me was glad. I'm sorry, but I was hurt and part of me was glad that you were going to forget me.

"But then you came back to school last week and I saw you. I regretted not finding you before The Program changed you. Before I could talk to you and tell you everything, I saw Tatum there. And she continued to be there, always at your side, just like before. I couldn't compete with your history—even when you couldn't remember it."

Kyle looks over at me, a flash of concern at what must be my deteriorating condition. "I'm sorry I didn't admit it to you sooner, Tatum," she says. "I honestly thought you knew. I figured you just didn't want to acknowledge it."

"Why were you at the hospital?" Wes asks suddenly, his entire complexion a sheet of white with shades of purple under his eyes.

"Like I told Tatum," she says. "Dr. McKee tracked me down after your session. He asked me about our past. I told him. He was pissed, said he should have known sooner. He asked me not to say anything to either of you. He said it would compromise your well-being."

"Then why are you telling us now?" Wes asks.

"Because you showed up here," she responds with a smile. "And because I don't trust doctors anymore." Kyle stands up from her chair, smoothing the thighs of her shorts. She walks over to the mantel, running her fingertip over the image of her brother.

"I miss that bond we had," she says to Wes. "And I'm sorry,

Tatum"—she looks over at me—"but Wes didn't love you anymore. Not the real Wes at least."

"You talk about me like I'm dead," Wes says. "But I'm sitting right here. I'm real, and I don't need you to speak for me. And definitely not about my relationship with Tate."

"And when your memories crash back?" she asks, glaring at him. "Will you want to die again? Will you hurt her again?" Kyle nods in my direction. "Or will you find another stranger to bond with late at night?"

Sitting there, listening to the two of them, I feel a million miles away. Nothing makes sense. None of this seems real, but it hurts like it is. I stare down at the floor and the specks of dirt in between the slats of wood.

"Where did you go?" I ask out loud. Both Wes and Kyle fall silent, and I look up at Wes. "The week you went missing—where did you go?"

Wes looks absolutely forlorn when he meets my eyes. "I don't remember, Tate. I don't remember any of this. Please—"

I stand abruptly, turning away from him. The world tilts sharply, and I grab the back of the chair and train my eyes on Kyle. I'm no longer angry about her presence in my life. Seems she's been there for a while. I just didn't notice. Somehow . . . I had missed it all.

I nod at her, thanking her for her honesty, and I start for the front door.

"Tate," Wes calls. "Don't walk away from me now. I need you."

I stop to look back. "No," I say, shaking my head. "You need to figure out your shared past with Kyle. Because, Wes . . . this has nothing to do with me. This is all you."

He shakes his head like he's ready to argue, but I don't let him have another word in this. My heart can't take any more. And so I leave Kyle's house without him. I leave Wes behind.

SUZANNE YOUNG

CHAPTER ELEVEN

I PROBABLY SHOULDN'T BE DRIVING, NOT WHEN I'M
this out of control. I take the turns at full speed, bumping
curbs, the windshield wipers slapping rainwater back and forth.

Wes and I broke up.

Did we? Could that be true? Would my denial really run
so deep?

A few blocks from home, something occurs to me. Something awful. The pills, the ones my grandparents have been giving me. What if . . . ?

I blink quickly, like I'm trying to blink away the thought.
But it doesn't fade. What if my grandparents gave me those pills
to help me get over Wes?

"No," I say out loud in my car. They wouldn't give me medication for that purpose without asking me. My cheek itches

and I reach up to scratch it, wincing when my fingernail digs too deep.

I glance in the mirror and see a thin line of red where I've cut myself. "You're cracking up," I say to my reflection, and then laugh.

I look back at the road, my mind swirling. I think about Vanessa, just before she died. She was right—I shouldn't have trusted anybody. Dr. McKee—he found out about Kyle and didn't tell us. He kept her out of Weston's memory. Memory control, just like The Program.

And I wish Vanessa were still alive. I wish I could have saved her and asked her everything. We should have been friends. My mind races, and I conjure up Sebastian and Alecia. I bring back all the dead.

I sputter out a cry. "I'm sorry," I say out loud. "I'm sorry I wasn't there." My head throbs; my vision blurs. But I keep racing for home, pressing harder on the accelerator.

My grandparents' car isn't in the driveway when I pull up, screeching my tires and skidding one tire onto the grass. I'm glad they're not home. I can ask them about the pills later. And I will. But if they see me like this now, they'll probably never let me out of the house again.

I climb out of the Jeep, moving slowly and letting the rain run over my hair. I glance up at Nathan's bedroom window. He's probably in there with Jana, and the thought of it annoys me. I'm not even sure why. I slosh through puddles and walk in the back kitchen door of my house.

SUZANNE YOUNG

I go directly to the cabinet and grab the bottle of pills. I dump them all into the disposal and turn it on, chopping them to bits. When that's done, I toss the bottle aside and start toward my room. I flinch once—like a shiver that contracts all my muscles. My headache deepens, and I groan in pain.

Halfway up the stairs, I strip off my wet sweater and pull my T-shirt over my head to toss it aside, walking around in my bra. I push open my bedroom door and head straight for my drawer of pictures.

I don't call Nathan—the thought of talking to anyone is unappealing. I'm sick with paranoia, and beyond that, I can't imagine retelling what Kyle said.

Wes didn't love you anymore.

I flinch again, and pull open the drawer hard enough to yank it out of the dresser, spilling its contents as it falls to the floor.

And there, spread out on my wood floor, is the history of me and Weston Ambrose. Our smiles, our kisses. I fold in on myself and sit down next to them, spreading them out. His dimples. His eyes. None of it looks fake, not one second of it.

Tears stream down my cheeks, and finally . . . I let myself fall apart.

Weston stopped loving me. He'd met someone else he connected with. And I denied it all. I drove the thought away—whether by sheer will or medication, it doesn't change a fucking thing.

Wes and Tatum are a lie. And now I have to doubt everything I thought I knew.

I curl up next to the pictures, gathering them up at my side. I should throw them away, but I'm mourning for the girl in the picture. I'm mourning for the future she thought they had. Because nothing is what she thought. Not even—

There is a sudden and devastating pain across my forehead. I scream, covering my face, and before I can even understand what's happening, I crash back into a memory.

"Tatum, wait up," Wes called as I rushed out of Casey's house, running for my Jeep. "Please," he said.

I slowed but didn't stop. I was angry, but more than that, I was hurt. Crushed. I knew Wes didn't want to go to the party; he'd said as much. But I told him if we didn't show up together, people would wonder. The Program would come. And although that was true, I was also hoping things would change between us—that he'd see me again the way he used to.

Instead he met up with her. The blonde—Kyle Mahoney. He didn't tell me, but I had a feeling something was going on between them. And his smile . . . I knew by his smile that it was true. Fuck, it was true.

I dashed around to the driver's-side door, my fingers shaking as I tried to get the key in the lock.

"Hey," Wes said softly, appearing at my side. He reached to put his hand over mine, steadying the key. "Take it easy, Tate. I'm here."

My expression broke, but I quickly pulled back and shook off his hand. "I've got it," I said. I unlocked the door and jumped in. Wes cursed and ran around to the other side, getting in the passenger seat.

He slammed the door shut, and we both sat there for a moment in the dark. I took in the scent of his cologne—more than usual. More for her. I listened to him breathe deeply.

"Do you want a ride home?" I asked numbly. Wes looked out the passenger window and said sure. He didn't seem like he wanted to leave, but I was glad he said yes.

We drove in silence, and I parked in front of his house. The lights were blazing inside. His mother had been acting worried lately; she said I wasn't myself. But I didn't care what she thought. Wes doesn't get out of the Jeep.

I looked sideways at him. "I love you," I said miserably.

Wes squeezed his eyes shut like my confession hurt him. "Tate," he said warningly.

I unclicked my seat belt and climbed over to the passenger seat. He kept his face turned away, but his hands rested on my hips like it was where they were naturally meant to be. I stared at him until I couldn't take it anymore.

"Look at me," I said, my voice hitching on a cry. Wes swallowed hard, and then lifted his eyes to mine. "I love you," I repeated, only I said it like it was the most painful thing in the world. Wes sniffled and he began to cry.

"I know you do, baby," he said, nodding. "I know." He gathered me up then, tucking my head under his neck, cradling me to him. He laid his cheek against my hair, and I could feel his tears when they dripped onto my skin.

"I never wanted to hurt you," he whispered. "Never. But if we don't end this now, it's going to kill us both. I'm worried about you, and . . ." He stopped to cry a moment. "We just can't be together anymore, Tate."

I sobbed against him, telling him I would do anything. I *begged* him.

"Please, Tate," he said, reaching to put his palms on my cheeks. "Please don't cry anymore. I can't . . . I can't take it."

And so I tried. I sniffled and took a deep breath. Wes and I sat facing each other in the dark, breaking up again—a breakup that was going on three weeks now. And then, despite all we said, I leaned in and Wes met me halfway in a kiss. Sad and slow at first, but then—as if we sensed it could be the last time—passionate and reckless. We kissed until we were both breathless. But it had gotten late and I was going to miss curfew. Wes said he had to go.

I nodded, fixing my clothes and moving over so he could climb out. He paused just outside the door, his eyes red from crying, his mouth red from kissing. He looked at me, long and deep.

"I don't know how to live without you in my life," he said. "I don't know how to leave you after all this time. I don't deserve you, Tatum. You know that, right?"

I smiled sadly. "Sometimes you do," I said.

He laughed, shaking his head. "So stubborn," he whispered. He looked down at the ground and I watched his smile fade away, replace itself with the same determination to leave me that he came outside with. But I didn't give him a chance to say the words again.

"Good night, Wes," I said quickly, and got behind the wheel. Guilt hung on Wes's posture, and reluctantly he shut the door of the Jeep, and he walked back toward his house.

And once he was gone, I didn't pull away. I sat there and I cried. And I cried.

And I *cried*.

I open my eyes and find myself on my bedroom floor. I stir awake, and slowly sit up. There's a tickle under my nose, and when I swipe it, there's a small streak of blood. I get up and grab a tissue, dabbing it until it's clear.

It's true. It's all true.

There's an ache deep in my chest, a shadow over my heart. I lost Wes once, and it wasn't to The Program. Somehow I'd forgotten that.

The doorbell rings downstairs, and I turn toward my bedroom door. It may have been ringing for a while. I'm still half in my head, but more settled now. My headache has passed completely, and I imagine it was the memory trying to get out. Crashing back on me.

I start downstairs, soaked in grief. More heartbroken than I thought possible. I still can't make sense of the memory, but I know it's real. And that's devastating.

"I'm coming," I call when the knocking starts. I get to the door and yank it open, a cold breeze blowing over my bare skin.

Wes sways, grabbing the door frame. He's dripping wet like he ran the whole way here from Kyle's house. In reality, his motorcycle is at the curb.

"Tate, you don't have a shirt on," he says, stepping inside like he means to cover me up. I push him aside, and cross my arms over my bra instead. Wes falls back, looking hurt.

I take in his appearance; the rims of his eyes are so dark, so red, that it looks like he's been crying blood. He's been beating himself up about this, seeming as brokenhearted as I am. He reaches for me again, but I sidestep his touch and close the door with him dripping in my foyer.

I'm hurt. And after the memory, I'm angry about his relationship with Kyle. That he moved on so quickly. But as Wes stands here, waiting for me to decide if he stays or goes, I realize that this Wes—the one here now—didn't break my heart. And so I'm not even sure who to be angry with.

"Did it work?" I ask. "Did you remember everything?"

"No," he says. "No, I didn't."

So it wasn't worth it. Destroying us wasn't even worth it—not to me.

When I don't ask him to leave, Wes goes to sit on the bottom stair, his elbows on his knees, his shoulders slumped. "I don't remember her, Tate," he says. "I don't remember us breaking up." He looks me over, pain coating his expression as tears well up. "I don't remember hurting you like this," he whispers. "It wasn't *me*."

And I can't bear to see him cry—it destroys me on the most

basic level; it unravels me. I walk over and place my hand on the back of Wes's neck, and he pulls me between his knees, wrapping his arms around me as he presses his cool cheek against my waist.

"Don't leave me," he murmurs into my skin. "I need you."

I am utterly heartbroken. Everything was a lie—everything I believed we were. And yet . . . here we are once again. We came back to each other; we always seem to come back to each other like muscle memory. Maybe we always will. We're young. We're in love. We're flawed.

I look down at Wes, running my hand over his shaved head, and he slowly lifts his face to gaze up at me. He's so beautiful that it's painful.

"I'm sorry, Tate," he whispers. "I'm sorry that I—"

I shake my head, telling him to stop. I don't want to hear his apology; I can't listen to an explanation. I lost him once. Or, rather, he lost me.

And it could be the residual pain from the memory, or maybe I just fell in love with him all over again, but I'm not willing to let this Wes go. Not in this moment. Not yet.

I lower myself to my knees to match his height, and he watches with apprehension, worry. I pull him closer, hearing him sigh out his relief just before I kiss him, his clothes freezing cold on my bare skin. And soon I find my hands slipping under the back of his shirt, my nails digging into his flesh there.

Wes moans, and I kiss him hard on the mouth, my eyes closed tight. It isn't romance, the way we tear at each other, the desperate way we feel for each other. But soon we're upstairs in my room, and I push him down on my bed and climb on top of him. He strips his shirt over his head and reaches for a condom in his wallet.

Because sometimes all you can do is feel; sometimes we're all nerve endings and we'll do anything to stop the pain there. We'll blast them with sex or numb them with alcohol. And sometimes . . . it's love. It's holding on too tight, dangerous. Suffocating. Consuming.

And as Wes moves inside me, we're all those things. We're emotional devastation. We're love. We don't know the difference anymore.

CHAPTER TWELVE

WE LIE TOGETHER, UNDRESSED IN MY BED. MY cheek rests on his shoulder, my thigh over his. There's a moment of peace, like our minds have quieted enough for us to talk rationally. I don't know how long this clarity will last. I wish it were forever, but every so often, Wes flinches.

He turns, running his fingertip over the scratch on my cheek. We stay quiet a moment longer, and then I close my eyes.

"Do you love her?" I ask, keeping the emotion out of my voice.

"No," he says immediately, like my question is dumb.

"Did you?" I ask.

And now he falls silent. I get up on my elbow and look down at him. He turns his face away, and his expression is all shame.

"I don't even know her," he says. "Please, just—"

A wild streak of anger flashes, and I have to rein it in. "Where did you go, Wes?" I ask. "The week you disappeared, where did you go and why did you come back? Why do you keep showing up at my house?"

He closes his eyes at the sound of my pain, but I can tell he doesn't remember those parts either. He was somebody else then.

The storm of my emotions begins to rage again, but this time they come with a side of humiliation. The image of me begging him not to leave me. The idea that he actually did, even after that. I sit up and grab a shirt from the floor and pull it on.

"Tate, can we just—"

"No," I interrupt. "I remembered something earlier," I say. "Before you got here." Wes listens as I give him a shortened version of our breakup, or at least one of them. I spare myself some embarrassment in the retelling.

Wes listens, his head in his hands. He feels guilty, when really . . . I know it's not his fault. People fall out of love. It sucks, but it happens.

I just didn't think it could happen to us.

"I don't know if it was those pills my grandmother gave me, but somehow I forgot it all," I say. "So it's my fault your memory was corrupted."

"I'm the one who ruined everything," he says. "But I'll fix it, Tate. I'll make it right."

But I know it's too late. The idea of us smashed, cracked beyond repair. I'll never be able to think of us without pain. I'll never be able to get past it. That version of me, so fucking broken in that Jeep, is all I can see now.

I shake my head, trying to clear away the pain, and tell Wes to get dressed. Reluctantly he reaches to grab his clothes. I watch him from across the room. And there's one question that I know I have to ask, even though it digs into my heart with claws.

"Did you sleep with her?" I ask.

"Today?" He looks offended by the question.

"Before," I say. "When you were together."

Wes curses and stands to pull on his pants, buttoning them quickly. "Don't talk about it like that," he says. "You know I don't remember."

"But she does," I say. "So what did she tell you? I have to know."

He keeps his back to me and crosses his arms over his bare chest. "No," he says. And then he adds, quieter, "I don't think so."

It shouldn't matter, I try to tell myself. We were (mostly) broken up. He's gone through so much since. We're both different people now. And, yet . . . the possibility kills me. I sniffle, and Wes spins to look at me.

"Tate," he murmurs so softly that I cry harder. He comes over and wraps me in a hug.

"What else did she say?" I ask, wanting it all. Needing to

get all the pain out now so I never have to feel it again. Maybe Kyle was right. Maybe I am broken.

"She said it was emotional," Wes says. "We brought out each other's misery. And that's it. I told her it was a mistake and she told me to go fuck myself. So that was nice. It's been a great day."

"At least you had her, right?" I say. "When I wasn't enough, you turned to her."

"I don't know her," he says, getting angry.

I pull away, taking a few steps back from him. "But maybe you would have," I say. "If she had gotten to your locker first the day you came back, she might have been the one you ended up with. Obviously my memories are skewed. Who knows," I say miserably. "She might know you better than I do."

Wes's eyes weaken like I've just invalidated our entire relationship. "*Him*," he says. "She knew him. Not me."

And maybe I'm being unfair; I don't even know anymore. I still don't even understand how I could have forgotten this, pills or not.

"Tate," Wes says, putting his hand over his heart. "I'm in love with you. I'm deeply and helplessly in love with you. Right now."

My heart swells at the words—not because I've never heard "I love you" before. But because I've never heard them like this. They sound like the first time. They sound honest and pure. And I know I feel the same way. Our shared past aside, we both fell in love again. We fell in love with the same people.

"I love you," Wes repeats. "And I'm a shithead for hurting you before. But that guy, that version of me . . . Fuck him. I hate him. I just want to be with you." His breath hitches on the start of a cry, but he holds it back.

And although I don't say anything in return, tears slip down from the corners of my eyes. I'm confused. I'm unsure of my place in my life, of the people in my life. I'm broken in so many ways that I wish my heart would dissolve into ash and drift away. That's not the way love's supposed to feel.

Wes takes a step toward me like he's going to keep apologizing, but I can't listen anymore. I need to think. I step out of his reach and pull on the rest of my clothes. My body is sore from him—from us trying so hard to hold on to something we wanted rather than something we had.

"You have to go," I say, and start walking for my bedroom door. Wes reaches out to take my elbow to stop me, but I look pointedly at him and he apologizes and lets go. Without argument, he follows me downstairs. I pull open the door and the sound of rain is loud on the rooftop. Cool air breezes in, chilling my skin.

Wes comes to pause in front of me, his eyes begging me to let him stay.

"You told me once that it would kill us if we didn't end our relationship," I say, making him wince. "I understand what you meant now. Because it seems the more I love you, the more it hurts. So I can't love you anymore, Weston," I say, my voice cracking. "I won't let myself."

"Tate," he murmurs, the tone so soaked in pain that I want to fling myself into his arms. Instead I motion outside. Wes lowers his head and walks onto the porch.

I turn away, about to close the door, when I hear a garbled scream. Startled, I swing around to see Wes drop to his knees, clutching his head with both hands.

"Wes?" I yell, and run outside.

His eyes are squeezed shut, his teeth gritted. And as I kneel next to him, a steady stream of blood begins to pour from both nostrils, running over his lips and off his chin.

"Fuck," he moans, and collapses onto his side, pressing his temples like he's trying to hold together the pieces of his skull.

I'm frantic, not sure how to help him as he rolls around in agony. I run inside to grab my phone and then come back out, one hand on his shoulder, telling him that I'm here. I dial 911 and beg for an ambulance. They tell me there's one en route, and I set the phone down to give Wes all my attention.

His breaths are growing ragged, uneven. I roll him onto his side, and lean down so my face is near his. Blood is everywhere, and I see a thin brown line running from his ear.

"Wes," I sob out, putting my hands on his cheeks. And for a moment his body stills when I touch him, and he opens his eyes to look at me, a sharpness there that's startling.

"I remember," he murmurs.

My lips part, shock rocking me back. "What?"

"I remember everything. I came back for you, Tate. I came back to save you from The Program."

He reaches out his hand, but before he can touch me, Wes's eyes roll back in his head, and his body begins to convulse with a seizure.

It's a blur. Nathan came running over when he heard the sirens, Jana waiting on his porch as she watched in horror. She ended up leaving, and I rode with Nathan to the hospital. He called Foster and asked him to meet us. As we drove, I left a message at the Adjustment office. I told Dr. McKee what had happened and begged him to help us.

When we get to the hospital, they admit Wes immediately. Nathan offers to call my grandparents to let them know what happened. I don't tell him about the earlier breakup—I'd kept it secret from him. I know that much. Seems I've lied to him before. And I don't tell him now about Kyle or about the pills. I can't think about any of that right now.

While Nathan makes calls, I sit in the waiting-room chair, my arms wrapped around myself. The nurse tells me that Dr. McKee has already arrived and that he's currently with Wes. She says he'll be over to talk to me in a moment. But that moment feels like eternity. The double doors open and Dr. McKee comes rushing out. I jump up and meet him in the center of the hall, my anger flashing when I see him in person, all of my rage suddenly pointed at him, deflecting the real source of my worry and concern. "You're a liar," I say to him. "Why didn't you tell me about Kyle? You knew something was wrong, and you . . . you—" But I start to cry because I don't care about the past right now. I just need Wes. "Tell me he's okay," I beg desperately. "Because it didn't fix him. The truth didn't fix him."

Dr. McKee puts his hands on my shoulders, looking devastated. "Tatum, I'm going to need you to calm down."

"Calm down? This is your fault," I tell him, pushing him away. "You tampered with his memories—you took Kyle out of them. What else did you change? You said you cared about us. You said you weren't like The Program."

Dr. McKee straightens his back, like he's getting ready to take a punch. "You're right," he says. "It's my fault. I thought . . . I saw the way his guilt was triggered by the memory of Kyle. I thought if he didn't know, it would be better for both of you." He stops and shakes his head. "I do sound like The Program," he says, mostly to himself.

"Wes said he remembered everything, but then . . . he started to convulse. And after that I couldn't wake him up. How is he now?"

Dr. McKee nods, but it's with a hopeless expression. "I'll be honest, Tatum. I'm not sure what I can do for him at this point," he says. "We've run into some complications. His memories crashed back all at once, but it was too strong. He had so many emotions. . . . He's not well. He might not make it."

I fall back a step. That was the same thing they'd said about Vanessa. And she'd died.

"But . . . you were the cure," I say weakly. "How can you kill him if you were the cure?" I nearly gag on my cry, holding my stomach, fear washing over my head and pulling me under.

"I understand you're upset," Dr. McKee says carefully, his voice taking on an edge. "But you need to be careful here. I don't want you to hurt yourself."

"I'm not going to kill myself," I spit out like he's stupid.

"That's not what I meant. Listen, Tatum," he says, redirecting, "I'm going to go back to Weston now. But his brain is in full recall mode. Memories are pouring in. Too many at once. Think of it like a fuse box. He keeps tripping the switch, and his body is shutting him down. If he continues on like this, he'll die."

"So what are you suggesting?" I ask.

Dr. McKee bites down hard. "We either let him reboot in the hopes he'll recover," he says, "or we remove the corrupted memories. We remove . . . all the memories."

Another wave of panic crashes. "What do you mean, *all*?"

"The problem isn't just with the implanted memories," he says. "It has skewed others. Infected his reality. His perspective. The only safe bet would be to remove everything from the day he left The Program. More if necessary."

"You want to reset him?" I ask, struck down with fear. "Like The Program did?"

"I'm not sure he'll recover otherwise."

I rub roughly at my face and turn away from him. I look around the waiting room wishing Nathan was back. Wishing my grandparents were here, or Foster. "What will Wes remember?" I ask the doctor.

"He'll know his name," he says quietly. "He might remember

his parents, but that's not a given. He won't know you or me. As far as he's concerned, he's never seen us before in his life."

Less than an hour ago I tried to end our relationship, but the truth is I fell in love with Wes—*this* Wes. And he loved me back. He loved me deeply and honestly, even without our past. But I was hurt and I took it out on him. This time I ruined us. And I can't fix it.

Because now . . . now he'll be gone forever. Like I never happened to him. Like I was never real. The horror of my erasure buries itself in my bones, a sharp pain that I think might never go away.

"It's the only choice," Dr. McKee says sympathetically. "If we hope to wake him up, it's the only choice. It's what his parents want."

"And what about the returners who are breaking down?" I ask. "Won't that still happen to him?"

"No," Dr. McKee says. "This reset will be complete—more thorough than The Program. There will be no chance of memory recovery. Not ever."

The wave of hurt is crushing—I'll never get him back. He will never ever remember me again. We're over.

I wipe my nose and turn to the doctor, fire burning up my heart. "Tell me something," I say bitterly. "Your Adjustment, your promises—did they ever work? Did you ever save anyone?"

His eyes glass over, and he grows very still and solemn. "Once," he says. "Our case study."

Nathan had been right all along. I shouldn't have trusted this. Yes, the returners are crashing back, but with therapy . . . maybe we could have figured this out. Wes could be here right now. Awake. Healthy. I ruined everything.

"I'm sorry," the doctor says, his voice sympathetic. "Weston did get his memories back, but he got them back all at once. Unfortunately, not everyone can deal with that. We can give him a chance to fight this on his own, but even if he does wake up, he'll need intensive therapy, the kind that doesn't even exist yet." He shakes his head. "The memories will crash and collide—they'll all be there in some form or another—but I'm not sure his brain will be able to make sense of them. Reset or recovery, those are the only two choices . . . and one could end up killing him. Ethically, resetting is only one answer. I'm just giving you the courtesy of letting you know why."

The decision's been made, but really . . . I lose Wes either way. Because the Wes before The Program left me; he was with somebody else. The Wes after The Program didn't know me at all. And with this complete reset, he never will.

I walk over to the nurse's desk, and she offers me a tissue. I thank her, sure I look a mess, and swipe under my nose. I can barely face the doctor when I say, "Save his life, Dr. McKee. Whatever you do, just save his life."

Dr. McKee nods, and then heads back to the treatment rooms. When the doors close behind him, I walk over to the waiting-room chairs and sit on the edge of one, shaking all over. The muscle above my right eye twitches.

Nathan comes back a few minutes later with Foster, who must have just arrived. I can't hear what they're saying, but I see the absolute devastation in Foster's eyes when he looks over at me.

They sit down with me, one on either side like they can protect me from the world. From myself. I tell them what Dr. McKee said. I tell him about me and Wes breaking up, about Kyle. Nathan curses, swearing he had no idea about any of it. But Foster falls quiet, and I turn to look at him.

"You knew?" I ask.

He shifts his jaw, like he can't believe it himself. "Yeah," he says. "I knew something was up." Foster glances at me, his expression apologetic. "I had no idea about Kyle, though. I swear."

"Why didn't you say anything?" I ask.

Foster shrugs. "The one time I tried to ask you about your relationship, you nicely told me to mind my own fucking business." He smiles. "Then I didn't hear from you for a while; I thought you were mad. But then Weston disappeared, and I figured . . . I figured it didn't matter what had happened before. You loved each other. All that mattered was getting him back. I didn't realize . . . I was never sure, Tatum. And when you didn't bring it up again, I figured it was none of my business. Just a bump in the road—or whatever bullshit relationship saying goes here."

"Could have mentioned it to me," Nathan says, glaring over at him.

"I could have," Foster says. "But I didn't think it was any of your business either."

Nathan sniffs a laugh, and then reaches to take my arm, letting me lean against him for support.

"God, I hate hospitals," Foster murmurs. I look over at him, reminded of Sebastian. I tell Foster again how sorry I am, but he doesn't want to talk about it. We all process grief in our own way.

The three of us are pathetic, three friends who survived an epidemic only to be crushed by its aftermath. But we have each other. At least we have that.

After some of the shock wears off and time ticks by with no updates, I find myself still in the chair, Nathan's jacket over my shoulders as I continue to shake. Foster had to leave, promising to check in with us later. It all feels like a bad dream.

"You sure you don't want me to get you a hot chocolate out of the machine or anything?" Nathan asks. I look over at him, my head feeling too heavy, and my appearance must answer for me, because he swallows hard and holds me tighter.

"He won't know me, so I'm not sure why I'm waiting here," I say. "I guess to make sure he'll come out of this alive."

"He'll be alive," Nathan says. "But it sounds like he won't be the same guy you've been sneaking around with."

"Yeah, I guess he won't be." And I miss him madly, wondering if I would have just told him I loved him too, if he would have stayed at my house—maybe he wouldn't have melted down. Maybe I'm the one to blame, just like his mother always thought.

Because all the things I was upset about . . . well, they're nothing compared to this. None of it matters like Wes does to me.

I straighten out of Nathan's arms and sniffle. "I loved him," I say. "What I thought we had was a lie, but I loved him anyway."

"We all get lied to, Tatum," he says, his raspy voice a little quieter. "Sometimes we're lying to ourselves. Seems there's a healthy dose of that going around. And sometimes we lie to others. Let's just agree on one thing," he adds. "No more tampering. No more fucking Program—even if they call it something else."

I agree and sit back, shoulder to shoulder with him as we watch the doors to the treatment rooms. "Do you actually think they'll ever stop, though?" I ask, not looking at him.

"Nope," he says simply. "Probably not. And from what Pop told me on the phone, it sounds like we're heading into some new kinds of regulations. The monitor wants safeguards. Which, of course . . . means control."

"How long until graduation?" I ask, as if that's our answer.

"Two months."

I lean my head on the edge of Nathan's shoulder. He's my best friend. He's always been there for me. But here, we're basking in sadness. Nathan reaches over and takes my hand to hold it, and I try to remind myself that I can find hope. Even when the world feels like it's closing in around me.

"Tatum," a soft voice says close to my ear. I stir, realizing that I've fallen asleep against Nathan. I blink quickly and look around in time to see the doctor coming toward us.

SUZANNE YOUNG

I jolt upright, dropping Nathan's jacket on the tile floor. I see Wes's parents in the corner of the waiting room with my grandparents, Wes's mom crying as my grandmother comforts her.

No, no, no, I think, fear chilling my skin. Nathan steadies me, but I'm worried that Wes is dead. That Dr. McKee didn't save him at all.

Dr. McKee heads over from where he was talking to Wes's parents, holding a clipboard in his hand. Just before he gets to me, he flips to peek at a paper underneath the top page.

"How is he?" I call out, needing him to look at me. He takes his time, though, and it isn't until he stops dead in front of me that he meets my eyes. He nods a polite hello to Nathan.

Dr. McKee glances down at the chart again, but I get the impression that he's using it more as a prop than an actual source of information. He lifts one corner of his mouth in a gentle smile.

"He's alive," the doctor says. "And there's no permanent damage. His brain functions are all normal now."

I cover my mouth as I sob my relief. Nathan murmurs that it's great, that he's happy for us. But when I look up, Dr. McKee's expression has grown serious.

"I'm sorry . . . ," he starts a little hesitantly. "The damage was severe. We had to take it all. His whole life. Even his parents. It was the only way to be sure nothing else was corrupted."

My mouth opens, but no sound comes out. Nathan picks up the cause for me.

"What the hell will he remember, then?" Nathan asks.

"He'll retain his knowledge—reading, math, world events," Dr. McKee says. "But his personal relationships, family and friends, those will have to be reintroduced slowly. He'll start therapy immediately, including family counseling. I know this is devastating," he says, turning to me. "And I'm sorry, but we had to be thorough. We had to be sure. We couldn't afford any more complications."

"He doesn't know me," I say, weighted down, underwater with cement shoes and sinking deeper.

"No," Dr. McKee says. "He doesn't know you exist, Tatum. And if . . ." He furrows his brow and I get that he has something to say off the record. I nod for him to continue.

"Forgive me," he says. "But it's honestly better this way. I don't know the entirety of your history together. None of this was in your files—I'm not sure how. We've never seen an instance of self-erasure. At this point, what we do know is that Weston had a meltdown and his mother attributes some of that to you, to your relationship. They've opted to exclude you from his reintroductions. And I think it's for the best. Some people . . . they're just not meant to be together. No matter how much they love each other."

The doctor's words sting me, and I recoil back from them. They're too personal. Too controlling.

"Thanks for the advice, doc," Nathan says coolly, and reaches to take my hand again, holding it firmly as if giving me strength.

Dr. McKee looks at his chart again, all business now. "There was one more thing," he adds quietly. "Weston woke up briefly, and he asked me if I could . . . he didn't want . . ."

"Didn't want what?" I ask.

"When I told him what was about to happen with his memory, he said he didn't want you here. He didn't want to hurt you any more. I have to respect his wishes." He lifts his eyes to meet mine. "It would be best if you left now, Miss Masterson. His family will take it from here."

My eyes feel heavy, sore from crying. Wes must have felt abandoned in those moments. My words of not being able to love him anymore haunting him. I did this to him.

I blink a few tears, and then swipe my palm over my cheek. I turn to look at my grandparents, and find them watching me—checking on me. I'm not alone, so I know I can weather this. For now, I just have to get out of here.

"Nathan?" I say, trying to keep my shit together before I walk out. "Can you drive?" He stares at me like he's confused why I'm not fighting this, arguing that I have a right to be in Wes's life. "Can you?" I ask again, more forcefully.

"Of course," Nathan says, shaking his head. "Anything, Tatum. Let's just—"

I grab his arm and we start toward the door, but before we get there, Dr. McKee calls after me.

"I'm sorry," he says. "For what it's worth, I really am sorry it didn't work out."

"Yeah," I say. "Me too."

CHAPTER THIRTEEN

I'M SITTING IN ENGLISH CLASS, TAKING NOTES ON the character arcs in *Wuthering Heights*, when Nathan leans up and pokes me with the eraser end of his pencil.

"Stop, idiot," I say, trying to get the last few lines down.

"Rockstar after school?"

"Gross, Nathan. How can you think about food when it's barely eight in the morning?"

"It's always a good time for pizza," he says, and swishes the back of my hair. I laugh and turn to push him backward.

"Better clear it with Jana," I say. He tells me he already did. Nathan and Jana have officially become a couple, making me the third wheel. A fifth wheel if Foster and Arturo are there.

Jana's nicer to me now. Hell, we even talk on the phone

sometimes. I guess we're friends. I helped her deal with Vanessa's death, and she helped me deal with losing Wes.

It's been nearly a month since I've seen Weston; he hasn't come back to school. My grandparents told me he made a full physical recovery, and that his therapy has been going well. They keep in touch with his mother. I called to check on Wes once myself, but I didn't go by the house—not that I was welcome to.

I apologized to his mother, accepting my part in his Adjustment. Surprisingly, she told me she was sorry about what happened between me and Wes. We called a truce, basically.

The pain is still there. All of it, right on the surface most days. Weston Ambrose broke my heart. But I don't let that define me. Truth is, Wes loved me twice. He just didn't stay in love with me the first time. And this time around, I didn't love him enough, I guess. Always chasing the idea of us—the past us. I wasn't fair to him. So this time . . . it was my fault. Maybe Dr. McKee was right. Love isn't always enough.

I still wonder, though, I wonder if it's possible that it's muscle memory, our hearts trained to love each other. That Wes and I are destined to fall in love over and over, no matter the cost. Because our hearts remember. Because our hearts can't forget.

I see Kyle Mahoney some afternoons, and I don't hold anything against her. I can't say she feels the same way, even if neither of us owes the other anything beyond common decency. But I'm sorry for my part in her unhappiness. And she's told me in passing that she's sorry for mine.

After leaving the hospital, I asked my grandparents about the pills in the cabinet. I didn't accuse them—I just asked for an explanation. My pop is the one who got them, and yes, he got them from Dr. McKee—the attending physician at the hospital. But he swears they were for my grandmother's migraines.

He had no idea about Dr. McKee's involvement with the Adjustment, not until I mentioned his name after my and Nathan's visit. After that, my grandfather was in full research mode; it's part of why he got his job back at the paper. He thought something was off, although he has yet to figure out exactly what that is.

He's sorry he didn't tell me sooner, but both he and my grandmother swear they had no idea the medicine would be for anything other than what was prescribed. I have no reason to doubt them. Besides, I'm tired of doubting and questioning people's motives.

They also had no idea about me and Wes breaking up. Have no idea how I forgot. So it seems I kept that secret from everyone, including myself. Dr. McKee claimed it wasn't in Wes's Program file either—the first instance of a hidden memory he's seen. Wes hid it too. Dr. McKee doesn't mention it, but I think he knows what that means for the Adjustment. It means donor memories can't be trusted either. It means the Adjustment is entirely fallible.

A few bits and pieces have come back to me, though. My therapist says I repressed it all after Wes was taken into The Program and that I might never remember all of it. For now, I accept that—not willing to dredge up my painful past. I hate returning to that time, even if it's just a memory. I'm embarrassed for myself. I'm hurt. And now I'm ready to move on. My therapist thought that was a good idea too; Dr. Warren has been a godsend.

The Program ruined so many lives. Suicide ruined so many lives. We're living in the aftermath, one where we're allowed to feel, allowed to love and regret and fear. We're free to do all of that, but it's not all good. A total of seven returners have gotten sick so far, and four of them have died.

And, unfortunately, the monitor has become a daily nuisance at school. Once in a while, Dr. Wyatt will come into the classroom, wander around, observing us. She says it's for educational purposes, but it feels more like the work of handlers to me.

Murmurs of their continued existence still make their way through the student body. Handlers—the paranoia they can bring. It's one conspiracy theory that won't die—maybe because it's the one we fear the most.

Assessments happen once a week, but so far, most of us have refused to answer them. Foster has even taken to drawing happy faces on his. But I worry about the strain it's causing on all of us. It's like we've learned nothing from The Program.

The door to the classroom opens, and when I look up, my heart stops dead in my chest. Weston Ambrose walks into my English class, only this time, he's not wearing returner clothes. He looks like himself: a T-shirt and jeans with heavy motorcycle boots.

There's a squeak as Nathan shifts in his chair, but I don't turn around to look at him. My eyes are trained on Wes's face as he talks to the teacher. I will him to look at me, not because I expect him to run to me. But because I want to know what he remembers. Part of me wants to think he will.

The teacher motions him to a seat, right next to the one he sat in originally. A few students glance back at me to see my reaction, and I imagine Nathan is wondering how I am. I lean forward on my desk, staring at the back of Weston's head, his hair slightly grown out from the last time I saw him.

Do you remember me? I think. *Do you still love me?* The last part of my question brings tears to my eyes and I do my best to push those feelings away. It's not fair, not to me or him. But I can't help thinking them anyway.

And then, as if he can hear my thoughts, Wes covertly puts his chin on his shoulder, and then he turns around and looks directly at me. I freeze under his gaze, trying to read his expression.

There isn't even a second of recognition, and his eyes travel over the rest of the students before he turns around. There's a part of me that's wailing on the inside, the girl who lost the boy she loved so dearly. He may have hurt her, but no matter what—he will always be her first love. He might even be her only love.

But we were reckless. Dangerous. I know that. And I know that none of us is who we thought we'd be when it comes right down to it.

SUZANNE YOUNG

I look down and my notebook page blurs slightly. I blink quickly to clear my vision. There are no tears, just the start of a dull headache, one that continues to return nearly every day, although some days it's worse than others. My grandparents ask me about it, but I don't want them to worry, so I play it down. It's just a headache.

In the front of the classroom, the teacher begins to write more notes.

"Hey," Nathan says just over my shoulder. "He looked back at you. That's encouraging, right?"

"I guess," I say.

Dr. McKee advised me to stay away from Wes, but just because Wes doesn't remember me, that doesn't mean he can forget me. I turn back to Nathan.

"He looks healthy," I say, sounding optimistic.

Nathan leans forward on his desk. "Indeed," he replies. "Weston is a strapping young lad."

I laugh, and Nathan watches me with a hesitant smile.

"I'm sorry, you know," he says. "For what it's worth."

"You have nothing to be sorry for," I say.

"I'm just . . ." He lowers his eyes. "I'm sorry I didn't help you sooner. I wish I could have done more. It might have made a difference."

"What do you mean?" I ask. "You've been here all along—even when I was totally annoying. I didn't tell anyone about me and Wes breaking up. Not even when Foster asked me about it. If anything, *I'm* the bad friend here."

Nathan shakes his head, looking up at me. "I may not have known about you and Wes," he says, "but I knew something was wrong last summer. That night you came to my house . . . it was obvious. But I didn't ask; I should have."

I have no idea which night he's referring to.

"And even when you came back," he continues. "I know I swore to your grandparents that I'd never talk about your time in The Program, not to anyone, including Foster, but I still should have asked *you*. I should have made sure you were okay, especially once Wes returned. So for that, I'm so sorry."

I stare at him, and suddenly time ticks to a stop; the classroom scene cracks, splintering glass, and crashes down around me. His words are a wallop to my chest. "My time in The Program?"

"I know," he says, holding up his hand apologetically. "I shouldn't talk about it. Your grandparents said it could trigger a meltdown, or possibly even bring The Program down on you again—I promised them. And you've never brought it up. But that means I've never gotten the chance to apologize. I've wanted to so many times, Tatum," he whispers. "And after what happened with Wes"—he motions toward him—"I want to make sure you know how I feel. Know that I will always, *always* be here for you."

He smiles. "You've done so well. I mean, nothing like the other returners. Pop said he had The Program seal your records so no one would know. He got to you in time."

I fight to stay calm, but my emotions stir, a cyclone in my chest. "He did," I murmur.

"Every day," Nathan continues his confession. "I was at your house every day with your grandparents, waiting for you to come home. Pop called in favors, made threats. He got to bring you back early. And we all agreed that we'd never let anything happen to you again. And it was only a week later when I saw you. And you remembered everything—well, almost everything, just like Pop said you would. You beat The Program. You were home."

I look down, trying to make sense of his words. I flinch, and reach up absently to put my hand on the front of my throat, my fingers ice-cold.

"Point is," Nathan says, as if he got off track, "I know we've kept secrets in the past, but no more. From this point forward, we'll tell each other everything, okay? I'll never betray you. I've got your back on all things. You know I love you, right?" he asks. "You forgive me?"

I turn around in my seat, my chest feeling like it might burst. My mind is racing too fast trying to put together pieces that don't fit—I'm bending and tearing them, but no matter what I do, the puzzle doesn't make sense.

"Of course I forgive you," I say to Nathan, staring straight ahead in class. I can't . . . I don't understand, but I feel a memory just under the surface. Something dark. Something about to break through. A tragedy scratching at the inside of my skull.

When I look up, I see the monitor standing at the front of class, a stack of assessments in her hands. Nathan groans behind me and swears. Dr. Wyatt begins to talk, although her words drift past me without comprehension.

As if he's still curious, Weston looks back at me again from the front of the room. Only this time, when his eyes meet mine, a tear drips onto my cheek. My world is completely turned upside down. Wes stiffens in his chair, his lips parting like he might call out to me.

And I think the boy who forgot everything, the one who will never remember again, might just be the only person I can truly trust.

EPILOGUE

MARIE DEVOROUX CLICKS THROUGH THE REPORTS and e-mails, searching for a name as she sits in the back office. The Adjustment facility has been stripped bare, with only a few chairs, a desk, and the picture of Tom still hanging on the wall, while they await the ruling by the drug administration. Investigators came through already, and Marie handed over all the files.

But maybe not all.

The Adjustment is nearing approval, and Marie knows she and Tom will have to keep the Adjustment out of the news for now, at least until they get it passed. The public will be quick to judge this time, not willing to wait for the full benefit. It might skew the board's decision.

And the monitor is getting closer; if Wyatt finds out about

the Adjustment, finds out she and Tom are running it, she'll do everything in her power to dismantle it—her ideology outweighing the benefits. They'll have to be careful.

"How is she?" Tom asks as he enters the office, looking over at Marie.

"Seems well enough," she responds. "Her grandparents are still pushing for us to tell Tatum the truth, but other than that, they say she's coping well. No setbacks."

"That's good," he says. "The headaches had begun to worry me. Tatum handled the therapy expertly, but after what happened with the others . . ." He sighs. "I'm not sure we could control another snag. If we hadn't rushed the boy, then maybe—"

Marie clicks off the computer screen, and turns in her chair to face Tom. "Don't blame me," she says. "His file was incomplete. Besides, you saw how miserable they were. He and Tatum had already met—we couldn't undo that. I thought if we could control the narrative, it would stave off any problems. The Adjustment should have worked on him, too. It didn't, but it doesn't matter. The boy would have had the meltdown either way. At least now . . . at least now he's out of her life. And he'll survive."

"Yes, well—Kyle Mahoney threw a wrench in the gears," Dr. McKee responds. "Showing up in the memory like that. Seems the truth serum is enough to cut through the implanted memories. We'll have to watch that next time."

"Tom," Marie says, growing concerned. "We need to think

this through. We have no idea how long this can last. Do you really think Tatum won't crash back? We have so much riding on her case."

"If she crashes, she'll survive it," Tom says curtly. "We only need a few more weeks. So long as we keep her and Weston controlled, the study shouldn't—"

The office door opens, and in a flurry, Jana Simms bursts in with Michael Realm close behind. Jana walks over to the desk and hops up to sit on it. Her bracelets jangle, her hair hanging long and wavy. Michael chews on his lip, hanging by the door.

"Yes, come on in, Jana," Tom says, making Marie smile. Jana often takes up the entire space she occupies. At least, she does when she's being herself and not some version of everyone's best friend.

"Hey, docs," Jana says. "Sooo . . . ," she starts dramatically, and turns to Michael. "Do you want to tell them or should I?"

"Tell us what?" Marie asks. Her heartbeats speed up, and she shoots Tom a concerned look. He straightens in his chair.

"Is there a problem?" Tom asks Michael Realm.

"Guess that depends," Michael says. "Considering I just saw Tatum Masterson and Weston Ambrose ride off together on his motorcycle. Looked like they were going to his house."

"Yeah, I thought you erased him?" Jana adds, looking at Tom.

The doctor curses and jumps up. He begins to pace, staring intently at Marie. She holds up her hand to tell him to stay calm, even if her concern has spiked as well.

"First of all," Marie announces, and looks at Jana, "get off my desk."

Jana's expression falters under Marie's scolding, and she hops down and wanders over to stand next to Michael, her cheeks glowing red.

"Now, Michael," Marie says, turning to him. "Did Tatum see you?"

He's quiet too long. "Yeah," he says. "But I don't think she remembers—"

"That was careless," Marie responds quickly, slamming her laptop shut. "Seeing a handler, especially one with your vast talents, could have been enough to cause a crashback. I told you as much when you saw her in this office. And you do realize this is on you, right?" she asks him. Michael lowers his eyes. "The memories she told you," Marie adds, "they weren't true. How did you miss that?"

Michael shakes his head. "I don't know," he says. "It's never happened before."

Marie tsks like his answer isn't good enough. She spins around and walks over to the window, slipping her hands into the pockets of her white lab coat. "I don't think the two of you grasp the importance here," she states calmly. "Tatum Masterson is the only person to complete an Adjustment, fully restored without complication. The only returner to do so. In case you weren't paying attention, people have *died*."

She looks back at her adjustors to make sure they're ashamed. Jana stares at her defiantly. "Yeah," she says. "I know."

"You were supposed to be watching her," Marie responds. "But instead of keeping an eye on Tatum, you've been running around with that Nathan kid."

Jana's mouth falls open. "He's her best friend," she says. "And you have no idea how hard it was to get close to her. Everyone is suspicious. Now I'm aware of her every move. It's *smart*. It doesn't compromise—"

"Really?" Marie says. "And what about Vanessa? You let her find out you were a handler. An oversight?"

Jana rocks back on her heels, the color draining from her face. Marie has a moment of sympathy at the girl's regret.

"A mistake," Jana says quietly. "A fucked-up mistake."

Marie nods that it was, and then she rounds the desk to sit in the chair. "You were the one who told us Wes was a good candidate," she says. "You were wrong. We won't trust you again on this matter."

Jana flares her nostrils, holding back an ashamed cry. Michael puts his hand on her arm to comfort her.

"You're both here because you wanted to make up for your crimes as handlers," Marie says, looking at both of them. "You wanted to set it all right, just like us. But understand: You are failing us."

Her words sting, but Marie goes on, sounding all business. "Now," she says, "Tom didn't fit The Program into Tatum's recall pattern; he took that memory with the permission of her grandparents. So in Tatum's mind, she was *never* sick. In her mind, she *never* left. We had those records sealed. At this point, any knowledge to the contrary would be devastating. Keep your distance."

Michael scoffs. "Marie, I would never—"

"Yes, of course, Michael," she says, agitated that the former handler would get so close to one of his patients again. "Always so ethical. You're lucky you didn't trip her memory when you showed up at the office during our meeting."

Marie looks at Tom, and the doctor watches her expression before slowly lowering himself back into his seat, confident in Marie's abilities to handle any situation.

"What should we do?" Tom asks her.

Marie purses her lips, thinking a moment. And then she nods. "It's time to make some calls, Tom," she says. "Let them know we have a complication."